The Empress Letters

A NOVEL

LINDA ROGERS

The Empress Letters

A NOVEL

Cormorant Books

Canada Council **Conseil des Arts**
for the Arts **du Canada**

The publisher gratefully acknowledges the support of the
Canada Council for the Arts and the Ontario Arts Council
for its publishing program. We acknowledge the financial support
of the Government of Canada through the Book Publishing
Industry Development Program (BPIDP) for our publishing activities.

Printed and bound in Canada

LIBRARY AND ARCHIVES CANADA CATALOGUING IN PUBLICATION

Rogers, Linda, 1944–
The Empress letters / Linda Rogers.

ISBN 978-1-896951-80-5

1. Title.

PS8585.O392E56 2007   C813'.54   C2007-900320-6

Cover design: Angel Guerra/Archetype
Text design: Tannice Goddard, Soul Oasis Networking
Cover image: Tetra Images/Corbis
Printer: Marquis Book Printing Inc.

CORMORANT BOOKS INC.
215 SPADINA AVENUE, STUDIO 230, TORONTO, ON CANADA M5T 2C7
WWW.CORMORANTBOOKS.COM

For Sophie, who asked for this story

Do not pray for gold and jade and precious things;
pray that your children and grandchildren may all be good.
— CHINESE PROVERB

My candle burns at both ends.
It will not last the night.
But ah, my foes, and oh, my friends —
It gives a lovely light!
— EDNA ST. VINCENT MILLAY

LETTER TO HERSELF BY POPPY VON STRONHEIM MANDEVILLE. MAY 12, 1927, 10 AM, ON THE FIRST CLASS DECK, THE *EMPRESS OF ASIA* EN ROUTE TO HONOLULU, YOKOHAMA, SHANGHAI, AND HONG KONG TO RESCUE PRECIOUS.

Once, when I was at a dinner party at a posh London Club, I went to the marble and gold ladies powder room and found a baby in the toilet. It was a foetus curled up like those dried medicinal seahorses they sell at Mah Leung in Chinatown, a little sea creature with its thumb in its mouth. I stood there, forgetting I had to pee. I didn't know whether to flush the nacreous flesh or fish it out. The toilet was running, perhaps broken. Was the porcelain head clearing its throat, preparing to sing its wet requiem for aborted foetuses? What if the abalone child plugged the drain and the water closet with a seat shaped like a seashell overflowed? Where would I hide the tiny body if I removed it?

I couldn't touch the curled flesh, flush it or pee on it. It hurt to look. I decided to leave the little creature. The gentleman's room was empty. I ducked in and locked the door, my heart racing. When I turned on the tap water and sat down, I couldn't go. I felt faint, leaned forward with my head in my hands. My nose started to bleed. I had to do something. My long absence from the dinner table would be noticed. If another guest found the foetus, she would assume it was mine. When my nosebleed stopped, I washed my face with cold water, dried myself with a towel, put on fresh lip rouge, went back to the ladies and flushed.

The dear little thing went down. I watched the foetus begin its journey back to the sea, where it no doubt encountered other babies from all different parts of the city.

There were twenty of us at dinner in the private dining room. I sat down, remembering to lift my skirt carefully, so I didn't harm the silk pleats, and looked around the table, a blaze of candlelight and diamonds and melting ice. The future king was there and I think he knew the sky was falling, or had already fallen with those of our generation who killed or were killed in the poppy fields of France.

Where I come from, most of the servants are Chinese, with sadness written in every expression and gesture we Occidentals call "inscrutable." I too have striven for inscrutability, and invisibility. My mother's secrets are planted in her garden. My secrets are hidden in the gardens I paint. But, like the foetus in the toilet, they are there to be seen by the right people.

I

MAY 13, 1927, 10 AM, ON THE FIRST CLASS DECK, THE *EMPRESS OF ASIA.*

My dear Little Shoe,

This letter is for you. Yesterday, I wrote to myself. I think it was practice, although I have been writing letters to myself ever since I was a child. In the first sentence, I used the ship's word "posh" — port out, starboard home. There are so many things we take for granted, and some we cannot change. That is life, ours subject to the same rules of the universe as everyone else's. What is the right way to ask that a positive force might protect you on your unfamiliar journey?

I am writing in the hope that you are safe and well, that Soong Chou has rescued you in Peking and brought you back to Hong Kong, and that we will have a happy reunion. I wish I could will this ship to move faster. Your Uncle Tony, my dear companion, has suggested that I pass the anxious time on board by writing to you.

There is no absolute truth, Precious, but we have lived with too many secrets and lies. I lie awake at night imagining the conversations we might have had. Now I intend to type what I might have told you. The sound of the keys is a great comfort. Much of what I will write is not for your little ears, grown up as you think you are, but for later. Because you will be a woman by the time you read this, I will not deliberately leave anything out. Tony and I are in disagreement about how much I should divulge but I want you to know all of it, even the parts that embarrass me in retrospect and might shock you. My life as a girl and woman has been based on hypocrisy, the parasite in our garden. Truth and beauty are co-dependent, my sweet. Are flowers ashamed of their thirst? Do flowers lie?

For years I have written to my stepfather, who gave me this typewriter when I was about your age so that I could express my feelings. He was unable to answer. I may not get a reply from you, but I can't think that letters written with so much love are wasted. My stepfather, who was a golfer, told me it was important to keep one's eye on the ball. I am keeping my mind's eye on you and the belief that we will be together soon. *Joy geen.*

Because I paint flowers, I will start with the place life begins. It is curious the words women choose for their intimate room. Some say nothing, as if the uncharted territory below the waist were the South Pole, all snow and ice with no identifiable landmarks. I know women who would rather be stretched on the rack than hear the word *cunt*. Others use it almost endearingly, as if describing the happy landscape of their childhood, where the hills are rosy and warm as cats sleeping at sunset. Then there is *pussy*. My mother said *koo*. The Italians call the round door *sorella*, which means sister. Sister is good. My friend Tallulah called hers *the plum garden*. I liked that. Plum garden. It had the taste of summer. I wanted to bite into the lips of summer, the peaches growing on trees espaliered on garden walls.

I worship the beautiful female shapes of nature. When the earth turns out to be flat, I will gladly sail off the edge into her perfect oval. I will slip through, head first, arms by my sides, fearless, the way I did the first time — so long as I know you are well and happy.

You are missing, lost, misplaced in China, your dark head floating in a sea of dark heads on the other side of the world. It was foolish of me to believe you would be safe in China, a country in the middle of a civil war. Because I have given in to people all my life, I acquiesced when you insisted on accepting Soong Chou's invitation to visit his family in Hong Kong. Who in their right mind listens to a child with an irrational request? I thought letting you go would ease the pain of separation, when I make my final journey. Now I have allowed you to be exposed to an even greater danger than my own, which is at least a controlled disaster, a weakness in my own body and not the irrationality of a country at war with itself.

AFTER I WATCHED the foetus swirl down the toilet during that dinner party in London in 1923, I looked for its mother, checked the maids in their black dresses and white organdie aprons for wet spots, checked their stockings for clots of blood, checked the guests for stains on their pale evening dresses, checked the chairs covered in striped silver and white satin for the heartbreaking evidence. Why would a woman leave her unborn child alone like that, unclothed and unshriven?

I have convinced myself that the foetus in the toilet was a girl, her plum garden unknown, un-entered, swollen, blushing with the surfeit of maternal hormones.

When I was a child, I dug holes in the sand with my mother's silver spoons. The other side was China. Nora reclaimed the heirlooms engraved with her family crest, what appears to be an orange tree, its branches symmetrical and laden with fruit. She believed in tree fairies and meadow fairies, our capricious deities. Now the bad fairies have taken you. I stand at the ship's rail and look in our wake for lost children. I see them pink in the foam. Good, I think, at last reconciled with my fear of saltwater. I would rather you were with the shape changers in the sea than with people who would hurt you.

When I say I will throw myself into the water, Tony puts a restraining hand on my arm, "She is not there." He is right. I am mad, but he says the madness will pass. "When you spill your petals into the ocean, Poppy, they will dissipate like blood. What good would that do?" he has written in the margin. We will find you. The East Wind will lie down and let us sail gently over all the children returned to the sea.

I am lying on a deck chair staring at the horizon, willing China to come into view. I know I will live long enough to get there. My heart still squeezes its blood; one unsteady beat after another — the way a child learns to walk. Each morning and evening on the voyage, I will type out parts of my story and he will save them for you. Hopefully, I will be finished by the time we dock in Hong Kong.

The Buddhists say that if we sit by a river long enough we will see the bodies of all our enemies float by. I am writing this so that you will be able to recognize your friends as well, the ones who have loved you more than you know.

I could paint you a picture, but my paintings fall short of the truth. Flowers dissemble. If I should end up eating with the fishes, Tony promises he will change nothing I have written. "Is this true?" he asks when he reads my words as they come out of the typewriter. Never mind. If I exaggerate the colours, that would be my perspective. Isn't exaggeration an artist's prerogative?

The difference between ordinary people and invalids is that invalids have the luxury of time in bed to listen to all the voices in our heads. For me, those voices are shapes and hues. I think of you when you took off your baby shoe, touching my velvet dress with your foot, saying your new word, "soft," as if it were the key to your sensual universe. I imagine a young bee touching down on its first velvet petal and, in the language of bees, uttering the same cry of delight.

Looking over my life, I would say I have spent more time in bed than out of it. That has given me a lot of time to ask questions.

While sunlight and firelight took turns dancing on the ceiling, I looked to their patterns for the answers. "Capture the light," our dear Emily said when she began to teach me everything I know about line and form and colour, and that is what I have tried to do.

⌒

CASANORA HAS BEEN our family home since we left San Francisco for Victoria in 1907, the year I turned seven. Used to living in hotels, I was at first overwhelmed by the large stone house surrounded by several acres of gardens. My mother's whole energy was devoted to cultivating her outdoor rooms decorated with flowering trees and fragrant blossoms. On the other side of Beach Drive, at the Oak Bay Golf Club, players aimed their balls at little holes in the grass. Sometimes, before Nora built her high stone wall, rogue balls sailed into sand traps and ponds and into her newly established flowerbeds. The gardeners covered my head and cursed and I learned to swear in Chinese.

When I was little, I felt the presence of death in Nanny's obsessive attention to my health and Nora's emotional distance, which I think might have been due to her refusal to bond with a child she might lose.

When I do finally leave this earth, I will have my ashes tossed into the ocean that hungers at the bottom of my mother's gardens. I do believe the sea desires us and, by and large, we don't deserve to live on the land. The land belongs to organisms with roots.

Do you remember what Voltaire said about our need to dig in the ground? We must, he said. Like dogs, we bury our bones and our dead. We are compelled to decorate our graves. He would have been astonished by our colonial city built on tunnels and graveyards and coal mines — one for the High Anglicans, one for Catholics and lesser Protestants, one for the Chinese, another for Jews, everything neat and tidy, in its place.

As a child, I believed that I could dig holes that went all the way to China. That is so odd given that we imported Chinese men to do our digging for us. They must have been exhausted. No wonder they sought the natural comfort of opiates. I am not sure why my parents called me Poppy. I don't regard myself as vibrant and intoxicating, but I have grown in difficult ground, like the volunteer plants that grow through the pavement.

Driven about the city as a child, first in Nora's electric car, and then in her Packard, I absorbed the demographic of gardens: Oriental market gardens planted with snow peas and *bok choy*, the elegant wind-sculpted rock gardens of Oak Bay overflowing with lobelia and succulents, the proud and tidy landscaping of working-class people who escaped the tenements of Europe and Great Britain to claim their small slice of paradise and plant it with dreams, tomatoes, roses and holy shrines. I have painted flowers because from my earliest memories they were my consolation. They say a kind heart experiences pain in order to recognize it in others. In the life and death of a garden, the innocent snowdrops and primroses of spring, summer's achingly sensual roses, fall's desperately flamboyant dahlias and dried leaves in the shape of dying hands, I discovered my life.

My mother, Stanford and I — along with Nanny MacDuff, and Miss Beach — moved to Victoria from San Francisco in 1907, just before the opium laws were passed. Because I was a child who didn't know anything about the adult cures for loneliness, even though I had experienced the opiated cough remedies still given to children in those days, I had my own prescription for night terrors. The first evening in our enormous Maclure house, I lay in bed saying our new address over and over — British Columbia, Victoria, Oak Bay, Beach Drive, Casanora — trying to reverse the frightening vortex of heaven.

I was weary of travel. In San Francisco, the death fairies had taken me to their glass city under the sea and found me wanting. That was a double unhappiness — being abducted and then sent back with a damaged heart. I blamed the God of our Presbyterian nanny. If God were as great as Duffie had said he was, then he would have cured the fever that made me vulnerable. Well-bred children, I was told, returned things in good condition. When I borrowed books on my visits to the library with Duffie, they went back promptly with no corners turned down, nothing written in the margins. I didn't want a different me with my words underlined. I should have been returned exactly as I had been.

Casanora was our first real home. Up until my father's death, we had visited with relatives and stayed in hotels in Europe and America. My father performed mercantile diplomacy while we moved *en famille*, following the social seasons of two continents. Duffie told me that my father had died of a massive nosebleed in the Waldorf-Astoria Hotel in 1905. I believed her because I had seen the blood. I saw, and then Nanny MacDuff took me away. Until I met Tallulah and found out the truth, I accepted Nanny's story. As you know, I also have nosebleeds when I am upset.

When my father died, Stanford accompanied us to San Francisco, where my mother had relatives. We only lived there for a year before she decided to move again, this time to Victoria. My mother intimated that it was the aftershock from the earthquake that devastated San Francisco and my illness that had exiled us to Canada. But that was not the case. The exquisitely carved and elaborately fenestrated doors of Nob Hill had been shut in Mother and Stanford's very surprised faces.

During all our moving around, Duffie had managed to teach me to read, mind my manners and avoid stepping on pavement cracks. I was clever, but that was a liability. It was Duffie's job to make a lady out of me. Ladies had good table manners, were not loud in voice or dress and not overly bright. Smart was the undoing of plain girls. Plain girls could be made attractive, but a plain girl with opinions was an anathema. I assumed I was ordinary, at least by comparison to the maternal butterfly fluttering about me, or, I should say, away from me.

Nora was only occasionally interested in children, but when she did pull me into her limited circle of radiance the experience was intense and memorable. "Look," she said when we found a bee's nest in a hollow in a tree. "Honey!" She stuck in her hand and pulled out a piece of wax dripping golden syrup. "Taste this." She thrust her finger in my mouth and I sucked.

She was an enthusiast. I believe her provenance, the rich and fragrant citrus groves of Southern California, had made her more vivid than had her brief proximity to café society. Where she had been an elegant cipher in our travels across the Atlantic Ocean, someone I saw drifting like smoke past a porthole, she became nearly real to me in California.

My most intense memories of San Francisco are all of flowers — my mother taking me out of bed to go barefoot into our walled urban garden and smell the night-blooming honeysuckle or inviting me to sit beside her in front of her three-mirrored dressing table while she took the glass stoppers out of crystal bottles, telling me which flowers were magically captured in each perfume.

Her favourites were the white flowers — especially gardenias. There was a hierarchy in the garden, just as there was in life. She loathed the sword- shaped gladiolas and the carnations. They were common, she said, and besides they gave us hay fever. I liked hay fever. Sneezing was pleasant. When I recently made the connection between sneezing and sex, I wondered why Nora had hated carnations so much.

I think it was difficult for the wild California girl to reconcile her restless intelligence with the expectations of an old world marriage. With Stanford, her second husband, there was no sense of him being in charge. If she had been a boy, I imagine my mother would have managed her family's farms and the fruit company.

The weather was cold and foggy in San Francisco. I had a sore throat. My tongue was coated with a bitter white substance. I was hot and my nightgown was damp. I cried at night and Duffie stayed with me. I don't remember seeing my mother during that time, but I was delirious and might have forgotten. Duffie made me an infusion of hollyhock leaves, which Nora believed would cure any illness caused by bad fairies, until our cook, Mah Lee, talked her into trying his special white tiger tea. The tea was delicious and it brought down my fever.

Nora blamed Mah Lee's tea for the damage to my heart. I now know that was a time of intense paranoia in the kitchens of the American rich. Typhoid Mary had infected her wealthy employers, and the new aristocracy was learning that money was no protection against the illnesses that ravaged the holds of coffin ships and the disease-breeding tenements where unlucky immigrants lived in poverty. Duffie eventually capitulated to my mother's notion that Mah Lee worked for the bad fairies; so he was relieved of the job that supported him and his extended family in China. My mother was wrong. There was no conspiracy. I drank his tea and the fairies brought me back.

I didn't like the damp smell of wood and stone that permeated our new house in Victoria. I feared the wind from the sea that blew rain against the windows. I refused to eat lunch in the children's dining room next to the kitchen. I didn't like creamed chicken and peas and baby carrots in puff pastry anymore, even if they were served on our familiar French pottery dishes with their blue and orange folk designs. My bathroom was too big. My bedroom, painted a blushing ivory with dusty pink silk curtains and matching quilt, was too big. The sea beyond the wildflower garden that bordered the beach was too big. So often, I have heard adults say their childhood memories were diminished when they returned home to find everything smaller.

I didn't want to go out on the balcony and look at the San Juan Islands. I didn't care if the islands were American: my old country just a skip and a hop away. My mother and stepfather had already stolen America. My real father, who ruined the Empire bedroom in his suite at the Waldorf-Astoria when he bled to death, had stolen America. When I looked back over the transom of the ship that brought us to Victoria, I would have jumped in and dog paddled back to my old life if I hadn't been so afraid of the water.

It was dark in my room. Victoria was dark. Canada was dark. I laugh now when I meet people who think Canada is one endless night made of ice and snow and all Canadians sleep in igloos, but my first reaction was to believe we had moved back to the Stone Age. Of course, Stanford didn't help. He told me about madmen who drove teams of dogs in the snow in pursuit of ferocious polar bears.

"They're just stories," he told Duffie when I pulled my blankets up over my face.

"She's nae t' be teased or upset," Nanny said, her Presbyterian lips uncompromising. Duffie had to sleep beside me on a cot while her own little son slept all by himself in a house I never visited.

That first night, Nanny MacDuff was in the kitchen giving Chan Fong, the new cook, her paediatric medicinal recipes. Nora and Stanford were having before-dinner drinks in front of the library fire. I strained to hear the familiar and reassuring sound of ice clinking in their glasses, the snap of the fire in the oak-panelled room. The library was too far away. I prayed Stanford would whistle and reassure me.

Duffie refused to light the fire in my bedroom. Sleepwalkers didn't get to have fires at night. Their nightgowns could catch fire. She knew a girl whose nightgown had caught a spark. No one could save her and she was burned to a crisp. "Och, she was a daftie girl too," Duffie said. I liked the idea of going up in flames. Maybe my mother would notice.

Nanny knew girls who had burned and girls who had tripped on their shoelaces and broken their noses, making them ugly and unmarriageable. She knew children who had crossed their eyes and couldn't uncross them. She knew a boy who had picked his nose and died of a massive nosebleed. She knew boys and girls who had touched their private parts and gone blind and some who went mad. I expected Duffie would soon have cautionary tales to project fear of the Maclure mansion, but she could have saved her breath. I was already terrified.

Nonsense, my stepfather had said when he popped in, wearing his familiar maroon smoking jacket, to say goodnight before going downstairs to join my mother. The bad fairies weren't coming into our new house. They couldn't get passports, and, besides, American fairies didn't like to go where it rained and snowed. They were afraid of the polar bears. Just whistle and they will stay away. My stepfather had a thin moustache. Before he went barking mad, he was a good storyteller.

When the stone wall that separates our house from Beach Drive and the golf course across the road was finished, Stanford took me there and placed a note between the rocks. "There," he said. "I have made a wish that will protect you. It's something your mother's people do." At the time, I thought he meant the fairies but later on I learned it was Jews. That was the beginning of the notes in the wall.

My mother married amusing men. My father had also told tales, old ones from Europe with characters called *nebbishes* and *schlemiels*. I begged Stanford to stay and tell me one more story, even a scary one, but he wouldn't. His drink was poured. The ice was melting. We haven't seen any icebergs on this voyage. Are there no icebergs in the Pacific?

Tony says that I am unbelievably stupid and now I am typing his words — unbelievably stupid. I love the way the English are able to be so rude and yet so polite at the same time.

A Chinese herbalist on Fisgard Street gave me the White Tiger Tea recipe. I recognized the taste right away. Afterward, I took my first cup to a psychic to have the leaves and petals read. She said I had once escaped a fire but that I would eventually die in one. As it turned out, she was more or less right. My sore throat turned out to be rheumatic fever. The valves in my heart had been damaged. I had no idea they were related.

With no siblings with whom to compare myself, I developed an interest in bodies that first year in Victoria. I wanted to know how they were shaped and how they worked. I was especially curious about boys. Duffie, who dressed and undressed in the darkness of early morning and late evening, hid herself with elaborate strata-gems. As far as I knew, the only difference between boys and girls was the cut of our hair and our clothes. I often wondered what it would take to change me into a boy. Perhaps, since opposites attract, a principle of physics I unconsciously absorbed, my mother might fall in love with me.

That summer, I decided I would transform myself. I did this in steps. When we took possession of the house, it had an English garden with large oak trees and acres of lawn sloping to the rocky beach. My mother, whose creativity had languished in our vertical domiciles, the hotels where we had perched like birds living in tall trees, began reorganizing the park. First she planted a fragrant kitchen garden surrounded by a neat boxwood hedge that smelled like cat pee. Further from the house, she oversaw the building of what is now the Japanese garden, with raked gravel, iris and grasses, bonsai maples and cherry trees, grasses nudging contempla-tive ponds with waterfalls, water lilies and the glass balls Japanese fishermen used to float their nets.

I only truly understood this maternal flourishing years later, when I saw a cartoon of an apartment-bound uniformed maid watering a floral-patterned carpet. How frustrated Nora must have been before she cultivated the gardens that allowed her to release her passionate and contemplative natures. No wonder she despised the religion that inevitably resolves in the human incapacity for tol-erance and compassion. Her redemption was in the garden where, if the soil is nurtured, the soul is fed. Without it, my mother would have been like one of those neurotic apartment cats. A child like me would use up her air.

My mother's cultural concession to Oak Bay, the most British neighbourhood between London and Singapore, was her wild tea garden with a gazebo circled by perennials. Every summer afternoon at four, rain or shine — in the fashion of our new community populated by the more delicate second and third sons of the British aristocracy who hadn't been banished to ranches in the Chilcotin and the Cariboo to play cowboy — we had tea and scones with jam in the gazebo. Then as now, Miss Beach changed from her blue lady's maid uniform with white cap and apron into her pearl grey uniform with white lace trim to serve us.

After drinking Nora's special blend of Earl Grey without slurping or clattering our cups, we walked around the park to investigate the progress of her expanding gardens. She took special pleasure in knocking the dead blooms off the lilies and rhododendrons and snipping the faded roses.

"Here," she said, handing me her secateurs. "Off with their heads."

Her enthusiasm for deadheading the plants frightened me. I liked the look of dying flowers. Their colours are exceptional, especially the pinks and peaches shaded by decay.

"No!" I said.

"I thought you'd enjoy helping, Poppy. You will learn from me."

"I don't want to hurt the flowers."

"It isn't hurting them. If you don't deadhead the roses, they will stop flowering and go to seed."

I knew that I was an imperfect flower. Was I being given the same ruthless treatment as her plants? I defended imperfection, and I still do. She required balance.

Following her instructions, the flock of Coolie gardeners using shovels and their bare hands interrupted the lawn with plantings of asters, and blowsy columbine in the graceful beds that meander on the slope to the ocean. Like light-deprived miners coming out of the ground with their tools, the gardeners emerged at daybreak from a tunnel under the house. Because Stanford had told me I could dig a hole all the way to China if I persevered in my excavation of the beach, I thought the workers had passed through the centre of the earth each morning. Only the head gardener, Guan Sing, spoke pidgin English with my mother. The rest, I was told, spoke Cantonese. They were crows in black pyjamas with straw sunhats shaped like the limpets we pulled off rocks in the sea.

I was in no hurry, but, one evening when Duffie was distracted by her barley water, I intended to follow the men home and find out what the their underground life was all about. Nanny liked a little taste of her homeland after supper, a time when Nora would be unlikely to smell it on her breath. There was a bottle of something with a tartan label in the back of my toilet and a carefully washed teacup she kept in the medicine cupboard. Duffie had no idea that I knew, but I have a strong sense of smell.

Like a child conditioned to praising a favoured sibling, I soon learned that complimenting my mother's garden was the way to curry her favour. If she'd had the gift for raising children as self-confident as her plants, my life would have been very different. In the beginning, I had no friends but Stanford and had to content myself with playing in my make-believe world. I made secret potions with the petals I gathered in the rose garden. I played marooned sailor at the beach, raiding the vegetable garden on the eastern border of our seven acres for provisions.

I heard Miss Beach whisper to Duffie that my mother kept Stanford on a short leash. Luckily that leash extended as far as the shoreline and my stepfather and I spent some happy times collecting shells and stones on the beach. I particularly liked the blue glass worn smooth by the waves. Stanford said I should not keep those but throw them back because they were water. The blue glass was tears, he said, shed for lost souls. The sea smoothed their edges to make grief more bearable.

The fairy glen was my private kingdom. The sea was dangerous for children, Stanford told me, and the garden was risky for fairies, where they could be disbelieved or caught playing naughty tricks. In the meadow that separates the garden from the sea, he told me, small things, the wildflowers, the children and the fairies, were safe. The adults were amused when I insisted they pay a toll before they were allowed to step past the clipped lawn into the wild grasses where I was the queen.

I still have the box of magical payments drawn from adult pockets — a tiny silver notebook and attached pen with an art nouveau fairy engraved on the cover, a cat's-eye marble, an ivory toothpick, a miniature card deck, a small opium bottle with painted chrysanthemums and a jade stopper, coins stamped with the head of Queen Victoria, and other treasures. Sometimes I exchanged passage through my fiefdom for a story or a song or permission to go to the library after adult dinner, to beg a puff on a cigar and the privilege of wearing the ring around it. No one could get to the beach by land without passing me, not even Stanford — especially not Stanford because his pockets were deep and filled with delights.

The fairy glen was a carpet of lilies in spring, small California poppies in the summer. My favourites were the chocolate coloured fritillaries. When I brought a handful to the children's dining room, Duffie told me there was a terrible punishment for picking the lilies and I believed her. She said the same thing about dogwood, the tree to which her Lord had been nailed. If I picked dogwood, which grew all around our house, I would bleed as Jesus bled, from the hands and the feet, and in my case, the nose as well. Even though the Christian religion was banned from our house, Duffie took her chances because she had told me that her Lord would make communion wafers out of my ground-up bones if I told.

My mother instructed me to respect plants the way some parents teach their children to handle animals with care, or books. I know the lengths that children will go to when they want attention. I once saw a little boy who was old enough to know better throw a handful of sand at his mother's oil painting when she was mesmerized by waves. My paintings of flowers and floral arrangements pleased my mother but I wanted to arouse stronger emotions, rage and delight.

The best way to test my mother's patience would have been to do damage to her beloved plants. I could have decapitated the purpurea orchids, whose stamens rested like placidly bonneted babies on lavender pillows. That would have been an offence as serious as infanticide in our household. Stomping the virginal calla lilies would get a reaction beyond the power of my childish imagination. What punishment short of sending me to be crushed with the grapes in her friend's California vineyard would suffice?

But, preferring appeasement to opposition in deference to my lonely muscle, I eschewed violence. Rather than directly oppose my garden-obsessed mother, I chose quieter strategies.

While I lay awake one winter evening, wishing my mother would come and tell me a bedtime story while she pored over her seed and bulb catalogues as usual, I made a decision that would please and displease her. I would steal packets of seeds when they came in the mail and plant my own garden in the fairy glen. She would question me and other members of our household. She would send complaining letters to the growers. Time would pass. My mother would fret, and I would comfort her.

That is exactly what happened. My mother fussed. I cultivated my small piece of the earth, carried seaweed up from the beach and stole compost from the large bin near the kitchen garden. I planted my seeds and watered them as they grew, carrying my sand pail back and forth from the house. Soon my rectangle of stolen flowers would bloom like an impressionist painting.

My mother's temperature rose from glacial to tepid. The gardeners were interrogated. Her annoyance was fertilizer to my little plantation. With every hour of sunshine and every tin bucket of water, the plants flourished. When the summer flowers opened their faces to the sun, I would show her what I had done. I would defeat her and show her how much I loved her all at once.

That was what was supposed to happen. One night in June, I dreamed I slept in a tiny open grave in the middle of my secret garden. There was only a thin fingernail of moon. In my dream, I heard munching and squirting, the sound of deer eating and eliminating.

In the real morning, all my plants had been eaten and trampled. Only the creamy Romnea poppy, which hadn't yet flowered, was saved. Now that one plant is the mother and grandmother of many. If my mother figured out what had happened to her seeds, she didn't mention it.

Slowly, in the summer of my conversion to the son she might adore, I gathered the paraphernalia I would need for my boyhood. In a metal box like the one where I kept my treasures, I hid a kitchen knife, a compass, a pair of sandals, an undershirt, a pair of men's shorts I had stolen from Stanford's drawer, and a woven belt with red and green stripes to hold up the shorts, which were much too big for me. Because Duffie was under orders to accompany me anywhere near the beach, I had to promise I wouldn't go there by myself.

Probably she was relieved to be left in her room under the eaves in the attic to read her *Nanny* magazine or write a letter to her ten-year-old son, Alec, whom she was only allowed to visit on Sunday afternoon and every second Thursday evening. Alec was the stuttering shadow that had followed us from Scotland to America and finally to Canada. Because he was not allowed to live with us, Duffie had to find a family to care for him each time we moved. When I was a child, I accepted that reality. Now, I am appalled.

On Christmas Eve, when Duffie brought Alec to the staff party and dressed him up in his scratchy new sweater, the twin to the one in a chastely wrapped parcel under the tree that was addressed to me, he stood self-consciously apart. Perhaps he was afraid to speak because of his stutter. There was no evidence of Alec's father, who, we were told, had died in a war.

When I came to know Alec better, we spent hours conjuring our ideal fathers, his and mine. Mine I could vaguely remember. His was fantasy. We imagined a Celt with black hair. Alec was much swarthier than his mother. If he resented me for taking Duffie from him, he didn't say; and I was too obtuse to think of the possibility. I think we both accepted our strange social orphanhood. Duffie didn't talk about Alec and, when I asked about him, she went stiff with sorrow. I wondered if my mother grieved over the mysterious social barricade between children and adults that kept us apart.

It didn't occur to me then that she might have had a choice where Duffie didn't.

All summer long, I hung my dresses like flags from the arbutus trees. Freed from satin bows and fragile cloth, I swaggered in my shorts and enjoyed my bare chest with nipples pleasantly erect in the wind. I built forts and climbed trees without fear of punishment from Duffie, whose personal mission and professional mandate was keeping me in box condition. When I returned to the house in my summer dresses, there were no tears or stains to betray my life as a boy.

I had to decide what to do with my hair, which was long and curled at the ends — the colour of corn silk Stanford said when he petted it. To his credit, he didn't make me feel awkward and unlovely the way my mother and Duffie did.

"How can we make her pretty?" my mother asked once, holding her ebony cigarette holder and blowing the smoke out the nursery window while Duffie struggled with untangling the fine knots in my hair with my ivory-backed brush. I now know there was nothing wrong with my looks. I just wasn't my mother, polished and manicured to perfection by her lady's maid. Nora was stunning, a glamorous gathering of light, one of those blue-eyed, black-haired Oriental-looking Jewish women, with skin as pale as beleek china. My mother understood about breeding hybrids. I was a mouse-coloured being, an irritating reminder of the failure of genetic planning.

I had the choice of hiding it under a hat, slowly trimming it with the knife in my tin box, or hacking it all off at once. I chose the latter. The cutting took place on a hot July afternoon while the adults rested after lunch. Wearing my khaki shorts and no shirt, I sawed with the blade. My hair fell to the ground and I gathered it up and made a nest with twigs, which I placed on a branch in an arbutus tree. I had the purse mirror I used to send unanswered messages to my mother on the other side of the garden. When I looked in it, I saw what I wanted, her boy.

Duffie didn't see it that way at all. When she was confronted with the new me, she saw her own reflection, a jobless nanny in disgrace. For the rest of the summer, she kept me under house arrest. She even arranged to take me on her days off, which must have been convenient for my mother, who did not protest this new arrangement. I wore a hat at all times — "for the sun" — even in the house. Nanny produced some gathered gingham and organdie bonnets, which she passed off as a whim of my own. I complied because, added to my crime of depriving Alec of his mother was the possibility that — were I discovered and Duffie sacked — she assured me he would starve to death or be taken to an orphanage where he would eat gruel and be beaten by sadistic priests. It wouldn't matter if I had cut my hair in one of my sleepwalking episodes while Duffie was snoring in her own attic bed. Nanny was supposed to be on duty day and night. Because I refused to go there with Duffie, enforcer of the laws of ladylike behaviour, the fairy glen was verboten. My wilding time was over.

My mother let the summer of hats pass without comment. I did catch her looking at me once with a strange smile. Perhaps I had satisfied the repressed anarchist in her with my small rebellion. I wish she had reacted with anger because I was tired of my pale invisibility in her life. Stanford, who was determined to improve his golf swing, spent hours each day knocking light balls with holes in them across the lawn. I was required to fetch them without trampling flowers. He said my straw hat was fetching.

Duffie was not about to give up her pleasures because of my selfishness. The time she had spent reading and writing in her room she now spent in my room, reclining on my *toile de Jouy* day bed while I read aloud or made neat copies of gothic stories about lost children fed by my memories of febrile delirium. If the friends my mother made in Victoria had children, they were a mystery to me. Before Dola came into my life, none were invited for tea and my mother didn't take me with her when she went calling in her new electric car. I wanted so badly to be asked. I was good. I knew which fork to use. I could make my nervous hands be still in my lap. Nora ignored my silent pleas. When she waved goodbye, I honestly couldn't tell if the gesture was for me or if she was simply shaking the pollen out of her gloves.

One after the other, the dog days of summer rolled over moments as uniform and unremarkable as the grey pebbles in our circular driveway. I was awakened by Duffie at six and, still wearing my nightgown and nightcap, taken out on my balcony to watch the sun rise over the San Juan Islands. Then I was bathed and dressed in a cotton smock with matching bonnet. For breakfast, I was given freshly-squeezed orange juice, porridge, and an egg with two pieces of Melba toast and jam. Since Stanford had alleged that he was allergic to eggs, I claimed allergy by association. If I ate the porridge very quickly, gulping air with each bite, I could manage to vomit all over the egg, but not until I had secreted the toast, jam sides facing, in the pocket of my dress.

Duffie cottoned on very quickly. She was, as she often told me, "nae Scottish fool." There was no such thing. All the Scots I knew — Nanny, our doctor, mother's bridge partner — were smart as foxes. My two-course breakfast became three courses. I was not given toast and jam until the egg had been eaten.

After breakfast, I was taken to say good morning to Nora, who had her meal in bed, on a painted wicker tray, a privilege only accorded to me when I had a fever. I watched her take tiny sips of tea and nibbles of toast. She ate so little. I still feel sad when I eat dry toast. Food was discipline. Life was discipline. When my mother dismissed me with a wave of her hand, Duffie and I would walk to Oak Bay Village where she bought meat for Guan Sing, our new cook. The rest of the morning was spent in my room doing schoolwork. After lunch, we rested.

I lay on my bed listening to seagulls and the curious tongues of water exploring the caves and crevices along the shoreline, wondering what miracles were occurring in the fairy glen that I was missing, what butterflies the grass had released from its side of the radiant line that divided my mother's gardens from the land of make believe, what birds called their young, which blossoms were opening their hungry mouths. Duffie would turn a few pages of the latest ladies magazine passed on by my mother or her own copy of *Nanny* and nod off. I waited for that.

Although Nora's sitting room is adjacent to my bedroom, I could not clearly hear the voices coming through the wall. As you know, the two rooms share a linen closet with a door at each end. While Duffie slept, I crouched in the closet and allowed myself to inhale the gardenia scent of Nora's linens and neatly folded lingerie. Sometimes Stanford would visit. I could see the tip of one well-polished boot swinging like a metronome over his crossed knees, punctuating his gossip.

One very hot afternoon, while I was sitting on the floor of the linen closet with a nightgown from my mother's laundry hamper pressed to my face, I heard female voices, my mother and Miss Beach. They were both laughing. I hadn't heard Miss Beach laugh before. Very carefully, I opened the door a crack, as I had so many times before. *Your mother is quite helpless*, I remembered Stanford saying. *She can't even tie her own shoelaces.* But she wasn't helpless in the garden, was she? No, she ruled her garden with a porcelain fist. And yet, looking beyond the French doors that separate my mother's sitting room from her boudoir, I could see her sitting on her satin quilt waiting for Miss Beach, who was kneeling on the floor in front of her, to untie her shoes. The shoes came off, one at a time. Miss Beach leaned lower. I could have sworn she kissed my mother's silk-shod feet.

Nora stood up and Miss Beach turned her around to undo the buttons on her dress. When this was done, I watched the maid's hands move over her shoulders and down her chest. I saw her bare shoulders and the plump arcs of her breasts as Miss Beach slipped the straps on her chemise over her arms and rested her hands on her bosom. My mother smiled as her nipples changed from pink to a darker colour and I felt an alarming current between my legs.

Miss Beach turned down the bed for my mother's nap and arranged her clothing over a chair. Nora got in, sighing approval of the coolness of her bed and lay exposed with the top sheet folded back. Miss Beach closed the curtains and the room darkened to a warm peach colour. My mother asked Miss Beach to rub her shoulders. She had been arranging flowers all morning, she said, and they ached.

Miss Beach rubbed and I watched her competent hands move in circles on Nora's back. Observing this intimate act, I was fascinated and repelled at once. Miss Beach's hands made smaller and smaller circles as they moved down her spine and caressed the small of her back and her bottom. One hand moved between her legs and circled and circled. I took the two damp fingers I had been sucking out of my mouth and touched myself in the same place. My mother moaned, her voice as dark as echoes in the caves along our shore. I moaned too, as my insides opened like a flower. I shuddered and wept into my mother's nightgown..

Nora's body relaxed in sleep as Miss Beach covered her with the top sheet, picked up the dress she had been wearing and hung it on a hanger. I held my breath when she gathered the discarded lingerie, walked slowly toward the linen cupboard and opened the door.

Miss Beach looked straight at me and said nothing. Perhaps she had heard my small cry of pleasure. I pretended I was asleep, but I could feel her disbelieving glance through my eyelids. She closed the door firmly and walked away and, after a few minutes, I tiptoed out of the cupboard past the snoring Duffie to my own bed. Neither Miss Beach nor my mother acknowledged they knew I had been in the closet, but the next time I went to spy on them, the door was locked on the other side.

2

MAY 13, 1927, 7:30 PM, IN MY STATEROOM, THE *EMPRESS OF ASIA*

Mon Petit Chou,
After two days, we are well out to sea. All I can see through the
porthole is ocean and sky. My life is guided by stars. I hope these
ones are lucky. I think of my mother and her superstition around
cutting the asters in her garden. Disaster, she said, means against
the stars. The ocean is calm and I look forward to moonlight on the
water. I will write until sunset and then we shall go out on deck and
watch the orange and purple horizon.

This afternoon I rested on my berth with a magazine, but I
couldn't concentrate on reading. Instead, I lay listening to the
rhythm of the ship's engine saying *chou, chou, chou*; the sound
pushing the ship like oars in the water. I thought of Alec's stutter
and the time long ago when I lay awake listening to the wheels on
our train say "mother" over and over.

Tony and I have ordered a light supper on deck. I don't feel up
to dressing for dinner and overeating, which is a terrible temptation
on board ship. Last night the sea was rough. I went straight to bed
after tea and stayed there. Tony, who has amazing sea legs, brought

me brandy and milk and thin salmon sandwiches, his remedy for seasickness and insomnia.

"Eat fish, Poppy, and you will become a fish."

"If I were a fish, how would I find Precious?"

"Don't take me so literally. I mean fish-like, immune to seasickness, dear Poppers. You are so deep and I mean to be superficial."

"You are not superficial, Tony. You are a miracle."

"Tell my mother." He laughed. Tony maintains he is a disappointment to Lady Bainbridge, who wants grandchildren. His mother, who made an heir and a spare, lost her elder son in the Spanish influenza epidemic, as did many others who had been spared the sorrow of an unmarked grave in French battlefields.

"And I am a fairy," he pencils in.

"Did you know," he says, "that the Romans believed illness was influenced by the stars, hence influenza."

"I thought celestial navigation was romantic," I reply.

Yesterday evening Tony told me that sex was the best sleeping medicine and we laughed when I asked him if he could guess which ladies on the ship were being helped to their rest by paid companions or randy sailors at that very moment. This will no doubt become a theme of our voyage as we guess which single women in the first-class dining room require nap assistance. Anything that distracts me from worrying is welcome. We chatted until I fell asleep.

⌐

WHEN WE BECAME ACQUAINTED in London after the war, Tallulah Bankhead told me that she knew someone who had met my mother at a women's clinic in New York where she had gone to be treated for depression by Emma Goldman. All her friends went for hand release, Tallulah said, and they gossiped about one another. It was through another Goldman patient, Anne Morgan, the neurotic daughter of the banker J.P. Morgan, that Nora had met Stanford.

Goldman specialized in something she called vulvular massage, an orgasmic treatment for women's hysteria. Tallulah informed me that Goldman, the social egalitarian, loved to name drop. My mother was a name.

During the beginning of this century, lots of rich American girls married into aristocratic European families. I have no idea about the dynamic of my parents' marriage, but I am sure that Nora felt constrained by my father's old world ideas.

Now, of course, it is different. That world no longer exists. Now there are not enough boys to marry all the girls who want husbands, and not enough fathers to continue the family lines, providing hope for grandparents. No wonder Lady Bainbridge is disappointed in Tony. He is the only one left carry on the family name.

Much of the fabulous Miss Bankhead's wisdom came from the wrong end of a bottle of *Old Granddad* bourbon, or her pipe dreams. One of Duffie's favourite proverbs, and she had many, was "where there's smoke there's fire." I think that Tallulah, as with many confabulators I have met, is more of an exaggerator than a liar. I do believe women adore her because she has given us the courage to speak out.

My father's family was a wealthy, well-connected banking dynasty that subsidized Austria's aristocracy for generations, earning minor titles in addition to interest on borrowed money. Perhaps it was the innocence of America that attracted him when he met my fourteen-year-old mother in her father's orange grove during a fresh-air break from a tea dance in her family's big Mission-style farmhouse. At bedtime, I often asked to hear the story of their marriage in a specially built gazebo made from a circular planting of echium.

"Echium?" Tony wants to know.

"You'd love it Tony. It has a single stalk and looks like a sixteen-foot penis."

"How remarkable."

Nora, the child bride, wore ivory silk embroidered with orange blossoms, and a circle of mixed orange and honeysuckle held her veil in place. It was easy to get my mother to talk about flowers. When my father died, he was forty-three and my mother was still in her twenties.

Before I met Tallulah, I'd heard only fairy tales about my father's death. Further, I was not told outright that we were Jewish, and I wondered if that information was common knowledge in Victoria, where anti-Semitism is a polite fact of life. There were clues, of course, that I put together later after Tallulah filled me in; certain words I remember my father using, the absence of ritual in our observance of Christian holidays. We had Christmas trees and Christmas presents, but there was no carol singing. We had Easter-egg hunts but the Easter meal was more like a Passover Seder that I attended in London. Even when anti-German sentiment erupted in Victoria after the sinking of the Lusitania, my mother refused to use our real heritage as a defense.

We were chic, but I could tell that my mother and I were outsiders. Even through she had a busy social life, she complained about certain snobs who excluded her. I barely remembered my father, except that he had a beard with gold and red highlights and a gold pocket watch. I imagine Nora was afraid of my questions, which were, of course, impossible to answer. There were no family photographs. I did, however, see a medal, the Iron Crown, in her jewel-box when she showed me the beautiful things — the perfect strands of pearls, emerald earrings and four-carat diamonds from Tiffany's — which Stanford had given her.

Tony asks, "What was Stanford like? You have mentioned that he was eccentric, and funny."

"Yes, he was. I imagine I regarded him as a crazy uncle, the kind children like, with pockets full of magic and good things to eat. I didn't resent him because he made no attempt to impose fatherly discipline. He was my friend."

"Your little sunbeam?"

"No. He had a dark side."

My mother's new husband was entertaining and kind when he felt like it, but he was also depressive and vain, given to what Victoria ladies of his time called the vapours. Even though I have been privy to excess, I haven't seen a toilette to compare with Stanford's. My mother's elaborately appointed dressing table with its crystal bottles, silver picture frame and gold brush and looking glass, was nothing beside Stanford's ritual vanities.

My stepfather spent a full hour getting dressed every morning and that was *after* his bath. He had creams and powders for every crack and orifice in his body, nose hair scissors, silver ear cleaners, triangular plasters to hold back the wrinkles in his forehead, hair nets, hair dye and perfumes, not to mention a full gymnasium adjoining the attic ballroom, and a cupboard full of vitamins and tonics, the elixir of youth. It is my obligation to take care of myself, he told me, and I wondered, but didn't say, for what?

My stepfather and I both endured the darkness, which may have been my mother's natural habitat. Stanford was a day person and his rituals started at dawn. Rarely up before ten in the morning, my mother was, in spite of her passion for gardening, a nocturnal character, given to reading detective fiction and playing canasta in bed. Victoria in winter was dull after sunny California. Hour after hour, I sat at the windows watching the rain slide down the glass, wondering when the weather would improve. Stanford was also sensitive to the changes. Sometimes he moped in his room for days, and I saw trays of untouched food being returned to the kitchen via the back stairs.

As part of my regular lessons, Duffie gave me a box of water-colours to decorate my written work and colour my maps. Those *Winsor and Newton* paints were my salvation. I pushed the colours as hard as I could, trying to find the intensity of hues that we had left behind in California with its palm, orange and lemon trees, and glorious sunsets.

When Stanford and Nora stayed home in the evening, I was allowed to visit her room for a few minutes before my bedtime. On those evenings, she played solitaire on her tray, while Ling Ling and Moo Pei lay like two Pekingese eunuchs on either side of her. I wanted to lie down beside her, but I was obliged to sulk on the end of the bed. Watching her spoil her favourites made me want to spit. When Mother was happy with the outcome of a game, she rewarded the dogs with chocolates she kept in a box on the white and gold commode beside her bed.

"Chocolates? Aren't dogs allergic?" Tony asks.

"Not these ones, apparently."

I brought my paintings to show her, hoping I, too, might be rewarded with a chocolate, but that didn't happen. Nora would look up and say that they were very good in an utterly bored tone of voice, then go back to shuffling her cards, a fresh deck once a week. I learned that if I wanted a real reaction I had to paint flowers. When I copied her beautiful arrangements, she commended my successful renderings and pointed out my mistakes with her beautifully buffed nails.

Eventually, Nora decided I needed company and more specific instruction than Duffie, who had a Scots passion for the written word, was capable of giving me. Two students, Boulie, a ward of Lady Cowes-Wentworth-Cowes, who was the widow of an English engineering advisor to the Chinese Imperial Family, and Alec MacDuff, joined my home school. I have no idea why my mother made this egalitarian concession to Duffie or how she talked Lady Cowes-Wentworth-Cowes into private tutoring, but Nanny was overjoyed and the bottles of Scotch she had been swiping from the pantry disappeared from my water closet. Our school was a godsend to Alec who, as the son of a servant, had been teased and bullied at school by the sons of the *nouveaux riches* who sent their children to learn the manners of upper-class English boys.

To teach us, Mother hired M. Bonheur to teach French, Miss Wiebe for history, Miss Earl for arithmetic, a complete waste of time in my case at least because I am indifferent to numbers, Mme. Danilova for dance and Miss Carr for painting. Our teachers came to the house, one on each day of the school week, just for the morning. The afternoons were for reading.

My large breakfasts were now served only on weekends. After orange juice, a cup of tea and an English muffin with Chan Fong's delicious green gage plum and ginger jam in the children's dining room, we were at work by nine o'clock. Miss Carr refused to transport herself. Stanford taught Soong Chou how to drive the car, and our servant fetched Emily from James Bay every Friday, returning her after lunch. She was the only teacher who was given her noon meal.

"Miss Carr smells," I wrote in my daybook. In my infant world — which ended in war, plague, prohibition and the first depression — women were graded by appearances. Miss Carr was disheveled. My mother smoked, drank, and took her sexual pleasures without regard for convention and yet she was, to all appearances, a lady. Mother dressed well, talked well, knew which spoon and fork to use, and ran her house like a medieval seigneur, everyone in his or her place, including me.

Nora said, while tending her garden as tenderly as any mother could be expected to care for a child, "It is not what you do. It's what people think you do." I felt constrained by the twine she used to train her plants. What if Boulie and I traded places, I wondered? Would Duffie and my mother be able to curb Boulie's spirit with proverbs and cautionary tales about what happened to "wee bizems" and "daftie girls"? I doubted it.

"Pure" was a big word with Duffie. Boulie and I called ourselves "the Pures" because Nanny was constantly warning us to keep our pinafores as "pure as the driven snow." The women in our house were all identifiable by their uniforms. Nora's pleated and beaded pastel gowns by Worth and her elegant suits proclaimed her status as a lady. I thought she was a goddess. Duffie, in her white nanny's uniform and veil, was a step above Miss Beach, not quite a lady's maid, not quite a nurse, in spite of some dubious qualifications as a midwife and masseuse. Misses Wiebe and Earl were spinsters. They were plain, "ugly as plates of snails," Boulie said, and they wore ordinary wool and cotton dresses with practical shoes and coats. Weep and Snarl, as we called them, had identifying hats of one sort or another, sensible shoes and practical gloves. The teachers wore dull browns and the servants wore shades of black, which Nora only put on for mourning.

Emily was something else. For all we knew, she slept in her clothes. They were dirty and covered in paint. She smelled like the dead sea-life I found washed up on the beach. To make matters worse, she was a great believer in classroom intimacy, coming in close while critiquing our work. We could not hold her off with a stick or a paintbrush. I won't forget the look on Alec's face when she grabbed him in a headlock under her arm, explaining that she would swim all the way to China using that grip should he try mimicking her instructions again. His grimace when he got the full force of her underarm odor sent Boulie and me into fits of laughter. We were sure that Miss Carr hadn't seen the inside of a bathtub even once in her life and dared one another to ask her if she was as afraid of bathwater as I was of the sea.

We never did, but one day she delivered herself of an impressive hygiene lecture. It was her opinion that too frequent bathing had weakened my health. I had destroyed all my protective coverings. It would be better if I let my natural oils and bacteria do their work. I didn't dare look, but I could hear something between a suppressed sneeze and a fart. It was Boulie trying to control her laughter. I pressed my fingernails into the palm of my hand and bit my bottom lip. When Miss Carr was finished, she sent Boulie and me outside to pick some anemones for a still life. We laughed so hard we had to leave our underpants hanging to dry in the monkey tree, pinching one another and making wishes — in case the fairies were listening.

"What did you wish for, Boulie?" I asked.

"I won't tell. It's bad luck."

"Oh, it's just me. I don't count. We're blood sisters." We were. We had pricked our wrists and mingled blood they day before, at Boulie's insistence.

"I wished to see Miss Carr naked in the bath."

"You're a pervert!"

"Yes I am, and so are you!"

"Am not."

Our classroom was set up in the ballroom on the third floor, which eventually became my studio. Even though it is a large room, it was not big enough to enable us to get away from Miss Carr's unattractive aura. She brought a big sheep dog with her and it was Alec's job to take her pet outside for watering or clean up if she didn't make it down three sets of stairs to the canine powder room in the garden. That dog got very excited and began to piddle when anyone paid attention to her. Miss Carr told us everything had a use. She told us that dyers used urine to fix colours and that she had seen children go about London collecting buckets of dog feces to sell to leather tanners. These, she said, were called *pure*. That got us giggling in our ink-stained pinnies. *Pu-ure* drivel, we said pulling out the vowel like shiny toffee.

"What are you going to draw?" she asked Boulie one morning.

"God," Boulie said, as if she had a personal connection.

"We don't know what God looks like," Miss Carr retorted.

"We will in a minute," Boulie demanded, with her tongue between her teeth and her pencil flying over the paper.

I wasn't sure if Miss Carr wanted to shake me up because she didn't like teaching the privileged children of Oak Bay or if she was trying to change my artistic direction. When I think of it now, I realise that she had recognized my talent and didn't want me to waste it on what she called "Sunday painting," the amateur efforts of ladies with nothing better to do.

"These ladies all have three names," she said. "They advertise their mediocrity."

I think all three of us liked her deliberate coarseness. I say coarseness as opposed to vulgarity because she was actually quite prudish and was offended by such things as nudity in painting. "Stay away from that muck," she said. When I grew up and Miss

Carr became Emily, she confided to me that she had been frightened by the inappropriate behaviour of her father, who had died when she was still a child.

Stanford said Miss Carr was a "bohemian" and I liked the word. On our next visit to San Francisco, Duffie took me to a matinee of *La Bohème*. Bohemians died beautifully. I remember the tenor tucked Mimi's pink satin hat in his cummerbund, and, while he sang "*Che gelida manina*," the pink ribbon dangled between his legs. From our seats in the loges, he could have been exposing himself. Duffie covered my eyes. It was a bit late, because, by then, I had seen far more than a pink ribbon.

Miss Carr thought I had talent and she did everything she could to distract me from my childish genre, the paintings of civilized gardens and well-bred floral arrangements that pleased my mother. I had to decide for whom I was going to paint, the mother whose attention I wanted or the teacher whose passionate enthusiasms were sometimes fiercely judgmental. I made the obvious choice, still hoping my mother's unconditional love would follow.

My forte was colour. Alec, who was a much better draughtsman than I, pleased and displeased our teacher because he was capable of photographic representation of anything put in front of him. His dogs looked like dogs, right down to the appropriate texture of fur and sharpness of incisors. His trees were trees, every branch and trembling leaf. Miss Carr shook him hard, ordering his soul to come out. "You must leave something to the imagination. Otherwise, take a photograph." Once she picked him up by his feet and hung him upside down until his face turned red. None of this was reported to our parents because in her way Miss Carr, unlike our other teachers, was *for* us, supporting our wild side.

I believe I learned from Emily that a girl could protect her independent spirit. She taught us that good manners have nothing to do with wealth or social position. Emily told me the real measure of a person was whether they treated others with respect. Her way was to assert her idealism. Mine was to fit in.

One Friday morning, Miss Carr asked us to paint from imagination something we had lost. I presented my America, a prismatic
shimmer walking out of the sunrise over the snow-capped mountains of western Washington. Alec drew a pretty woman I did not
recognize in black pen and slowly filled in the colours. She had
auburn hair that flew out of its pins and large dark blue eyes.
The appealing woman wore a teal dress with soft pleats and she
was reaching toward the foreground. "Who is it?" I asked and Alec
refused to tell me.

I still have the painting. It took me a while to figure out it was
a portrait of his mother. To me, Duffie was all business, nothing
feminine at all. Much as I loved her, I would have drawn Duffie
without grace, defining her chin hairs and beginning wrinkles. "Do
wrinkles hurt?" I once asked her when she tucked me in. Nora,
our female genius, sucked all the radiance out of the women of our
household, but Alec saw what he needed — an intact and vital mother.

Miss Carr called her own dead mother Mrs. Father. We could tell
she loved and hated her father and much of her determination to
shock was rebellion against his autocratic ways. She warned us not
to become Mrs. Fathers, wives who lived vicariously. It was obvious to us there was no danger of Boulie becoming that sort of
woman, but our teacher made it clear she was worried about me.

Boulie's painting was a cross section of a woman falling down a
well. Her picture was made in washes of gray and the woman was
wearing white pyjamas. White, I later found out, was the colour of
mourning in China. The woman's mouth was open. Her face,
beauty betrayed, was chalk white with bright red lips.

"Who is that," I asked?

"That is my mother," Boulie said flatly, and put down her brush.

"Liar," I said, and that was that, or so I thought.

One of the things I liked about Boulie was her ability to colour
any situation, so that even the most mundane event was transformed into high drama. Boulie had the gift of the gab and she kept
Alec and me spellbound with her stories during our lunches in the

children's dining room and our operatic garden adventures. My two friends were the only non-fairy beings allowed to pass into the fairy glen without paying a toll. Boulie was taller than either Alec, who was small with a slight stutter that made his Scottish accent almost unintelligible, or myself. She was larger than life, and her stories, spilling from her as she sat astride an arbutus branch or lay flat on her back in grasses sprinkled with wildflowers, were enthralling.

I hadn't thought of Boulie as an exotic, beyond my awareness that she was beautiful. She had gray almond-shaped eyes with black lashes and straight dark hair to her waist. Her clothing was somewhat eccentric — she sometimes wore colourful silk brocade jackets with toggles — and her favourite colour was red, which she told us was lucky in her mother's culture. Now I found myself staring at Boulie, trying to determine what her painting was telling us, if anything.

She didn't mention her provenance again until the evening Lady Cowes-Wentworth-Cowes invited me to a sleep over to celebrate Chinese New Year. It was the year of the monkey. When Lady Cowes's houseboy, Quon Sam, served dinner in her red and gold dining room, he told us lurid stories about Chinese banquets, where monkey-brain soup was presented in the skull of a freshly killed ape. My porcelain soupspoon trembled in my hand. Lady Cowes-Wentworth-Cowes's carved Oriental furniture cast long shadows in her dimly lit dining room. Her long-nosed face — red lips, black charcoaled eyebrows and powdered skin — more made up than the Anglo-Indian ladies of our acquaintance — was a scary mask in the candlelight. Frightened, adding shadow to speculation, I began to wish I could rush home after dinner, even though I had looked forward to this party for weeks.

I tried to focus on navigating the astonishing meal from my bowl to my mouth. This was the first time I had used chopsticks. That night, Quon Sam made a beautiful melon soup, eight-jewel duck, a boneless bird stuffed with meat and rice and rare spices, *Szechuan* eggplant from his winter garden, Chinese broccoli with shrimp from a trap that floated in front of the house, and a quivering almond pudding for dessert. We drank a delicate jasmine tea called *Dragon's Tears*.

"That was a delicious dinner," I said to my host and Quon Sam, because Duffie had taught me that compliments should also be given to the servants. "I especially liked the eight-jewel duck. What was in the rice?"

"Ginger, onion, and pork," Quon Sam beamed.

"Pork?" I asked in a weak voice.

"Yes," Lady Cowes-Wentworth-Cowes smiled as if she had swallowed a whole pig. "Pork is the most delicious meat."

I was not allowed to eat pork. I thought it had something to do with my heart. Duffie had said I must not eat it *on pain of death*. The forbidden food bounced in my stomach. Too cowed to say anything, I swallowed hard and took a deep breath.

After dinner, Lady Cowes-Wentworth-Cowes wrapped us in blankets and led us through the French doors in the dining room to a stone terrace, where we watched Quon Sam set off fireworks in the garden. He said that fireworks chased away evil spirits. Boulie and I covered our ears when the houseboy lit the fuses and set off his pyrotechnics, glittering waterfalls that exploded in the dark winter sky. The spectacle was gorgeous and terrifying. As the garden filled with smoke, I leaned over the balcony wall and threw up my dinner.

Boulie had two beds in her room, but after Quon Sam turned down the covers and left us alone, I scampered out of mine and got into hers. In the dark, she told me the story of her mother, who had been the third wife of a Chinese warlord the Cowes-Wentworth-Cowes had befriended in Peking. Her mother was beautiful and young and the warlord, who was much older, had married her to produce more children for his bloodline, and because she was a very talented musician.

"What did she play Boulie?"

"The *pipa*. It's a Chinese lute. Women play it. My mother was a master."

"Soong Chou plays the *pipa* too."

"I know."

The warlord suffered from migraines and music was the only thing that soothed him. Boulie's mother, who had little to do but lie around waiting for her husband to have headaches and give her a son, fell in love with a young attaché at the French Embassy where she had been going for lessons in the French language.

"*Elle est boulversée*," Boulie said. "That's how I got my name." She had a Chinese name as well. It meant Moon Lily. "When my French father came to see me at my one-month ceremony, my Chinese father saw a glance between him and my mother and he knew. The next day, a rickshaw driver on the street outside the French Embassy stuck a chopstick through my real father's ear and stirred his brain and my mother was thrown down a well. I had to watch, even though I was too young to remember. The second wife held me in her arms."

I shivered in fear. Recognizing that Boulie was a fabulist, I only half-believed her story. She didn't look particularly Chinese. In Victoria, that would have been a good thing. Duffie told me to wash my hands after I handled money because the Chinamen might have had it. Her advice made no sense to me when all our food was grown by Chinamen and cooked by Chinamen. I wondered what Boulie thought of the hurtful skipping rhymes about *Chinky, Chinky Chinamen* that children chanted in the park where Duffie took us to play on the wooden two-seater swings with hearts and initials carved in them by people in love.

Boulie told me Sir Latham and Lady Cowes-Wentworth-Cowes had kidnapped her in a daring midnight raid and had hidden her at the British Embassy in Peking until they left China to retire in Victoria. The excitement of leaving gave Sir Latham a stroke and he had died en route to the port of Hong Kong. Lady Cowes-Wentworth-Cowes and Boulie sailed to Canada incognito on the *Empress of Asia*, ironically this very ship, to avoid Chinese spies.

"There are Chinamen with sharp knives crossing the Pacific right now. They're coming to get me," she said. "They have orders to take me or kill me."

I could hear myself hyperventilating in Boulie's dramatic pauses.

"To them, all white people are ghosts with big noses. My mother's husband does not want me raised by ghosts because I am a Han."

"What's that?"

"My mother's married name. The soldiers could come at any time, probably at night. Tonight could be auspicious." Boulie usually blinked when she lied, but I couldn't see her face clearly in the dark.

"We are all orphans," I protested weakly, "But I don't believe you are Chinese. You look a lot like my mother. You could be my sister. We could pretend to be sisters."

"We are, aren't we? Our blood is mixed."

"Damn right," I said, one of Stanford's favourite expressions. "And sisters don't lie to one another."

I clung to Boulie that night. When I finally fell asleep, I saw my own mother, wearing her silk nightgown and Stanford's pearls, her face painted white, her mouth open and red, falling in the crack between two buildings in New York City. I dreamed there were men with chopsticks and knives, guided by fireworks, landing on the beach below Lady Cowes-Wentworth-Cowes's house. I saw Quon Sam holding a torch, leading the Chinamen up past the rocks to the lawn, up the stone steps to the terrace, through the French doors in the dining room where we had eaten our New Year's feast.

"*Gong hay fat choy*," Quon Sam whispered in my sleep while the knives flashed over my head. I woke up, my damaged heart beating wildly. Boulie was leaning over me, holding a candle, her face — so close I could see her breath — painted, with red lips and cheeks and covered with a stocking so her eyes were pulled back in a fold. She looked Chinese, all right.

"I *am* Moon Lily, Poppy," she said. "I am."

3

Oh Beauty,

The sunset last night was spectacular. In all that intense colour the silhouette of a girl appeared on the horizon and walked over the water toward our ship. Tony saw it too. I am so encouraged. We decided to go straight to bed so we could get up for the sunrise this morning. I will type like a fiend and then we will go to the last breakfast call at nine. In the meantime, a steward has brought us coffee and scones with marmalade. We are discussing, of all things, the empirical philosopher Bishop Berkeley and China.

"If you believe in China, then it is real," Tony said.

"That's ridiculous. Then we would have to say fairies, Santa Claus and the Easter Bunny were real."

"They are."

Will you make China real for me? I have been in rooms that felt as though I had been there before. Certainly, Europe feels familiar to me. I wonder if China will be the same. Will unfamiliar sounds and smells throw me off your scent? Are you really lost, or just mislaid? Tony has been reassuring me. He has been in China before.

Sometimes I think I might be imagining all this; that I might have died already and this journey is part of leaving my life behind. Am I tricking myself? Is that what the mind does when it is deprived of oxygen?

It is a comfort having Tony with me. I have spent most of my life trying to figure out why, given that the whole human struggle seems to be about connecting in some way with the larger community, so many are alone. Tony was an accident that has turned out to be fortuitous. He came with Olivier. He wasn't in our marriage contract, but there he was and I am so grateful for him now.

"I am not your mother." He interrupts me again.

"Oh Tony, I'll never get my story told."

"Where are we?"

"Chinese New Year with Boulie."

"Carry on."

I was enduring another year of loss that wore away at my belief in the constancy of human relationships. As soon as Boulie revealed herself to me, she scared me literally paralytic. Fear is my enemy. Try as I might, I have been unable to leave it behind. The only way I can live with it is to embrace it. I am afraid of human beings with their infinite intellectual resources for betrayal, afraid of my heart and its damaged valves, but I do lie in bed, enjoying the sound of my secret self.

When Boulie leapt out of the dark, her candlelit face distorted by a cotton stocking, I realise she needed me to feel what she felt. She wanted me to hurt, to be afraid of the dark, whatever might crawl out of the night and grab her.

When I tried to get out of bed and run I did not know where — just away from Boulie — I collapsed on the floor. There was no feeling in my legs. I lay helpless on top of the dragon carved in her Oriental carpet and screamed. Lady Cowes-Wentworth-Cowes appeared without her teeth, which was almost as horrifying as the apparition of Boulie.

When he heard me screaming, Quon Sam ran into Boulie's bedroom fastening the toggles on his white cotton jacket. There were no horses at Lady Cowes's and neither she nor anyone on her staff drove a car. I heard her say it was too late to call *Winter Carriages* in Fairfield. She didn't want to alarm my mother, because I was only having an attack of hysteria and Nora had been through enough. I clearly remember that, the word "enough." What did she mean? What level of intimacy did she have with my mother to know about her emotional state? As far as I knew, they only shared an interest in dogs and gardens.

My nose bled copiously. Quon Sam carried me all the way down Beach Drive from Lady Cowes-Wentworth-Cowes's house to my own. I sometimes wonder what would have happened had we been intercepted on the road between our properties — a distraught child in her bloody nightgown being carried off in the night by a Chinaman with limited English.

In another of my recurring dreams, I see Quon Sam hanging, lynched by a mob of irate quasi-Englishmen, from one of the large oaks lining the Oak Bay golf course across the street from our house. Such violence is not so unusual. I know that men of colour are not often given the opportunity to explain why they have rescued young ladies in white nightgowns.

There was no lynching that night. The only sounds were wind in the oak trees and waves on the beach rhyming with the slap, slap, of Quon Sam's black slippers. He handed me over to Stanford, who came to the door in his pyjamas, carried me upstairs, tucked me in and talked me to sleep.

"Nothing to be afraid of, Poppy. You've got me here."

"You're not as big as the sea, Stanford."

"But the sea is good."

"What about the ghosts and the pirates?"

"What pirates?"

"The ones who are coming to get Boulie."

"What would pirates want with Boulie?"

"They will take her back to China and throw her down a well."

"No one is coming after Boulie. Girls hardly count in China."

"Do they count here?"

"They do with me."

He told me about silkies who live in the sea, but visit the land when they hear music. Silkies fall in love with girls who sing while they weave and embroider cloth. The girls fall in love with the silkies, but rarely follow them back to the ocean. Sometimes they have babies.

"What do the silkies look like, Stanford?" I asked.

"Like seals, Poppy. They are harmless as seals.

"Sleep, Poppy. Everything will all be right in the morning." He stroked my forehead.

The next morning, when I was still unable to feel anything below the waist, the doctor was called. Since there had been no apparent physiological cause, he assumed I was dissembling. In the beginning, Duffie, when she straightened my bed or turned me for washing, pinched me to see if I would respond. When I didn't, she seemed satisfied that I wasn't performing.

Except for Soong Chou carrying me to the balcony to sit in the sun, I stayed in my bed for six months listening to the ocean and watching the sea changes. Lying in my room day after day, hearing the gulls and the waves pounding the rocks below, I amused myself by imagining the stories brought in by the tide. Page after page of drawings piled up on my bedside table. Using charcoal to draw and adding vivid colour with my oil pastels, I drew Stanford's silkies coming out of the ocean and girls running to meet them.

Right after Chinese New Year, Boulie sent a note apologizing for scaring me. She didn't intend to do harm, she wrote; she just wanted me to believe her. My friend was right. Now I know her mother's murder was brutal and common and that sort of thing does happen to women in China. There are many Chinese wells filled up with the bones of beautiful, unhappy women who died because they reached out to take what they desperately needed.

I didn't know how to answer Boulie's letter, but I still have it. Now and again, I take it out of the inlaid lacquer box where I keep my most precious correspondence and read it to remind myself there is no grace in forgiveness without trust.

Boulie was no longer welcome in our little school. We had classes in my bedroom, where everyone indulged my hysterical paralysis. Except for dancing, lessons went on as before. I missed Boulie's ebullience, but I was too proud and too injured to accept her apology with grace. Her free spirit had proven to be a real danger. I am not sure my forgiveness would have guaranteed her re-entry to our household. Remembering the nanny dictum that children should be seen and not heard, I kept my head down and my voice low.

In the shakeup that followed the revelation of Boulie's eccentricities, my mother allowed Alec to continue attending my home school. Because Duffie had a limited intimacy with her son, I am thankful for their time together. For his part, my company must have been a relief after his unhappy experiences with previous schoolmates.

We were both anomalies. It didn't matter that Alec was several years older than I was. In our own little school, we were encouraged to be curious. Duffie, who was wise, told us that genius was not a gift, but rather the willingness to act on curiosity. After meeting a number of so-called geniuses in my life and work, I have come to the conclusion that the word "genius" means the social talent for linking the "I" to the "us."

Compliments from Duffie were generally hard earned. She was less likely to praise than call us "cheeky wee buggers" when we made competent observations about the books we were reading. She did hold out the possibility of genius, even for me, and I bless her for that — especially now that I have seen how women struggle. Duffie encouraged us to think independently, my constraints being determined by privilege and gender and Alec's by his mother's rotten luck.

When Mother and Stanford traded the electric car for a Packard touring car, Alec and I had to sit in the rumble seat while the adults rode in the front. Given that I'd had rheumatic fever, it was inexcusable to leave us out in the weather while Nora and Stanford rode in comfort. My mother said that fresh air was what I needed. We were the cabooses, a status that made me wary. When Soong Chou chauffeured us without adult passengers, he would stop a safe distance from the garden wall and bring us up front with him. He told us the Chinese labourers who built the Canadian Pacific Railway were made to sit at the back of the train until there was an accident that killed people at the front. Then the Coolies were told to sit at the front.

I think most girls fall in love at least once with a fantasy. Teethed on fairy tales, I had my exotic Prince Charming. I adored Chou. He was the essence of elegance. His voice enthralled me, as did his playing of the Chinese lute, which I could hear from my mother's oriental garden, where I went secretly to hear him. I liked to sit beside him in the car and watch his graceful wrists while he changed gears.

Soong Chou spoke English well. He had a *savoir-faire* and grace that belied his status as an employee in our household. Alec and I agreed he must have been an undercover spy. Duffie told us he was a younger brother in a rich Chinese family. Because we thought he was too smart and too handsome to spend his life in service, we spied on him looking for clues that would reveal his real reasons for living in Canada. I adored his smooth aquiline profile, his fine almost feminine bones and tapered fingers, and his jade ring.

Even though Chou didn't appear to be old enough, was it possible that he was romantically connected to her mother? I was frightened and thrilled. Unlike the Coolies, who vanished under the house, Soong Chou had his apartment over the stable, where we kept our car and a white Arab gelding inappropriately named Sheik.

On Thursday evenings, Soong Chou rode Sheik to Chinatown, where he played Fan Tan. During my convalescence, he brought me little gifts, which I assumed he bought from his gambling winnings. I kept all these treasures on my bedside table — a jar of ginger, a painted fan with singing ladies, a pair of jade and pearl earrings that I would wear when I was old enough to get my ears pierced, a set of ivory chopsticks and a small porcelain Buddha. Soong Chou told me to rub Buddha's tummy and make a wish. I wished to become the concubine of Soong Chou, whatever that meant. It was a word I had come across in a Chinese fairytale.

He also brought me flowers, explaining how comforting it was to find some of the same plants in our garden as the ones that bloomed in the large courtyard of his family compound in Hong Kong. When he smelled the fragrances, he said he could ride their perfume like a magic carpet, all the way back to China. One day he brought me a sprig of wisteria, explaining how the budding stem had the same silver cocoon shape as a silkworm. He called it the Empress flower. When the individual blossoms opened, they were yellow-skinned ladies with voluminous violet skirts sitting on fan-shaped Imperial thrones. There were rows and rows of Empresses on every vine. One Friday morning, Soong Chou interrupted our drawing lesson, bringing a wonderful gift. It was a small teak box filled with tiles made of bone dovetailed into bamboo. There were characters on the tiles, which he explained to us.

"This game of four winds was possibly invented by Confucius, who loved birds. It is called *mah jong*, which means 'hemp bird.' It is the game of one hundred intelligences and it will teach you patience."

"Och," Duffie said. "That would take a miracle."

Mah jong has been a miracle in my life. We all learned to play — Duffie, Miss Beach, Alec, me, even my mother, who taught it to her bridge-playing friends. Cook gave up one of his bed trays, which we kept constantly ready for games that sometimes lasted all day as we built our walls, North, South, East and West. The clicking music of the tiles became as familiar to me as the rhyming of the waves.

"The East Wind is yours, Poppy." Soong Chou told me. "See how the Chinese character looks like a woman running with skirts. She is very powerful, but she must be careful not to trip on her dress."

I have often tripped and fallen, but if life is a game, the East Wind has brought me so many gifts I count myself lucky. Lost and found three times, I am asking for the fourth blessing. I want to find you.

I accepted the efforts of my friends and family to cheer me up during my convalescence after the fright at Boulie's. During the six months of my paralysis, I adapted. Duffie brought all my hospital meals, insipid junket, custards and broths, on trays from the kitchen. She made sure I ate my bowl of stewed prunes. Nanny had an unnatural obsession with my bowels. My favourite meal was tea: sandwiches, scones and lemon tarts. She made my sandwiches herself: egg, cucumber and honey bunnies, made with a rabbit-shaped cookie cutter, the love of which I have passed on to you.

On fine days, Chou carried me out to the balcony. Sometimes I dared to press my face in his neck, just for a moment, and smelled the jasmine and ginger fragrance of his soaps. The scent made me giddy. If I weren't already paralyzed I think infatuation would have done it. One morning, he went straight into my bathroom and half filled a copper bronze bowl, which he placed on top of a towel he had folded on my bed.

"This is a singing fountain bowl. My father sent it to you from Hong Kong. Wet your hands and rub the handles forwards and backwards, Poppy. Do not make a circle. You want certain vibrations."

I dipped my hands in the water, which was warm and comforting, and greeted the four dragons at the bottom, as he instructed. "What will happen?" I asked, moving my hands back and forth, feeling the water respond in a pattern of dancing waves in a matter of seconds.

"The water will sing. Watch the dragons."

What I now know is something called the Chladni pattern caused the waves to reinforce one another and push water droplets into the air. The bowl was indeed a fountain, as the four dragons appeared to spit higher and higher. I was ecstatic and Soong Chou was pleased.

"The bowl will stimulate activity in your mind, improve your concentration and strengthen your muscles. You will be well, Poppy."

Soong Chou wanted to leave the bowl in my room, but I knew it would have more power if he brought it to me. Releasing the fountain became our ritual. Each morning after breakfast, we made the bowl sing. He was convinced that if Chinese magic had injured me then Chinese magic would make me better.

I was patient and the days passed pleasantly. My mother brought me flowers to paint, carefully explaining their genealogy so I would understand why they had a certain smell or colour or shape of petal. While we "visited the flowers" she taught me the fairy recipes. She did not extend these familiarities to what I understand to be normal mother-daughter affection. It has taken me most of my life to comprehend that a woman who has almost lost a child will guard her heart.

"Did you love me before I got sick?" I asked her one day while she was arranging a bowl of creamy roses with lemon frills in a *famille verte* bowl.

"What a silly question."

"Well, did you?"

"You can be so tiresome, Poppy."

"Was my father tiresome?"

Her secateurs hung over the stem she was de-thorning. I thought she might use them to cut out my tongue, so I put my head under the covers. I waited for a hug and reassurance, but I think I would have preferred an act of violence to nothing. I got nothing. My mother sighed and left my room.

"Why don't you love me?" I whispered my mantra over and over until I fell asleep.

In spite of Chou's spiritual ministrations, I was half-resigned to spending my life in bed, comforted by the attentions of Duffie and the rest of the staff. When my mother, still dressed in her evening gown, paid me a morning visit, she told me she and Stanford had climbed seventy-one steps to dance in the ballroom at Craigdarroch castle, which had just been sold by the Dunsmuir family. She said she could see all the way to Japan. I wished I could go there, but I would have to be content with waiting for the volcanic Mount Baker to erupt and watching the beautiful sunrises through the French windows that opened onto my balcony.

Stanford, bless him, gave me the folding typewriter in a case lined with purple velvet that I am using now. He set it up on a special tray without sides so I could write in bed.

"Tell your stories," he said.

"I don't know how," meaning I couldn't type, and besides, my stories were locked inside me.

"Write letters to yourself," he advised. "I will give you stamps and envelopes. Address them and I will mail them."

"You won't read them will you?"

"No, Poppy, not unless you ask me to."

His plan worked. Duffie taught me the "seek and ye shall find" method of pecking the keys, and here I am. Despite my two-finger method, I can type as quickly as Tony. The tapping rhythm is a kind of semaphore. I wonder if you can hear it?

He also transported my messages to the wall. I made hundreds of wishes and many of them were granted, for which I was grateful to Stanford and the fairies.

Duffie softened during the year of my paralysis. I began to see the woman Alec had painted for Miss Carr and not the *strega nona* I loved and feared. My first memory was from San Francisco, when Duffie had rubbed my poor surprised face in my soaking wet underpants.

I couldn't fully forgive Nanny MacDuff for that early bullying, but she did rise to the occasion of my hysterical paralysis. I have no idea how many times she went up and down the back stairs to fetch me a drink or a hot water bottle from the kitchen. For the first month after my terrible fright, she slept on my chaise longue, with a knife under her pillow to scare off the intruders I was sure would come from the sea and climb up the back of the house to my balcony. Duffie, who was such a believer in fresh air, even accommodated my obsession with open windows, locking them all securely at night.

Miss Carr sympathetically related the story of a similar hysterical experience of her own while she was studying painting in London. She suspended judgment of my tame subject matter, encouraging my interest in nature, even if it was this side of the garden wall, not the wilderness that beckoned her. Now the three of us worked side by side in my bedroom, me in bed with a board propped against my breakfast tray and Alec and our teacher standing at easels. "Unplayed music wastes away," she admonished us and we persevered.

Even though Alec and I endured our arithmetic lessons with Miss Earl, whom we decided was incapable of smiling, lacking the proper muscles for supporting a grin, we progressed well in our reading with Duffie, taking turns reading Dickens, Shakespeare and her beloved Sir Walter Scott aloud. M. Bonheur's Gallic snobberies made us laugh so hard that we couldn't say the word "cheese" without becoming hysterical. I still can't have my photograph taken without remembering M. Bonheur's haughty distinction between mere cheese and the French *fromages*. Miss Wiebe, who had been shunned by her Mennonite family for loving art, made history live for us. Tapping into our obsession with visual art, she taught us history through colour reproductions of paintings and sculpture. We learned about Greece through the Elgin Marbles. She had us emulate Medieval Books of Hours by writing poems about our daily lives on pages we illuminated with watercolour and gold ink. We made funny Bruegheloid cartoons of the stratified world we lived in. Even at the time, I regretted that we frequently gave into the temptation to make fun of Miss Wiebe's spinsterish ways.

Miss Carr was the icing on our cake. We got used to her smells and eccentricities and came to love her. She told us stories about the native friends she made in *Lekwungen*, the Songhees Village across the inner harbour from her house in James Bay, and on her painting excursions into the wilderness on Vancouver Island. We shared in her awareness of the new Canadian painting styles and the importance of landscape. Neither she nor I was particularly interested in drawing and painting the human figure. Our eyes were turned to plants and animals. Aboriginal people and small children were the only two-legged species Miss Carr tolerated.

I marveled at how Alec, who faltered over every consonant, could have such a steady hand, such articulate lines, an unbroken legato, and could represent the forms in nature. Miss Carr reconciled herself to our aesthetic shortcomings and there were days when we actually forgot the time and had to be reminded to eat the food on our lunch trays. Freed from instruction and criticism, we were allowed to do what we liked, so long as we did it with passion. It was a very happy time. I was comfortable with the status quo and I almost dreaded the prognosis of the various specialists who trooped through my bedroom and tapped my shins and feet for signs of life — she will get better when she makes up her mind.

Stanford took quite an interest in Alec's lifelike drawing and began hanging around my bedroom, which did not please either Duffie or Miss Carr, who weren't as amused as we were by the stories he told us. He was spending a lot of time in Chinatown, doing research, he said, for a book he was going to write about the contribution Chinese workers made to the national railroad. As far as I was concerned, Stanford was the cat's pyjamas. He had so often rescued me from boredom. I thought the book was a good idea. If Stanford wrote as well as he talked, the project would give his life meaning the way her garden defined my mother.

Stanford said that Fisgard Street was filled with brothels and opium factories connected by a system of alleys and passageways like the one under our house. I think I believed Victoria was a city built by moles. When I was younger, my favourite stories were about animals living in mansions under the ground. I spent hours constructing city maps of subterranean civilizations.

Stanford told Alec and me a story about a flood in the old Chinese cemetery in the inner harbour.

"I talked to people who saw zombies pushing through the mud covering their shallow graves. Dogs ran through the streets with human hands and feet in their mouths. The stench was terrific."

We were enthralled. Immediately, Alec got to work with his pencil, drawing the macabre scene. Duffie must have reported and perhaps underlined her allegations of Stanford's improprieties to my mother with his gruesomely realistic portrayal. I wasn't in the least upset by the ingloriously risen corpses. The dead, including my gentle, almost forgotten father, were my secret friends. I accepted Stanford's feverish and highly coloured accounts as entertainment. It hardly mattered whether they were true or not, we loved them.

When my mother came into my bedroom to ask what Stanford had told us he stood in the doorway with a look of smirking defiance on his face.

"What has Stanford been telling you about the Chinese cemetery?" she asked quietly while I watched the throbbing blue vein in her forehead.

"Nothing," I said, wringing the edge of my sheet.

"Nothing?" Her voice rose a little.

"Nothing much." I heard Alec clear his throat to cover a giggle and saw Duffie slip out of the room through the linen closet door.

"I would hardly call a gross exaggeration designed to scare you out of your wits nothing, Poppy."

"I liked it." I said.

"She liked it!" My mother turned to Stanford. "You twit!"

"Better a good twit than a bad mother, Nora."

"Get out!" she said, her voice as cold as snow.

I gather Stanford had been told to stay away from our school, but he was not the obedient sort. One Friday morning in May, Miss Carr, Alec and I were quietly drawing when my unrepentant stepfather came into my bedroom wearing his white silk dressing gown. I heard Miss Carr take in her breath, but she said nothing as Stanford arranged himself on the chaise longue with one arm over the back and his legs stretched out in front of him and crossed at the ankles. He asked if we would like him to model for us and Alec thanked him, saying we were already occupied with the arbutus trees at the bottom of the garden.

I tried to keep my head down as the silk slipped away from Stanford's remarkably smooth legs, but something made me look up. My stepfather had undone his sash, revealing his erect member. I was transfixed. Vicarious pleasure in his rebellion made me almost levitate in my bed. Whatever this performance was — perverse comedy, or madness — I was ecstatic.

"Idiot!" Miss Carr ran out of the room in a rank fury of skirts and came back with Duffie who picked up the fire poker and went after him.

"Away wi' yew, yew daft bugger!"

I don't know whether I was more surprised by my first glimpse of a penis, Stanford's frantic performance, or hearing Duffie, who had promised on many occasions to wash my mouth out with soap if I uttered anything even close to profanity, letting loose some very colourful Scottish language.

"Yew bad stick. Yew pervert!"

Stanford left by the door to my balcony, his dressing gown flapping around his legs, and scrambled up the lattice to the top of the house, two floors above my bedroom. While Miss Carr and Duffie fumed and discussed whether they should call the doctor, the police or the fire department first, Alec stood on the balcony and reported back to me as Stanford paraded on the roof, holding his dressing gown like a white flag ripping in the wind.

While Stanford sailed his pale ensign over our ostensibly inviolate stone house, I watched my mother separate from the gardeners, take off her gloves, and stare up in amazement. I willed my paralyzed legs to move, but they wouldn't.

The decision made, Duffie ran to call Dr. Creighton. Stanford sent his dressing gown flying from the roof. Filled with wind, it sailed past my windows, graceful as a gull, and sprawled on the lawn at my mother's feet.

Our doctor, who had just bought his first coupe so he could respond quickly to Oak Bay medical emergencies, ran puffing up the stairs within minutes and joined Miss Carr, Alec and Duffie on the balcony. Doctor Creighton, who could have been a plantation owner in his linen suit, asked Stanford to be reasonable and come down.

"Let's pour ourselves a drink and have a man-to-man talk."

"Bugger off." I could hear the high pitch in his voice that meant he was on a roll. Stanford was having fun. "I am the king of the castle."

I began laughing hysterically.

"Yew shut your mouth, Miss." Duffie pointed her finger at me. I felt my face cracking with mirth.

My mother rushed into the house from the garden. It didn't look as though Stanford meant to jump. The doctor picked up his black bag, went through the linen closet to her sitting room and gave her an injection to help her sleep. While Miss Beach got my mother ready for her therapeutic nap, Duffie found Soong Chou and asked him to take Alec and Miss Carr home. Dr. Creighton asked for a whiskey and Duffie brought him the whole bottle and a glass.

The doctor sat down on the balcony and waited while Stanford shouted beautiful things on the roof. He blessed our house, the sea and the white dragons of China. At one point he urinated, splashing the balcony rail, causing Dr. Creighton to move the white wicker chair he was sitting on. I got the giggles again and Duffie told me once again to shut up, or people would believe I was barking mad like the rest of them. I wasn't sure whom she meant. Were my relatives all insane or was this a normal family? How many times had Dr. Creighton carefully pulled up the creases in his pant legs and sat patiently sipping Scotch while one patient lay in bed with hysterical paralysis, another took a drug-induced beauty sleep and the third made his bid for Mount Everest or whatever he was calling the top of our four-story house?

Just before dinnertime, my mother, who had guests coming, went out on the balcony and told Stanford enough was enough. She wasn't angry, as she had been the time Stanford told me the story about the Chinese cemetery. He simply laughed at her, so this time she called to the Coolies and asked them to climb up and fetch him.

When he saw the Cantonese army climbing the side of the house, Stanford came down himself and surrendered to Dr. Creighton, who brought him into my room and injected calm into his trembling bottom right before my eyes. I noticed the bit of skin that had shot up perpendicular while he languished on the chaise now dangled helplessly between his legs.

That night, while my mother entertained dinner guests, Stanford quietly disappeared from my life. Duffie told me he was taken to a sanatorium for the rich in Connecticut. I knew he wasn't completely mad because he remembered to whistle while the men in white hustled him down the back stairs. I whistled back.

I wouldn't have found his behaviour funny if I had considered the consequences. His madness crept up on us so slowly it had become the norm. I loved Stanford and I resent that he was taken from me so abruptly. He had family in the eastern United States, but I could see no reason why he should be so far from us. The afternoon of his magnificent performance on the roof was the last time I saw him.

I have mailed many paintings and drawings to my stepfather over the years and he hasn't responded. I wonder if his doctors have neutralized his brain with drugs or shock treatment. I hope not so much that he is insensitive to the love I have sent him. All that remains of Stanford is my whistle, which I have passed on to you. When I call and you respond, I think of my stepfather and how he had the sanity to notice the needs of a lonely little girl.

After he was taken away, my mother spoke of her mad husband with compassionate exasperation, as if he had been a fish that went off. Whenever I asked about him, she sighed and rolled her eyes.

"Don't nag, Poppy. I don't know much more about Stanford's illness than you do."

Nothing lasts, Duffie was fond of telling us, and I covered my ears and sang because I knew, for one thing, she was telling me that I was going to lose more loved ones. At the end of the school year, Miss Carr gave her notice. She had decided to take a job teaching at The Lady's Art Club and Crofton House School for Girls in Vancouver.

I assume it was the sound of the ocean where life begins and ends that eventually cured me. Sometimes the cause is the cure, as we have learned with the discovery of modern vaccines. Just as the smoke from fireworks dissipates, my paralysis lifted as suddenly as it had come over me on the night of Chinese New Year.

One summer afternoon, while my mother took her nap and the house was quiet except for the ticking of clocks and rhythmic spitting of lawn sprinklers, I slowly got out of bed and went down the stairs, outside and across the lawn, past the amazed Coolies with their secateurs and bamboo rakes, to the fairy glen where the hollyhocks and orange California poppies were blooming. Light sparkled on the water. I crossed the glen, left my nightgown on the beach and walked into the sea up to my waist. The water was bitterly cold, but I could feel it. I decided then that even though I was afraid of man-of-war jellyfish, death, darkness, pirates and the withholding of love, I would not give in.

I lost my teacher, my friend and my stepfather that summer, but I gained a greater awareness of my resilience. When I stood in the water between two continents and two countries on the afternoon that feeling returned to my legs, I thought of myself as an old building being wired for electricity for the first time. I felt the currents of America and Asia running through my body and I knew, in spite of the weakness of my heart, that I was strong.

⌒

"ENOUGH, POPPERS, or the fat ladies in first class will eat all our breakfast." Tony is hungry.

"Oh Tony, you know there is plenty of breakfast for all the fat ladies and all the ladies with broken hearts."

"And the mermaids."

"Are there enough mermaids for all the dead souls, Tony? Do poor Alec and your brother Charles have merwives?"

"If you believe it, Poppy."

I love Tony. He is willing to accept any idea short of cruelty. No wonder Olivier adores him.

Human beings must eat, even ones like me who are only hungry for the arms of their loved ones, and now Tony and I shall go to breakfast. Every meal on this ship is so opulent that I can't imagine the waste. Tony said he saw the remains of last night's dinner leaving in the ship's wake when he took his walk around the deck this morning. I am going to make a watercolour of carved ice swans swimming alongside the towering cakes and salad, and the babies, of course. I wonder why they don't give the leftovers to the people in steerage?

4

MAY 14, 3 PM, IN THE FIRST-CLASS SMOKING ROOM, THE *EMPRESS OF ASIA*

Dear Miss Waldorf Salad,
Life is a strange mix of cabbage and apples, with a few raisins thrown in. I didn't think I would mind as much as I did when Stanford was taken away. My stepfather had been getting more and more irrational as his addiction or demons took hold. Still, he remained kind and funny and I missed him. When my mother came into my room and found me crying one evening soon after his departure, she surprised me by asking what she could do to make me feel better. I told her about Stanford and blue beach glass we had collected and returned to the sea. I had nowhere to put my tears. She gave me a lovely blue bottle and told me to save them up until I could walk down to the sea again.

"How will he know?" I asked.

"Make a drawing and we will mail it."

It was her idea in the beginning. I have to give her credit. My mother had recognized the value of my art. Her advice didn't advance to praise, but it was recognition.

"Was Stanford nicer than my father?" I asked, smudging a line of charcoal with my finger, not looking up.

"You do ask hard questions." She felt in her pocket for the gold cigarette case Stanford had given her, took one out and put it in her ebony holder. I was learning that my questions made my mother fidget.

TONY IS RESTLESS. He doesn't think we should be sitting in the lounge because people are smoking. I have spent my life breathing other people's smoke and a little of my own and I doubt if taking a little more into my lungs will make much difference. It's a "get down to work" room with a table large enough for spreading out my typewriter and papers. I am inspired by the vision we saw last night. All I have to do is close my eyes and remember. When I see your silhouette coming toward me, you remain real, and safe.

"Where do you suppose we are now?" he asks, looking out the porthole.

"In the summer of anarchy."

"Aren't they all?"

MY MOTHER SAILED FROM San Francisco through the Panama Canal to Europe in the summer of 1912. When she left, I stood at the iron gate that separated Casanora from the real world and watched the car disappear into the green hills around the Oak Bay Golf Club. "Take me!" I yelled until I had no breath left.

Miss Beach had been left to run our household, which included Cook and Daisy, the daily maid. Chou oversaw Chan Fong and the Coolies and Duffie had me, which she said was the biggest job of all. I was twelve and nothing fit me any more, not my waistless dresses with smocking over the bosom and certainly not the transparent politeness that had so far kept me out of trouble.

"Never cast a clot till May's oot" Duffie importuned, ordering Alec and me to wear our woolen undershirts until the very end of May. We laughed and took our rough undies off, hanging them on the first available branch as soon as she was out of sight.

Without my critical mother to please, everyone in our household relaxed that summer. I heard laughter in the kitchen and music from the phonograph in the library, where Miss Beach and Duffie played Stanford's records and danced with one another. My mother said that noise gave her migraines. I can't remember a time when I wasn't told to keep quiet. "Think of yourselves as Red Indians," Duffie shushed me, "tiptoeing up to your meat."

The windows were left open in the heat, and I believe the spicy mix of smells that came from the kitchen and the garden intoxicated us. Duffie's idea of nursery flower arrangement was to cram a handful of sweet peas or roses in a vase and leave them until the water was fetid and all the petals had fallen on the table. I collected these petals in a hatbox with the intention of adding lavender and making potpourri for our linen drawers.

Normally, the servants had every Thursday evening and alternate Sunday afternoons off, but that summer Miss Beach went out almost every night. She looked quite different out of uniform. One evening when I met her on the back stairs she was wearing my mother's gray fox stole, her pearls, and a periwinkle blue wool suit that I remembered seeing Nora wear in San Francisco. The suit was a tighter fit on Miss Beach, but the colour suited her fair hair. I could see her breasts and her bottom quite clearly. When I came upon her, all got up in my mother's finery, panic passed over her pale blue eyes, and then defiance. She put a gloved finger — my mother's white kid — to her lips and I remembered how fierce she had looked the day she had found me in the linen closet. We both had secrets.

The very day my mother left, Chan Fong forsook western cooking and began serving bowls of rice with tender slices of vegetables stir-fried with garlic and ginger from our garden. At first, I was given a fork with chopsticks, but soon after, the fork disappeared. By the end of the summer, I was so competent with my new implements I could pick up a single pea without dropping it. "Cookie in charge of kitchen now," he said, when I complimented our new menu but complained about the missing puddings. "Missus no pay Cookie for puddings extra." When Duffie importuned him, he threatened to cut off her braid with his sharp kitchen knife. In China, Duffie told me a man would kill after suffering such an indignity.

"Never mind," Duffie said, "I'm wise to men. He won't get his dignity back by taking mine."

We ignored the threats, picked our own raspberries and ate them with the thick cream at the top of the bottles.

Fong's day off turned into *days* off the time he disappeared. The morning he returned he told me that he had been to Chinatown to honour a family occasion. His wife had given birth to a new baby boy and he and his friends had been celebrating. Duffie was not impressed. The wife was in China, she told me. Fong's brother "helped out" with the baby. Duffie didn't tell me what "helping out" meant. I remember Chinese birth announcements coming with a great deal of mirth, as if the absent fathers had been cuckolded or were under the impression that gestation could take as much as a decade or two. Because I knew so little, I simply accepted the news as comedy. It was only later that I realised the extent of misery and resentment that came from exile and discrimination that penetrated the fabric of family life for those whose husbands and fathers might as well have lived on the moon.

THE EMPRESS OF ASIA will arrive in China in about ten days, after stopping to drop mail and passengers in Honolulu and Yokohama. The Orient is only the other side of the pond. How appalling that so many men have spent entire lifetimes away from families that are little more than a week away by ship.

"I wonder," I ask Tony, "if being separated from Precious is my punishment for benefiting from the separation of our Coolies from their families."

"You weren't responsible, Poppy."

WHEN I HELPED Soong Chou polish the car shortly after Fong's birth announcement, I asked him if our cook had a wife in Chinatown, to see what he would say. Presumably, he knew more about Fong's family matters than Duffie did. "There are comfort wives in Chinatown," he told me. "Men need the company of women." Chinatown was full of *sing-song* girls necessary to the mental health of the men who laboured in the factories and households of Victoria. China was a big and poor country, but no one told me these men *had* to leave their families behind, that they came to Canada on overcrowded and miserable ships to work and send back money to support their loved ones. No one told me that women weren't allowed to emigrate and the head tax on every worker was five hundred dollars, which had to be paid back to the employer. I had no idea the Chinamen were lonely. They were different from us. I thought they had been put on earth to cook our food and make our gardens beautiful.

A few years later, I went to a garden party at the O'Reilly's, a *nouveau riche* Irish family who lived at Point Ellice on the Gorge. The O'Reilly's were quite boring and they exuded the snobbish confidence that money had bought them breeding. While the others played croquet, I sulked about and did some drawing. When I had sketched every flower in their garden, I went to hide in the barn until Soong Chou came to pick us up. Soon after I had settled my sketchbook and myself in the hayloft, I heard singing.

I cleared a spot on the floor and peered down through a crack.

The O' Reilly houseboy, his faced pressed in the soft neck of their Jersey milk cow, was crooning and stroking its flank. He sang a beautiful, sad song. On the way home, I hummed the melody for Chou, who told me the song was about a man who lived far away from the woman he loved and he knew he wouldn't see her again. I understood right away. Chou told me he knew that the O'Reilly's houseboy had no other servant to talk to, and that was why he sang to the cow. All the Chinese in Victoria know one another, he said. It was a long time before I understood how essential that was to their survival. They helped one another.

I was fixated on Chou's beautiful fingers and the jade and gold ring he wore on his right hand. "You have perfect pitch, Poppy," he commented.

I trailed around after Soong Chou offering to help, and he told me stories, just like Stanford had before aliens in white coats abducted him. I was fascinated with the Chinamen and their families. He explained that they lived with despair, something much wider and deeper than the Pacific Ocean that separated them. The men were little more than slaves oppressed by bigotry, low wages and laws that discriminated against them and their families. There were businessmen in Victoria who illegally rented indentured Chinese labourers to Americans. A white deckhand on one of the ships that transported workers across the Puget Sound told Soong Chou that one group of men had been handcuffed to an iron rail with an anchor attached to the end of it. When an American immigration boat approached the ship to question the human cargo, the Chinamen had been sent to the bottom of the ocean.

How can Chou respect me, I wondered, when my people did things like that? I desperately wanted him to like me. In the fairy glen, I closed my eyes and tickled my lips with fireweed, pretending it was his kisses.

While my mother danced with strangers and played canasta on the deck of a trans-Atlantic liner in the summer of 1912, Duffie had her own voyage of discovery. For the first time in Alec's life since he was a "wee bairn," she actually lived full time with her son. Fong rebelled against this added obligation, especially since Alec was a hungry adolescent. "The earth will provide," Duffie admonished the cook.

Duffie was right. First thing in the morning, while the dew was still on the grass, Alec and I went to the garden to pick vegetables for our lunch. I don't suppose I will ever eat anything as delicious as Chinese peas on the vine or the sweet baby carrots tasting of the earth even after we washed them with the garden hose. When Cook went AWOL, Alec and I boiled the smallest of the new potatoes and ate them with parsley, mint and butter. We called the new potatoes "summer candy."

Duffie wasn't going to install her son in one of the punishingly hot servant's bedrooms under the eaves in the attic, where she and Miss Beach had their limited private lives. When Alec was fetched by Soong Chou the very day my Mother sailed to San Francisco, he and his little brown suitcase went straight to my stepfather's room, which had been left as it was the day Stanford was whisked off to bedlam.

Even though my mother didn't speak of Stanford's eventual return, I had been led to believe that the possibility existed. There were ways in which she had depended on him. Not only was he a handsome addition to a bridge game or dinner party, but also there had been the invisible "business" that had transpired in the library, where he had meetings with people who came from San Francisco. My mother didn't appear to understand or care about business so long as Stanford was around to take care of it. Flowers were her world. I often wonder how differently her life would have turned out had Stanford kept a safe distance from the deep end.

Perhaps it was my almost silent Mediterranean blood prematurely asserting itself, but I was beginning to mature. I sat naked to the waist in front of the beveled oval mirror on my dressing table, amazed by my swelling nipples — pink as baby roses and sensitive to the touch. I heard someone say the hair and fingernails grow after death. Had I died in San Francisco, would this still have happened to me in my grave? Could my breasts possibly have grown into womanhood while I lay sleeping?

While Mother was off cruising for suitable Stanford replacements or whatever transpired on her trans-Atlantic journey, I once again refused to put on the baby dresses she insisted I wear in spite of the changes in my figure.

"Are we getting to the good bits then?" Tony wants to know. He is putting the neat stack of pages in his portfolio and keeping these letters safe for me.

"Oh there's lots," I tell him. "You will be surprised."

"Moi?" he says.

Alec and I ransacked Stanford's closets and wore his monogrammed shirts and boxer shorts. His billowing untucked blouses sailed us down the lawn to the sea. We ran wild as dandelions and the temporarily liberated adults seemed to approve, even Duffie. That summer, she allowed herself to relax and be a mother.

Stanford's dressing table, with all its cosmetic paraphernalia, amused Alec and me for hours. We tweezed our eyebrows and darkened the peach fuzz on our upper lips. We discovered we could ignite puffs of cologne and create flames. We wore Stanford's hairnets and the triangular bandages that kept his brow from folding into accordion pleats.

In one of Stanford's drawers, we found bags of saltwater taffy in pastel colours. We put these bags in an animal-proof cracker tin stolen from the pantry and took them to our summerhouse, an elaborate fort made of driftwood and boughs that we were building on a high rock looking over the ocean. From this superior location, we could, with the help of Stanford's binoculars and a vast arsenal of sticks and stones, protect our interests from pirates making their way from the South China Sea.

I was still haunted by the possibility that Boulie's kidnappers might choose to land at our beach and make their way to Lady Cowes-Wentworth-Cowes's false Tudor house on a night with good cloud cover.

While Miss Beach and Duffie played grand ladies, entertaining one another at tea in the gazebo and games of cards in the library, Alec and I investigated every inch of the house and garden, paying particular attention to the trap door that led to we knew not where, except that it looked like an old root cellar. Could eight people possibly be living in a space designed for storing vegetables? Where did the Chinamen bathe and go to the bathroom? I assumed Chinese people also used the toilet. Stanford had told me that even the King and Queen went to the bathroom, his statement of egalitarianism which I am sure his peers would have taken as evidence of his insanity had they heard.

Spying from the trees and shrubbery and paying close attention to the time, we knew that the gardeners came out at eight o'clock in the morning and began work. Just before noon, Guan Sing hit a gong and they all gathered on the lower lawn for tea and rice with what looked like a stir-fry similar to the ones Fong had been giving us since my mother left on her holiday. Fong gonged for us to come in for our lunch after the Chinamen were fed. At four in the afternoon, they went back into the hole in the earth that spat them out in the morning. We got to watch this because during my mother's absence afternoon tea was abandoned. It had become Miss Beach and Duffie's "drinky time," which they announced by rattling ice in the cocktail shaker and laughing.

Some days three gardeners came out to work, some days seven or eight. We could not tell who was who. The men all dressed the same and their hats shaded their faces. Every second Thursday, most of the gardeners left to take the tramcar to Chinatown. One vigilant guardian of their enigmatic mole home stayed behind. We planned our raid. Nighttime, when discovery was a real possibility, was potentially dangerous. We decided that the only time to investigate was during lunch break on a day when all eight Chinamen were working. On that day, we would ask Fong to make us a picnic.

One rosy July dawn, we counted eight crow-like humans in black pyjamas emerging from the hole in the earth. All morning, we lurked in the shadows, peeing nervously behind the shrubbery. We ate our picnic of cheese and crackers and transparent apples. I was so nervous that I threw mine up behind a large rhododendron. At exactly eleven-thirty by Alec's pocket watch, lunch came out for the gardeners. We skulked along the side of the house, past the herb garden to the trap door, which had a sliding fastener. I slid it open and Alec raised the door while I took a last look around. Sickeningly sweet smells, a combination of milky smoke and herbs I remembered from our trips to Chinatown, came out of the dark opening.

We breathed in the threshold to another world. My heart beat wildly. I went in first. Carefully putting one foot after another down the ladder that connected the garden we knew intimately to the unknown underground, we descended. While my eyes adjusted to the dark, I wondered where the curiosity that Duffie had described as my finest attribute was going to take me. Imagining my severed head boiling in a pot in a subterranean kitchen or hanging from the mast of a Chinese pirate ship, I shivered in fear. It was chilly underground. Our feet touched the earth and Alec took my stone cold hand. He led, feeling his way along the damp walls.

I had been right. The space felt like a tunnel, about six feet wide and six feet in height. This was no root cellar. We were exploring an underground village. I imagined doors opening on secret streets. There was no sound, only a silence filled with damp and exotic smells. We saw cracks of light and came to wooden doors opening off the tunnel. Alec chose one and I chose another. Both led to identical cells, each with two beds, a light bulb hanging in the centre and, at the foot of each bed, a black lacquer box.

More doors led to similar rooms. We counted six. One room was filled with boxes. I wish we had looked inside them, but we were too frightened to disturb the neat stacks. We did snoop in an unlocked lacquer box in one of the dormitory rooms. It held exotic smells and personal items — a pair of glasses, a wooden comb, some neatly folded black cotton pajamas, photographs of women and children, parents and grandparents stiffly staring at the camera.

The storage room boxes, covered with Chinese calligraphy, were more intimidating because we could only think of sinister reasons for their being there. If we'd opened them and found something dangerous, who knew what might have happened? Treacherous genies lurked in those boxes. Neither Alec nor I spoke much while we were investigating. The last door we opened revealed a room with a large wood stove with a chimney, a table and chairs, a shelf holding teapots and bowls and many shelves with rows of tins lined up on them. An inlaid box filled with *mah jong* tiles sat on the middle of the table.

There were no windows. We hadn't seen a toilet or a bathtub. I still wonder if they came up in the middle of the night and enjoyed a tub in one of my mother's luxurious bathrooms. When I was old enough to understand that Chinatown "listening wives" were comfort women who accommodated the lonely émigrés with the pleasures of the flesh, I hoped at least a few of them got to enjoy my mother's house and garden when she was off on her little holidays.

When Chou reported that you were missing in China, I felt right away that you had not been injured or killed. I did however fear that someone who would abuse your innocence had stolen you, because you are at the age when girls often appear to be women. When I can get to sleep, I see you rouged and bejeweled, besotted with opium in a Shanghai singing house, or sold by Boulie's family to an old warlord as a virgin concubine.

"Bury those thoughts," Tony remarks. "They aren't good for you. We have no reason to think that has happened."

"Okay. We'll go back underground." I am trying very hard to stay focused, but it is difficult.

In the corner of the room with the table and chairs in the tunnel, there were rough wooden steps leading to another trap door. I led Alec tiptoeing up the stairs, opened the hook at the top, lifted the hatch just a crack, and listened. We heard voices. It was Fong and

Duffie. I opened the hatch a little more and saw that the opening led to the pantry. Duffie was having a cup of tea at the kitchen table and Fong was chopping on the cutting board. "It's your mum," I whispered to Alec, letting the trap door drop softly back in place, and we scuttled back down the stairs.

Whatever went on under the house, Chan Fong was privy to it. Sinister or not, we didn't want him knowing that we were suspicious. We could leave the way we came in or risk discovery by going through the pantry. Alec suggested we keep moving through the tunnel, to see where it led. When we left the doors behind, it got darker. We began going downhill, we guessed toward the sea. Close to the end, we saw light. In no time at all, we came to an opening partly obscured by a large rock that allowed a few feet on either side. There was just enough room, I saw, to allow a man to carry a box out of the tunnel. We blinked in the bright sunlight. In front of us, across the Pacific Ocean lay Asia and America.

5

Dear Brussels Sprout,

The weather cleared up last night. After dinner, we had a dance out on the deck. There must have been a party in second class as well. I could hear music coming from below. The banter was comical as the war of the bands went on well into the night. We thought we might as well stay up, because the likelihood of sleeping through the noise was remote. I sat on a deck chair, wrapped in my shawl with the usual ship's blanket across my knees, watching the women promenade in their evening dresses.

In between dances, Tony checked on me, making sure I was comfortable and properly warmed up by hot rum. Knowing how much I like dancing, he tried to cheer me with a story circulating in London about Tallulah and Dola hiring little girls to come to Dola's mother's garden to dance for them. Word had it the children were naked as spring. Instead of laughing as Tony had hoped, I was miserable thinking of you, possibly performing for some perverted warlord.

I tried to distract myself by visualizing steerage, where the human cargo goes back and forth from Asia to North America.

Were the men losing their Gold Mountain money in games of *fantan*? Was anyone playing the *Yang-qin* and singing those painful Chinese songs, or perhaps a lively fiddle tune on the two-stringed *erhu*? Was there dancing down there where there is no deck to take the evening air? Do men dance with men in China the way they do in Greece? I have my *pipa* with me, but I can't bear to play it.

All is quiet this morning. The travelers who stayed up late are sleeping in. At the moment, the only other person on deck is Brooke Hartley, a young American diplomat going to Japan with his family. When Brooke caught me looking dejected, he offered me a candy shaped like a lifesaver, which he says will cure hangovers, seasickness and just about any ailment. I wanted to ask him if the candy would return you to me, but that would have been unfair. Why would I burden Brooke with my sorrow when he was only trying to be kind?

My thoughts of the men below decks are still with me. I think of my mother's servants crossing the ocean without seeing the sea and then living in the tunnel beneath our house.

Exhilarated by our underground discovery, Alec and I began to explore other thrilling opportunities offered by the summer of 1912. After fine-combing the house and garden and the mysteries below stairs, we turned our curiosity on one another. Since I had seen Stanford naked, I was anxious to examine Alec without his clothes on. In our humble fortress on the rock, we shyly undressed one another and examined our bodies. He was lithe and golden lying under our roof of sword ferns and cedar boughs. I explored the smooth skin behind his elbows and knees and the boy thing between his legs.

I marked each passing day on my calendar, as the summer slipped through my fingers as easily as sunlight. One hot afternoon at the end of July, while Miss Beach and Duffie had "drinky time" and played canasta in my mother's hand-me-down slips, Alec and I looked up from our primitive housekeeping and saw Soong Chou walking across the lawn to the fairy glen. He had Boulie with him.

I still see her standing there, her red dress blowing in the wind, her hands clenched by her side. Rather than cross our *No Man's Land* without permission, Chou waited for us to walk through the meadow to meet them. The trespasser also waited. Alec and I, two wild things in Stanford's torn silks — our bodies tanned and caked with salt from the sea — walked barefoot across the glen. We stood in the long grass and waited for one of them to speak.

"Lady Cowes-Wentworth-Cowes sent you a St. Honoré cake," Chou said, tantalizing us. We all loved this specialty of Quon Sam, a sponge cake covered in custard and marzipan and raspberries from his garden.

Miss Beach pulled herself together and served a special children's tea made of dried fruit, mint and edible blossoms in the gazebo. We devoured the cake. There was no discussion of Chinese New Year's. Boulie didn't beg for forgiveness and I didn't offer it.

"Are you still Chinese?" I asked her, putting down my teacup. I remember the sound of the thin porcelain hitting the saucer.

"Yes," she said.

"I thought so." I don't know why I asked. She had risked my friendship in her desperation to make me believe it.

"They took Stanford away," Alec changed course.

"Yes, he was mad."

"I know," Boulie said. "It was the opium."

"Liar," I said.

"I heard Lady Cowes-Wentworth-Cowes tell Quon Sam. She said he shouldn't have fouled his own nest."

"You make everything up, Boulie. Come to think of it, I made a mistake. I don't really believe you are Chinese." I lied.

"My mother used opium. Your mother uses opium."

"Sometimes, Boulie, I feel like tearing off your cheeks and putting them in the toaster." In a moment, I had swept Boulie off her chair and was lying on top of her. One of the lovely teacups tottered off the wicker table and bounced. I watched it and when I knew it was safe, I pinned her hands behind her head and spat on her face.

Alec picked up the teacup and saucer and pulled me off. "W-we ought to show B-boulie the t-tunnel," he said. I knew then that, for whatever reason — perhaps fear of the intensity of my undivided attention — he had decided we were three again.

Boulie was re-assimilated in our summer household without consultation with Miss Beach and Duffie, who were not only lolly-gagging themselves but willing to regard us children as another oppressed class entitled to enjoy a our brief hiatus from totalitarian rule.

Without instruction, Chou continued to pick Boulie up each morning and return her after tea. Alec and I spent our evenings in my room reading Stanford's copies of plays by Oscar Wilde.

"Do you suppose Alec was a fairy?" Tony asks.

"What a ridiculous question. One doesn't have to be a fairy to like Oscar Wilde! I'm not a fairy."

"Oh no. You are the Virgin Mary."

"Alec was in love with me, Tony."

"So was Olivier. I rest my case."

"Rubbish."

"He was. He is."

I am so confused. Everything is upside down and topsy-turvy. Was love as we imagined it buried in the poppy fields?

That summer, we were simply curious kids. Whenever Fong went to visit his Chinatown wife and there was a full complement of gardeners, we tested the trap door in the pantry. Our Coolies were occasionally careless. We had gained entry and were standing in front of the boxes with Chinese writing in the room below the stairs.

"Tell us what they say."

"Just because I am Chinese doesn't mean I can read it, stupid." Boulie spat.

"What do you think is going on down here?" I asked.

"It is smugglers," she confirmed my suspicions. "We have to find out what is in the boxes."

The boxes were piled high. Alec pulled over a chair and climbed up on it. He wasn't all that tall yet. In the next year, he would grow eleven inches and his voice would change, but for the moment, he was about the same height as Boulie and me. He reached for a carton and pulled it down, indicating Boulie was to grab it. Boulie took hold, but the box was heavy. It slipped out of her hands and crashed to the floor.

In my entire life, I have never heard such a terrible loud sound as the thunder in that box. An icy fear grabbed us as we froze in the near dark. I saw three wriggling sacks being thrown overboard in the freezing Straights of Juan de Fuca. We were about to be dead detectives. We suspected the boxes contained opium, but we didn't stay to investigate. Alec, Boulie and I ran up the stairs and slammed the hatch behind us. That night, I lay in bed waiting for furious Coolies to come and get me. I had a stolen kitchen knife under my pillow. So did Alec. When the clock struck two in the morning, I saw a flash in the dark and I screamed.

"Sh-shut up," a non-Coolie voice ordered me in the dark. "C-can I sleep in here w-with you?" Alec asked.

He slept on top of the blankets, his knife by his side, but the pirates didn't come. However, the next morning, Boulie tore out of my mother's car and we ran straight to the fairy glen and lay down in the warm grass. "Soong Chou told me to tell you to stay out of the tunnel. They knew it was us."

"What does Chou have to do with it?" I asked, my heart making a sharp little pain that traveled across my chest. Soong Chou was the one who would save me at the same time he rescued Boulie from the pirates and our intransigent colonial caretakers. I couldn't bear to think that he might be involved in something deeper than indentured labour with my mother.

"I don't know. He told me that we had to respect the gardeners' privacy downstairs."

"It isn't downstairs," I said indignantly. "It's a tunnel."

"They're s-suspicious n-now," Alec said, sensibly. "W-we've g-got l-lots of t-time. I vote we l-let them think we b-believe his story and that w-we've l-lost interest."

We agreed to that. Since it was Thursday and Miss Beach had gone off in my mother's clothes, we decided to investigate the master bedroom for clues while Duffie was occupied in her own room with her well-read ladies' magazines. "You're daft," she said at lunch, when we announced we were going to spend the afternoon sewing sachets of potpourri in the linen closet.

I kicked Ling and Pei out of the sitting room where they were lounging and locked the door with the skeleton key. "Let *them* taste banishment," I said. My mother's rooms were permeated with the scent of gardenias. I could sit there for hours watching the colours change from the palest ivory to butter to rose as the light through the French windows from her balcony transformed her apartment in the time between dawn and dusk.

Boulie was intrigued with Nora's hooded bathtub. She immediately took off her clothes and turned on all the taps. Alec followed her. We left our things in a heap on the floor and jumped into the bath, all of us barely suppressing laughter as we splashed water over the side of the large claw footed tub in the centre of the room.

"Let's dress up," Boulie said, stepping from the tub and wrapping herself in one of my mother's fluffy bath sheets embroidered with my real father's initials, M von S, and his family crest, a lion with a crown. We kept the shower hood running until the hot water ran out, and then stepped out, flushed and wicked. While Alec and I dried off, Boulie ran into my mother's dressing room and opened all the closet doors. Nora had dozens of dresses and rows and rows of shoes and hats, all carefully laundered and mended and currently worn by their custodian, Miss Beach. Her evening dress closet was an iridescence of dresses shimmering with beads and silver embroidery. I plunged into them like a desperate swimmer, sniffing the waves for her smells.

"It's like d-diving into the ocean," Alec said, stroking the watery silk.

Boulie pulled a silver nightgown with pearls sewn in the bodice and hem from a lingerie drawer. "I'm wearing this." I was next, and then Alec. When we were all dressed in gowns, dancing slippers and the jewelry we had found in her dressing table drawers, we sat in front of my mother's mirror and took turns covering our faces with rouge, powder and kohl. I lit matches and blew them out, painting our lashes with the charcoal, as I had seen my mother colour hers. Alec made a very good girl. He had the longest eyelashes of us all.

"Do you want to play Mother and Miss Beach?" I asked Boulie, knowing she would agree.

Alec had to be Stanford. "You don't say a word," I ordered him. "Just watch."

I turned down the bed and sat Boulie on the edge. Down on my knees in front of her, I lifted one slippered foot and carefully removed the satin shoe with its glittering marquisite buckle. I kissed Boulie's arch and felt her shiver, then covered her leg with little kisses from her ankle to the soft inside of her thigh. I took off the other shoe and traced the inside of her leg with my tongue, risking a glance at Alec, who sat still as a statue with his mouth slightly open.

There were stale dog chocolates in the box in my mother's bedside drawer. I took one out and bit it in half, feeding Boulie one half and taking the other to Alec, who took it from my mouth and swallowed it. I licked my lips and chose another, bit it and put half in her belly button. Boulie lay there slowly sucking her toffee-centered sweet while I licked around her belly, smearing my face and her smooth stomach with candy. Then I leaned over and kissed her, felt her chew the sweet treacle from my lips.

"This is w-weird," Alec said as he stood beside the bed, watching us. I put the half chocolate I was saving in Boulie's mouth, watching him all the while I did it, observing his face and the tender swelling in his gown. "Eat it," I ordered and he lowered himself to his knees, leaning into Boulie, who lifted his skirt and took his little hummingbird in her hand while I lay back and touched myself.

We shared a lovely, mysterious shiver, the beautiful group surprise rising like a cake with Alec releasing a thin white stream of icing, and then we laughed and got up and jumped on the bed, hitting one another with my mother's down-filled pillows.

Boulie and I were twelve and Alec fifteen, discovering sex the way animals do, I suppose, putting together instinct and what I had observed through the door to the linen closet. This was a game. I still had no idea how babies were made and Duffie hadn't as yet told me about "the monthly curse."

⌐

BECAUSE I HAD been raised to ignore certain realities, it didn't occur to me that the fairies wouldn't be cleaning up after our romp in Mother's bedroom. The next morning, I woke up and found three nightgowns soiled with cosmetics and chocolate, a pair of sheets and four similarly desecrated pillow-slips laid over the end of my bed, with a furious unsigned note saying *Take these things down to Wash Martha yourself.*

"Yourself" implied blame and damnation, Judgment Day in the scullery. Wash Martha was the Songhees woman who came every other day to do the laundry. I would have to explain the laundry to her, but I wasn't unduly worried. She would turn her dark face from me and mutter in a language I couldn't comprehend. Then it would be over. The note was from Miss Beach, but she wouldn't tell. I knew it was a preemptive move to keep me from ratting on her that lacked any insight whatsoever into my discreet character.

We left Miss Beach behind that morning. I took one moment away from my pleasure in sitting up front, listening to the pea gravel crunching under the wheels, to watch her standing forlorn in the driveway as Song Chou drove me, Boulie, Duffie and Alec through the wrought iron gates. There was no room for her in the car. None of us was willing to sit in the rumble seat to make room for her after I had reported her nasty blackmail attempt to my friends.

"So unkind," Tony, faultlessly polite, comments on my rude behaviour.

"Oh I know. Poor Miss Beach. She became such a friend. I was jealous of her in the beginning, because my mother was attached to her."

We were off without Miss Beach to watch the canoe races on the Gorge. In the days before the inland waterway became crowded and polluted, the Gorge was heaven on earth. Now I think of the laughing Selkirk Waters and mourn for the summer days we spent watching the swimming and diving, paddling in boats or having our afternoon tea at Mr. Nishimoto's *yakata*, his floating teahouse decorated with cherry blossoms and paper lanterns at the Tramway Gorge Park. I treasure those boats with lanterns floating down the Gorge, Chinamen with long queues and embroidered pyjamas paddling in unison, and Victorian houses with elaborate gingerbread and cupolas shaped like wine glasses blown by Venetian masters.

Soon, most of the old houses would burn, the children who bravely jumped off the rocks into the sparkling water would be sent with guns to kill or be killed in the muddy fields of France, or die of typhus, tuberculosis or influenza. The next generation would swim in sewage from the houses proliferating along the sheltered inlet, and the Japanese Garden and teahouse would fall into ruin.

Soong Chou drove us as far as Yates and Government Streets. He had business in Chinatown. We took the open tram over the bridge to Victoria West. Duffie loved the ride. Her rust-coloured curls flew away from her hairpins as she held on to her straw hat with its plaid grosgrain ribbon. She put her arm around Alec and laughed with her head thrown back and her mouth wide open. Alec said she was going to catch flies.

"I was a love child." Alec said to me as we waited while Duffie and Boulie searched out a location for our picnic.

"What does that mean?"

"I don't know. I want to find out."

"I don't think I was," I said finally, then got up and brushed the grass seeds from my clothes.

I didn't mind that Duffie was paying more attention to Alec than to me. I missed my mother, but I also dreaded the routine that would be reinstated when she returned. She had decided to send Alec back to regular school in the fall and we were none of us going to mention Boulie's reintroduction to our household during my mother's absence. Anticipating the loneliness that was coming made this day and a few others like it very poignant.

Duffie had brought a picnic basket for the canoe races. After she decided between sunlight and shade for our lunch, she spread a white linen tablecloth on the ground and we lay under the trees eating our picnic. We didn't care who won or lost the contests. It was beautiful to watch the Songhees and their rivals from the Nootka, Cowichan, Bella Coola and Kwagiulth nations paddling in unison. The half-naked bodies of the Aboriginal athletes must have excited Duffie. Deprived of romance, her cheeks flushed when the red silk flag from the Chinese Benevolent Association was given to the winning team.

She told us the legend of the reversing falls, the rapids at the Tillicum Narrows, where careless boaters capsized during adverse tides. The spirits of Snukaymelt and Camossung — warriors who had been turned to stone by Halys the Transformer so they could protect the fish and game in the waterway — were imprisoned in the dangerous rocks. Camossung would give natives who survived diving into the rapids special powers and guidance. Clothes washed in the foam from the turbulent waters would protect the wearer from drowning. I asked Duffie if she believed in magic and she told me she only trusted in prayer.

"Were you not taught any prayers?" Tony is incredulous.

"Duffie made me say, 'Now I lay me down to sleep' at bedtime. I had to promise not to tell my mother. Nora was ferocious about religion. 'People kill one another for religion,' she said."

After the races, we got back on the tram and rode down to the Gorge Tramway Park. Three people in the seat behind us talked about going for tea on the *yakata* moored at the Japanese Tea Garden.

"Can we go?" we begged Duffie.

"Anything your wee hearts desire," Duffie said.

We were over the moon with excitement. Aboard the barge pulled by a small launch, bowing waiters brought us green tea ice cream and a woman wearing a kimono played a small piano while we drifted under cedar boughs leaning over the water. I wondered if Boulie felt at home in this little piece of the Orient, if drinking tea on a boat was as familiar to her as the orange groves of California were to me. Her face, luminous as the moonstone on a silver chain that Soong Chou had given me for my twelfth birthday, said yes.

We saw common seabirds and garden scavengers as we floated along the Gorge, but also spotted eagles, cormorants, and herons competing for fish, and stellar jays pecking the dead trees, hunting for insects. The man at the canoe club gave us a tin can full of herring chunks to feed the curious seals that swam alongside the boat. Alec pointed out deer and otter on the shore.

Oddly, our Japanese tea consisted of black tea and milk, cucumber sandwiches and scones with wild blackberry jam.

"Is this what they eat in Japan?" Boulie asked.

I had to be the queen of the upper waters, one of the chosen few lucky enough to have a perfect day, but I ached for the girl with the perfect heart that used to be me. I wondered if my spirit was trapped in a rock somewhere waiting to be released. In any case, going on the water without fear was, I realised, my first step toward freedom.

After we disembarked from our cruise, we sat for a while with Duffie and listened to the brass band playing in the bandstand. Duffie chatted with everyone around us, particularly a man wearing a peaked cap and a tweed suit with the jacket thrown over his shoulders. His white shirtsleeves were rolled up. Just this one day, I was wearing girl's clothes, a sundress and straw hat, as was Boulie, and Alec was dressed in his gray cotton shirt and plaid tie with khaki shorts. I pitied the suit-man and all the other gentlemen dressed in their Sunday best on this hot summer day. Perspiration ran down both sides of his face.

Alec must have been glad of the man claiming his mother's attention. He had been complaining about an excess of public affection from her. I wouldn't have minded such behaviour from my mother, but it bothered him to be petted like a dog. Boulie and I had been calling Alec "the greyhound" and he didn't like it. We didn't say much to one another while the band played on, but there was a current passing between us. The romp in my mother's boudoir had taken us to the wild side and we were alive to the possibilities of further investigation. When the suit-man asked Duffie to dance, Alec seized the moment, asking if we could rent a rowboat to further explore Portage Inlet.

"Mind Poppy's wee heart now. She's not to row," Duffie commanded him as she took a dollar from her purse. "And don't go near the rapids."

"Are you s-scared?" Alec asked, as we got in the boat.

"No!" I lied.

It was my job to sit in the bow and look out for other boaters and swimmers and any peril that might be floating on or under the surface. I trailed my fingers in the water, scaring off silver smelts.

"Lazy Mary!" Boulie yelled at the top of her lungs and the spirits in Pulwutsang Creek, the Songhees River of ghosts, answered her. None of us said it, but we were looking for a hiding place under the shady trees where we could tie up the boat and lose ourselves in the woods.

"Let's go to the rapids," I said, more bravely than I felt. Without argument, Alec and Boulie began to row in the direction of the Tillicum Narrows. I closed my eyes and enjoyed the now familiar thrill between my legs. Our first pass went without incident. We slid through the waterfalls and spitting foam without losing control of the boat. The other side was calm.

Alec pointed to a good landing spot on the bank. We paddled into the cove and, tying the bowline to an arbutus that leaned out over the water, made for shore. Boulie and I had taken off our shoes and stockings, leaving them in the boat. Our skirts lifted and tied around our waists, we scrambled out of the muddy water and headed into the bushes, scaring a brilliant cock pheasant out of our path. A crow scolded from a cedar branch above us. I can still smell the warmly composting forest floor. On the way to bliss, we collected sword ferns to make a bed for our humble *ménage à trois*.

Boulie found the spot. Pointing without speaking, she led us to a clearing under a clump of ash trees. Silent as deer, we stacked our ferns in a spot already thick with fallen leaves. The three of us lay down, side by side, holding hands, with Alec in the middle. "It aches between my legs," I whispered. "It feels like whirlpools pulling me in."

"Sssh," Boulie put her finger to her lips. We heard laughter. Someone was near us in the woods. We got on our hands and knees, crawling closer, carefully pushing aside Oregon grape and low ferns. Whatever we were about to see, we knew we shouldn't. Flesh moved between the sun-dappled leaves. It was a man and a woman lying on a tartan blanket, naked, Duffie would have said, as bad sticks.

"Aren't they the people who sat behind us on the tram?" I whispered.

"Where's the pregnant lady who was with them?" Boulie asked.

The woman was lying on her back on a Hudson Bay Blanket, her long honey-coloured hair fanned over the dirt, legs wrapped around the man riding her. She was moaning. At first I thought the man was hurting her, and was about to mobilize Alec and Boulie to help me save her. The woman cried out and thrashed at his back, scratching him. Then they kissed and he fell off her.

I was at once repelled and fascinated as the pieces fell together. This was how babies were made.

Awed and silent, we crept back to our canoe and stole away. The miracle I had felt between Alec's legs was as ordinary as mud. Anyone could do it. I kept watch and my friends pulled hard on their oars. The boat skimmed over the water. Boulie giggled as we approached the bridge with its string of electric lights arching over the rapids. "K-keep rowing!" Alec ordered, and she did. Turbulence splashed water over the sides of the boat. I lay back terrified as the sea swirled around us, turning our small boat in a complete circle. It shuddered as we crashed against a rock. Alec dropped his oar and got it back again.

The tumult only lasted a few frightening seconds; and then, just as quickly, we passed under the gates to heaven or hell and found ourselves safe on the other side of the narrows where the water was still. Alec and Boulie rested on their oars as we sat in the middle of the Gorge and watched the sun sink behind the dark silhouettes of trees. A high diver, carrying a torch, flared in the darkness. We rowed toward the fairy lights and the music calling us from the shore.

Duffie was, of course, pacing the float by the boathouse, while her suit-man lurked in the background. As we got out and tied up the boat, she leapt on us and hugged us in relief. None of us was going to mention our frightening adventure at the rapids.

"Yew wee dafties are a sight for sore eyes" Duffie clucked and pulled out a hairbrush. We allowed ourselves to be groomed, smirking at one another.

Duffie ordered Boulie to collect bark, while she sent Alec and me to buy fresh buns from the concession in the tea garden surrounded by wisteria-bound pergolas and large rhododendrons. The Japanese garden was a fairyland of electric lights and lanterns. Alec grabbed onto me as we stopped at the end of the path and looked back at the land of make believe, fairy-lit shapes of bamboo, red pines and lily ponds surrounded by stone lanterns. He squeezed my hand then let it go as we turned around.

Suit-man had made a campfire on the beach, over which he boiled water for tea. He cut off chunks of sausage and handed them around with the bread we had fetched. Starving, we tore into our late supper, "like wee savages," Duffie said, laughing. Savages or not, our day on the water and in the woods had made us hungry. For dessert, Duffie had a bowl of peaches in her picnic basket, which she sliced with Suit-man's pocketknife. I noticed when she fed him sections he touched her with his tongue, licking the sweet juice on her hands. Suit-man and Duffie hardly looked at one another, the studied indifference I now recognize as sexual attraction.

Branches hung with lights and paper lanterns marked the paths through the forest. We had until just before midnight when the last tram left. Soong Chou would be waiting with the car at the station after his day in Chinatown. Duffie set us free, but I was told not to ride on the shoot-the-chute water slide. Boulie, Alec and I exchanged meaningful looks and wandered off to watch the moving pictures while Duffie and Suit-man paid to dance to raise money for the survivors of the *Titanic*. In the outdoor theatre surrounded by twinkling lights, film stars with ten-foot faces flickered on a large screen. The actors took pratfalls and kissed, robbed banks and waited to be rescued from moving trains and whizzing arrows.

I heard Duffie calling to us, her "wee hens." Grief began as a wail, then faded to a whisper. As the crowd lifted and moved as one, the way a school of fish startles when disturbed, the moving picture stood still and the band stopped playing. Alec, Boulie and I held hands so as not to lose one another. Like sea-creatures carried on a tide, we floated to the fire on the beach.

The three of us circled the crowd and went to the place where two bodies were laid out in the sand. The rest of the crowd was still. The only sounds were the crackling fire, wind chimes tinkling in the trees, and the sobbing of the pregnant woman holding her drowned husband's head in her lap. He was a ghostly blue in the firelight. Laid out beside him, her long gown, wet so her red flannel petticoat showed through, clinging to her legs, and her honey-coloured hair fanned out just the way we had seen it earlier in the afternoon, was the woman we had seen with him in the woods. Someone whispered that their rowboat had been found smashed on the rocks in the Tillicum Narrows an hour earlier. Another hushed voice said the dead woman was the widow's sister, who had come from Seattle to help with her confinement.

Boulie squeezed my hand and I squeezed Alec's. We said nothing; our eyes large while Duffie went on about the wages of sin. Was this what she meant? We too had been naughty. How had we avoided this terrible fate? There would be much to talk about later.

6

My Dear,

Tony and I are having dinner in my cabin tonight. Sometimes it is too much effort just to get dressed, let alone deal with the complications of eating with strangers. It is amazing how ships create instant social hierarchies. Exclusion is colder than the ice boxes in the ship's kitchen, but, once accepted, one is in for rash-inducing intimacy. The other passengers don't know what to make of Tony and me or why we are going to China. That is none of their business, and besides I am too tired to explain that I am a careless woman who has misplaced my loved one.

Tony has ordered crab bisque with caviar *blinis* and a bottle of champagne. The typewriter is set up on the little writing desk and we are cosy in our pyjamas. "We are nesting creatures," I said, thinking of all the times my nest has been disturbed. As always, typing makes me think of Stanford and my unanswered letters.

Later this evening, Tony has plans to go on deck to watch the shooting stars. Olivier once told me about viewing James McNeill Whistler's "Nocturne in Black and Gold: the Falling Rocket," a beautiful painting of a night sky full of turbulence. "I realised," he said, "the impressionists are right. We are all fragments of light in the same sky." That is comforting.

꜁

ON MY THIRTEENTH BIRTHDAY, Duffie left us. She said she wanted to go home to Scotland before war broke out in Europe. Alec was to stay in Canada and finish his education. So long as he was in school, Duffie confided, he would be safe.

Duffie, who had told me more times than I care to remember that she was the only one who truly cared for me, was about to jump ship. I don't know which is worse, death or abandonment, but I was devastated when she left. My beloved Nanny MacDuff didn't look back once when Soong Chou drove her to the C.P.R. dock. Now, as a mother, I am amazed that I didn't realise at the time that she *couldn't*.

With the exception of an insulting birthday card that arrived the following year, Duffie didn't write me a single word from Scotland. By sending the greeting signed Violet Pringle from Edinburgh, she was telling me she had found a husband. Angry and betrayed, I tore up the card and burned it in my waste paper basket.

Even stranger than leaving me was Duffie's desertion of Alec. I think her decision, which may have been intended to save him, left Alec vulnerable to making impetuous decisions, like so many of our boys who gave into the glamourous notion of wearing a uniform and seeking glory in war.

My mother excused herself from celebrating my thirteenth birthday dinner with me because she had a migraine. I ate by myself in the children's dining room. Fong watched me open my present, a watch with a striped canvas strap. After dinner, I visited Chou in the stable. I had been going to Chou's apartment for secret lessons after hearing him play his *pipa* in the garden. His music had moved me to tears. The first time I stayed hidden in the bamboo and listened, but eventually I asked about the pineapple-shaped four stringed instrument. Then I persisted in asking for lessons until he relented. Neither Chou nor I mentioned my musical adventure to my mother.

Soong Chou's apartment, accessed by an exterior stairway with a lattice arch covered by Virginia creeper was a world apart from the rooms off the tunnel under the house. Perhaps I was right about him. He had the bearing of an aristocrat and smoked his cigarettes in a carved ivory holder. The rugs on his floor had dragons and chrysanthemum patterns woven into them.

"Walk on the flowers," he said. "You can't crush them. But stay away from the dragons. It is bad luck to walk on a dragon." While Chou made tea, I tiptoed around the dragons, but they still must have been awakened. Now I wonder who and what we are offending as we cross the Pacific on this ocean liner.

Soong Chou's furniture, carved dark wood with mother of pearl inlay and silk cushions on the chairs, was not unlike the exquisite furnishings that Lady Cowes-Wentworth-Cowes had brought from China. A far cry from the small lacquer trunks, which appeared to be the sole possessions of our Coolies, they spoke of privilege. Soong Chou had large and small *pipas*. He gave me the child-sized *liuqin*.

I had my lessons in his kitchen at the wooden table. On my birthday, he invited me into his sitting room and gave me jasmine tea brewed from a single flower that opened in the small round cup like a fairy skirt. I buried my face in the steam and breathed. The jasmine, which had been picked in the moonlight, smelled of enchantment. He put an orchid and a small package wrapped in silk and ribbon on the low octagonal table in front of my chair.

"Sometimes the injured bird sings better, Poppy," he said, urging me to open it. My birthday present was a *tabatière*, a small oval box made of tortoise shell. It had an oval enamel on top, which, when a small catch in the side was engaged, opened and allowed a tiny mechanical bird to rise up, raise its wings and sing. The bird, decorated with hummingbird feathers, was no larger than my thumbnail. The hummingbird's song was similar to a tune I had heard Chou play in the garden.

I curled myself around the *liuqin* and felt it respond to the rhythms of my heart. Chou left my instrument in its case on a shelf in the garage. That way I could play it when he was busy elsewhere. When the car was parked there, I often climbed in the rumble seat to practice.

The more I played, the more I needed to paint. Emily was back from her travels abroad. While away, she had sent me affectionate letters with little drawings of amusing people and animals she had sketched, and sometimes a plant she knew I would fancy. In spite of these friendly gestures, she refused to come back to our house.

Soong Chou drove me to her new house, which in the beginning she called *Hill House*, and later, during hard times when she was forced to give lodging to rougher trade, *The House of Allsorts*. One of the reasons she'd started having all her classes at home was because she was now raising dogs that competed for her attention, as did her unruly tenants. My private classes were constantly interrupted by demands from one or the other and sometimes, as you know, Emily was an abusive landlady. When she didn't want to address a complaint, she often sent me to deal with a tenant. I once had to stop her from hitting one of her boarders with her frying pan.

Emily and I were both changed. I was a young woman and Emily, who had been handsome before, was now matronly. In acknowledgement of my maturity, she told me to use her Christian name. Where she had been familial, almost maternal with me when I was a child, she was now sometimes cruelly forthright, which I accepted, considering it a deeper level of intimacy. Otherwise, I would have been offended by her criticism. This honesty did not extend to personal revelation. While she tramped through my private garden, she protected her own with a thorn hedge. Emily only revealed herself to me in the oblique manner of Soong Chou, through proverb. "Depression is anger without enthusiasm," she told me once, and I realised that channeling her creative energy was a deliberate antidote to despair.

I liked the classes at *Hill House* because Emily and I had both felt intimidated by the level of cleanliness in Nora's fastidiously maintained house. *Hill House*, though Emily struggled to maintain it all by herself, was full of dogs and people and their mess. No longer restrained by the presence of Duffie or a maid or my mother, our canvases shouted the new freedom.

It was good for Emily to have me as a student. We helped one another. There had been times when she painted on butcher paper because she couldn't afford canvas. When she didn't have money for turpentine, she had substituted gasoline she'd "borrowed" from parked cars. My mother paid a premium for painting supplies and her largesse provided plenty of paint and canvas for both of us. I was happy to help with my teacher's chores and with diplomacy, not just with the tenants but also with shopkeepers who had to be paid and often placated.

By 1914, I knew I was a painter, and Alec had found his vocation as well. He wanted to sign up as a war artist. The idea made me physically ill. We rambled over the rocks on the beach in Oak Bay, shouting into the wind. I tried to take the part of an outraged mother.

"Yew daft wee bizem. Ye'll get yerself killed. I won't let yew."

"You c- can't stop me, P-poppy. What k-kind of a m-man would I b-be if I d-didn't stand up for m-my c-country?"

I reverted to my frustrated self. "You're not a man, Alec. You're a boy."

"I'm a m-man P-poppy and you know it."

Did I? Alec and I had taken our childish games one step further, having pledged our virginity to one another much as Boulie and I had decided on blood sisterhood, but we were still just playing house.

"It's f-for you, P-poppy."

"I need you here, Alec." The wind chilled my tears.

He lived a continent away from war; why go? Deciding whether or not to enlist wasn't a matter of courage or cowardice. It was common sense. Why waste the lives of children created and raised in love? He argued that it was not relevant in his case. The war would define him as a person in ways his mother had been unable to manage. I swallowed a lump in my throat, wondering if it would mean anything to him if I apologized for stealing Duffie. I looked over the sea to the flat composure of the San Juan Islands and wondered what I could say to convince him that he was needed here. In the end, I took his hand and told him that it would kill me if anything happened to him.

"We have to make our baby," I said and led him away from the beach.

My soldier artist and I went to the fairy glen and lay down in the grass. We didn't undress. It was too cold. My heart was a lump of ice in my chest. When we kissed, I tried to swallow his lips, wishing I could consume him and keep him safe inside me until it was safe to let him out again, but I couldn't. The boy Alec no longer existed. It was a man who confidently lifted my skirt and unbuttoned his trousers. I put my hands on his chilly bottom and we rubbed against one another. When he shuddered, I felt as though his precious life was emptying into me. "I l-love you," he said.

I loved him too, but I was *in* love with someone else. "You are precious to me, Alec."

"And you to me."

"Are you mad at Duffie?" I asked while we shook off grass seeds.

"No, why should I be?"

"I am. I thought she cared. She was the only one."

"I l-love you, P-poppy," he repeated.

I put my hand over his mouth. "Don't say it again, until you come back."

It is hard to write these things, but they are an important part of the story.

When we walked back to the garden through the fairy glen, I saw Nora watching us from her balcony. The next day she came into the children's dining room and suggested that I eat with her in future.

On my first night of gustatory adulthood, I came to dinner, my stomach in a knot. Would she notice that I had become a woman? Would I pass muster, as Stanford liked to say? I wanted to be included in my mother's charmed circle, but was afraid I would ruin it once and for all. She had an agenda. I could tell by the bright manner in which she attempted conversation.

"You must come with me to see the Dunsmuir's Corot."

Cows in fields, I thought, echoing Emily. Why do rich people only buy safe art? "I'd love to."

The dinner proceeded with polite conversation. Fong, who acted as cook and maid when there were no guests, served dinner. I looked to him for affirmation or amusement, but there was no reaction — not in front of my mother, who was wearing a pair of gold Chinese pyjamas. I kept my eyes on her toggles, not daring to raise them to her face. We maintained civility until Fong served the coffee. My mother stuck a cigarette in her long ebony holder and told me that Alec and I were too old to play together.

"It is time for Alec to move along."

"You can't tell him what to do."

"I can so long as I am paying his expenses. I told him that it is time for him to become independent. He is old enough to join the army."

"You told him to sign up? When?"

"He came to talk to me about his education, and I told him that serving our country was a matter of honour."

"This isn't about honour. This is war. People die needlessly in wars. Besides, this isn't his country. He is Scottish."

"All the more reason. Serving is his duty, Poppy."

Duty? Oh, could I ever give her a lecture about duty. What about a mother's duty to her child? What about her duty to Alec? I was incredulous. So that is where his stupid sense of obligation came from. My mother had casually condemned the child of a woman who had given a good part of her life in our service. I could not think of a greater cruelty. All my animosity toward Duffie deserted me. "You promised Duffie that you would help Alec go to university," I argued. If I ever let my longing for her trespass into the dark forest of loathing, it was at that moment.

"He can do that after the war." She put out her cigarette. Then she got up and left the room. Fong, who had been clearing the table during our conversation, looked at me and raised his eyebrows.

The following Friday, Emily sent me to answer a knock at her door. It was Alec. He wanted to show me something. I didn't have to ask Emily to keep his visit a secret. She didn't like my mother.

I got on the handlebar of Alec's bicycle and he drove me down Government Street. Several years earlier, a fire had devastated the downtown core. The block between the Five Sisters Building and Trounce Alley was a wasteland. Some entrepreneur had the idea of making money off the property while it lay fallow. When we arrived downtown, Alec parked his bicycle against a wall, took two quarters out of his pocket, and gave them to a soldier guarding the vacant property, which had been excavated by the army. He explained he was taking me on a tour of simulated trenches, like the ones dug by Coolies in France.

In the schoolroom, Duffie had indulged us with a fantasy game. We had imagined and built, in words and pictures we kept in scribblers, an underground world populated by small people who lived like rabbits and moles transporting food and raising their young in well-appointed dens that were invisible to adults. In cross-sections of the garden and our burrows, we created a Utopia where children and parents cuddled, keeping one another warm. Alec was trying to convince me that life in the trenches was an extension of that childhood game. "L-look," he stuttered, showing me the shelters. "They are p-perfectly safe. I w-won't even h-have to stick my h-head up. The army has p-periscopes for looking over the b-battlefields."

The Victoria boys went off like sheep to war. No one mentioned gas in the imprecations to young men to sign up. No one mentioned septic wounds, gangrene and filth in the trenches. No one mentioned tuberculosis, typhus or influenza. No one mentioned the psychologically damaged men who would cripple the generation to follow. Most of this we learned in hindsight. War was glorious, for God and country. A young man should feel privileged to go, his family proud of the sacrifice. The simulated trench we toured didn't have the stench of latrines and festering injuries. Just a cheery little fantasy, it was neither damp nor cold, but I wasn't fooled. We rode back to Emily's in silence.

I didn't see Alec again before he left. He sent a note in June telling me he had joined the Seaforth Highlanders and would have shipped out before I got the letter. In it, he included a photo of himself looking serious in a kilt, and also a ring in the shape of a flower, an amethyst surrounded by pearls. I put the ring on my baby finger and touched it whenever I thought of him.

One morning, as I was heading for the garage by way of the kitchen door, I saw my mother inspecting the herb garden. She called me to her. "Rosemary," she said, pointing to the spiky bush, "is protection from evil. Basil is for bridegrooms, the right ones. What is this?" she asked, taking my hand.

"It's a friendship ring." I kicked the dirt. "Alec gave it to me."

"How vulgar," she said, removing his gift and putting it in her pocket.

"You're being unkind," I pleaded.

"And you are being immature, Poppy. It's time you grew up. I should have sent Nanny and Alec packing years ago."

"Sent them packing. What do you mean?" My eyes were slits; so narrow they could have been the windows in tanks. I took aim. In my mind, I fired.

"It was high time for you learn to get on without Nanny and for her to move on to younger children. I gave her notice."

"So, it was you. She didn't leave me," my voice rose. "Or Alec." At that moment, I purely hated her.

"Don't be silly, Poppy, and don't take jewelry from any man unless you intend to marry him."

I will marry him, I said to myself, and have his baby.

I should have fought her tooth and nail for that ring. She had no right to it. Instead of wresting it from her, I went straight upstairs and cut my hair. That night, my mother went to a dinner party with friends. As soon as I heard the departing tires in the gravel, I went to the stable and took my *liuqin* down from the shelf. Soong Chou had been sitting at the kitchen table doing accounts on his abacas. Having heard me on the stairs, he opened the door before I knocked. Chou was so splendid in his white silk pyjamas, I could hardly breathe.

"Your hair is different," he said.

The hair on my arms stood up. I was surprised by that intimate remark. Hard as I had tried, Soong Chou would not comment on my occasional use of perfume or a new dress like the one that had recently arrived from Paris. I wanted him to notice that I now had a woman's figure with a small waist and gently rounding hips and breasts. Chou had primed me for Alec. I was so sexually charged I could barely think straight.

He made black tea. I sat on a cushion in his sitting room, sipped and listened while he played his *pipa*. When Chou played, he held his Chinese lute as if it were a woman he was coaxing to sing. The notes, while clear and individual, came together in a beautiful legato, gentle as the water running over the rocks in my mother's Japanese pools. I watched his face, with nut-shaped eyes and circumflex eyebrows and divinely sculpted profile. I watched his mouth set in the most exquisite sorrow and his graceful hands and wrists. If I had to choose a part of his body to worship, I think it would

have been his wrists. When he played a tremolo, my body responded
in little waves.

"This song is 'The Great Wave Washes the Beach,'" he said.
"The composer, my friend Hua Yan-jun, is a Taoist monk. The
water changes constantly, Poppy, and the beach remains. It is the
same with us."

I was not sure what he was telling me. I knew very little about
him, only what I had learned from his oblique teachings, but I was
sure he had suffered. I was not unfamiliar with loneliness myself,
and his, I knew, was mixed with humiliation. I kissed his hands and
he looked at me for a long time. Then he told me to play the song
I had been practicing — "Spring Rain." When I finished, he stood
up and said, "In this country, Poppy, we Chinese are invisible,
except when people are angry with us." Then he took me to the
door.

The next day, Dola Dunsmuir came for tea with her awful
mother. Dola was about as amusing as a potato and it was clear
that my mother expected me to entertain her. She was two years
younger than me and deadly dull apart from her passion for flowers. At the dinner party the night before, my mother had offered to
teach her about herbs. I realised Nora's hospitality had nothing to
do with her overwhelming love of children, but with cultivating the
immensely rich Dunsmuir family.

I could determine the degree of importance my mother attached
to a visitor by the quality of the tea. When there was no one but
us, we might have oatmeal biscuits and scones with jam. The
next level included cucumber sandwiches with the crusts cut off.
For guests like the Dunsmuirs, whom my mother described as
"common" behind their backs, she had Miss Beach produce the
priceless Staffordshire tea pot, her best China tea, sherry, cucumber
and watercress sandwiches, scones, shortbread and lemon tarts.
After feeding her already overfed compadres, she would confide to
Miss Beach that they could do well to exercise their arms, pushing
themselves away from the table.

"Except for Kathleen and Doulie, the girls are all as ugly as mud fences."

Dola's grandfather, a working-class Scottish immigrant, had become the wealthiest man on Vancouver Island. His coal mines were scars on the green hills. Maybe Dola understood, even as a child, that it was her responsibility to compensate for him, just as another of my mother's friends, Mrs. Butchart, was building gardens around her husband's hideous cement works. I already knew, after going to a Christmas party at Hatley Park, that Dola's mother had a green-house full of orchids.

"Why doesn't Dola stay home and play with her mother's orchids?"

My mother laughed. I think that, being rebellious herself, she enjoyed my small outbursts. As it turned out, her garden bond with me wasn't as strong as the one she would forge with Dola. We girls had so much in common, she argued. "Be nice to her." Dola's brother, Boy, had sunk with the *Lusitania* in May and her parents were bereft.

I was incredulous. Who was helping *me* with *my* grief? My father was dead. Stanford had been banished. Nanny was gone. Alec had jumped into a hole in the earth. Why was it suddenly so important that I become the patron saint of bereaved rich girls? Of course, I could guess at the answer. Nora wanted to make us socially unassailable. We were not overtly Jewish. Therefore, with an Austrian name, we were, by default, German. After the Germans had scuttled the fifteen Victorians aboard the *Lusitania*, there were anti-German riots in Victoria. What, I wondered, would the good citizens of Victoria make of our secret tunnel?

I took Dola to the fairy glen and talked to her about dying. She said she had dreams about her brother going down on the ship. He was banging on a porthole, begging her to help him get free. His horse was in the hold. She heard Boy and the horse screaming in unison, and she woke up weeping and drenched in perspiration.

"I died when I had Rheumatic Fever and I came back," I said.

"It wasn't so bad. You fly through a tunnel of clouds to the light."
I tried to comfort her. Why complicate matters? The Dunsmuirs
were already wrecked on the beach where their son should have
washed up. They weren't going to find his body. Was that what
Soong Chou meant when he told me about the song he had been
playing?

Dola said her father cried all the time and kept playing a song,
"Where, Oh Where Is My Wandering Boy Tonight?" over and over
on his Victrola. I wondered if Soong Chou's family felt the same
way, if they believed they had lost him on these foreign shores.
Perhaps he sent them money. Duffie told me the Coolies sent all
their money — after a few indulgences like gambling, opium and
comfort women — back to China, since my mother provided room
and board, such as it was.

On the way home from Emily's the following Friday, I began to
cry. Emily had been in a bad mood and had spoken sharply to me.
All the emotions of the week caught up with me and I became quite
hysterical. Chou stopped beside the Chinese cemetery at the beach.
"The *feng shui* is good here," he told me as we got out of the car.
"We are standing on two continents. The tectonic plates meet under
our graveyard." He opened the gate in the picket fence around the
burial ground and led me past the tombstones and the furnace
where the joss paper and Hell money is burned when someone dies.
"The people buried here want to go home. They have to wait seven
years in these graves and then their bones are cleaned in wine and
sent home in boxes," he said. I imagine he wanted to distract me
from my own pain, but I cried harder because I knew that he too
would leave.

We walked down to the beach, took off our shoes and walked
along the tide line letting the cold water shock our feet, forcing the
blood, Chou said, to go to our brains so we could think more
clearly. "Our dead," he said, waving his arm over the sea, "know
that China is right over there. They are happier waiting." He took

me to a tombstone and read the inscription, "It says *Yi bu wang hua*, which means the righteous one does not forget China."

"And you," I asked, "Are you happy here?"

"I do my duty to my family," He answered. "That is enough happiness for now."

"What about later?" Of course Chou was waiting too.

"Later will tell me what it wants me to know." Chou sat down on the gnarl in a huge tree that had been uprooted by the sea and brought up on the rocks. I knelt and kissed his foot. I heard him sigh. I kissed his pant-leg and his buttons. I kissed his jade ring. I kissed his shirt and nuzzled the soft warm skin of his neck, which smelled familiar from all the times he had carried me when my legs went to sleep. He didn't move. I kissed his eyes.

The shadow of Alec briefly stepped between the sun and us. I blinked and he was gone. I looked to the right and left. There was no one tending the graves in the Chinese graveyard and no one on the beach. We were alone. Fully realizing what would happen to a Chinaman found on the bluff with his employer's daughter, I stepped out of my dress and my slip and they fell into the tall grass growing in hollows in the rocks. Then I took off my underwear, watching his face as I did so.

"I am not a virgin," I said.

I spread my dress in the meadow foam and blue camas and lay down on it, my feet pointing to the Orient. Soong Chou stood up and unbuttoned his shirt and his trousers, laying them neatly over the log. When he stood between China and me with the sun behind him he could have been male or female, a shadow with a radiant outline. Then he lay down on me. His body felt light and smooth. We kissed, his tongue tasting my mouth and mine his, exotic caves filled with silky crevices.

Then he lifted himself up, bent to kiss my feet and ankles, the inside of my thighs. I moaned and held onto the grass lest he sweep me away out to sea. He played me with his fingers; made the lovely tremolo, and I released the sound he was waiting for, my body aching, opening I imagined like a sea anemone. Then, when I sang for him, he entered me, kissing my face and hair. I smelled the Orient on him, as if he were a boat sailing into me with its cargo of spices.

We lay in the sun for a few moments, until the water came up and almost touched us. Soong Chou told me the Olympic Mountains across the ocean were a friendship gate to China, and when the dead souls went home the gates opened for them. On this day they were formidable, the peaks sharp and gleaming, protecting our secret. With changes in weather, the mountains transform themselves. Sometimes they disappear in the fog and I see how easily the homesick could slip past their rugged peaks and begin the journey across the Pacific Ocean.

My lover dried me with his shirt, wiped the sand and grass from my legs and the place where he had entered me. Then he dressed and I dressed. "This is our secret," he said, as we walked to the car, and I knew it wouldn't happen again.

7

My Cabbage,

"Weren't you the naughty girl?" Tony laughs as he tucks the page he has just read under the pile.

"I loved Soong Chou. I still do."

"What about Alec?"

"I'm glad it happened. He deserved to be the first."

"You are right, dear Poppins. You are kind, and I am not."

"You are the kindest, Tony. But sometimes you go for the joke."

"And I will confess I was a mindless bugger at Eton."

"Aren't all the boys at Eton mindless buggers?"

So far, I have avoided contact with the other passengers, buggers and otherwise, and they seem to respect that. Can they see that I am an invalid? I would love to hear the speculation about Tony and me, their tongues gossiping like the silver place settings rattling in inclement weather. Perhaps they are deferential because Tony made our reservations as Lady Coverton and Lord Bainbridge. That was only to make sure we jumped the queue, as there was no time to waste.

I thought of Alec's sea voyage and wondered what he and his fellow soldiers said to one another as they approached the shores of France. Did he show them my photograph? Did he tell them we had made love in the wild garden below my house? Were the virgins among them in awe, wishing they too had experienced carnal love before sacrificing themselves? Did fear excite them sexually?

My mother handed me Alec's letter written on Thanksgiving, 1916, with a look. Her so-called harmless war had already taken Boy and the sons of other families we knew in Victoria. She opened her mouth, but remained silent. There was nothing for her to say, no point in trying. She had other things on her mind.

I took the letter to the fairy glen, sat down on a rock facing the sea and read it. Alec started by asking if I had been to the Gorge. He said he lay on his cot at night and imagined rowing Boulie and me to a garden party. He included sketches of us sitting in the stern ordering him to row faster. "Faster, Alec, row harder!" laughter fluttering like birds on the water. Sleek heads turned when he walked up the dock to the lawn with the two most beautiful girls at the party, one on each arm.

The food was lovely, every imaginable sandwich, sponge cakes with sliced strawberries buried in the icing, China tea, lemonade, and punch in a crystal bowl — all of it set out on long tables with lilies in crystal vases, fine linen and gleaming silver. There was music and dancing in the gazebo. The band played waltzes by Strauss and the new American songs from Tin Pan Alley. Alec had to fight off men and women both to get dances with Boulie and me, but he didn't mind. He loved watching us. Instead of being afraid of the gunfire and bombing at night, he told himself it was fireworks lighting up the Gorge, illuminating the water and the last rowers out romancing.

I felt nauseous when he went on to report that the trenches smelled bad and the food left a lot to be desired. The Canadian boys had better rations than anyone — tinned meat and butter and puddings — so he wasn't going to complain. The war would be over soon and the boys would be home by Christmas. He would really like to hear from me. His mother was fine. She had found herself a husband almost as soon as she returned to Selkirk. Mr. Pringle was older than Duffie, a widower with a bad heart.

"I hope you think of me when you look at your ring," he wrote. "I think of you all the time."

I rode my bicycle to Boulie's, with the letter in the carrier. "He's going to be killed," she said when she had finished reading it. "I just know it; and it will be Nora's fault."

"My mother didn't start the war," I surprised myself in defending her.

I had something else to show Boulie. She was the only one I could trust, even if she was, in Duffie's words, a daftie girl. We went down to the beach below Lady Cowes-Wentworth-Cowes's house and found a place, almost a cave, in the rocks that was out of the wind. I looked out at the ocean and asked Boulie if she thought Boy Dunsmuir might find his way home and wash up in the lagoon in front of his parent's monstrous house, his drowned flesh a reproach to their pride. Boy's ship had gone down near Ireland but he could have floated the polar route from Ireland, past Greenland, through the arctic and down the Alaska coast.

"Why are you obsessing on Boy Dunsmuir?" she asked. "You're even starting to sound like Nora." We had both started calling my mother Nora and Lady Cowes-Wentworth-Cowes, Fanny and sometimes Cow Fanny. These cheeky familiarities made us feel sophisticated.

"I'm not. I just wonder how much trouble the dead will take to come back. Dola says her father cries all the time and begs her brother to come home."

"Fanny belongs to a spiritualist group. They talk to the dead. Maybe she could get a message to him."

"Do you ever talk to your Chinese mum?"

"I don't speak her language, remember."

"Do you want to know my secret?"

It was cold now, October. Even though the sun was shining, there was a bitter wind off the sea. I took off my sweater and then my blouse. Goosebumps rose on my arms. A seagull called over the water. Boulie watched me, her eyes narrowed. I pulled up my chemise and lowered my skirt to my knees, exposing my swollen breasts and the slight rise in my abdomen. She looked hard. I imagine she was expecting ringworm.

"So?"

"Can't you see it?"

"See what?"

"There's a baby in there."

"Go way wi' yew! Ye canna'." She really had Duffie's accent down.

"It's true. I *am* old enough."

"Fifteen!" Boulie scoffed. "Is it ours?"

I expect Boulie meant was it mine and hers and Alec's, so I said yes. In a sense it was true. What was ours was hers. "You can be the baby's secret godmother." And Soong Chou would be the secret godfather, I thought, since he had already blessed it.

"Does that mean we are keeping it?"

"What else can we do?"

"We could get rid of it." Boulie went to Angela College now. There were levels of information circulating among the girls who went there that I, a home prisoner, could not access.

"What do you mean?"

"One of the girls at school got pregnant with her stepfather. He gave her gin and quinine. She took a hot bath and threw herself down the stairs. Then she lost the baby. Easy as pie."

"Go away."

"Otherwise, you'll be shopworn, used goods." Boulie's cheeks were frantic. "They'll throw you down a well."

"Oh Boulie, hardly. This is not China. Besides, I want it."

"Nora will die of embarrassment."

"Good. She is hardly in a position to talk."

My mother hadn't even told me the facts of life, which I had pieced together from Boulie's jokes and gossip and Duffie's demented warnings and judgments. Good, I thought on the beach with Boulie. My outrageous transgressions might make Nora pay attention. I would show her how to be a good mother.

Even though I was attached to the little being inside me, Boulie wore me down and I eventually saw some wisdom in her advice. Would Alec really come back from the war and claim me? In my heart, I knew I didn't want that. My infatuation with Soong Chou would lead nowhere, but that didn't mean I would want to be married to someone else. Alec was my brother, my friend, but he couldn't be my husband.

"I will try the mischief spell first," I suggested to Boulie. "All we need is sand, water, oak leaves and acorns."

We tried mixing the ingredients and shouting "Banshee" over and over as we ran through the garden, but nothing happened.

"Back to Plan A," Boulie advised me several days later.

We chose a Sunday afternoon when the house was quiet. The servants were out. My mother was next door playing bridge with Mary Todd. I waited by the gate with a stolen bottle of gin hidden under my coat and watched Boulie cycle down the road toward me. We had no idea where we would do the deed. There was a higher risk of detection inside the house, should someone come home. She chose the fairy glen. We hid her bicycle and walked down the lawn, arm in arm. It was a grayish blustery day, but Boulie and I were both warmly dressed. We sat on a log where the glen met the beach, and stared at America. I remembered the time I had seen China behind Soong Chou's incandescent silhouette and felt as if a gray sack had been pulled over my head.

"Just plug your nose and drink it as fast as you can," Boulie told me.

"Where am I going to jump from?"

"The rocks."

"Are we trying to kill both of us?" I asked morosely.

"Nae daftie girl," she imitated Duffie and I felt double unhappiness. "You're going to jump from that rock," she pointed, "into the sand."

I did as she said, plugged my nose and swallowed. The gin was hot in my throat, and coarse. I gagged and swallowed again. Within moments, my blood hummed and my body started to relax. I drank again and again. The horizon tilted. Then I felt sick. Boulie, to her credit, held back my hair while I vomited in the beach grass. "Oh God," I moaned, wiping my mouth. "I can't do it."

"Yes, you can. You're almost there."

I took another gulp, and then Boulie got me to my feet and led me over the rocks to the place she deemed safe to jump. I held out my arms like the seabirds swirling around us and laughed. The wind blew in my face. I jumped. Boulie told me to do it again. And again.

"That's enough," she said after many jumps. "Now we have to sober you up."

"I'm going in the sea," I said, trying to pull off my scarf. Boulie undressed me gently and folded my clothes on a log while I stood shivering in my birthday suit, trying to get up the nerve.

"Go for it," she said as I headed toward America.

The sea was a dreadful shock. I vomited again and the sick circled me as the waves lapped at my stomach and my breasts. I plunged in and paddled — one stroke each for all the dear names. It was enough. Boulie beckoned me from the freezing water — then she covered me with my coat and hers and carried the rest of my things to the house. Safely inside, she locked my bedroom door and poured me a hot bath.

The cure didn't work. I felt absolutely awful, but my little passenger hung on for dear life. I lay in the steaming water, visualizing an alien creature with its fingers curled into my womb, refusing to let go the way I had hung onto the bedpost in my room in San Francisco the day we left for Canada.

Eventually I crawled into bed — still shivering — and Boulie lay down beside me, convinced that sooner or later a little blob of flesh was going to make its way out of me.

"What do you think it's going to look like?" she asked.

"I don't know."

"I could take it to school and show the kids," she teased.

"Where would you say you got it, Boulie? What a perfectly disgusting idea."

"I'd tell them I found it."

"Oh sure. Where, under your pillow? Will the tooth fairy be leaving it then, yew wee bizem?"

"Actually, it's none of their damned business."

"In that case, you wouldn't take it, would you?" Boulie sure had a knack for making me mad. I wanted her gone. In fact, I wanted my baby.

"Isn't it your dinner time?"

"No way, Poppy. We're in this together."

"You are not the father, you know."

"I have other girlfriends, Poppy. In fact, I am going steady."

"With a girl."

"Yes, she's my special friend. We have a fort in the woods behind the school. Her name is Mason and we lie in the woods petting one another. She loves it when I put my fingers inside her."

"You are full of shit, Boulie. There is no such person as Mason. Whoever heard of a girl called Mason? Besides, I heard everyone thinks you are stuck up at school." I was just guessing, but my reaction shut Boulie up.

"Lies," she said, but I knew she would be quiet for a while.

Nothing happened that night. As expected, Boulie was visited by another idea over the next few days. If hiccoughs could be cured by fright, then perhaps abortions could be effected the same way. Lady Cowes-Wentworth-Cowes had recently given in to the demands of life in the modern world and bought herself a car.

Unlike ours, which was a convertible, hers was enclosed except for the chauffeur's seat in the front. In the coach, there were Venetian glass vases chased in silver, which she kept filled with flowers from her greenhouse. She'd had her initials F.C.W.C. painted in gold on the doors. We laughed and, putting on British accents, chanted, "Cow Fanny's water closet" — nothing funnier than a moving toilet to two hysterical girls looking for any excuse to be silly. Boulie had taught herself to drive in order to help Lady C., who liked to do her own marketing.

One October afternoon, Boulie took me for a spin. Lady Cowes had asked Boulie to borrow some orange Chinese lantern flowers from my mother, but my mother was out. Normally, Boulie would have taken them without asking, but this time she said we should kill some time and come back later. When I got in the passenger seat, I smelled the freesias in the vases and they made me feel sick, so I moved up to the front seat and sat outside, beside Boulie.

We started tooling along Beach Drive, heading toward Fairfield and the Ross Bay Cemetery. "Too fast, Boulie," I said, gripping the dimpled leather in the seat beside her.

Boulie laughed and accelerated, taking the curves on two wheels. I told her I was going to be sick in Cow Fanny's beautiful new Pierce-Arrow automobile and she laughed harder. I recalled Duffie's admonitions about the shoot-the-chute at the Gorge and my frail heart. She turned abruptly at the road to the Chinese cemetery and sped toward it at top speed. It appeared as though we were heading straight for the rocks and the sea beyond. I screamed as we approached the fence, and she stopped.

"Who is the father?" she asked.

I answered by throwing up all over the seats. Boulie had scared me half to death, but I survived. And so did my dear baby.

Soong Chou was watching when we returned in Lady Cowes-Wentworth-Cowes's formerly pristine car. I got out and picked the Chinese lanterns, which I thrust onto the vomit-smelling seat beside

Boulie. She left, her laughter drifting out of the open window like petals in the wind.

I was still having my *liuqin* lessons. There was no outward change in me. I knew if I told him I was pregnant, all contact would cease. We went on as before. Sometimes I sat in the Japanese garden at night and listened while he played the haunting songs of his lost friend over the water and I wondered how long he would stay.

Sooner or later, my mother would discover my perforated condition. I decided it would be later and continued with my music lessons. All I could expect from her was callousness and I wasn't going to have her views forced on me.

Just after Christmas, I had another letter from Alec. He wrote about his wonderful holiday feast, everything from tins. The Seaforth Highlanders had an armistice with the Germans, so the skies were quiet for once. After dinner, some of the boys who had instruments got them out and, while they played their squeeze-boxes, harmonicas and pipes, the rest of them sang. There wasn't a dry eye in the trenches, or dry feet either. The battlefields were a sea of mud. He enclosed a sketch of men in kilts sitting at an elegant table with candelabras and wine glasses with stems, floating in mud and eating from open tins. After a while, they heard a German soldier calling, "Ladies, ladies!"

The Highlanders were called the Ladies From Hell, he explained, because of their kilts and their fierce fighting. The lookout came down and reported the German was carrying a white flag. When a party went out, the enemy soldier told them in perfect English that the German boys wanted the Scots to come and sing for them. They didn't have anyone who could do that in their trenches. Alec felt an exquisite sadness, he wrote, when the Hall brothers from Vancouver sang "Silent Night" in German.

The Canadians took some of their rations to the Germans because the Krauts didn't have any meat or chocolate for their

Christmas dinner, he wrote. Boxing Day, the Scots challenged the Germans to soccer, and won. The day after, they went back to war and a cousin from Selkirk, who had given most of his tuck away to the German boys, had lost his eye. There had been reports that the Germans had used mustard gas in a recent battle and the Highlanders who'd been without gas masks had pissed in their kilts and put them over their faces to protect themselves from the sweet smelling fumes.

Boulie, meanwhile, was in a state of near hysteria about my condition. Frustrated by my inability or unwillingness to abort and the tenacity of my baby, she did everything in her power to draw attention to herself. It was as if she were saying, "Look at me. *I* need you." She drove recklessly. She dressed outrageously. She spoke inappropriately. By and large, I ignored her, believing that by not participating as her audience I would discourage her strange behaviours. One night, though, curiosity got the best of me.

I woke up to find Boulie sitting at the end of my bed, a high-strung ghost in a white nightgown.

"I want to show you something," she whispered.

"Not now. I'm sleeping."

"If you don't come, I will tell."

"Go right ahead." I knew she wouldn't. Snitching was the last thing I expected of Boulie. She had no respect for whinging of any kind.

"Come on, Poppy. It's something beautiful."

Boulie's nightgown was long and diaphanous. I had no idea where she'd got it. Lady Cowes was hardly likely to be seen in a get-up like that. Later, Boulie confessed she had gone into my mother's closet while she was asleep and helped herself. I got out of bed and the two of us tiptoed down the carpeted main stairs, because they didn't creak like the wooden stairs that led from the children's dining room up to the second floor. She was beautiful in the light from the large stained glass window over the landing. Boulie realised the impression she was making in the painted moonlight. Seeing the shape of her body through the nightgown, I shivered.

"Are you cold?"

"No."

Sheik was tethered in the *port cochère*. I had no idea how she'd managed to get him out of the stable without alerting Soong Chou, who had extra eyes and ears, but there was our white gelding with a rope around his neck and no saddle or bridle.

"Now what?"

"Shhh. Let me help you on."

"No, I'm not allowed to ride."

"Just to the glen. We'll walk."

She helped me mount by taking my bare foot in her cupped hands and then jumped up behind me. I held onto Sheik's mane and Boulie held onto me, her hands around my waist. I could feel the power of the horse between my legs and the tension in Boulie's body as she pressed her breasts against my back and put her face in my hair. We walked slowly toward the glen, listening to the horse's breathing and the retreating noise of waves on the beach. It was a clear night with a full moon. We were made of ice, Boulie and me, but Sheik was warm. I could feel the heat of Arabia moving from him to us as easily as blood moves through sand.

"Get off," she said, jumping down, and helping me. Then she remounted and touched the gelding's sides with her bare heels. The tide was out. Sheik took off along the beach, with Boulie bending low on his neck, holding a handful of mane. With her encouragement, Sheik climbed up on the rocks and stood there, still as sculpture, pale against the dark sky. Sheik pawed the ground and Boulie laughed, her voice bouncing on the water.

"Come here," she said and helped me up behind her. This time I pressed my woman's body into her back with my child between us. We rode back to the house together, and I noticed a dark shape heading toward the stable.

"It's Soong Chou," I said, frightened of his disapproval.

"Never mind," Boulie helped me down and rode on the lawn, crossing the driveway when she came to the gate. I imagine Chou was waiting for her in the stable, but neither of them mentioned it later.

Miss Beach noticed my changing figure first. "What have you been up to?" she asked, her arms crossed in front of her maid's apron.

"Nothing you haven't done, Miss Beach, I am sure," I answered, crossing my own arms in front of my disappearing waistline.

She would do her worst, I was certain. This situation would override the *entente cordiale* based on our previous revealed indiscretions. If I reported Miss Beach's behaviour during my mother's absences now, she would say I was lying to cover my own breaches of conduct.

A few hours later, Miss Beach returned Alec's ring to me and told me to hide it. She had retrieved it from the waste-paper basket the day Nora had taken it from me. My mother knew my secret, she said, and would speak to me after dinner.

Now the cat was not only out of the bag but also tearing up the floral needlepoint carpet in front of Nora's fireplace. We had our fireside mother and daughter chat, appropriately at night, when the servants were upstairs.

"It's too late to get rid of it," I said, somewhat defiantly.

"I wouldn't want you to," she said in a soft voice that surprised me "We mustn't kill what we love, Poppy."

It was my mother's idea that we sail to San Francisco for a holiday "visit to my aunt." I had eliminated all the other options since I was, by then, nearly six months pregnant. My mother would think of a story. In the meantime, I was not to tell anyone else about my predicament. Miss Beach, who had previously worked as an assistant midwife and baby nurse, would take care of me as well as her. Since I had seen how Miss Beach "took care" of Nora, I was more than curious to find out what that involved. There were no recriminations, no breast-beating about our good name. Perhaps my mother knew that I knew she lived in a glass house with a secret tunnel. Perhaps her early marriage had been precipitated by a similar indiscretion that she had the grace to remember at my time of great inconvenience.

The next day, Miss Beach brought up my breakfast tray and produced a bottle of lily oil, which she told me she would rub on my nipples, stomach, and perineum. "You don't want stretch marks," she said, "And you don't want to tear." Her massages were very pleasant. First, she warmed her hands by rubbing them together; then she poured the fragrant lily oil into her palms and rubbed it into my skin, making circular movements around my breasts, gradually moving toward my nipples. "You have beautiful nipples," she said. "Your mother has decided that you will feed the baby for the first few months." When my breasts were warm and alert, she moved her hands down to my stomach, circling my belly button, then moved on to my groin and then between my legs, her fingers all around my perineum. Aroused but wary, I was excited by her massages.

"It's all right to enjoy it," she said. "Most women do. How often are they touched like this?"

The first time, I didn't give in, but, after that, in Victoria and San Francisco where we "hid out" in the Palace Hotel for three months, I began to crave Miss Beach's clinical ministrations to break the tedium of waiting.

At the Palace, we took walks at night, sketched the fresh flowers the hotel staff delivered every other day, and played cards and a curious three-handed mah jong to pass the time. A heart specialist and an obstetrician paid regular visits to our rooms. Miss Beach told me, after I had safely given birth, that the cardiologist had told them I would probably not survive the delivery.

We read a lot of books during those few months and I made the pictures for a children's story about the Palace Hotel. Below Market Street, there was an underground world that serviced the hotel. Bakeries for bread and pastry, butcher shops, wine cellars, root cellars, a cobbler and a laundry all thrummed in the subterranean civilization that laboured to satisfy our every desire. The twin heroes of my story, a boy and a girl, found the keys to the feudal village left in an elevator and eventually discovered the little people living and working underground.

Even though I was to maintain a discreet non-presence in the hotel, I made friends with the maids and bellboys. Domestics sometimes lingered long enough over bed making and deliveries to talk with me. It was through them that I heard about the various hotel scandals: robberies, famous liaisons and mysterious deaths.

Because guests had complained that they were harshly audible and had unpleasant accents, the bellboys were having speech lessons during our stay at the hotel. They told me in their newly modulated voices about the world below stairs and the magnificent mural in the bar downstairs by the American painter Maxfield Parrish. I had been given a book showing Parrish's work in reproduction and was dying to set my eyes on an original.

One night, after Miss Beach and my mother were asleep, I threw a coat over my nightclothes, went down to the lobby and tiptoed into the bar, where a few stupefied guests were spilling their troubles to a bartender preoccupied with polishing glasses. The darkened room was more like a temple than a den of iniquity. At one end, over the bar with its collection of bottles, hung a glowing masterpiece, the landscape as alive as the childish figures following their musical genius. I practically sank to my knees, which were trembling under my nightgown.

While my well-oiled body swelled into motherhood, Nora went out shopping almost every day, and, when she dined or played bridge with friends at night, left Miss Beach and me in the hotel. Miss Beach, whose job it was to help me relax, extended her mandate for pleasure. While I soaked in my mallow and chamomile baths, she brought me cinnamon tea and later, toward the end, licorice tea and warm towels.

Over the years, I have alternately felt exasperated and inspired by Miss Beach's anarchist leanings. I think she comprehends the vicarious pleasure I take in seeing others take risks. We took one or two together at the Palace Hotel. Apart from the opportunity to breathe fresh air, our rambles in the dark barely satisfied my need for freedom. Miss Beach understood this better than my mother, whose irritation with our situation was mostly expressed in sighs and impatient reaction to my frequent requests for a longer leash. I suppose the ultimate desideratum of protecting my child from gossip carried some weight, but I wasn't thinking that far ahead.

One evening, when my mother was doing whatever it was she did in San Francisco at night, Miss Beach asked me out for dinner. "Out" was downstairs in the Great Court, which could just as well have been Ali Baba's cave. I had watched beautifully dressed men and women glide in and out of the magnificent domed restaurant on my infrequent visits to the lobby and had spent many evenings lying in bed imagining myself sitting at an elegantly set table with Soong Chou dressed in a dinner jacket. In these dreams, Chou dropped an imaginary jade and diamond ring into my drink and asked me to marry him. His sperm had, after all, anointed my baby.

On the appointed evening, Miss Beach and I dressed for our date, both of us in my mother's gowns. As soon as the coast was clear, we romped, giggling, into our bubble baths. Miss Beach painted my toenails because I couldn't reach them. Maid's black was not good with Miss Beach's complexion. She looked better in a colour. I helped her into a silver blue chiffon dress with crystal beads and she did her best to squeeze me into a teal pleated silk gown. Thank goodness for the new shapeless dresses and pleats that expand. We powdered our noses and twirled in the mirror.

Miss Beach and I both wanted to avoid the elevator for security reasons and my claustrophobia, but I couldn't possibly have managed the stairs in my mother's silver sandals, which were tight on my swollen feet. The Palace had an indescribably gorgeous elevator. "It looks like the Empress Josephine's boudoir." I was giddy with fear and freedom. Having memorized the menu in our suite, I ran through the dinner choices in my mind, practicing the French pronunciations.

"Do you *want* to lose your job?" I asked, giggling nervously, as soon as our very handsome waiter had seated us.

"What do you mean?"

"Well, don't you think that Nora would sack you if she found out what we were up to?"

"Nothing ventured, nothing gained. Your mother admires people who take risks," Miss Beach replied, looking around the dining room for conspicuously rich people and actors, not, she assured me, for possible snitches.

"What about you, Poppy?"

"Oh, I've already been sacked." I laughed so outrageously that heads turned in the dining room. "Seriously, why are you doing this?"

"The value of adventure," Miss Beach said, "is constantly underestimated."

"What if adventure gets you in trouble?"

"I would say, in your case, that it got you a San Francisco holiday."

"You can't mean that," I laughed.

"No, I don't, but right now, right here, we are on vacation. What are you having for dinner?" The waiter was hovering with a laboured patience.

"I want the coquilles St. Jacques, anchovies on toast, sweetbreads and *Babas au Rhum* with a nice chardonnay." I said, trying to sound chic.

"Are we going to see that dinner again upstairs, Poppy?"

"Probably, but I'll enjoy eating it."

Miss Beach ordered for us, as she was the elder. I wondered if she was going to pay or if, hoping my mother wouldn't notice, she would charge it to our bill. She had mock turtle soup, striped bass Dieppoise, quail, and whipped cream and strawberry kisses for dessert. I had to admire her. If Miss Beach went down, she'd go down in style.

"Tell me your story, Miss Beach." I sipped my wine. My mother's maid had to be more than a servant who gave hand release to rich ladies. This was my chance to find out. Once the cork was out of the bottle, she would spill. She leaned toward me, speaking confidentially, and I noticed for the first time that her teeth were two rows of seed pearls. When she smiled, which was not often, the pink gums showed.

"I am a lady's maid, Poppy. We're all the same, aspirations and broken dreams. We learn how to do everything just right without going to finishing school. I know which gloves go with which dresses, when to wear a hat and when not to, how to take care of silk stockings and embroidered lingerie, how to keep furs cold in summer, when not to wear certain colours and which flowers are tasteful in a bedroom. I know about food and wine and caring for the skin. I know about women's health. I know how to cover up for marital infidelity, drunkenness and drug addiction, in other words, how to keep a secret. I know not to say 'drapes' and 'serviette' — that 'looking glass' is *comme il faut* and 'mirror' is not. In short, I am a snob for hire."

"How does that feel?"

"I'm here with you, aren't I? Doesn't that tell you something?"

"How do you know you can trust me?" I wolfed down my toast. I love the salty taste of anchovies.

"We are both survivors."

I gave the room a long panning gaze as if I were planning a mural, taking in the potted palms, the mirrored doors, the elegant diners and most of all, the gilded glass dome and crystal chandeliers. I thought about Alec's letters from France describing meals in the trenches and the toast stuck in my throat. "It's so unfair."

"Life is unfair. We have to seize the day." She held her glass in the air. "I heard the hotel has a gold service for every place setting in this room."

"Ours isn't gold."

"The good stuff is for royalty."

"Baronesses aren't good enough?"

"Baronies are usually bought, especially Austrian baronies."

"You know everything, Miss Beach. I underestimated you."

"You are a child becoming a woman, Poppy. Life wouldn't be worth living if we weren't learning along the way. I think you were jealous of the time I spent with your mother and I can understand why, because I had a mother who gave all she had to her children."

"I guess you're right, but I like you now. Did you ever wonder what it was like to have a baby?"

"I had a son and I gave him away." Miss Beach examined her fork.

"You did?"

"There was no choice. I wasn't married and my lover was. I had no income and I had to work."

"Was it hard?"

She picked up her knife. "Imagine taking this and sawing your arm off. That's what it was like." She looked away for a moment. "Your mother gave me a job when I was pregnant. She saw me through it. After I gave away the baby, she brought me cold cabbage leaves to comfort my breasts when the milk came in."

"Really? Nora?"

"There is much more to your mother than meets the eye. You'd be surprised how tough and knowledgeable she is. She has kept all of us together."

"Are you and my mother lovers?"

"No, nothing like that. We have our places. We are both women who take what comes and make the best of it."

We finished the bottle of wine and left the sadness behind.

"I think it's time I knew your first name, Miss Beach."

"It's Alexandra, or Sandy!"

We laughed all the way up the elevator, undressed and got into bed seconds before my mother unlocked the door to our suite.

Sandy Beach. Wouldn't you know?

Nora told us matter of factly over tea the next day that we would return to Victoria soon after the baby was born and resume our normal lives. A baby could be hidden for some time. The servants wouldn't talk. I looked at Sandy Beach, with whom I now had a certain intimacy, and she stared into her teacup. Gradually, the story would emerge that Nora had adopted the orphaned child of a cousin in California.

If I'd had the maturity to think ahead, I might have realised how difficult a bargain I was making. At the time, it seemed easy, the right thing to do. No one told me that I would fall head over heels in love with my baby, that every moment apart, every deception to protect our secret would be an arrow in my heart.

Beachy and I talked about analgesics during childbirth and what was appropriate for a fussy baby. She told me not to worry about labour. She had special tea for that and she made a mixture of opium and wine for babies. Everyone used it, even the royal family. *Adkinson's Royal Infant Preservative* was a laudanum mixture taken by Queen Victoria's children.

"Where will you buy the opium?" I asked.

"Chinatown."

"What about downstairs?"

"Don't ask so many questions, Poppy. It is against the law now."

The foggy April morning that my water broke and I went into labour, my mother received a telegram. I watched her read it, turn red and put it in her pocket.

"What is it?" I asked.

"Nothing," Nora lied.

"Mother, if it is nothing, why can't you tell me?"

"It's none of your business." She began to cry.

I felt something brush by me. It was Alec.

"It's Alec, isn't it?"

8

My Precious,

Tony's eyes are still red from yesterday. We wept together for Alec and for his brother who had survived the war only to die of influenza. "What saved you from despair, Poppy?"

"Alec couldn't be killed because he lived in our child."

"Oh Poppy!" Tony's eyes fill with tears again. "How awful. You were in shock."

"It was harder later. I had dreams where I saw him getting ready to leave the trench. I tried to stop him, but I couldn't. He was only an artist, Tony. Alec wasn't even armed."

Last night Boulie's drawing of her mother came alive; only it wasn't her falling down the well. It was you. I went weeping in my nightgown to Tony's room and he had the ship's physician paged. The doctor gave me a sedative and I finally went to sleep. Tonight Tony has promised to stay. I said he could share my bed, which is almost a double, but he said he would have the steward bring in a cot, so I can thrash about without elbowing him.

We are having breakfast in my cabin, but I plan to go to the dining room for lunch. Since I am at the point in my story where you come in, perhaps today will slip by a little more easily than yesterday. I have had a shower and a cup of tea and I feel much better. After lunch, I will go to the beauty salon to have my hair and nails done.

Whatever her reason, because I had told her nothing, my mother registered the birth of my daughter with Alec MacDuff, deceased Seaforth Highlander, as the father. The good people of Victoria could hardly shun the child of a man who had given his life for them. That child, you must have guessed by now, was you.

This is where the lying stops. I hope you can find it in your heart to forgive me. There was no other way I could think of to tell you. If you read on, you will find out that no matter how difficult it was for you not knowing who your real parents were, there wasn't a day I didn't ache to hear you call me mother.

You were born with a shock of black hair that stood straight up as soon as you were washed. My mother, who smoked in the next room while I laboured on the third floor of the Palace Hotel with the help of the gas fairies, said you looked exactly like her. Miss Beach thought you looked like Alec. You were a breach birth and there was not a mark on you except for a tiny bruise shaped like a cabbage on your spine.

Everyone had opinions about your name, most of them unfavorable, but Precious you were, and mine, no matter what story they concocted about the tragic death of your alleged birth parents. You took to my Miss Beach-anointed breasts and I fed you for a year, every four hours for the first three months and thereafter only at night. I had to resist my mother's efforts to shame me into taking you off the breast after three months. The more she derisively called me "the wet nurse" and described extended nursing as "common" in my hearing, the more I was determined to ignore her.

I have played "house" and "doctor" with children and made love with men and women, but nothing has approached the pleasure of breastfeeding. Feeling your tiny lips nudge and tug at my nipples was the equivalent of being the epicenter of an earthquake. I couldn't get over the joy. Every time was the same, surprise and ecstasy. I hope, when you read this, you will know how closely we bonded when you were a baby.

Amazed that I survived childbirth, my mother acquiesced to my insistence on caring for you myself. Later on, I would agree to accept you as a cousin. Before sailing back to Victoria from San Francisco, I spent a month sleeping and feeding you in our hotel suite with help from Miss Beach, while my mother said her prolonged goodbyes to California. That month was our mother and daughter honeymoon.

The voyage home was smooth and uneventful. I spent most of my time in our stateroom with you, taking a walk on the deck every few hours. Miss Beach brought my meals on a tray and played *mah jong* with me while you slept. Since going home was the beginning of the big lie, I was increasingly anxious about our planned domestic arrangements. Not sure I could keep up my end of the bargain, I continued my performance of acceptance and amiability for Nora and Miss Beach; but the closer we got to Victoria, the more my heart protested.

I was the first on deck the morning we arrived home. As promised, Daisy waved a sheet from the balcony when we passed Casanora. When we sailed into the inner harbour, we could see Soong Chou waiting beside the car at the C.P.R. dock. Miss Beach held you while my mother explained to her chauffeur that you were an orphaned niece she was adopting. I didn't find Nora's rehearsal of a performance that she would repeat very convincing. Soong Chou opened the car doors and helped us in. My mother hesitated and then asked me to sit beside her. We were all quiet during the ride from the inner harbour to Oak Bay. Fort Street hadn't seemed so long before. Only once, Chou found my eyes in the rear view mirror and I looked away.

Boulie, I think, was jealous when she realised how attached I was to you. We introduced you gradually, as things normalized at home.

It wouldn't do to have you rooting for my breast while someone was visiting. I couldn't be seen with milk leaking down my dress. Boulie was the exception. She already knew. Part of keeping her quiet was having her involved. Hoping she would fall in love with you, I reiterated my request that she might be your secret god-mother, but she held you as if you were gunpowder about to go off.

It was May and my mother's garden had been growing wild without her. Nora attacked her plants the way a gourmand would eat after months of starvation. Soil was sifted. Loads of compost got wheeled across the lawns to the vegetable garden. Trees were transplanted. Flowerbeds were moved around. Annuals were planted among perennials. The Chinamen were busy. Dola, driven all the way from Hatley Park each morning, came back on the scene. Under house arrest while she was there, I watched this activity from my bedroom windows. Dola, a cumbersome child becoming an awkward woman in her shapeless dresses, was eager to assist my elegant mother. Privately, I called Dola "The Earth Mover." Why on earth wasn't she helping in her own gardens at home? I imagine I felt about Dola the way Boulie did toward you. She was in my way, obstructing my view, hogging my mother.

One evening, after Boulie had dinner with us, I headed to the stable to find Chou. We had not been alone in the few weeks I had been back in Victoria and I wanted to talk to him about resuming my music lessons. As I began to walk through the jasmine-scented garden, I heard a whispered argument in Chinese. The combatants were Soong Chou and Boulie. It wasn't the foreign words that stunned me. I only understood their inflection. Chinese, I have learned, is a language of nuance, each word having multiple meanings conveyed by different tones. It was the intimacy of their tone that shocked me through and through.

"I don't speak Chinese." I heard her say it again in my head. "*Liar, liar, pants on fire!*" I remembered our childhood chant. How stupid could I have been? Boulie was five when she came from China. How many times had I heard Lady Cowes-Wentworth-Cowes give her houseboy orders in Mandarin? Of course Boulie spoke Chinese. What a witless wonder I had been to believe her.

What language were they speaking? If Boulie, the so-called aristocrat, spoke Mandarin at home, what common language did she have with Soong Chou, who conversed in Cantonese with the Coolies, or so I was told? Why was she having such a passionate conversation with him anyway? Was *she* involved with him sexually? My blood leached into the ground.

Feeling as though the sky had fallen, I crept back to the house and, lifting you out of your crib, took you into my bed. All night long I lay awake listening to you breathe and wondered what I was going to say to Boulie. I knew better than to bring the matter up with Chou. If I so much as breathed on his intentions, I knew our limited trust would crumble as quickly as a mummy exposed to the light. Boulie was my best bet. I could confront her or wait and see. Boulie was a careless girl, and she was also volatile. Common sense told me to trust her carelessness.

However, I hadn't been relying on my common sense lately and so, the next day, I impulsively jumped in, without waiting for her to expose herself. We were sitting on my balcony, drinking iced tea.

"You said you didn't speak Chinese," I attacked.

Boulie squinted at me. "What do you mean?"

"I said, you told me you didn't speak Chinese. Was that pig Latin I heard you speaking with Chou last night?"

"Oh," she said, "I thought I heard you sneaking around in the garden."

"I wasn't sneaking around. It's *my* garden, Boulie. I was going for my lesson."

"OK, so you happened to be tiptoeing to your *private lesson* while I was having a *private conversation*."

"You shouldn't be having private conversations with our chauffeur," I protested.

"Why ever not, Poppy?"

"Because he's a servant." I felt foolish even as I said it.

Boulie laughed so hard I could have sworn she was going to fall off the balcony right on top of Nora who was deadheading the magenta peonies directly beneath us. I am ashamed to say I visualized Boulie lying in my mother's lap with her secateurs piercing her heart.

"A servant?"

"Yes." I swallowed hard and looked down

"If you say so." Boulie rolled her eyes.

"You were angry. Was it a lover's quarrel?"

"Poppy, you've got a nerve. Of course he isn't my lover. I was calling him a fool."

"Why?" I asked, bravely.

"You know perfectly well why."

"No, I don't get it. You will have to spell it out." I was dying to know what she knew.

"P-R-E-S-H-U-S." Boulie was a terrible speller. I tried not to smile. "No!"

"And you called me a liar. I would say talking to a servant was hardly comparable to dropping one's knickers for one."

She repeated the word servant with contempt; then laughed again, so sharply and abruptly my mother looked up from her peonies.

"It didn't happen, Boulie," I lied. "Precious is Alec's." Then I put my fingers in my ears and whistled, while Boulie rambled on, *sotto voce*. Of course, she was Alec's. I had done it *later* with Chou, who had simply blessed her. As romantic as the idea of having Chou's baby would have been to me, it would have made your life unbearably complicated. I didn't entertain the idea, even for a moment. Chou had no claim on her. Would he not have *known* in his heart if she were his? Wouldn't I?

I had to bandage my breasts when I went back to Miss Carr for painting lessons. She of all people would not have been pleased by what I had done. Soong Chou drove me back and forth and we chatted in an impersonal way about the landscape, Chinese customs and my mother's niece.

One evening, I went into the nursery to kiss you goodnight and found my mother leaning over the bassinette singing a lullaby I could not recall hearing before. She was rubbing your back singing "*Go to sleep/ Go to sleep/ Go to sleep you little baby/ When you wake, have some cake/ Ride the pretty little horses.*" Her black head almost touched your black head. You were connected; and I was touched beyond anything I can remember. I stood in the doorway watching you until Nora felt my presence and turned around.

"Where in the world did you learn that?" I whispered.

"My mother." She took me by the elbow and led me out to the hall, shutting your bedroom door.

"You never sang it to me."

"No. Duffie wouldn't let me near you."

"She wasn't my mother."

I stood with my hand on my cheek where she touched me before she turned and disappeared into her sitting room. I would have followed my mother, held her shoulders and shaken her if I thought it would rearrange whatever was faulty in her mind and being, but I knew it would do no good.

Duffie had by then returned from Scotland, a widow and a War Mother. She looked a hundred years old, but she took wonderful care of you. Nora had arranged to have Stanford's bedroom painted a dusty pink with cream trim and had curtains with big tea roses made to cover the floor to ceiling windows that opened onto his balcony. Poor Stanford had been exorcised. Duffie, who had a cot in your room, just as she had in mine when I was small, only went to her own room on her days off. She had nowhere else to go now. "Och, nae other fish to fry," she said. I was glad for her sake. By giving her a secret granddaughter, I hoped to balance the debt we owed her.

We spent hours together rocking the baby and reminiscing about Alec. She commented on my ring, telling me that it was a family heirloom she had saved for Alec to give to the girl he married. It would have been presumptuous of her to say anything more to me, despite the fact that she knew me better than anyone. To my mother, she was a servant. To me, she was your other grandmother. I know Duffie would not have left Scotland again had she not known that her son's heart beat in your chest. We went over Alec's journal and his letters and the hundreds of drawings that Duffie kept in a drawer in her attic room. I told her Emily had called him a genius. She wanted to hear that. "Perhaps wee Precious is gifted," she said, hopefully, when you coloured on the wall, something I would have been punished for doing.

In sharing you with Duffie, I felt I was giving back some of the valuable times she had missed with Alec. We were content to sit together and adore you while you coloured or danced around the attic ballroom, one end of which we had made into a playroom. I could even paint while you played with your toys, secure in knowing that Nanny was ever watchful.

Motherhood focused my work. I made good time at Emily's, "Painting up a storm," she said. Just as Emily was able to capture the spirit of the trees in her forests, I was able to find the *anima* in the garden, pushing my brush past the cultivated garden, painting the rocks and wildflowers and windswept trees along the edge of the sea. Barely seventeen, I was a mother and painter almost ready, Emily said, to have her first exhibition.

Boulie, meanwhile, was resisting Lady Cowes' attempts to marry her into one of the acceptable hyphenated families she was exceptionally good at mimicking. She ruthlessly pilloried the chin-less wonders from the remittance list forced upon her at tea dances and debutante balls. When I marveled at her acting skill, she would say, "It isn't hard. They're all the same — inbred monkeys toilet trained by gorillas in nurse's uniforms. Wankers! Baboons with silver spoons."

Boulie was an inevitable revolutionary. Precocious in her aware-ness of her real origins and her sexual preferences, she was not particularly malleable to Lady Cowes' idea of a young lady. In her circle, Lady Cowes herself was considered to be a bit of a Bohemian and slightly outrageous by virtue of having been in China rather than India and having kidnapped a child, albeit for virtuous reasons. Boulie expected she should be more understanding. This was a flaw in her intuition. Lady Cowes was socially ambitious, and Boulie found herself at war with her otherwise benevolent guardian.

"I wonder," she said one November afternoon while we were climbing the rocks bordering the fairy glen, "what effect smoking opium would have on your painting."

"What do you know about opium?" I asked, remembering our fight in the gazebo when she had slandered what was left of my family, and recalling her later comprehension of the evidence we had found in the tunnel.

"They're still smoking opium in Chinatown. I know people who do it all the time."

"What kind of people?"

"All kinds. Caucasians, Orientals, you name it. Most of the women are prostitutes, but some of the men would surprise you."

"I wouldn't mind having a look." I was curious. As Duffie used to say, curious was my middle name. Then she would add that curiosity killed the wee cat.

"One puff of the magic dragon won't kill you."

We made a date. On a Friday night, after dinner, Boulie picked me up in Lady Cowes's car. I preferred risking another ride with her to asking Soong Chou if he would drive us to Chinatown at night. I was certain he would refuse and furthermore he could have had me put under house arrest. Long after you and Duffie retired, and when my mother was safely asleep with her face held together with her tape arrangement, the anti-wrinkle apparatus she had inherited from her indisposed husband, I slipped out and walked around the noisy gravel driveway, on the lawn and rock gardens, avoiding beds where I would leave footprints. My apparently reformed driver waited outside the gates.

Boulie drove soberly and directly to Chinatown, taking Pandora Street to Wharf Street; then turning right on Fisgard. While she was rolling along at an acceptable speed, she told me what she knew about the opium trade out of Victoria.

"Most of the opium is imported from India by the Fook Hing Company in Hong Kong. Making it illegal didn't change the fact that people are addicted. Some of the factories shut down after the law was passed in 1908, but it's still refined and sold. There's a big demand in the United States and most of their opium comes from here. They tried growing it in California, but the climate wasn't quite right. When opium was legal the American government had a huge import tax and that made it desirable for smugglers to move it out of Canada."

"I wonder if Stanford and Nora attempted to grow it in California and failed, then came up here to try their hand at smuggling. That would explain the tunnel." I guessed.

"It would. Chinese fishermen on the American side pick up opium at San Juan Island and deliver it to San Francisco. They dump the crates in the harbour and the people there pick them up."

I was ready to believe her. There had been enough evidence here and there to convince me that something venal was going on under our house. I wondered what Chou had to do with it, but I decided not to ask Boulie. She was half- Chinese after all and I already knew that the famous Chinese inscrutability had more to do with not trusting Caucasians, and why should they? I had noticed the same reticence among the Songhees people I met and I realised the less information given to one's oppressor the better. Like it or not, I was on the wrong team.

We parked the car on Fisgard and walked to Fantan Alley. Boulie knew exactly where to go. She knocked at the door to the Sing Yee laundry. A woman who recognized her let us in. Four men were playing *mah jong* at a round table with a thirsty looking jade plant in the middle. A single bulb hanging inside a red silk lantern lit the room. The men didn't look up as we passed, but I could feel them watching us. Boulie opened a door and led me down a flight of stairs. We were in a tunnel. "This goes under the street," she said. I saw a rat the size of a cat run by us.

We arrived at a door and I smelled the same sweet smoky odor that had come from our tunnel. Boulie knocked and an elderly man wearing an embroidered silk jacket opened the door. "This is an ordinary *joint*," she said, passing the man who let us in. The room was dimly lit and full of smoke. Half a dozen semi-conscious men lay on bamboo mats covering wooden bunks built against the walls, their opium pipes resting on small tables beside them. There was only one window high on a wall and it was just slightly open. The smell was sickening, like the fetid water that flowers have stood in for days.

"Come on," Boulie pulled me through the room. "We're going to Ah Bing's." She led me further along the tunnel and we went down a few stairs to yet another room, which sounded as if it may have been under the Dart Foon Club, where Soong Chou told me Chinese musicians met to play music. By comparison, the second room was luxuriously appointed. Men and women lay on couches covered with Chinese brocade, with colourful pillows thrown about. Each couch had a small table with a glass lamp for cooking the opium, and pipes and bowls for smoking. Boulie gave the attendant some money and we were taken to adjoining couches and given lemon pipes, called *Yen Tsian*, which supposedly gave a better flavour to the heated resin. The attendant heated some opium on a pin held over the lamp and put it in the bowl for me, showing me how to tip it over the lamp and draw from the pipe, which had an ivory tip. Boulie didn't need any help. She knew exactly what to do.

As soon as I inhaled the pale lemony smoke, the colours in the room ran together. Very soon, I was one with everything; the living, the dead, earth, water, air. I laughed and my laughter splashed like water on stones. My loved ones and I were transparent beings running in and out of one another, laughing the way babies laugh, with absolute delight, in a liquid world.

Boulie shook me awake. I must have slept for hours. "Time to go home," she said and we went out yet another door to a tunnel, up a flight of stairs and exited from the front door of a dry goods shop with bolts of embroidered satin on the shelves. The sun was rising on our side of the city, lighting up one of those mornings that falls out of the horizon the way an egg yolk slips from its shell into a bowl. My breasts leaked milk. I couldn't wait to see you, and to feel your hungry mouth.

On the corner of Fisgard and Store Streets, we noticed a sign painted on the side of the British Welding Company building that said, "We weld all brakes but the break of day." "And broken hearts," Boulie said and we threw back our heads and laughed while our pipe dreams merged with the morning. There were no cracks in our opium experience, nothing to mend. We were one with the universe, and that was seductive. I would not do this with her again — nothing in excess. The opium experience enlightened me in the same way I am transformed by witnessing a sublime poem or a painting. All matter is one. I decided there would be no lines in my paintings and no borders between my dear ones and me. Most important, lying on that Chinese bed, I had once again recognized death as a friendly passage.

You were very glad to see me. I stole into the nursery, lifted you from your crib, and crept past Duffie's sleeping form. Nora, asleep with her own fairies, didn't notice my absence. I could now definitely identify the pungent sweetness lurking under the top note of gardenia in her rooms.

By the next day, Chou had heard from his friends in Chinatown that I had been there with Boulie. I knew because Boulie was red-eyed and quiet when she came for tea with Nora and me. He must have intercepted her in the driveway. When I went for my *liuqin* lesson, Chou told me he was busy and closed the door in my face.

Victoria is a city of closed doors. I was beginning to understand that it was not one but several cities. To the English ex-pats, living in Oak Bay was a chance to access a hierarchy closed to them in England, where pedigrees are known. Second sons and remittance men with minor titles could lord themselves over émigrés of another ilk, driving them to bitterness, and sometimes, to convenient opiates. For the Chinese, it was the Gold Mountain, *gum sum*, the prospect of finding fortune and changing the luck of working-class families back in China. To the Songhees, it was home. And, as the incredible city of tunnels and canals beneath the city was constructed to accommodate the alternate economy of pirates and smugglers, the ground shifted uncomfortably beneath us all.

Emily told me she had heard that there was a canal wide enough to paddle canoes both ways from the Empress Hotel in the inner harbour to the new Parliament Buildings. She also informed me that there were people in Victoria who whispered that my mother was a collaborator. Von Stronheim was a Hun name, and we smuggled Germans into Victoria. I had to laugh. Perhaps Emily's stories were as fanciful as her paintings. I wondered how many houses along the coast of Oak Bay had tunnels like the one under ours. I said I wanted my paintings to express the paradoxes in this new fallen world. Emily told me I could do it so long as I didn't become a part of it. I think I know what she meant. We were both outsiders.

9

My Own,

Tonight Tony and I have changed identities to lift my spirits. After my nap this afternoon, we spent an hour fixing him up. His perfectly manicured nails only needed a coat of red polish. I parted his hair on the side and pinned it with my mother's marquisite barrette. Without pomade, his hair is fluffy like mine and about the same colour. Since I have a bob, mine isn't much longer than his. We could be brother and sister, or sister and sister. He was going to wear my diamond pendant, but when we couldn't get it over his big konk, he decided to wear it as a *ferronière*. That meant taking out the barrette, but the effect was much more dramatic.

"So Egyptian," I said, adjusting the jewel on his forehead. It matches the *faconne* pattern in the dress we chose for him to wear tonight.

"Neat but not gaudy," he admired himself in the looking glass.

"Should we both go *femme*?" I asked, while he held his lips apart for me to rouge.

"Only if you will hold hands with me at dinner and bite my neck."

"No, I think I'll stay with the plan."

Tony looked brilliant in my ivory Chanel dress and, when he was done twirling in my stateroom, I slicked back my hair and put on his tropical dinner jacket. We were a handsome pair, Tony just slightly taller than me in a pair of open-backed evening shoes that allowed his heels to hang over. I remembered tripping to dinner in my mother's shoes at the Palace Hotel.

"You make a jolly boy, Poppy."

"Do you think we could fool Olivier?" I asked.

"Probably. I think we do confuse him."

"Remember the first time we met?"

"Yes. It was a foggy night. I was to meet Olivier for a drink at a club in Soho."

"Yes, the *Oasis*."

"You had stopped to meet with a friend and were on your way out," he said.

"I was already on the street, wearing a fedora hat and a gray suit with a camel hair coat. Olivier ran into me on his way in. He hugged me and said..." I didn't get to finish.

"Hello, Tony!"

"He thought I was you. You were right behind him," I laughed.

"He was quick. 'Tony meet Tony,' he said. 'Poppy meet Poppy.'"

"We had drinks together. I should have guessed then." But would it have changed anything, I wondered?

My new sister and I have come out on deck to get used to our new old roles; and Antonia, as I have dubbed him, waits patiently while I hunt and peck. We have ordered a pitcher of Singapore Slings to prepare ourselves for dinner and the frost-coloured glasses are a delight to touch, as it is humid in the South Pacific.

AFTER THE WAR, my mother had less need of Coolies. It only took a few to manage her garden now that it had been transformed into all the outdoor rooms which would comfort but not contain her spirit. In 1919, Soong Chou sailed home to China with three of the men who had lived and worked for over a decade in our house, and whose names I still didn't know. I had by then learned to drive the car, so it fell on me to take the travelers down to the docks.

I had dressed you in a pair of red Chinese pyjamas and slippers the gardeners had given you for Christmas, but Duffie intervened, "We'll nae dress our wee lassie like a Chinaman," and changed you into a kilt with a sweater she had knitted.

On that frosty January morning, Chou sat beside me in the front seat with you between us. Of the four travelers, only Soong Chou intended to return to Canada. He had family business to attend to in Hong Kong and would be staying until late in the summer. "These men are attached to my family," he explained. I had limited comprehension of the complex Chinese social and familial relationships. "Attached" could mean anything. They could be cousins, neighbours or indentured labourers.

When we got to the dock, Chou got out, lifted you and held you a moment. "*Joy geen*," he whispered, "See you again." Then he gave you back to me. "Take good care of the child," he said and his hand rested on mine. I had a moment of panic where I wanted to beg him not to leave, but resisted, as I had trained myself. I had heard Boulie's stories about plague, revolution and starvation in China and pirates in the South China Sea. Soong Chou could vanish into China's red earth, along with the thousands of others who were dying during the various wars for liberation. After a war that had swallowed so many people we knew and loved, I had no faith that we would ever see Chou again, but I did know he would not deliberately abandon us. I was so thankful that we had become friends again after my evening in Chinatown.

For young girls like Boulie and myself, the war and the terrible influenza that came out of it had diminished the pool of men from which we might marry. We grieved for the friendships interrupted, for the damaged veterans who came home with tubercular lungs and missing eyes, arms and legs, for the shell-shocked, and for what might have been, resenting the ones who had chosen to stay safe at home. I watched Emily and her circle scramble to find meaning in their pictorial definition of the new order. I saw Boulie lose meaning. One day, she said to me, "I'm disappearing. Am I like soap, Poppy?"

Perhaps it was a premonition. So many had died and now there was this new wave of suffering, a disease that was killing more than had died in the war. I wanted my painting to capture and hold onto what had been essentially good in our lives. Watching my mother and her gardeners dead-heading the spent flowers and culling the sleeping garden every fall taught me optimism and heightened my appreciation of young flowers and small children. When my mother, who had, after all, named *her* daughter after a lowly flower, asked why I had named you Precious, I countered by telling her I that had come to believe my own name was a curse.

"It's a flower," she said, "a beautiful and tenacious flower."

"It's death," I said, and I knew I was right.

Painting on my balcony in good weather, I was reminded that it was that view of the world that I valued most. If I have any regrets, it has been my inability to climb high enough to see everything around me in miniature — the small farms, houses, animals, plants and people blending in the great pattern of life. My heart will not allow me to ascend stairs or mountains. I had to stand on the sidewalk and watch you climb to the top of the Eiffel tower. I suppose I should treat myself to a ride in a hot air balloon or an airplane. This voyage may be my great adventure, and I have the comfort of knowing that, when I first see you again, that view from the upper deck will be far more beautiful than the one from the top of the world.

If I couldn't have a bird's eye view of the world, I would celebrate the foreground, whatever passes for goodness in nature. I wanted to find the intimacy between species in my painting. It was my great good luck that Emily respected that, right from the beginning. I suppose observing our household and comparing it with her own, she was able to see clearly where I came from and to understand that finding my voice as a painter was as important to my survival as the same process was to her. In her case, the wilderness was a safe place to explore her repressed feelings.

"Look, Poppy," she said, pointing her brush at my face, as if she might paint it blue. "It's right in front of you; paradise, the New Jerusalem. That's what you should paint, the new beginning, the new world. Forget civilization. Civilization is a big mistake. What has it given you, flowers in rows and rows of crosses. What good is that?"

"Voltaire said we should cultivate our gardens, Emily. That is the best we can do."

"You are a stubborn girl."

"I learned it from you."

No matter how much she protests, there is no doubt in my mind that painting is a sexual act for Emily. I know it is for me. Every painting becomes an obsession, like falling in love. Emily must respond the same way to her trees and story totems. It is clear to me that she lets herself become the beloved, the dynamic vortex of the forest.

We are both driven. Anything beside painting and mothering is, to me, unwelcome distraction. I was lucky to have Duffie when you were small, because there is no doubt she did all the hard work. For me, you were kisses and make-believe, stories at bedtime and delightful visits to the fairy glen, where you blew dandelion clocks, your "wishies," and marveled at the wildflowers, which I taught you to protect, just as I had been instructed by my mother. Duffie made it possible for me to stand at my easel in the ballroom upstairs or on my balcony without having to coax you down for her nap or tease you into eating your vegetables with games about hungry rabbits. Not that I didn't relish those moments when they came my way.

Emily's children are her animals, the dogs and Woo, the monkey she dresses as a child and takes for walks in the perambulator. Between dog breeding and running her boarding house, she has little free time for painting. In the beginning I felt guilty that I was so protected and have tried to make my lessons a work time for Emily as well. I learned by painting beside her. Olivier said that I was like the ordinary horse at the track that calms and paces the nervous thoroughbred. There was some condescension in his observation, but it is true. If I have helped Emily to realise her genius, then my working life has had a good enough purpose.

As far as my own work is concerned, I don't mind being regarded as what Emily calls "a society painter" whose decorative canvases hang in the drawing rooms of the privileged. I know they have more meaning than that, and I realise the privileged need comforting as much as the under-privileged. There may be some small way in which my paintings are a window to hers; that those who really see what I am expressing will step into the garden's frantic sensuality and find innocence again.

For me, you were the new garden, the first green of spring. Through you, I experienced the childhood I had missed. My mother, apart from aberrant moments like the time I found her singing in the nursery, kept a benign distance from you as she had with me. This time, I understood and I felt compassion for her. I didn't push you on her, but I gave her plenty of opportunity to express her affection. Duffie was the incarnate nanny-granny, filling you with all her wisdom and the fussy protectiveness you comprehended without resentment of the loss of freedom it meant. With me you could be free, and with Boulie too. As you grew, Boulie became more accepting, sharing her mad enthusiasms with you.

Boulie was increasingly wild. She was furious with China, furious with Victoria, furious with her guardian, her mother and her mother's murderers. That made her one difficult character. She had become a very beautiful woman, tall but tiny, built like boys in that exquisite moment before slenderness gives way to muscle and puppy enthusiasm becomes wary. Boulie didn't stop moving. She wiggled and squirmed. We all bobbed our hair now: mother, Boulie, and myself — only the servants clung to their buns. We teased Duffie and Miss Beach, sometimes chasing them with scissors. Why wouldn't they also cut their hair? It was so much easier to maintain a bob that dried in minutes and could be combed with the fingers.

Now I wonder if our servants believed that their long hair was all that belonged to them. Perhaps when they let it down each night, brushing it one hundred times by the old prescription, they had their only experience of freedom and femininity.

I was worried about Boulie. She spent a lot of time in Chinatown and I knew what that meant. I couldn't talk about it with my mother because that was a line we didn't cross. I knew and didn't want to know too many things. Painting is my addiction, and, given the condition of my heart, it is a safe one. Perhaps things would change when Soong Chou came back from China. Who else would understand about these things and know what to do, if anything, to help my friend.

One night, when Boulie and I were sharing a room at Hatley Park during a weekend party, she woke me up, babbling about flight. As I rubbed the sleep out of my eyes, she stood on the end of her bed, looking like a great moth in her white nightgown. Her eyes were wide open.

"The well is deep," she said, over and over.

I still had dreams about Boulie's Chinese mother falling down the well in her red lipstick and white pyjamas, so I knew what she was talking about. I should have put my arms around her, taken her into my bed and held her all night long, but I didn't. I simply stared. She was beautiful and sad standing there — mesmerizing.

Boulie jumped off the end of the bed, her arms stretched out and fell face first onto the floor. In the morning, her forehead was black and blue and blood had hardened in two red lines that ran from her nose to her chin. She didn't remember any of it.

I counted the minutes until Soong Chou came back from China, every one a petal torn off a daisy, "He loves me. He loves me not." In June, my mother had a telegram from Hong Kong. Soong Chou announced his marriage to Wei-lan, a scholar from Hunan, and the particulars of his return voyage. He would be in Victoria toward the end of September. I felt my blood leave my body. Under no illusion that Chou belonged to me or I to him, I had made myself comfortable with the status quo. I had been celibate since that time with him on the beach but I wasn't fooling myself that he went to Chinatown just to play *fan-tan* or *mah jong*.

A wife was a different matter. Wives were deep roots, commitments that overtook sentimental associations. A Chinese wife would give him Chinese children. She would know what to wear on every occasion, how to walk, speak and sing. She would know how to prepare the food he liked and could quote from his favourite poets. I didn't like hearing her described as a scholar. That meant she and Chou might form an intellectual bond. Recognizing that Chou was a fantasy left over from my childhood, I was nevertheless devastated.

I invited the little hummingbird in my *tabatière* to come out and sing, but he did not comfort me. I locked myself in my bathroom and wept. Curled up in a ball under my bedcovers, I imagined the new wife, her face powdered white, her lips painted red. I saw her being carried to the wedding in a red litter followed by a procession of musicians, the appreciation on Chou's face when he saw her for the first time in her red wedding dress with her hair garlanded in jasmine and lotus blossoms.

I was on edge. Emily, who had returned from one of her pilgrimages north with a stack of astonishing paintings and sketches, was on edge. Both of us were frustrated and inspired by boundaries. She told me about "country weddings" between white settlers and Aboriginal women, couples that generally lived in harmony, working side by side and having children until the husband was re-called to England and expected to marry within his own class and culture.

"Some men sent money and some returned, but most did not. Men usually end up choosing the familiar," she told me.

One afternoon, on the drive home from Emily's house in James Bay, I stopped at the Chinese Cemetery and wandered among the gravestones. My one-time "country husband" could be buried among the unhappy expatriates, but not me. None of the grave-yards fit my pedigree, neither the Chinese, the Catholic, the Anglican, or the Jewish. I wondered if Soong Chou would ever lie there longing for his bones to be returned to China and his Chinese wife or if he would in fact go home for good one day.

One a blustery spring day, I stood on the rocks at the shoreline. Across the water, clouds impaled themselves on the cold mountain peaks. China was the other side of the world. Just as on that day when Boulie and I tried to abort you, I pushed past my fear of the sea and waded in. My body grew numb. I had just to put my face in the water and keep it there to end my sadness. But I couldn't do it because of you.

Chou arrived as expected on September 26, 1919. I didn't want to pick him up at the boat, but it fell upon me to meet him. If I had refused, my mother might have guessed that I was angry about his marriage. I arrived early and stood by the gangplank. As I watched the passengers disembark, I wondered if marriage had made a stranger of him. My knees shook; and, I must admit I felt erotically charged, even if I was heartsick, by what I perceived to be his betrayal.

He came off the ship last, wearing a white linen suit and carrying a leather suitcase. We stood in uneasy silence on the dock while he waited for his trunk to be unloaded and taken through customs. I remember drying my sweating palms on the skirt of my dress, thinking how unattractive a gesture that was. Chou appeared cool. I resented that. Now I know better. He simply knew how to cover his feelings.

At immigration, the officer tried to charge the Chinese head tax again, even though Chou had his immigration card with him. There was no possible reason for it, except to harass and embarrass us both. "He is my mother's employee," I said. "She paid the five hundred dollars years ago." I half wanted to say "servant" because I was so angry with him, but I didn't, because he had already been humiliated.

On the drive home, Chou told me about his homeland, and the great social change underway. The people were rising up and the future was uncertain. Either the *Kuomintang* or the Communists would take over China. The old ways were vanishing. Women would no longer have their feet bound. His wife had unbound hers on the day of their wedding. One way or the other, they would be liberated, just as women in the West were arriving at political freedom.

"Not an ideal time for old-fashioned marriage, I imagine." I could have bitten my tongue off for saying it, but there it was.

"I put off marriage as long as I could, Poppy. My family expects it, just as your mother will expect you to marry."

"Why didn't you stay then?" My knuckles were white on the steering wheel.

"I have obligations here."

"To whom?"

He didn't answer, but he did slip something in my pocket, which he told me to open later. A year earlier, we might have played twenty questions as I guessed what it was. Now I was too proud and too angry to let on that I was even interested. Since I was driving, I went straight to the garage, parked the car and left without another word, before Chou had even taken out his trunk. I passed my mother on the gravel path to the house, keeping my head down. When I got to my room, I immediately took the small green brocade purse fastened with a silk frog out of my pocket. Inside was an exquisite choker — four strands of seed pearls held together in the front by a marquisite dragon with jade eyes. I went to bed naked that night, except for the choker, wishing he could come to me and explain that the story of his marriage had been a joke, but knowing he wouldn't.

The next day there was a regatta in honour of the visit of the Prince of Wales, who was staying at Hatley Park with the Dunsmuir family. As everyone in Victoria headed to the Gorge on regatta days and the traffic was awful, we had decided to spend the whole weekend with the Scott-Thornton's at Selkirk across the water from *Ashnola*, Dola's aunt's house. The Gorge is changing now, its waters polluted and its farmland developed into suburbs, but ten years ago it was still magical. Unlike the houses in Oak Bay, many of which, like our own, were made of stone and built in the Arts and Crafts style, the Gorge houses were elaborate Victorian follies with turrets and cupolas, elaborate fenestration and milled "ginger-bread" trim imported from California. The Gorge people were a monied aristocracy and our pedigree, such as it was, paved our way into their over-decorated drawing rooms. The Scott-Thornton's, newly minted from plain Scott and Thornton, were no different, but they had wonderful parties.

The Prince of Wales would open the regatta and there was a rumour that he would drop in at various celebrations along the Gorge, traveling in the Lieutenant -Governor's steam launch. This year, all the socially anxious families along the Selkirk Waters were outdoing themselves to impress the visiting royal as were the Dunsmuirs who were having a dance at Hatley Park.

Elspeth Scott-Thornton, whom I'd met at a party at Dola's sister's house across the Selkirk Waters, had asked if I would like to have a *vernissage* during her weekend party and there was last-minute work to be done getting the paintings ready to travel. As I was anxious for a reaction to my work and desperately needed diversion, I was happy to forgo a boring evening with Dola's still grieving, unhinged parents. My pictures would look well in Elspeth's beautiful rooms, otherwise decorated with lavish bowls of flowers. Even though I realised I was being used to further her social agenda, I was looking forward to the *spettacolo*.

Boulie drove you, my paintings and me down in the morning. I knew that with you in the car Boulie would behave herself. En route, she chattered away about the dance the night before. A louche friend of the Prince had stalked her. She hoped he wouldn't show up this afternoon. We arrived in good time to lean the pictures on brass easels set up in the conservatory and drawing room. I have to say, the effect of my floral canvases was so stunning I almost forgot my unhappiness.

Elspeth had sandwiches and lemonade sent to our room and we had plenty of time to get ready for the tea dance that afternoon. You had an astonishing dress, pale green silk with a ragged fairy skirt and pink rosebuds smocked all over the bodice. My dress more or less matched yours, with a layer of net over the silk and a pink satin band below the waist. We had wide-brimmed straw hats made at Young's, and satin slippers in green.

"Twins," you said, standing in front of the mirror with me, and my eyes filled with tears.

As you and I twirled in our party dresses, Boulie lay back in her slip and drank from her hip flask. She wasn't keen to get ready because Olivier Mandeville, the Prince's friend and equerry, had taken a shine to her. Boulie wasn't generally very keen on men and Olivier had inspired an allergic response, as did all the men on her regular dance card. Perhaps, like me, she was revolted by the snobbery of girls who went into hunt mode at the scent of a peer. At least this one was intelligent in spite of his inbred English gentleman's demeanor — confident self-parody, auburn hair curling at the nape of his neck and a slight bowleggedness from riding too much. Olivier, to his credit, was not so tall as to be an awkward dance partner. Later, I learned that his mother was French, which would explain his stature. The French are proud of their *physiques maigres*. Boulie was disinterested. She wasn't keen on anything but mischief. I kept wishing she would find something concrete to be passionate about, as I had.

My paintings weren't for sale at the party. That, my mother said, would have been coarse, but they could be bought privately after the exhibition and the money would be donated to charity. I could tell by the excitement in the rooms where they were shown that my energy had transferred itself to the viewers. A small but elegant blonde man, surrounded by girls and their mothers, was admiring my work. Elspeth clawed my forearm, an irritating habit of hers, and told me that the man was the Prince of Wales. I turned the other way and he followed me, as men will. I kept walking out to the front drive toward the beautifully scented rose garden in the circle in the front drive, looking forward to a royal compliment.

"Your paintings are extraordinary," he said, and I turned around. The Prince would have to do better than that. Artists prefer specific knowledgeable comments to abject praise.

"Thank you, Sir."

"I mean this sincerely. They are very beautiful. Should you come to London, be sure to let me know. I would be happy to introduce you and your work to my friends."

I could hear my pulse in my ears as my heart shook its cage of bones and I begged it to settle down so I could catch my breath and answer.

As luck would have it, Soong Chou drove up at that very moment with my mother and Duffie. He got out first, helped my mother from the front seat and Duffie with her overnight bag from the rumble seat.

"Where is Precious?" Duffie called to me, not recognizing the Prince. "She's watching the boats with the other children and their nannies," I said, pointing to the garden; and my mother and Duffie hurried off without acknowledging the man I had been talking to.

"Why did you leave her?" Chou accused in a low voice, facing me in the drive. At that moment I hated him. How dare he interfere? My voice throttled by rage and jealousy, not to mention absolute humiliation in front of the prince, I slapped him hard across the face.

For a moment we stood facing one another listening to the cold silence of our two worlds colliding. Chou turned, expressionless, got in the car and drove away.

"You are a woman of spirit," the Prince said, laughing. He was the only one. When I looked about me, I saw that no one else, guests and servants alike, was impressed with my outburst. They all turned away.

"My mother has been very good to Soong Chou," I said, "He thinks that entitles him to be rude." Hysterical with remorse, I laughed and put my hands behind my back so he couldn't see them shaking.

"You shouldn'ae done that, Poppy," Duffie said later. "Trouble follows trouble."

Night followed agonized day. Boulie and I bathed and dressed for dinner and the Prince stayed at Elspeth's party because he was having such a good time. The special iced-tea spiked with gin had done its work. One side of the dock had been made into a dance floor with latticed walls wound with honeysuckle and an ornate Byzantine roof. Elspeth and her husband had hired a full orchestra, which was playing Viennese waltzes.

Dozens of canoes had lined up in the Gorge to listen and catch a glimpse of the royal visitor. By nightfall, the boats had paper lanterns to light their way and fireworks were set off on the lawn across the Gorge at *Ashnola*. I wasn't particularly interested and you had already been put to bed. You inherited my fear of fire and fireworks, something that must have begun the night of Chinese New Year.

Blue eyes followed me. Having heard that the Prince liked assertive, androgynous women, I was aware of a certain attraction. After admiring my new choker, which I explained was Chinese, he asked me to dance and I agreed. We danced several times and I found out he was musical, a wonderful dancer, and a witty conversationalist who, in spite of his outrageous reputation, cared about social issues. We stood on the sprung dance floor and talked intensely while the musicians checked their set lists. Boulie was not amused. She advanced on us in her shockingly red chiffon dress, slightly unsteady on her feet.

"Can I cut in, sir?" She asked.

"What about all three of us?" he asked and Boulie smiled her egregious smile, which I knew was about as sincere as a pitch for snake-water. We danced, arm in arm.

"I smell smoke," I said.

"It's the fireworks across the water," the prince observed.

"Do you know what Poppy paints?" Boulie was famous for her non-sequitors.

"No," the bemused royal replied.

"She paints what she loves."

"And what does Poppy love?"

"Flowers," I answered for myself as Boulie said, quite clearly, "Vaginas."

"Oh Boulie," I said, not knowing whether to laugh or slap her, but decided two slaps in one day might be too much, even for this odd little Prince.

Just then, as if to save me, a barge decorated with coloured lanterns came by with the Orion choir on board. They were singing "My Jerusalem," and the Prince's eyes filled with tears. We turned to the music, all but Boulie who was taking off her red dress. She left it in the middle of the dance floor, and, standing on one of the low sections of lattice, dove stark naked into the Gorge.

"My," the Prince said. "Your friend is quite a character." The band kept on playing, just as the musicians on the *Titanic* had when the miracle ship went down. Anxious-looking aides circled the Prince. I excused myself, picked up Boulie's clothes and went into the house to get a towel. The day had been warm, but it was late in September. The evenings were getting shorter and there was a nip of fall in the air. Mad as I was at Boulie, I didn't want her to catch her death of cold and I was damned if I was going to watch the spectacle of my dearest friend sauntering naked up the lawn and into the house in front of everyone there, amusing as I would find the story later on.

Your fairy dress hung from the picture rail in the bedroom we were sharing. Boulie and I were to sleep in one large bed and Duffie and you, in spite of the music, fireworks and laughter outdoors, were already asleep in the other. Duffie lay on her back making the purring sound that is not quite a snore, with her hand lying across your stomach, as if to protect you. I stopped and looked at you, then took off my choker and put it around your neck. You had wanted to wear it that night. I kissed your sleeping eyes, fetched a towel for Boulie and tiptoed out. Apart from the servants and you, there was no one else in the house. The adult guests and older children were all down by the water, boating or watching the boats and the spectacle of Boulie, swimming stark naked in front of a member of the royal family.

It had been a perverse day from beginning to end. Sometimes I wonder if I could have stopped it somewhere short of disaster. Should I have followed Chou home? Should I have noticed the smoke in the house smelled different from the fireworks outside?

Jesus, Boulie, I thought, if you were doing this to draw attention to women's rights in China, or anything but your own demented obsession, I would join you. I called, but Boulie just swam in angry circles. Straining to see her in the dark among all the boats, I stood there for ages, calling her name, wishing I had the courage to take off my own clothes and the ability to swim after her and calm her down. No one else seemed to care. She was just being Boulie.

"Best to ignore her," I heard someone say, but I couldn't. I was enchanted by the spectacle of Boulie swimming inside the reflection of fireworks dancing on the water. I didn't hear the roar of the fire or feel the heat on my back.

Suddenly, she stopped circling and swam quickly toward me, her arms chopping the water. She snatched the towel from my hand and dropped it in the sea, retrieved it, then ran past me, and, as I turned, I saw that the great wedding cake of a house was on fire. The blaze could have been fireworks sparking in the night sky, another entertainment for the guests, the ultimate amusement, but it wasn't. The inferno was a real house and you were in it.

Screaming your name, Boulie raced naked into the flames and was gone. When I got past the frozen moment when I couldn't believe what was happening, I ran after her, my heart beating wildly. In the drawing room, everything was burning, the curtains, my paintings on the wall. There was so much smoke, I couldn't see or breathe. "Boulie!" I screamed. "Precious!"

I found the stairs, but Boulie was already crawling down, trying to stay under the smoke, carrying a bundle in her wet towel. It was you, swaddled and, hopefully, safe. She handed you to me and we felt our way out the same way we had got in, through the French doors to the terrace. My dress was on fire. I dropped you on the lawn and my mother fell on me, putting out the flames with her own body. Miraculously, neither of us was burned, but Boulie had fallen naked and unconscious on the grass, her flesh blistering.

"Get a doctor," my mother screamed.

"Precious!" I folded into you. "Boulie!" My friend just opened her eyes and sighed as her soul left her body.

"Duffie!" I stood up, but a man held me back. My nose bled all over his dress shirt. I remember that.

"She's gone," someone said. I slumped to my knees, picked you up and removed the wet towel and your nightgown. You were naked except for Chou's necklace. The man who had held me gave me his coat to wrap you in. The crowd pressed in around us. I heard more voices asking if there was a doctor present, and strangely, noticed one pair of glittering dark eyes.

"What does that mean?" Tony asks.

"Everything pointed back to the moment I slapped Chou. From then on, the day was ruined. Our lives were ruined. I started it."

"You aren't to blame."

"I am if I think I am."

"Poor Poppy. It wasn't your fault."

We were taken to the gazebo to wait. I held you wrapped in the dinner jacket in my arms and my mother held me. Someone brought tea from a neighbour's house. After what seemed forever, a pale and shaken Elspeth came to tell us she had been informed that Duffie was dead. I was numb, but not so unconscious that I couldn't think. There wouldn't have been a fire if I had ignored Chou's remark. I know that. The fire was my fault.

Because Selkirk Road was choked with fire equipment and fire fighters, the guests were eventually taken by boat to the inner harbour, where volunteers waited to drive us home. The Prince of Wales had slipped away on the Lieutenant Governor's launch, I presume right after Boulie disrobed, when his party separated him from the crowd, and I had gone into the house to get the towel to hide her shame. Boulie, covered with a canvas tarpaulin, sailed with Nora, you and me past the gaily-lit yachts and rowboats in a police boat.

Duffie stayed in the house. The volunteer firemen found her teeth, her thin gold ring, and some bits of bone the next day. She was the only one. The other servants in the house had been in the kitchen on the main floor and they had got out as soon as the fire started. We were in shock, crossing the River Styx as we made our way down the Selkirk Waters toward the city. Glad to be dead, I thought this had to be Hell, the fire that destroys memory.

Chou was waiting with the car at the foot of Pandora Street. He took you from me, laid you on the back seat and covered you with his jacket. When he noticed the dragon choker, he looked at me. His mouth opened slightly, but he said nothing. We drove home in silence.

When we woke up in our own beds the next morning, Nora and I both said we believed we had been dreaming the night before. But we hadn't been. We smelled of smoke and my mother's hair had turned completely white. There would be no more Duffie, no more Boulie. They had gone into the vortex that took everything. At least Duffie had died knowing she had left a grandchild to replace the son who was taken from her. Poor Boulie left only the air she had disturbed.

10

My Precious Cabbagina,

Dinner last night was a treat. We locked my worries in my stateroom. Tony and I sat at the Captain's table and the other guests pretended not to notice that we had traded roles. For an hour or two I let myself be carried off with the charade. Tony made a wonderful girl. He flirted with all the men and they handled it in good spirit. Even Mr. Stuffed Shirt, the truly boring Thomas Cook man, made himself agreeable by helping Antonia with *her* chair and suggesting a dinner wine.

"There's something I forgot to tell you, dear boy," Tony leaned over and whispered in my ear.

"What?"

"There's another meaning for Willie."

"Now you tell me."

"Would you rather I didn't?"

"Of course not. Don't list too far. The stuffing in your décolletage is about to abandon ship."

"A Willie is a man who wears make-up."

"Oh Winky, you are full of surprises, you shameless slut."

I drank a little too much; and by the time we got back to my cabin I was weepy again. Tony helped me into bed and, instead of sleeping on the cot which was brought in while we were at dinner, he lay down beside me and held my hand as we talked. He told me that before we left Victoria he had been to a joss house in Chinatown and had his oracle bone read.

"Precious is fine. She will be returned to us."

"How can you believe that?"

"Because I am an Anglican and Anglicans are raised to believe everything they hear."

"Oh Tony, what does the Church of England have to do with oracle bones?"

"It has to do with the colonial mind, which is a labyrinth. I know Precious is waiting in the garden. There is no dragon there."

"But it's a Chinese labyrinth, and she is a girl."

"The oracle bones don't make mistakes, Poppy. Trust me."

I have to trust somebody, but in a life of tragic surprises and ethical confusion, trust is in short supply. Sometimes in the dark, I used to ask Duffie how she could have believed in a God who would allow so much cruelty. My mother was right. God, if he or she ever existed, was just as dead as my beloved Alec and Duffie and Boulie. The more they retreated into the darkness, the more I called them back. I woke up at night in sweats, screaming their names.

"You needed someone to hold you, Poppy."

"I had Precious."

We are up early this morning, watching the island of Hawaii come into view. The sky and water are so blue, and the beaches dazzlingly white. I can't wait to put my feet in the sand. My great regret is that I have not been able to explore more of the world. I am sure there are many colours I have not yet discovered. I wish I could see them for the first time with you.

We will leave the ship while the mail and the Honolulu-bound passengers are unloaded and fresh provisions are brought on board. Tony has arranged for a car to pick us up and take us to lunch at the new Royal Hawaiian Hotel just down the beach from the Hotel Moana where I spent the summer of 1901 with my parents.

~

BECAUSE LADY COWES-WENTWORTH-COWES wished it, Boulie Desjardin had an Anglican funeral with the full choir at Christ Church Cathedral, which would have made her laugh. Han Moon Lily, Boulie's doppelganger, had a Chinese burial at the cemetery in Gonzales Bay. Soong Chou, who had negotiated privately with Lady Cowes, insisted on that. She gave Boulie back to her family.

"Boulie will wait for seven years for the gates to open," Chou said. "And then I will take her bones home to China." I watched my friend's Hell money twist and turn to ashes in the crematorium and prayed that it would buy her peace. Hopefully, Boulie's ghost would not be creating mayhem by driving recklessly through the leaf-strewn streets of Oak Bay. In seven years you would be almost full-grown. It would be time for Chou to pay attention to his family. I still believed Boulie was part of it, but Chou said nothing to me.

Life is a cycle. I accept that. I celebrate it. On the other hand, with the fire and its aftermath, mine was a tight circle with death overlapping life to an intolerable degree. I began to think of ways in which I could enlarge the circumference of my experience without disturbing you any more than you had been by the death of people you cared about.

Now I understand that running in circles is a form of insanity. For my mother, with her ever-expanding garden, freedom was as large as the cycle of seasons. For Chou, it was as small as bigotry in this country and tradition at home in China. For Boulie, it was the diameter of the well where her adulterous mother had been cruelly extinguished.

After the fire, I felt my own world shrinking into a small vortex of grief. My mother told Miss Beach to take what she wanted from Duffie's room, but I wouldn't let her touch anything. Duffie belonged to you and me. I knew it was selfish, but I locked the door and kept the key. When you were safely asleep, I would climb the narrow stairs to the attic, get into Duffie's bed and smell her pillowcases. I wore her slip and the brooch she kept in the blue velvet box from the shop in Edinburgh where my ring had been purchased. There were gray and ginger hairs in her hairbrush, and remains of dried toothpaste on her toothbrush. I collected these things and saved them.

Lacking the inventory that kept Duffie present, I drew Boulie as I remembered her, as if I could make her real by capturing her impossible essence. Drawing and erasing, I soon realised that I was obsessed. I needed to get away from Boulie in order to survive her.

I didn't want you to see me running in circles, because it would confuse you. I had to listen to Emily. Even though my decision would run contrary to her advice, it was her deeper wisdom that I needed to hear. More than how to apply paint to canvas, Emily was teaching me to be myself, to run as fast as my damaged heart would let me.

Boulie had told me that the opium business was in trouble. It was harder to procure and process the poppy resin and riskier to smuggle it out of the country now that it was illegal in Canada. I noticed more suspicious buzzing below stairs and sniffed around trying to figure out what the new activity was all about. Very soon after the Volstead Act was passed in the United States, the stench in the tunnel changed from the cloying odour of opium to the smell of alcohol.

Because I had grown up in the belief that financially at least we were secure, I had resisted assimilating Boulie's information about my mother and the others. As the evidence piled up, I had to accept that my friend had been right all along.

I began to see my mother as an adventuress. Constrained by

her sex and social position, she sought ways to avoid conformity. Gardening was a ladylike occupation, no matter how dirty she got her hands. Perhaps Lady Cowes-Wentworth-Cowes had also been party to the opium trade. Now, certain that smugglers were coming across the water from the United States at night, I lay in bed and listened for the powerful engines that meant there was a delivery leaving the tunnel. Having heard stories of gunfights and ruthless enforcement of the prohibition laws by the American authorities, I feared for you.

Like horses' hooves when they are are muffled in funeral processions to avoid intruding on the mourners with percussive noises, we inhabited our lives so soundlessly that winter we could have been wearing socks. My mother hired a practical nurse called Elsie Dumont to help with you; and you insisted on calling her Duffie. No one said much. The garden was silent too, black sticks and mud. Rain and fog left us damp and bewildered.

My mother kept to her domestic regime, even though her social life was curtailed. Most of her friends, respecting mourning, stayed away. Every morning and evening she took Ling Ling and Moo Pei to Lady Cowes and they walked their four yapping Pekingese dogs together along the beach. Then she met with Soong Chou and did her correspondence in the library. In the afternoon, she napped, but the naps were longer, lasting from after lunch until just before dinner. Evenings were for listening to records, playing *mah jong* with friends and reading.

You were invited to the *sanctum sanctorum* to say goodnight. The dog chocolates became a joke. We had our own tin of fairy cookies, little round crackers with coloured icing, and you were allowed one each evening before brushing your teeth.

When I turned twenty-one, I went over my father's will with a lawyer, who explained the terms of my inheritance. For four more years, my mother would be in charge of a trust administered jointly with the Bank of New York. Between that money and her family legacy, we should be in the chips.

It must have been late February when the sun finally forced its way through a fluff of cumulous clouds. I put on a warm coat and went for a walk on the beach. I stood on a rock and felt the wind blow through me. On my way back to the house, I found the first snowdrops poking through the grasses in the fairy glen. I picked a bunch and brought them up to the house to show that life was starting over.

I had arranged the bouquet in a small silver bowl and was carrying them up the stairs while Nora was on her way down, followed by her infantilised dogs. I remember thinking how beautiful she looked in her cream cashmere suit. When she saw the flowers, her face paled. She grabbed the bowl and threw it down the stairs; then she grabbed my shoulders and shook me.

"What are you trying to do? Don't you *ever* bring these flowers into my house!"

I was so shocked at first that I didn't react. While we stood head to head on the stairs and the dogs retreated to her bedroom, you ran to see what the noise was about, and knelt to pick up the flowers.

"Don't touch them!" Nora screamed again, then began sobbing.

No one had told me that snowdrops, which are scattered in graveyards, are thought to bring death and that touching them is bad luck. In her ferocity, I saw fear; and at once her emotion claimed and liberated me. The next morning I sat with her during her extended morning rituals at her dressing table and told her that I was going to exhibit my paintings privately in England and Wales. And further, I was taking you with me.

"I won't let you."

"You can't stop me. I am an adult."

"I am Precious' guardian."

"I am her mother. How dare you!" I was shouting at her for the first time in my life.

"You have no money."

"My father left me money Nora. We both know that. You owe it to me and I intend to take it."

"There is influenza in London."

"The worst of it is over."

"Travel will kill you."

"I am already dead! You have suffocated me just as effectively as you killed my father."

"It was an accident. I didn't mean to." She looked stricken.

My jaw dropped. It was true. She had killed him with her infidelity. I asked nothing more, fitting the words "I didn't mean to" like a sliver of glass into my mosaic of received truths, and regained my composure. She never lost hers, just sat rigidly at her dressing table with her hand on a perfume bottle that I suspected, no hoped, she would fling at me. I wanted her to smash it against the wall, then tell me it wasn't true. But she didn't.

She kept on. What about my heart? After the fire, I had less energy. How could I cope with travel and with a child? I noticed she was looking at herself in the mirror while she argued with me, and I wondered why she couldn't turn around and take my hands in hers and implore me, as a mother, to stay. Was she watching her performance, or couldn't she bear to look at me? Would I too start a fatal nosebleed? What terrible things had she said to my father to make that happen to him?

At that moment, I remembered watching her open her mail one long ago morning while I told her about some childhood problem. She had paid more attention to her letters, running her finger down the front of her invitations, checking to see if any were printed rather than engraved. The printed invitations went straight into the wastebasket. I felt myself sailing in the same direction and I liked it. The arc of the card was my arc. Freedom.

"I'm going. Precious is coming with me."

"I didn't mean to." Her words resonated on every rise and fall of the waves crashing on the beach.

A few days later, my mother asked me to come down to the garden with her. We walked past all the formal beds, under the oaks and chestnuts, over the lawn to the fairy glen. Nora stood on the edge of the lawn, the toes of her brown and white spectator shoes not quite touching the wild grass.

She told me the fairy glen was there for a reason. It was to contain bad spirits and keep them away from the house, where fairies could do evil business. Fairies stole children. If parents forgot their prescriptions — certain flowers, certain potions — if they forgot to pick the first daisy of spring or the first daffodil, if they neglected to pick the correct medicinal herbs at noon on the day closest to the full moon, then their children would die and be turned into bad fairies anxious to recruit others to their practice of the dark arts.

I had no idea my mother was so deeply superstitious. I had ascribed that attribute to Duffie. Perhaps, with the cumulative tragedies, she needed to comprehend the sources of evil in order to protect herself and us.

Perhaps she believed that the bad fairies had transformed me into one of them so that I could come back and pinch her for the great sin she had committed. Her husband had died mysteriously; her child was damaged. Were we all the victims of infidelity and indifferent mothering? Did she hope the fairy glen would separate land from sea, family from smugglers? If I was the wicked fairy in her opium dreams, then no wonder she couldn't trust me with my own child. It was ridiculous, but given what she had been through and her proclivities, not beyond imagining.

Fairies or no fairies, I was determined. Since the fire, all the emotional energy that hadn't gone into you was focused on my work. Except for the Fridays with Emily, I spent most of my time painting in the ballroom upstairs. I enjoyed being with you and you were happy to paint at your own little easel beside mine.

I tracked the progression of grief through my paintings, which, I could see, were more a map of my unconscious than a reflection of the landscape I represented. During that period, they were more like Emily's, gyres of colour disappearing into abstract backgrounds. Where Emily's palette was mostly the blues and greens and browns of the Rainforest, mine was progressively louder, tending more to the blood reds and red violets, oranges and yellows. Clearly, I was in the fire, but I was also barricading myself against my winter of grief with the colours of summer.

Your childish paintings were swirls of red. Even your people were red. "This is an operation," you told me once, handing me a curled and dried painting on newsprint. "I'm going to be a cut-open doctor when I grow up." Did you think it was your job to cure us? The idea breaks my heart.

Somewhere between my mother and Boulie in appearance, your blue-black hair was cut in a bob, but it was thick and shiny and straight. Rather than bangs, or a fringe, as my English friends say, we parted your hair on the side and held it back with bows that matched your dresses. Your eyes, almond shaped and a deep olive green, are fringed with the thickest black lashes I have ever seen. Right from the start, you were long and slender. Already, it was obvious that you would be a stunning woman. I rejoiced and feared for you at the same time. Beautiful flowers attract bees.

Remembering my solitary childhood meals, I ate as often as possible with you. I relished our conversations, because you gave me a fresh perspective on everything under the sun. Sometimes I had two dinners, the first in the children's dining room and the second with Nora, who ate like a mosquito. I didn't want to make my parenting a reproach to her, but I was constantly astonished by what she had missed.

You were a serious child, and like me, more inclined to watch than to act. I thought that was a good thing, given that I had seen where recklessness ended. It was recklessness that took Alec to France and Boulie into the fire. However, I also realised that if Boulie had not been careless with herself then you would have died with Duffie. Perhaps she had wanted to die doing something beautiful.

Soong Chou withdrew from me that year. I still had my music lessons, and I took you along, but there was something sadder, more reserved in his demeanor. He was kind to you, but there was a sense of holding back that went beyond the requirements of his station. It took me a long time to realise how seriously he had lost face in the outcome of the fire and how profoundly he felt the loss of Boulie. As I slowly realised the meaning of his depression, I knew he would not fail in what he perceived as his duty to return Boulie's bones to her family in China. I also knew he wouldn't come back the next time.

We had all been depressed that winter, and to tell the truth, I didn't have time to waste. I had to make my own life and it became clearer that it wouldn't be possible if I continued to stay in my mother's house. I needed a different reality and I wasn't going without you. When my mother continued to object, I went a little further, saying that I didn't trust the situation downstairs. She told me to mind my own business. That was the end of the discussion. I had made my decision.

I spent months planning our great adventure. My febrile paintings were packed up and shipped by the Kent Brothers. I read you colour-plated children's books about English history. You wept over the brothers in the tower and poor Mary, Queen of Scots, whose little dog hid under her skirt when she went to the executioner's block. You learned the names of all of the royal palaces and all the kings and queens of England. You couldn't wait to eat fish and chips wrapped in newspaper and watch the Royal Family ride by in golden coaches and the changing of the guard at Buckingham Palace.

I finally allowed Miss Beach and Daisy to clean out Duffie's room. They could have what they liked after I took her silver reading glasses and gave you her gold bracelet with a heart of pearls around an amethyst centre. Duffie was a thrifty person, who saved every ribbon, every envelope for re-use. Each piece of jewelry in her small collection of personal remembrances was in its original box. When I went through her things for the last time, I wondered who had given them to her. Was it someone in love? Perhaps he had died before they had time to get married. Perhaps he had another wife. He might have been in prison, the descendent of one of those lowland *rievers* who stole cattle and sheep from the English and cut their throats while they slept. Maybe her story was true and she was widowed by an unnamed war. Someday I might know.

11

My Own,

With the exception of an exasperating interlude with a shipmate, we had a good day today. Honolulu with its extravagant birds and flowers was beautiful beyond my memories. If I weren't on a mission, and you were safe, I would happily have jumped ship and stayed there.

We breathed in the mixed scents of pineapple, plumeria, and turquoise sea and sighed. "This is heaven on earth," I said to Tony, who must have been missing Olivier terribly at that moment.

Tony and I had lunch as planned at the Royal Hawaiian Hotel, a pink Moorish building with a terrace overlooking the extraordinary Waikiki Beach with its blinding white sand and majestic palms. Raked, I was told, by sun-burnished gods every morning, the shoreline was perfection. I had one drink; something made of rum and coconut milk with shaved ice, a delicious shrimp salad and pineapple sorbet. Tony chose *mahi-mahi*, a Hawaiian whitefish. Noticing that most of the hotel guests were either elderly couples or American honeymooners, we talked about my marriage. "You must come back here with Olivier," I said, and Tony assured me that he would. I was afraid that he would say, "Wouldn't it be fun, the three of us," but he didn't, and I was grateful.

"What do you think of the hotel?" I asked.

"Too pink, Poppy. It's rather like being trapped in a man-eating orchid."

"Spoken like a man!" I protested, braiding a lovely white plumeria flower into my hair. "I love the way the light changes on Diamond Head," I pointed at the volcano across the harbour.

"If we were staying, I'd have climbed to the crater and brought you back a cactus flower."

"In a perfect world, I'd climb it myself." I said, tumbling sand from one hand to the other. "Maybe Precious will one day."

We picked an armful of tropical flowers to take back to the ship. Tony made me promise to draw them for him.

On the drive back to the *Empress of Asia*, we got in an argument with Mr. Woodhouse, the pompous stuffed shirt who is en route to Japan to work for Thomas Cook. Mr. Woodhouse had lunch by himself at the Royal Hawaiian then begged a ride back to the ship when we met in the lobby. Perhaps he was punishing us for teasing him at dinner. Heaven knows he might have been attracted to Tony as a girl or maybe even as a boy. What confusion for him. Tony told me that at school the worst bullies picked on boys that they had decided were "light on their feet."

"The thing is," he said, "We could see that they had erections while they were beating on us."

Having been to China twice, Mr. Stuffed Shirt was a self-proclaimed expert on Chinese culture. He told us the Suffragettes had ruined western civilization. Women didn't need to vote. Their husbands could vote for them. He thought foot-binding was a beautiful tradition and all any woman needed was to follow the prescription of the four virtues, the accomplishments of a Chinese lady.

"That is fine," I said, "But did you know that a Chinese gentleman is expected to have the same accomplishments? And, since you are going to work in Japan, I should tell you that the most revered Japanese writer is a woman, Lady Murasaki."

Tony was amused by my indignation. My dear friend does an absolutely riotous imitation of Mr. Woodhouse. This evening we are dining in my cabin again. The day, interesting as it has been, has depleted my social energy. We are about to revisit the journey that brought me to Tony and his very special friendship.

I'd had no eye contact with Chou the crisp fall day in 1921 when you and I sailed to Vancouver en route to England on the *Princess Patricia*. We'd finished our oblique conversations in the stable during my final *pipa* lessons. He gave you a jade *pi* on a gold chain to wear around your neck. "*Joy geen*," you said, "See you again," as he had taught you.

My mother commented on the gift without judgment. There was a curious intimacy between my mother and her employee, and sometimes, when I noticed a look between them, I felt left out.

I wondered if Chou had left a child in China during the brief weeks of his marriage. Which wife did he think of in the moments before sleep? Perhaps both of us came to mind. In China, I have heard, a man doesn't have to choose. He might care for all his wives or concubines. Nevertheless, I wanted to ask him if he lay in the dark thinking of me, as I did of him. Did his hand wander into the placket in his silk pyjamas and wake up the small bird in its nest? Did he hear my reply, so near and yet so far, farther even than his wife in China, my own *belle chose* roused to song by thoughts of him?

There was no doubt that our duets on the *pipas* had the parry and thrust of intimate conversation. My playing had improved so much that I could forget technique and throw myself into the passionate string dialogue of two instruments tuned to unspeakable loneliness. I wonder how much of the feeling between us you absorbed. You were making astonishing progress yourself. Chou told me that he was surprised that a Western child would have so much natural feeling for Chinese music.

When Chou drove you, Nora and me to the C.P.R. dock the day we left for England, we shook hands and you kissed him goodbye, something of which my mother, even though she believed in the separate dignities of employer and employee, approved. I could tell. Nora had tears in her eyes when we were called on board. I remembered the proverb, "*When a child dies, the future is lost. When an elder dies, the past is lost.*" She was losing me and I believed I was about to be reborn. She wrote to me later, "*Why didn't you look back when you went up the gangplank?*" I could have answered, "*Why couldn't you have seen me before?*" but I didn't. "*Joy geen,*" I heard Soong Chou say. We were off.

It took almost a week to cross Canada on the train. You and I shared a roomette. You had the top bunk. I had the bottom. We perfected taking sponge baths, washed in the tiny metal sink, and enjoyed the intimacy of a small room. Three times a day, we put down our books, sketchpads and puzzles and made our way to the dining car, which you believed was the height of elegance with its brass sconces, crisp white napery and shivering cutlery. It's a moving picture, you told me, looking out the window as we slid past forest, mountain and prairie.

I thought about all the immigrants running away from the past, as I was, only in the opposite direction, and wondered how many had realised their aspirations. As our train rushed through mountain passes and fields of waving wheat, I compared them to the gardens I was leaving behind, each one a small utopia, somebody's dream — from the tiniest plot thick with rows of vegetables in Chinatown to Hatley Park, where a Scottish coal-miner's son had made his own little Versailles.

What of Robert Dunsmuir's ambitions? He got rich off the backs of poor men like himself and his dynasty had turned to tragedy in one generation. Already one grandson, Boy, was dead and another, Robin, was drinking himself to death. Already there were quarrels over land and money between his wife and their son. I thought of Dola's father James' beautiful Japanese Garden, designed by

Yoshihiro Kishida and Hayato Tanaka, the men who built the Tea Garden on the Gorge, and how its serenity — the pond, elegant shrubberies, half-moon bridges and rest houses shaded by bamboo and wisteria — failed to give peace to the family who lived there. The garden might have impressed The Prince of Wales, but in the end it was just a folly.

And my mother — what purpose did her garden serve if she was undermining its serenity with clandestine underground activity? If I were to draw her world in cross-section, it would look just as shaky as one of Dunsmuir's unsafe coalmines. What is the purpose of building beauty on top of dangerous excavation? I was angry with her for taking unnecessary risks. I have heard it said that women experience anger as depression and that depression is bad for the heart. I couldn't give in to depression. If I were to have a short life, I was determined to make it useful in some way. The only means I could think of was making something beautiful, and my life in Victoria had become ugly and small.

A very handsome girl got on the train in Calgary. She was tall and blonde and had an actor's mobile features. You watched her slouch into the dining car and started winking. The girl, about my age, winked back. "I think your daughter just invited me for dinner," she said, presuming herself into the empty chair beside you as if we should be honoured to have her at our table.

"She's my cousin," I explained as our white-gloved waiter set another place.

The lovely girl's name was Daphne and she was traveling to Toronto to get married. Daphne told us that her father was a rancher. I studied her smooth tanned face, sun-bleached shoulder length hair, and strong hands and pictured her on a horse. She was wearing men's clothes, a pair of camel hair slacks and a white silk shirt with a cardigan loosely tied around her shoulders. In London and Paris, I would meet more women like her, who dared to dress with elegant practicality. Her fiancé, she told us, was a newspaper publisher. They had met at a boarding school dance. She wasn't sure she would like living in the city. As she stared at her home country passing by, weighing her options, I guessed, I found myself looking at Daphne's pillowy mouth and white teeth, wondering what it would be like to kiss her.

My thoughts at dinner disturbed me, because, ever since my childish sexual experimentation with Boulie and Alec, I had thought of myself as a man's woman. Over the past year, I had often wondered if unnatural sexual urges had pushed Boulie into even deeper water than the well where her mother had been drowned. My own daydreams had all focused on the safely unattainable Soong Chou. I finished my beef tenderloin and tossed a remedial glass of claret after the Dubonnet *digestif* I had ordered before my dinner, looked out the window at the prairie night and forgot about it. Daphne was showing you tricks with a coin and a box she'd pulled out of her pocket.

We said goodnight and you and I went back to our roomette, put on our nightgowns, brushed our teeth, got into our up-and-down bunks and began telling stories as the night hurtled past our window. Soon you were breathing the even breaths of the unconscious and I lay awake wondering what lay ahead.

Around midnight, there was a knock at our door. I opened it a crack, anticipating a porter with a message. It was Daphne in her nightgown, carrying a bottle of brandy. I put my finger to my lips and nodded toward you.

"Do you know the definition of negligent?" she whispered and then answered before I had a chance to say no. "It's answering the door in your negligée. You have glasses I presume, or do you want to drink straight from the bottle?"

I let her in and we sat on my bunk, poured two brandies and clicked glasses. "It's *Daufnay*, you know. Not *Daffnee*."

"Like the Dauphin," I said.

Daphne took one of my pillows and stretched out on the bed, explaining that she was having pre-wedding jitters. She plumped my other pillow and gestured for me to lie beside her so that we could look out the window together. The bunk was narrow and, even though she was pressed against the wall, I had to turn myself toward her to prevent from rolling off the bed. We sipped our brandy from tooth glasses as the car rocked from side to side.

The car rolled and Daphne, raising her glass to her lips, spilled some brandy on me.

On the bunk above us, you breathed deeply, muttering in your childish dreams.

"It's time for you to go back to your own bed, Daphne." She had a face like a Renaissance Madonna.

There was a bump in her nose. "My father broke it." I kissed my finger and touched it.

"Thank you," she said and left the roomette, closing the door with a soft click. Disturbed, I lay there wondering if making love with a woman would be like pleasuring myself but without the loneliness.

I lay half-awake, looking out the window, imagining that she was watching the grasslands pass and fearing the sharp shapes of trees that would rise in the morning when we came to the forests of Western Ontario. I smiled when an angel passed by — the luminous shape of a desert flower tossed from the train, then turned and went to sleep.

Our new friend had promised to show you some card games. At breakfast, you and I both watched the door to the dining car. When would Daphne and her wonderful magic tricks reappear? "Daphne might be a late sleeper," I told you. "She needs her beauty rest because she's getting married."

At the next table, an elderly lady was talking loudly. A passenger had reported they had seen someone jump from the train the night before, but by the time they'd roused a sleeping porter it was too late to stop. Their porter had told them this morning. The engineer telegraphed a message, but no one was found — just a woman's nightgown. I laughed and covered my mouth with my napkin. "I think it was our friend." Daphne was no Anna Karenina. "It's just a joke," I said.

Daphne had ridden horses. Perhaps she couldn't let a man ride her. When you persevered, I said not to worry. She had disembarked early because she didn't really want to be married.

After we left the train two days later, you and I spent a day and night in Montreal, waking up to a fresh snowfall. We dressed quickly and left the Ritz-Carleton before breakfast. I wanted you to make the first footsteps in the fresh white morning. We lay down and made angels. I wondered if I could hire a *calèche* to take you for a ride, but it was Sunday and the city was deserted until the bells started ringing for church.

At noon, we took the train to New York and immediately boarded the *Aquitania* for England. Since my father had died in that big and incomprehensible city, I was glad to pass through without stopping to visit. Our lives would have turned out differently had our story not taken such a sad turn in New York.

The evening we left America, I stood with you at the stern of the ship and watched the Statue of Liberty get smaller and smaller in our wake, thinking of all the lost souls that had stood there on their way to and from the Great War. I thought of the panic — fear of death in those who were going and fear of living among those who returned damaged in body and shell-shocked minds from the killing fields. I thought of the *Aquitania's* delightful rooms filled with pain and suffering when the liner was requisitioned as a hospital ship, and with relief when it brought soldiers home from the war. Alec could have been one of them, and Boy Dunsmuir.

Would there soon be a gap as wide as the Atlantic Ocean between poor Boulie and me or had I been right in the beginning, when I believed the dead had been borrowed and transformed by fairies? Perhaps I would find her disrupting an English garden. I laughed and lifted you up, so that you too could look at the sea and see what I saw.

During the crossing to England, we hardly ever left our stateroom. On the second day out, we ran into a storm and we were ill most of the time, subsisting on crackers and the soda water I had intended to use as mix for drinks parties in the event we made friends on the voyage. From our portholes, we could see waves coming up to the rails of the ship. Even though I knew fresh air would be good for us, I was afraid to go out on deck, lest one of those hungry surges reach up and take you from me. Poor Precious, I had promised you sumptuous banquets and swimming pools. The reality was quite awful. We didn't even have the energy to type letters or draw or read the books we had brought along.

I was too sick to worry about Daphne and where she might have ended up. In any event, there were no further opportunities for misadventure. Convinced my bed was a coffin, I dreamed I was sharing it with all of my ghosts, none of them, thank God, sexually demanding.

"What a shame. The *Aquitania* is such a lovely ship. Precious would have adored the Egyptian pool." Tony is drawing an obelisk in the margin.

"We were nowhere near the pool. Most of the time, we just lay on our beds and stared at the ceilings."

"The fate of many women I imagine."

"Well, now that you mention it, I think I would rather be seasick than pinned to my mattress by some of the men I have met."

"Poor little Butterfly," Tony sings.

"Don't feel sorry for me. I make lethal secretions." Sadly, it might be true.

It was my first Atlantic crossing since the *Titanic* had gone down. This frequently crossed my mind during the voyage. I kept checking our life preservers, thinking about the people who sank with her, most of them immigrants in steerage full of hope for a new life.

You may remember the relief we felt when we entered calm waters again and steamed into Cherbourg and, at last, Southampton. There was no one to meet us in England. As two apparently helpless sisters, twenty-one and five years old, we got all the necessary help with luggage and transport from gallant men.

We made our way by train into London and Claridge's, hung up our clothes and lived in our nightgowns for two days. In the spring, I intended to find a cottage in the country, possibly Dorset or the Cotswolds, and live more simply, tramping the countryside looking for beautiful English gardens to paint. But for the time being, we gratefully accepted the luxury of a comfortable home base.

In those days, I didn't think about money. My mother was not foolish, but there was no sense of worry. It didn't occur to me that staying at a hotel like Claridge's, which was just undergoing its beautiful deco renovation, reeked of privilege. How many twenty-one year old girls had the freedom to live in such luxury? I wasn't wise enough to feel guilty. Hotel life — comfortably appointed rooms with maid service — was exactly what I was used to.

I promised you that we would live wild as berries in the summer. In the meantime, there was London to see. Until after Christmas, we were tourists. I devoted myself entirely to you. There is a limit to the endurance of five-year-olds, but you have an appetite for beauty that is equal to my own. I could sit you down at the Tate with your sketchbook for an hour and you would work away at copying the paintings you liked. Unlike myself, you were obsessed with the human figure, particularly the sensuous lines of the Pre-Raphaelites. I took you to Lord Leighton's house near Holland Park. You loved the theatrical interiors with the Moorish fountains and tiles in the Arab hall, and its Oriental furnishings, including a number of opium beds.

We spent a weekend in Brighton, visiting the exquisite Royal Pavilion with its domed roofs and exotic rooms. When we returned to London, you wanted to paint murals on the walls of our flat like our new friends who were followers of John Ruskin, and I promised you that we would have our own house one day where you could do whatever you liked to your room. I was delighted with your colour sense and your appreciation for art and architecture, but had to make our plans keeping in mind that there were limits on my heart and your little legs.

That Christmas Nora sent a package from home with books and oil pastels, nightgowns for both of us and preserves and remedies from Chan Fong's kitchen. She included my copy of *A Child's Garden of Verse*, signed by Robert Louis Stevenson, whom Nora had known in California, which we had left behind. I opened the jars one by one and smelled the pears, mint and quince from Nora's garden. We would have our own preserves the following summer; I was determined. In Harrods' food hall, I bought a duck, plum pudding with hard sauce, Christmas cake, crackers and a Stilton cheese in a pot. You had stopped asking about Duffie. That Christmas, with just the two of us, was our best.

In the middle of lunch, there was a knock at our door. A smiling bellboy delivered another large package from home. It was from Chou. He had sent flattened paper lanterns, candied ginger, and, as promised, my *pipa* and your *Liuqin*. You were ecstatic and wouldn't stop playing the songs you knew.

In January, I enrolled you in Miss Chester's School for Girls in Kensington and settled down to work, contacting people I already knew and names I had been given to follow up. My first show was in February at the Dulwich Picture Gallery where all the paintings from Victoria had been delivered before our arrival. I was anxious to start work again.

The hotel provided me with Miss Brown, a part-time nanny, and I started going out in the evenings to *vernissages* and the houses of people recommended by my mother. Strangely, the Prince of Wales, who had promised to be helpful, did not return my calls to his secretary. Later, I learned that he had distanced himself because of the embarrassment over Boulie, even though he had written a kind note after her death and an invitation to show in London.

I was too young to remember anything more than the London

Zoo and the parks from my early childhood, but it was clear to me that nothing would stay the same after the Great War buried and maimed our generation of boys. Everywhere I went, women outnumbered men. The women I met were more interested in careers than marriage, more interested in one another than in sorting through a diminished supply of boys. There was a real sexual *frisson* among the pretty girls with short hair and shorter skirts. Having been let out of the box, they were hardly ready to go back in. Middle and upper class women talked about careers on the stage or as painters and writers, unthinkable before the war. I started to wear black — which my mother had taught me was only worn by Mediterranean grandmothers and servants — because it suited me and brought out the gold in my hair.

There was a gaiety in London that was completely unlike Victoria. Ideas generally reverberated in Victoria. I was energized by the enthusiasm I felt all around me — new attitudes, new politics, new art. Women's emancipation, which bred moral conservatism in Canada and the United States, where women used the franchise to vote for prohibition, was giving creative and sexual freedom to women in London. Crushes had become full blown passion in that atmosphere.

The enthusiasm for anything Oriental, which was a natural phenomenon in Victoria — where east literally met west — was *avant-garde* in London. Glad that I had packed my *mah jong* set, because it was a great icebreaker, I do believe I introduced the game to London. When I realised what a wonderful thank you gift *mah jong* made for weekends at my new friends' country houses, I wrote to my mother and asked her to get Soong Chou to send us more boxes of tiles.

Soon, it seemed that everyone in London was playing *mah jong*. I liked to close my eyes and listen to the bone tiles clicking on the tabletop. Perhaps the game was people touching people at the deepest level, bone to bone, and that was why we found it such a comfort. I imagined elephants touching tusks in gestures of affection. If we were stripped down to the bone, would we sound like the gently percussive sound of the game? Did it take us closer to the soldiers sleeping in the mud?

You were quite *au courant* in the toggled pyjamas and slippers we brought from home. Everyone wanted a chic *cheongsam* dress like mine. Dola's brother-in-law, the designer Edward Molyneux, was having a vogue with his Chinese-influenced couture, as was Fortuny with his Greek and Arabic designs.

Art deco was the rage. Women, sick of the restraints of bustles and stays of Victorian and Edwardian couture, wore Egyptian make-up, Fortuny dresses and Chinese jackets. Gin and champagne flowed. Women smoked in public, most of them using long cigarette holders. I knew a few women who smoked cigarillos, but didn't use them myself because of my heart. These post-war years were an exhilarating time to be a young woman. Women without men were relieved of the necessity to conform. Everyone I met in London seemed hungry for life, and like me, giddy with freedom.

I wanted to paint this freshness, a continuum of the organic lines of Art Nouveau and the more geometric representation of shapes in Art Deco. Most of all, I hoped to express the sexual freedom of flowers. It was as if I was realizing for the first time that to be a woman who could reproduce herself in body and spirit was the greatest gift. Now, I hope to share, woman to woman, mother to child, what we missed talking about, cousin to cousin.

I saved every drawing you made, sending all but the ones we kept to decorate the Chelsea flat, home to Victoria. You drew fairy after fairy, fairies in Kensington Garden, fairies at Kew where we spent a delicious April afternoon picnicking in the wisteria covered gazebo, transported by the scent of fruity blossoms, fairies on the barges in Regent's Canal and in the rowboats on the Serpentine, fairies eating with us at Claridge's and sleeping in our beds. I hope they were the good kind. We had given them food and drink.

12

My Angel,
Tony has found a well-appointed room, just for writing, off the first
class lounge. It is long and narrow with windows on the deck and
a fireplace on the dining room side. There are comfortable chairs
where Tony can relax and read his well-worn copy of *Vanity Fair*
while I peck away. I doubt we'll be needing the fire, because, even
though we are heading Northeast to Yokohama, it is still quite
warm.

I rested well after our day in Honolulu and Tony, bless his heart,
has gone back to sleeping in his own cabin. He got up very early
this morning and explored the ship from top to bottom. It is like a
city, he says, a civilization. You traveled to China aboard the
Empress of Asia. And Boulie, long ago, sailed on her when she was
abducted from China. Because I haven't the energy to go up and
down the stairs from deck to deck, I am more or less a prisoner in
first class.

Tony and I are conjuring London from the middle of the Pacific.
The room we are inhabiting could be in a London club. This is a

difficult part of the story for Tony and me. We met in London. Our lives became entwined for better, or for worse, and now he is enduring the worst with me — helping me through it.

"Type what I am about to say Poppy. I am here for the happy outcome, because you girls are precious to me."

During our first year in London, my mother wrote to tell me that she was vacationing in Los Angeles, renting a bungalow at the Garden of Allah, owned by her friend Alla Nazimova. She couldn't endure another dreary winter in Victoria, staring at dead plants. There was nothing dead about the Garden of Allah. I had heard about it from my friends in London. Nazimova's pleasure plantation on Sunset Boulevard was a garden of sybarites, women without men, where Prohibition was the only dirty word. Nora was meeting lots of film stars inside its honeysuckle hedges, and eating oranges and grapefruit from the trees outside her windows.

I wondered if business or recreation took her there. In the London salons I had heard stories about gangsters fighting turf wars over smuggled liquor and government agents shooting on sight. As stories, they were exciting filler in bohemian cocktail conversations, but the reality was numbing. While I worried for my mother, I was glad you were half a world away from her clandestine life.

In London, the weather was foggy and damp, but I hardly noticed. What mattered was that I was working near your school in the Chelsea studio I had rented for three months. My rent was just enough to cover running expenses and I felt privileged to be able to work there. I had half the first floor, which was a relief because there were only the front steps to climb. Luckily, my studio had a large bay window, which let in whatever light the London sky afforded, a toilet that sang when I flushed it, and a sink and a hotplate where I could clean my brushes and make tea. The parameters of your school day forced me to discipline my time.

With my "flat-mate" Genia Stevenson, a Slade student who used the rest of the first floor, I took a strict half-hour for a picnic lunch.

We took turns providing provisions, which we spread on a blanket on the floor.

Genia asked me to model for her, as she was very good at figure painting. She has written to tell me she intends to send one of her paintings of me to you. It is a special portrait because, while I was posing, I told her our complicated story. Genia, a warm soft-built redhead from Manchester, the unspoiled daughter of a textile manufacturer, was someone I knew I could trust. It was such a luxury for me to be able to say "my daughter" to a real friend.

"Say it again, Poppy." Tony has hold of my wrist, so I have stopped typing.

"My daughter."

My London work reflected the freedom I was experiencing as a woman. The blazing grief that marked my post-fire paintings had been transformed, my red moving to violet and the blazing yellows and oranges to pale apricots, the flesh tones inviting the viewer in. Many times, I wished Emily had been there to see what I was doing. My letters to her came back unopened. I was hurt by her childish behaviour, even though I should have been used to it, having often seen her treat others badly.

My two hemispheres intersected constantly. I realised that for the privileged, London was a small place. In the drawing rooms of Belgravia and Bloomsbury, I met artists, politicians, writers and landed aristocrats. As an outsider, I was fascinated.

Because my first exhibition ended in the fire, I was extraordinarily nervous about my Dulwich *vernissage*. With the help of the gallery curator, I spent the morning of the opening hanging my paintings. By lunchtime I hated them. If I had thought of it, I would have taken them all down and thrown them in the Thames, where too much London garbage ends up. As it happened, the pictures stayed on the walls and, after making sure the gallery had fire doors and fire extinguishers at the ready, I went home to rest.

After trying on several dresses, I decided on my Poiret *directoire* dress made of a cranberry and moss green silk crepe. As I slipped on my cami-knickers, I thought how lucky I was to be small. The new dropped waist and waistless dresses looked like sausage casings on buxom figures. I felt sorry for dumpy girls like Dola, with their pigeon chests and piano legs.

I was ready for battle. My paintings were framed and I was too, more or less. I wished that I had Nora's green velvet opera coat with the mink cuffs. Then I would have been unassailable. However, by the time the cab I had hired picked me up at six, I felt posh enough in my very Canadian sheared beaver. As I got in the car, you and Miss Brown, your hotel nanny, waved from our third floor window.

They say crying and laughing are good for the heart. I know turning oneself inside out in public is not. By seven o'clock that evening, my chest heaved as desperately as a sack of drowning kittens. I accepted a glass of merlot for my nerves.

That Poiret dress was lucky. That night I met Tallulah, who came with the entourage of besotted debutantes she called her gallery girls, and all my paintings sold, one of them to Moulie and Edward Molyneux, who said he would make a tea gown inspired by my palette. Dola had only one more term at her finishing school in Paris, Moulie told me, and was dying to come to London, where her mother was going to do her damnedest to get her presented at court.

The Molyneux's brought Olivier Mandeville, the Prince's friend who had followed Boulie around in Victoria. Fortunately, I had no idea what he did for a living, and I might not have cared anyway because by then I had downed several glasses of wine. He asked what my paintings meant and I was irritated. "Really, what are they?" he persisted. "They're not just flowers."

Unable to tell if his question was intuition or condescension or both, I answered, taking a page out of Boulie's book, "They're cunts."

Luckily, the only other person who heard me was the deep-throated American actress who had taken London by storm. She threw back her amazingly lush hair and laughed. "Olivier is an art critic, Poppy. Your outrageous remark will be in the morning paper."

The next day, I had flowers from both of them. The actress sent white flowers, casa blanca lilies and tuberoses, never a mistake. The critic sent the most foul smelling Shasta daisies and skunk cabbage with a card that read, "Did we get off on the wrong foot?" I laughed. About hour later, he sent a note asking if I was free for dinner. I replied that I was staying in with my little cousin, but he could join us if he knew how to amuse a five-year-old.

He did. Olivier was the soul of grace, perfect as an extra man for dinner or a fourth at bridge. Slender with patrician features and wavy auburn hair combed flat, he knew what to wear and what to say; and, amazingly, he was not insufferable. Spending time with him was as valuable as reading a good book. He had firsts from Oxford in Classics and History and he knew everything about everybody. Olivier has what Stanford called a well-furnished mind, and, *miracolo*, he isn't a raging bigot like so many of his fellow aristocrats.

You were as intrigued as I was. Like Daphne on the train, Olivier could produce coins from his handkerchief and make palm trees out of newspapers. You clapped your hands and laughed as you hadn't since the fire. When you called him Olive he begged you not to eat him. "Not until I am old enough to drink martinis like Mummy," you said, and I winced because you meant Nora.

We adjusted very well to one another in London. Olivier showed you and me how to get around on the underground and took us to galleries and museums, *à trois*. I studied the Nocturne paintings by Whistler and compared them to the Turners.

We saw matinees in the west end and watched Isadora Duncan and her precocious Isadorables dance at an afternoon house party. Duncan and her adopted protégées were all wearing beautiful Doric costumes by Fortuny. When I heard that Isadora had strangled when her scarf tangled in the wheel of her car, I wondered if it had been the Knossos scarf she had used so effectively in her dance that day.

You and I were both getting an education. London was the capital of the world. The city of villages had the art of antiquity in its museums and the cant of reform in its streets. I wanted to absorb as much as I could without depleting my energy. Unlike the bright young things who danced all night in the clubs with their stockings rolled down, I made quick appearances and went home to bed by nine o'clock. We spent the morning at our jobs, which is what you called school because I called my painting work. In the late afternoon, after a nap, we visited the galleries and museums.

Olivier took me to Mrs. Henning at the House of Cyclax where I learned the beauty secrets of English ingénues, most of whom arrived at her back door wearing veils, leaving the same way with leaves of *papier-poudre* and geranium and poppy petal lip rouge hidden in their purses. The only store in London with cosmetics for sale was Selfridges, but as Olivier's mother Claire sniffed the first time I met her, Selfridges was an *American* shop.

When I came to know and appreciate Tony, who had been Olivier's Oxford roommate, the three of us had fun shopping and gossiping together. It was as if I had two brothers. One of my amusements with Tony and Olivier was people watching. We had fun tracking the *garçonnes*, as the androgynous young girls with rolled stockings were known. Many of them were in Tallulah's posse. To them, the name Tallulah Bankhead was an emblem for sexual freedom, license to continue the girlhood crushes that usually ended with their schooling. They copied her deep voice and her lifestyle, which meant everything in excess.

There were so many myths about Tallulah it is sometimes hard remembering her exactly as she was. I especially liked the story that she kept her lip rouge on ice and dipped it in bourbon before applying the colour to her lips. This was the kind of behaviour her claque adored. They loved the sense of liberation she exuded. She gave them license to act on their own impulses after years of repression.

"The boys are dead, poppy compost in Flanders," they might have been saying. "Long live the girls."

All the bad fairies ended up in London sooner or later. One Saturday afternoon, while you and I were sketching from the pre-Raphaelite portraits in the Tate Gallery, someone approached me from behind and put her hands over my eyes. At first I thought it was you, but the hands were too big. I couldn't guess. Dola had no interest in paintings. It was too early in the day for Tallulah to be out of bed and it couldn't have been one of my English friends. The English don't do potentially embarrassing things like that in public places. "Guess" the voice said and before I recognized it I heard the sound of wheels on a railroad track.

"Daphne, I thought you were dead." Of course, I had known all along that she wasn't.

"No, the rumours of my death were greatly exaggerated." She laughed.

"I wondered what you wore. They found your nightgown in the rail bed."

"I got off at the next stop."

"I gather you didn't marry what's-his-name."

"That was the point."

"What did happen?" By this time you had put down your sketchbook and run over to embrace Daphne, who kissed you so hard on the lips her lipstick imprinted on you. I made a mental note to tell her not to do that again, an opportunity that may or may not have presented itself depending on whether Daphne did another one of her fabulous disappearing acts, this time, perhaps, jumping from London Bridge into the Thames.

Daphne crowded onto my bench with you beside her. "I decided to follow you to England."

"Follow *us*?" I pointedly included you as a warning to her.

"Why not? However, on the voyage over, I met an amazing Scottish woman who invited me to stay. Her name is Fiona and, apart from her doddering parents, she is refreshingly bereft of relations. Fiona raises sheep on a farm by the River Tweed where I am right at home except for occasional episodes of cabin fever, during which I come to London and paint the town red."

"Red?" I saw the angel of death with her paintbrush charged with blood flying over our door.

"Just an expression, Poppy. Fiona gives me lots of rope and I like it that way."

"So you and Fiona are special friends?" I watched you carefully to see if there was a flicker of recognition, but you were simply as mesmerized as you had been the first time we met Daphne. This time, the object of your adoration was wearing a very handsome beige cashmere coat with mink cuffs. Daphne poured herself like barley water into her golden moments.

"Yes, she is Lady Moncrieff. Since she has no brothers, Fiona is Lord of all she surveys, including me."

"I thought you didn't want to be owned."

"I love Scotland, the green hills, the sheep, the *dry stane* walls, the salmon in the rivers and the Scotch whiskey. The only problem being that Fiona is overly fond of the latter."

"It sounds to me as though you have made a deal with the devil."

"We all do, sooner or later," Daphne said.

"Not me," I told her. "Never. I live to paint." I hesitated. "We live to paint."

"Is that so?" Daphne tickled you under your arms.

"Yes," you answered between giggles. "Poppy and I are almost famous."

Daphne left the gallery in a flurry of beige and *Arpège* and we went back to our sketching.

"Did that really happen?" I asked you.

"We're never sure when the fairies have been," you said.

By mid-March, it was clear I wouldn't have nearly enough new paintings for the exhibition in Abergavenny. The Dulwich Picture

Gallery agreed to send twenty of their canvases to Wales prior to releasing them to the buyers at the end of the exhibition. I gave my share of the proceeds to the war veteran's fund, happy to help a few boys who came home missing parts of their bodies and their minds.

Olivier had invited us to stop at his mother's house in Dorset on our journey back to London from Wales. She had a cottage, he said, that I might want to consider renting. The place was on a working farm, less than a ten-minute walk from the sea.

The night before we left, Olivier and I went to a dinner party at Tony's house in Kensington. "*J'aime votre poitrine*," Tony joked, staring down my décolletage in the drawing room after dinner. The Duchess of York was at the piano singing show tunes with a brilliantly funny young man. Olivier was trying to talk to her husband, who stutters. I thought I should rescue him, but decided to ride it out with Tony and Tallulah. I went to a window to check. There was no sign of her claque either inside or outside the house.

"You came without reinforcements," I said to her; and Tony smiled and wandered off in search of another drink.

"I'm the hunter tonight," she answered, looking where Tony had just been. "Where I come from, your neckline would be considered downright indecent."

"Lucky for us both that I don't then, isn't it?" Someone had told me Tallulah wore a Symington side-lacer to flatten her bosom. "Do you know where the little girls room is?" I asked. "I have a fierce need to powder my nose."

"I will show you."

I was trying to get away from her, but she pressed in after me. There were candles burning in the powder room and she put them out with her fingers, which she licked first. "Shhh," she said. I wondered if I could find a light switch if I needed to.

"Tallulah, I." She covered my mouth with hers and I thought I tasted the juices of a woman — perhaps her own. I could imagine her shocking a cab driver by pleasuring herself in his car. I wanted to laugh. The Duchess of York was sitting within spitting distance of London's most outrageous acting sensation, who was committing a heinous crime in the loo. She put her hands down the front of my dress, caressing my breasts. I didn't know whether to smack her or laugh out loud.

"Lift your skirt," she ordered, and kneeled in front of me.

Outrageous. "I want you to beg," she said, and who knows, I might have if someone hadn't tapped gently at the powder room door.

"It must be the Duchess," Tallulah said, standing up and we both exploded in laughter. "To be continued."

We put on our best faces and walked out past a startled guest.

"Your dress," Olivier said when I came back into the drawing room, and I straightened it. Tony winked. Later they would call it "Loo skirt" whenever they saw my hem in disarray.

"No, I am not responsible," Tony now exclaims. "That was Olivier. I like pretty bottoms. What reason on earth would I have to warn you when yours was showing."

"Oh, dear liar." I say. I am not changing a word.

The train trip from Victoria Station to Cardiff took about two hours. "No wonder English people smell," you noticed, "They are so close together." Wales was filled with unsightly black mounds of coal. It would take more than my paintings to brighten this landscape as quiet as death. It was horrible to think that men toiled and died in the dark under those green hills curled up like temple dogs guarding the valleys and the sheep that grazed there. I thought I heard the dead speak.

I wonder if all those boys and men who died in the muck in France were relieved when their war ended? Were they happy to leave behind the smell of septic wounds and latrines, the bad food and unwashed bodies? Did they welcome the bullets parting the air as they came toward them? Did they lie down to sleep in the mustard gas as willingly as Boulie and I had embraced our opium dreams that night in Chinatown? The real victims, I am sure, are the ones who remember.

Meanwhile, those of us who had survived the war and the subsequent plague that took millions of lives did our best to dance around our beloved ghosts because life must go on.

I couldn't wait to write to Nora and tell her about our hosts', the Rhys-Llewellyns, grass parterre, a labyrinth pattern of gravel paths and lawns enameled with seasonal wildflowers and bulbs that grew right through the grass. She would have delighted in the sod benches planted with chamomile and other fragrant herbs from which the various gardens were viewed.

The exhibition at the lovely country house went well. Dulwich Picture Gallery sent a man down to look after the loans from their sale. I wanted to go straight back to London and my bed at Claridge's, but we were expected at his mother's farm near Beaminster. We got off the train at Bridport, where we were picked up and helped into a pony-cart by her shepherd, who, if I heard him correctly, because his dialect was almost impossible for me to understand, resented our intrusion because he was in the middle of lambing. His employer was away in Monte Carlo. I wanted to turn right around, but the train had already left. I am glad we didn't because the farm, Meadowgrove, was heaven sent.

We knew as soon as we saw the cottage, one of a handful surrounded by meadows enclosed by singing hedgerows and stone walls and filled with grazing sheep, that we would take the let. Tom, the shepherd, carried in our bags and lit a fire in the stone fireplace. He pumped water, lit the woodstove and kerosene lamps and told us his wife had put provisions in the icebox. She had also made a loaf of bread, which was still warm on the cutting board. After showing us where to find dishes, tea and sugar he left, giving directions so we could find him or his wife if we needed anything. She would come down each morning to tidy and cook.

"What is an outhouse, Poppy?" you asked. We would know soon enough.

The farm was a dream. I thought of Marie Antoinette playing farmer at the Trianon and laughed at myself, thinking no doubt

Tom the shepherd and his good wife Alison would be laughing too. After eating our country dinner, you and I carried an oil lamp up the narrow stairs to the low-roofed second floor and found our bedrooms. You were thrilled with your cupboard bed with drawers beneath and a window that looked toward the main house, a small Norman castle. My bedroom was also tiny with a large double bed, a chest of drawers and a commode with a bowl and pitcher for washing crammed in. The third bedroom could be cleared for painting.

I could be well and strong in Dorset. You could go a little wild. We would eat good food and live as the farmers did; rising with the sun and settling down like the birds in the hedgerows at dusk. I couldn't wait to return in spring and see the wildflowers growing in a field that was not used for grazing, where Tom told us his employer had allowed the soil to sour in order to allow some space for flower seeds to take root.

You slept with me the first night. We lay in bed and told our stories. You sang a song about fairies. As summer followed spring, I would gather flowers with you and teach you the recipes for Nora's potions. I couldn't wait to mix rosebuds, daisies, and dew, the ingredients for joy. While you went to sleep, I wondered how we could possibly think we understood the world without knowing how the earth sustained us. I thought of all the children who believed milk appeared by magic on the doorstep each morning.

In the morning, I woke up first and went downstairs to light the fireplace, which had kindling and a few days supply of wood neatly stacked beside it. There was a letter on the mantle, sent to me care of Tom. It was from Olivier.

Marry me? The note said.

13

My Lovely Love,

I couldn't face a crowd this evening, so I had a tray by myself in my cabin. Tony went to the dining room to eat and do reconnaissance. The strangest thing happened today. We were just clearing our things from the writing room and about to go back to our cabins to dress for lunch, when a man approached us. He was Chinese, about fifty, wearing a business suit and round glasses — some kind of *petit fonctionaire* I thought, or a businessman, as he approached us.

"I am Mr. Lee, an associate of the Soong family," he said, bowing to us. Mr. Lee handed Tony a card and gave me an envelope with my name on it. It was Chou's handwriting. My hand trembled so badly I couldn't open it, so I passed it to Tony, who took out the letter and handed it back to me.

"Dear Poppy," it said. "I hope to meet you in Singapore. All will be well. Precious is not in danger. Yours faithfully, Chou."

"What do you make of it?" Tony asked.

"It's his writing." I was torn between jubilation and rage, because Chou was being his usual enigmatic self. What did this mean? Had Chou rescued you, or was he part of a plot with God knows what Byzantine purpose? Did "not in danger" mean "safe" or something a degree or two more precarious than that? At home, Olivier, Tony and I had gone through all the possibilities for your whereabouts. Had you got lost in Hong Kong and been abducted into the white slave trade, your virginity highly valued on the Asian market? Perhaps the Han family had come down from Peking and claimed you as reparation for the dishonour of Boulie and her mother. As I saw it, China was a labyrinth with no way out, now more than ever with political instability in the North.

"Mr. Lee," Tony asked. "Please tell us what you can. This lady is frantic about the child and she is in delicate health."

"I am sorry." Mr. Lee spoke English, I realised, with a posh accent. "I have only the letter and instructions to leave the ship with you in Shanghai. If Soong Chou says she is safe, then she is safe. Please don't worry"

"He didn't say, "safe," Mr. Lee. Our agreement was that Precious would be *safe* at the Soong house in Hong Kong."

"Try not to worry. Mr. Soong will explain when he meets you."

"Mr. Lee," I begged "*Jang-xin-bi-xin*" — Imagine my heart was yours. Chou had taught me the Confucian expression when I was a child.

"I do." When Mr. Lee bowed again, I thought I saw tears in his eyes; but before I could be sure he was gone.

After seeing me to my cabin, Tony went to inquire about Mr. Lee. The purser had no idea who he was. There was no Mr. Lee on the passenger list. We hadn't seen any Orientals in first class. In fact, we had remarked on it, wondering if there was a prohibition. I hadn't made the arrangements for you to travel with Chou. In which class would you have made the voyage, I wondered? I hadn't thought to ask. How stupid of me. Now I would give anything to know where you had and had not been on the ship. I know if I can get close to a fingerprint or a shared empirical experience, a sheet or napkin, I will be helped in tracking you. You will tell me, just as you did in the game of hot and cold, if I am getting closer.

Tony went to dinner, thinking that Mr. Lee must have joined the ship in Honolulu. Perhaps he was traveling under another name and would turn up during the evening meal.

"Was he there?"

"No, and no one else has seen him."

I wondered if all Asiatics were invisible to my fellow passengers, if the person who washed their clothes or served their meal in a favourite restaurant turned up at dinner on the *Empress of Asia*, would they recognize him? I certainly had lived for years in the same house with men whose identities were unknown to me.

Tony and I are carrying on with my letters, partly because they have their own momentum and partly because I truly will go mad if I am not distracted. Mr. Lee has, if anything, complicated things. His presence is at once reassuring and unsettling.

In ship's language, I am trying my best to keep a steady course, even though that has not been my habit. If having a baby out of wedlock had been a navigational error, I went even further astray when I married Olivier. Tallulah, who is nothing if not exacting with language, called him a *lymph*. When I asked her what that meant, she said, "He walks with a lisp, Darling. Olivier is so frail an ejaculation would blow him off the face of the earth." I must admit I was surprised by his proposal, having decided he was one of those men I could count on as a friend, but would hardly consider as a lover or husband. Besides, Olivier had courted Boulie in Victoria. That was a bit off-putting.

I had thought of the cottage in Dorset as independence, not a tender trap. Olivier was smart, funny, and kind, but hard to imagine as anything but a bachelor. As I turned his letter over and over while I waited for the kettle to boil, I made mental lists. Perhaps if I married, I could put my sexual demons to rest.

Alec was dead. Chou had a wife. There was no way in this world that I could marry him. You adored Olivier. He would be good to you, as Stanford had been to me. I could depend on him, and there would be lots of breathing space in our life together. He spent so much time on the continent that I would be left alone to paint to my heart's content. Besides, I had already fallen in love with the farm.

On the other hand, there was a strong possibility I would not survive another childbirth. I would have to tell Olivier and that would put an end to it. I was sure he had a dynastic incentive for getting married. In the meantime, he was very respectful. I couldn't believe he thought I was a virgin, but the topic never came up.

Whether people consider the reasons to marry or not marry, they still make mistakes. At the end of the day, Olivier and I took the risk. You would be our "pretend" child. I assumed Olivier, as a man of the world, meant he knew how to avoid conception. We got on together. I made him laugh. He made me laugh. That was as good a reason as any for marriage. Perhaps, I hoped, romance would follow. It wasn't unheard of. Without any courtship, except some amusing times *à trois* with you, we decided to be married in London without telling either of our mothers.

We invited a handful of wedding guests — Edward and Moulie Molyneux and Dola, who came over from France as Daphne had from Scotland *sans* her lover, HRH, who now took my calls, Olivier's great friend Tony, and you, of course, as flower girl. Edward made our frocks, ivory silk with dropped waists and matching jackets with peony-shaped buttons made of the same fabric. My cloche hat was also made of the silk, with yet another peony on one side. Your wreath of freesias and lily-of-the-valley looked beautiful in your black hair. I carried a small bouquet of calla lilies, white roses, rosemary and myrtle.

"The rosemary and myrtle are for longevity and loyalty," I told you.

Tallulah, the bad fairy who wasn't invited because of Olivier's loathing for her, told me I should sit in a warm comfrey bath to restore my hymen to a virginal state. I asked her whatever gave her the idea I needed it.

I was so nervous that all I can remember of our wedding was trying to still you and the trembling flowers in my bouquet. When we
came out of the chapel and walked through the graveyard to our
waiting cars, there was a light spring rain, which intensified the
smell of the lilacs blooming around the church. Olivier covered us
with his umbrella and I felt sure he would protect us.

A few more friends joined us for lunch at the Savoy, so we were
twenty. We had shrimp bisque, lemon sorbet, beef Wellington, my
favourite St. Honoré cake with rose petals dipped in sugar and lots
and lots of champagne. Almost everyone made funny speeches,
especially Tony, who followed every verb with "willy nilly," where-
upon Olivier's friends laughed like mad.

When we were on the train to Dorset, where we honeymooned
at the cottage, I asked Olivier what was so funny. "Willy is my
little fellow," he said. I doubted I would ever adjust to English potty
humor, but I was excited nevertheless about my wedding night. We
were husband and wife and our lovemaking would be blessed. I
couldn't wait to tuck you into bed and put on my new silk nightgown. Because we had waited, the consummation of our marriage
would be that much more romantic.

That evening, when we got between flannel sheets warmed and
sprinkled with lilac blossoms by Tom's wife Alison, Olivier explained
he wasn't much good at the sex part, but he knew I wouldn't mind
abstaining because of my heart. I felt as if I had been slapped.

During our short engagement, when he had kissed me on the
cheek and otherwise avoided contact, I thought he was delightfully
old-fashioned. When I objected on our first evening as husband and
wife, he kissed me on the forehead, turned his back to me and said
that when I had come into the room with Tallulah at Tony's he
thought I'd made my sexual preference clear.

Willy nilly. So *this* was how Olivier practised birth control. Lying
in the dark wearing my beautiful new nightgown in our nuptial bed
strewn with flowers, I realised I'd made what Nora called a lavender
marriage. I was furious. Many of my somewhat ambivalent friends

had settled down, just as I would have. Olivier had betrayed me.

"You lied, Olivier," I kept my voice down so you wouldn't hear in the next room.

"Don't be silly, Poppy. You must have known. Many of our friends live this way. We'll have fun; don't worry. I'll be a good husband."

"I want to be loved."

"I do love you Poppy, in my way. Can't you tell?"

"How would I?"

I have to say that for all the snobbish condescension to Americans in Canada and Britain, at least the Americans are candid. "When I buy a horse, I look at its teeth," my mother said, and now I knew what she meant. Primed for a night of conjugal pleasure, it was all I could do not to help myself with Olivier lying like lox beside me. I turned from my enigmatic bridegroom and stuffed the corner of the pillowslip in my mouth so he wouldn't hear me weeping for Chou.

I wondered what this marriage made me. Not a wife, surely. Not a mistress. I wasn't even an acknowledged mother. I would have to be content with being a painter. I imagine I was supposed to be grateful for the opportunity to be *something* and make the best of it. When I finally fell asleep, I dreamed Daphne winked at me while she drank champagne from my wedding slipper.

The next morning, Olivier was up first, and, when I came down to the kitchen, he had made us a full English breakfast. Olivier kissed me on both cheeks, and, asking if I had slept well, poured me a cup of tea. If you hadn't been there, I might have cheerfully dumped the scalding liquid in his lap.

After breakfast, he took you to feed the chickens and I sat at the kitchen table warming my hands on my cup of tea, wondering how my life managed to make itself extraordinary every time. I just couldn't do anything simple. It had to be fraught. Looking down at my chaste nuptial nightgown, I started to laugh. I'll bet my new friends were laughing too.

There was a knock at the door and I opened it to a woman who could only be Claire Mandeville. My new mother-in-law was wearing a beautiful tweed skirt, a cashmere sweater set with three strands of pearls held in place with a diamond fastener, and rubber boots, or Wellies as the English called them. Claire had naturally curly auburn hair, like Olivier, and, as it fell over one green eye, she was constantly tossing her head. Her other characteristic gesture was a turned down mouth, stiffened by her assumption of a British upper class accent. I thought it made her look rather like a codfish, even though she was very pretty in that petite French way.

Claire looked me up and down, as if to say she was as surprised by my appearance as I was by hers. "You won't be feeding my chickens in that negligée, will you?" Not that feeding chickens was my responsibility. I suppose she just had to let me know I was inappropriately dressed. Bloody right, I thought, all tricked out for my farcical wedding night with your son.

I told her that Olivier and my cousin Precious were possibly doing just that and asked if she had received my post-dated cheques for the rent. Oh no, she told me, she didn't *do* money, and at least we were on common ground there. Probably, assuming I was an American, she thought I did money all the time. Then she narrowed her eyes, asking if Olivier had just come, and I thought, no he didn't, the bugger, but said yes. Just. He could tell her about our marriage himself.

After she left, I poured myself another cup of lukewarm tea and laughed some more. I could hear Boulie doing a sublime Claire impersonation. It occurred to me that Claire might have been impersonating herself. I am not expert at English accents, but hers was so tweedy it smelled like wet sheep.

Olivier slept in his mother's house for the next two nights, and he fixed up my studio in the daytime. On the third day, he arrived with an invitation asking us for tea with Claire. Since I was used to my mother's social evaluations being reflected in the quality of the tea, I was curious to see what Claire would offer us. I wasn't disappointed. We were obviously judged members of an almost untouchable caste, the fare consisting of potted cheese and toast and not a drop of sherry. I wished for Boulie to materialize at that moment. How could I summon her from the bone house to haunt this woman, who sat beside her son and petted him hard, as if he were one of the half-dozen hunting dogs that lounged around the enormous fireplace in her hall? Where *do* these mothers come from, and why do they find me? Where was Boulie when I needed her? She would have made faces, and I would have laughed so hard I might have peed myself and ruined one of Claire's precious Chippendale chairs.

Clearly, Olivier had no intention of telling his Mama that we were married. Two can play at the same game. I wondered if I could prevail on you to keep it quiet. The marriage was just a lovely game, I told you. We played wedding because we wanted to wear new clothes and have a party. Wasn't it fun? I wasn't pretending to laugh. You clapped your hands and laughed with me. My, we were laughing a lot.

We relaxed in the country. You and I ate simply, buying produce from my undeclared husband's family farm. The farmhands were too busy with their work to do anything beyond routine maintenance of the cottage and garden, so we didn't get our own vegetable patch. In the mornings we painted and in the afternoons we took picnics and sketchbooks, explored the hills and streams and beaches along the coast, turning up bird's eggs and wild flowers, naming the swallows and finches and gulls that lived in the trees and by the sea. Once we found wild strawberries growing among the beach grasses and, amazed that we had beaten the birds to them, stuffed ourselves with the small, sweet fruit. We dozed in the late sun, listening to birds, squirrels and rabbits making their homes in verges made of dog roses and filled in with wildflowers I had previously thought of as weeds. Perhaps because of the buttercups and the rich cheese and butter we ate in the sun, you turned a delicious golden colour. We girls went wild in Dorset, even as the cod-mouthed Claire deadheaded the roses in her ubiquitous pearls.

Olivier wrote regularly from Paris and London. He sent wonderful letters, filled with details, to both of us. You asked if we could have a pretend honeymoon in Paris. I thought that was a very good idea. You slept with the books and toys your pretend step-cousin had sent under your pillow, so you would dream of your own bridegroom.

"Wasn't it wedding cake we were supposed to dream on?" I asked you.

"It's pretend, Poppy," you said. "Don't you understand pretend?" You were six, just the age when children begin to disbelieve. I wonder how much of this you remember? This is my version of our story of course, but I do hope they are mostly happy memories for you.

One afternoon, Claire lumbered down the drive in her dusty Rolls and said that since she was going into town to run some errands, my little cousin might like to go with her and have an ice cream at the teashop. This gesture was unprecedented and I wondered if I could trust you to keep our secret. Ice cream is ice cream and I couldn't deny my beauty a treat, so you and your favourite doll, Pinchy Baby, got into the car and sat beside Claire.

I lay on the wicker chaise longue, enjoying the peacefulness of the garden and its lengthening shadows in the late afternoon, as butterflies and birds returned to their homes in the trees and hedgerows, and flowers, exhausted after a day of blooming in the sun, withdrew into shade. From where I rested with an unread copy of *The Voyage Out* and a glass of lemonade, I watched the trail of dust following Claire's car up the drive and experienced one of those moments of absolute bliss. Soon you would step into my arms, bringing me the story of your afternoon.

Claire drove right by our cottage without stopping. I was disappointed. Perhaps she was taking you to see something at the house. Fifteen minutes, perhaps a half hour went by. The chill of evening began to settle and I shivered. At seven o'clock, I walked across the field, annoyed by Claire's complete lack of manners. She was surprised to see me at her kitchen door. When I asked for you, she told me she had left you in town. She had gone to the wharf to buy fish and some children who were cod jigging off a float intrigued you. Claire had left you to find your own way back to the farm.

How would she do that? I begged my heart to calm down so that I could at least live long enough to rescue you. In a quiet and dangerous voice, I ordered her to give me her keys and then I drove her enormous, terrifying car into Bridport. No one in her right mind leaves six-year-olds alone in a strange or potentially danger-ous place, where they can drown or be abducted. By now, you could have been half way across the Channel, floating upside down in a school of dead babies flushed from the shores of England or France, or in the company of a desperate man.

In town, I asked the first person I saw to give me directions. The elderly lady jumped in the car, bless her heart, and led me to the wharf. I parked the car and got out and ran. That wharf could have been five miles long. I couldn't run fast enough. It was the only time I ever took the risk.

There you were, first a speck and then a real girl sitting all alone on the end of the wharf with your doll. I stopped and whistled with what little air I had left, but you couldn't respond.

"She left me," you said, between sobs, and I sank to my knees and hugged you until you begged for mercy. The lady who had helped me dug in her pocket for a piece of barley sugar to cheer you up, and we drove home.

That night, we asked the banshees to pinch Claire until she was black and blue.

I have learned there is no space at all between life and death. A moment can go by and everything changes, even though all appears to be the same in the outer world. The clocks keep on ticking, the tides go in and out. You could have vanished as easily as a fish leaves the sea for the last time or lost children move through the sewers of London. How does one know who would be reckless with the life of a child? That night, when I sang you to sleep, I half believed that you were already gone and I was imagining you. I touched you everywhere, your face, your arms and legs, your round little tummy, fearing my hands would pass right through you.

While you slept, I lay awake wondering what makes people the way they are. I had assumed there might be something in Claire that I would respect because Olivier had a gift for certain kinds of intimacy, friendship at least, but I was wrong. Like my mother, she could nurture plants, but not people. Their children flourished in spite of them. Olivier and I understood that about one another. I decided there was no point in confronting Claire. Since she appeared to be completely out of touch with her own maternal feelings, she wouldn't understand.

As the days got shorter and the rams were let out with the ewes, I began to feel restless, wondering about my friends in London, longing to go to the theatre or visit the art galleries to see what was new. When I told Claire that I was going to go to London with my new paintings, she offered me the key to her flat, which had recently been redecorated. I protested that I had rooms at Claridge's, but she insisted. We were invited for tea and she would hand over the key. I thought she was offering reparations and wondered how on earth I would explain to her that there was no compensation for risking the safety of a child. This time, we were offered scones with current jelly. There was no mention of the wharf incident. She suggested I might like to trade a painting of her farm for a month's rent. "I don't want to Jew you down," she said. "You must tell me what they sell for."

"I don't *do* money," I told her, coldly. "My gallery will be happy to make arrangements with you."

There were dozens of times I had held my tongue in the polite drawing rooms of London where anti-Semitism was as common as the jokes about Chinese cuckolds in Victoria. No one questioned it. In retrospect, I am so proud of my mother, who, although she accepted the position of bosses and workers, did not disrespect her employees' culture or change our surname as so many Jews, fearing prejudice, did.

We checked in at Claridge's and I got Miss Brown to sleep over while I went with Daphne to see Tallulah in Noel Coward's *Fallen Angels*. I was in a dangerous mood. "Jew you down," I kept thinking, "Jew you down?" My God, I thought the English prided themselves on their manners.

Tallu was already drinking in her dressing room with some of her gallery girls by the time we got backstage. "Want one?" she offered.

"I'll have a double," I answered.

My actress friend asked about married life and I filled her in while she removed her make up and dressed for dinner.

"I told you so," Daphne laughed. We clicked glasses and toasted the men we had loved and left. Tallu announced that she had an impossible crush on Naps Alington, who was about as *lymph* as it gets and had a reputation for sleeping with the help.

"Did any heterosexual men survive the war?" I asked.

"I doubt it, but I haven't tried all of them yet, so there is hope," Tallulah laughed.

"To my bridegroom, Olivier," I said, laughing.

"To Lord Alington," Tallulah drained her glass and gathered her gallery girls. "Are you and Daphne joining us?"

"Poppy needs her beauty sleep." Daphne replied.

"Where to?" she asked when we got in the cab. There were two keys in my evening purse.

"I have an idea," I said, and gave the address to the cab driver.

The house was very chic — Art Deco, silver and white, devoid of blood, like my mother-in-law. I poured Daphne a boggy tasting Scotch, from a crystal decanter on the butler's tray in the drawing room and led her up stairs where we found a bedroom with a huge round bed with a round-mirrored headboard that matched the dressing table. She knocked back her drink and lay on the bed, spreading out her arms. I turned on a lamp so I could see her, and put a record on the Victrola.

"We are very synesthetic," I said, taking off my shoes and lying down beside her. She was wearing midnight satin with bugle beads. I was in my Luna moth dress, slate velvet with winged *devoré* sleeves. We watched ourselves in the mirror. She started singing along, "*Can you tame wild wimmen?*" in her voice the colour of prairie wheat and I laughed and laughed. How did that record find its way into this temple of urban chic?

"Do you want to dance?" she asked. We stood on the bed and put our arms around one another's waists. I felt her breasts, her stomach and her thighs slithering under the satin dress. Daphne was still singing, her breath warm in my ear. She took my earlobe in her mouth and my earring. I could feel the pearl floating on her tongue and I wanted her to swallow it and me with it.

I put my hands on her shoulders and pulled down her dress. She was naked under it. I kissed her shoulders and her stomach, taking the skirt the rest of the way down. I felt her breath on my neck as she unbuttoned my frock and pulled it over my head, running her hands over my body as she did so. "Time to stop beading around the bush," she said, taking the beaded hem and my silk panties in one gentle handful, and laughed. I closed my eyes and imagined I was passing through her, emerging trembling and weak as a chrysalis from the darkness inside.

We slowly pleasured one another, sipping the elixir of desire, our tongues circling, arousing us to the moment when we opened — shuddering — the way butterflies emerge fantastic and wet to dry in the sun.

"Whose bed are we blessing tonight?" Daphne asked as we sank into our pleasant sleep.

14

My Precious,

Now you know your mother is a naughty, vindictive girl. I believe Claire deserved to have her bed defiled by Daphne and me after what she did to you, and I don't regret it. Sometimes we have to stand up for ourselves. I wouldn't make a habit of Daphne. She was too dangerous. But she did, as they say, fill the bill on that occasion.

Tony has already done his morning tour of the ship. No sign of an early bird Mr. Lee or whatever his real name is, doing his *tai chi*, greeting the morning sun on any of the decks. I find his disappearance infuriating. Maybe that is a good thing. I have moved from grief to rage. Rage will push me toward you.

"Perhaps Mr. Lee is a ghost who came out of the sea," I say to Tony.

"I don't think so Poppy, because we're on the same page. We can't both be delusional, can we?"

We are getting closer to Japan. I can feel it in the agitated rhythm of the ship. The passengers are getting restless. Expectant chatter and laughter erupt all around us. The unknown engages and intimidates my shipmates, as it does me.

Perhaps I chose to befriend dangerous women because I needed to understand my mother. That is what my Harley Street psychiatrist told me, when I went to see him after my disappointment with Olivier. I suppose one has to be a little mad in order to become an artist.

Tony and I have been having the usual discussion about how much to put in this account of my life. He is beginning to think like an editor, suggesting that I prune here and there. I realise the part about baptizing my mother-in-law's bed doesn't put me in the best possible light, but you should know that women can and should rebel when they are violated. I am not saying every bride should have an affair when her husband is dishonest and her mother-in-law is a bitch, but that is what I did. The heart can only hold so much pain.

You and Miss Brown were still in bed when I came home from Claire's flat. I would love to report that Daphne and I were awakened in the middle of the night by the sound of a key in the lock in the front door, and that Claire came in and discovered her rumpled bed while we made a hasty departure down the fire escape, naked and laughing, our shoes and evening dresses in our hands. Or, better still, that Olivier turned up with his good friend Tony and we had Scotch and eggs together. That didn't happen either. I woke up at dawn, shook my friend awake, helped her dress, pulled the bed together and half-carried her out to the street where we hailed two separate cabs.

I waited for Claire to have a word with me about my little visit to her flat, but she said nothing when I returned the key, or afterward. I can't believe we didn't leave evidence, a lipstick-stained drinking glass, or an earring.

I had deliberately careless friends. Not long after my night at Claire's, Tallulah left her silver cigarette case with the cabochon sapphire under my pillow. When Olivier, who was sitting on the bed waiting for me to get dressed for a party, found it, he asked whose it was. I shrugged my shoulders. I hadn't noticed Tallu's initials and the date engraved under the sapphire. Unless it belonged to someone with lung disease, Olivier acidly remarked, we only knew one person with the initials T.B. Tallu and I were never in my bed together, although we sometimes had afternoon tea in my room.

In October, we packed up the cottage and returned to London for the winter. Olivier moved in with us at Claridge's and we shared the master bedroom. He thought it would be brilliant to let Claire in on our domestic secret, and so he invited her for lunch, *à trois*, on one of her visits to the city. We chose the Savoy because it was public and, since it was likely that one or more of her friends would be in the restaurant, she might not make a scene.

To say that Claire had a hissy fit when Olivier announced our marriage would be gross understatement. Olivier's distraught parent threw around a lot of strong language, including the blasphemies "American" and "Jew," irrevocably alienating me and disgusting her son. I had to give it to Claire, with her cunning insight and discreet sources of genealogical information she probably knew more about me than I realised. I drank too much and laughed too loudly. Short of throwing my drink in her face, I couldn't think of anything else to do.

I wanted to see our abysmal lunch through to the end, but Olivier, who was pained by his mother's appalling behaviour, walked out, leaving us girls staring our mutual loathing over the cheese. Since Olivier and I had invited Claire, I paid for lunch. Then I took out my lip rouge and applied it in public while she winced. I was so glad we hadn't taken you along. Afterward, I went back to Claridge's and slept for the rest of the day.

"Are we still pretending?" you asked the following spring. I realised that the veil of infancy was lifting and I had to give you some kind of real life. We simply couldn't live like gypsies forever.

Camping in a hotel, no matter how luxurious, is no life for a child. My marriage was a farce, albeit a pleasant one. Olivier remained a very good friend. He called me *Poupée* and was otherwise affectionate. Even though I was homesick, I was still hesitant about throwing you into whatever situation my mother had created in Victoria.

The very fact that Nora didn't mention the Prohibition in her letters was suspicious. Under normal circumstances, my mother was the first to enjoy at good story at someone else's expense. She would surely have told me all about the romps and lawlessness if she were not part of it.

It was chic among London's *avant-garde* to talk about outlaws during our time there. From Mayfair to Bloomsbury, the latest gossip about Mafia gangs and rumrunners went through the city as quickly as bushfires. There were stories about speakeasies, illegal clubs where girls and whiskey could be bought, and non-stop parties on floating bars outside the three-mile limit on both coasts of America. We heard about hijackings and machine gun murders, things that wouldn't have been discussed in polite circles before the war.

A raffish looking man from Vancouver told me that he was from a fish-packing family that slipped mickey bottles into the bellies of freshly killed and cleaned salmon and then exported them to the United States. Someone else one-upped him and commented that they were also using human cadavers to transport whiskey. Smugglers were getting rich, reportedly making seven or eight-hundred-per cent profit on liquor they moved across the Canadian-American border. I didn't dare to ask my louche party companion if he knew any bootleggers from Victoria.

As I grew more worried about my mother and Chou, my desire to paint diminished. Used to living in a big house by the sea, I began to feel claustrophobic at Claridge's and experienced frequent heart palpitations. Olivier suggested that we go to Dorset while Claire spent the winter in France. I told him he must be mad. I would have preferred death on the rack to another moment in the symbolic lap of his mother, who mercifully ignored us after her inexcusable behaviour at the Savoy. I suspected Olivier popped down to see her at the farm once in a while. I didn't hold it against him. Mothers are magnets, no matter how evil.

There was no question of my buying a house and staying permanently in London. England was not our home, and you and I were two-thirds of the family arrangement. I needed to see Soong Chou before he took Boulie's bones home to China. Even more, I wanted to say a proper goodbye to Boulie. Once I had made the decision to be at home before her seven years were up, I settled down to work again.

Olivier couldn't bear the sight of Tallulah. Despising her had nothing to do with jealousy, he said, but was because she was so common. That simply wasn't true. If my friend was coarse, her vulgarity was deliberate. She was a revolutionary, rebelling against the conventional wisdom, especially in the American South, where women were treated with Marian subjectivity. When I protested that common and vulgar was not the same thing and, in her culture, Tallu was something of an aristocrat, albeit a renegade one, he just sniffed. He wasn't fond of theatre people in general. They were so *artificial*, he said. I realise now that he was uncomfortable around the sexual openness of theatre people. Olivier was trying to pass, and he didn't want to be exposed.

That made our social life difficult because as soon as Dola had been sprung from Mademoiselle Ozanne's in Paris and brought to London where her mother was attempting to launch her youngest and two of her granddaughters, Dola went crazy for the London stage and one actress in particular. I felt obligated to help our old friend make social contacts and I didn't like the constraints Olivier was putting on my efforts.

In no time at all, Dola had become the ultimate gallery girl, forsaking her mother's social ambitions. Excited beyond reason by the incendiary vision of Tallulah in her infamous lacey underwear in *Fallen Angels*, she decided it was time to pledge her troth. By the time she had worked her way backstage one night Tallu and I had already left. Poor Dola stalked us all over London, and finally found us at the *Eiffel Tower*, a private club in Soho. Dola and her cousin Jimmy Audain couldn't get in, but they sent a note, which Tallulah used to light her cigarette.

"Dola is sweet," I argued. "She's a friend of my family." I finally convinced Tallu to answer the note and promise to include her in the post-performance festivities if she showed up the following night.

Dola, if nothing else, was dogged. Olivier actually called her "the little dog." I have nothing bad to say about her, apart from the fact that she is rather pathetic, more so now that she has picked up Tallulah's bad habits. After much wooing and spending, her prey warmed up to Dola's maternal qualities and willingness to treat at all times and they became something of a twosome, insofar as Tallu was two with anyone.

Olivier didn't learn many of my secrets — either through intuition or pillow talk — because our marriage lacked the kind of intimacy that comes with physical bonding. He knew nothing of my suspicions about my mother, or Chou, nor did I feel at that time that I had to tell him that you were my child.

In the spring of 1923, my mother wrote to tell me that the Exclusion Act, designed to limit Chinese emigration and prevent the reunification of Chinese families in Canada, was being rushed through parliament. Another insult. I drew Chou as I remembered him and then slowly rubbed him out with my art eraser.

Tony, Olivier and I had become inseparable. When Olivier traveled, Tony was my surrogate husband and a brilliant second step-cousin to you. Tony loved games. We spent many happy family evenings together playing Dictionary or Truth or Dare, which heated up after you went to bed. The way to Tony's heart was through my silver cocktail shaker. Two or three martinis with only a breath of vermouth and I had him in the palm of my hand. I realise I am *showing* my hand by revealing this, but there it is.

"Truth or dare?" I asked one night.

"Truth," Tony said bravely, because the dares were easy. He was fearless about running down the hall in his underwear, standing no hands on the windowsill, or eating a whole tin of chocolate covered bees.

"Tell me about your most unforgettable sexual experience."

"With a man or a woman?"

"Both, of course." I smiled, pulled his drunken head in my lap and massaged his temples until he purred.

"Can I exaggerate?"

"No."

"Long ago and far away, I fell in love with a Prince," he began.

"Not *the* Prince." I relaxed my knees and let his head loll dangerously. "How banal. Everyone has had a go at the Prince."

"This was a metaphorical Prince, Poppy. My Prince lived in a tower with his Princess sister."

"Was he in love with both of them?"

"Yes, actually, yes. Everyone loved everyone."

"Was the princess beautiful?"

"Not quite. She was very pretty."

In London I *had* evolved from moth to butterfly. Attractive and somewhat androgynous, diurnal by necessity, I was the right kind of girl for the time. All my life, I had compared myself to my mother, an extraordinary looking woman. Now I could see that a slender girl with approachable if not classically beautiful features and my father's reddish blonde hair needn't feel dull. Because of my new confidence and my marginally eccentric status as a painter, I became more assertive about the way I dressed and the manner in which I expressed my opinions.

I wondered how I would be received at home; if Emily would find that I had grown and if she would forgive me for ignoring her advice. I think she was worried I would become my mother, someone she didn't understand or like, even though they had their similarities. Emily failed to see the artistry in Nora's gardening, because it was a traditional feminine occupation. As far as I know, she had no idea about the other world my mother inhabited.

Critically, I found myself in a similar situation. Painting, like gardening, is a traditionally acceptable pastime for ladies. Certainly, some of the *avant-garde* painters regard me with condescension. I admire Cubism and the new abstract approaches to painting, and indeed, I think there is an element of abstraction in my work. It is just that I don't have a statement to make, or a name to make for myself, outside the mainstream of life. That is my personality and my *ars poetica*. I don't believe that I will care when I die that my obituary says nothing about changing the direction of modern art.

No effort guarantees immortality except giving life to the next generation. I haven't the desire or the vigour to struggle for affirmation. I leave that to others, some of them remarkable, some pathetic in their quest for recognition. Emily Carr is extraordinary and she will overcome the limitations of a woman's life. I admire her, but I do not envy her.

During our last Christmas in London, Olivier surprised us by giving us two months in Paris as a gift. There was a studio free in *la ruche*, the building occupied by Chagall and Modigliani before his death, and Olivier sublet it for the months of February and March. When I think of how things have turned out, I am so glad we had that time in Paris together. There was just the two of us, except for Olivier's three-day visit at the end of the first fortnight and the weekend he settled us in. Having thought of France as Olivier's private room, I was amazed and touched by his thoughtfulness in inviting us.

Olivier was a quite different person in Paris, as he is in Victoria. He had his Paris wardrobe, which was much less *comme il faut* than his somewhat stuffy London kit. In Paris, he eschewed the handmade silk shirts and fine leather shoes for sweaters with holes in the elbows and scuffed brogues. I took his lead and brought minimal luggage, with only one party dress in case I stumbled on a festive occasion.

Our studio was rough. We shared a bathroom and, if we didn't stay on top of feeding the coal-burning stove, it was colder, Olivier said, than a nun's jewels. We sent our clothes out to be laundered by a model who needed the money, but washed our own underwear and hung it over the stove to dry. *La ruche*, a building shaped like a beehive and surrounded by a little garden, was in the unfashionable Vaurigard district. Our closest neighbor was an *abattoir*. We could smell the blood.

In that bohemian neighbourhood, I would not be distracted by café society or by elegant shops and restaurants. We artists understood one another's need for privacy. Socializing when we chose to, we lived in a pleasant communal isolation. *La ruche*, with possibly one hundred studios, was its own city, even a world as the languages of many countries leaked through its thin walls. We could hear guitar playing from the Spaniards, singing from the Italians, argument from the Russians and sobbing from models taking abuse from irritable painters after sitting stiff and naked for hours in their cold studios. Our unconventional Paris nest was indeed a beehive of activity. There was never a moment at *la ruche* when we were cut off from the sounds and smells of life around us.

I heated onion soup from the market on our wood heater and we subsisted mostly on bread, cheese, beautiful French sausages, fruit, and cheap *vin rouge*. You loved eating warm croissants dipped in chocolate. The richness was in the quality of time you and I spent painting side by side, visiting the galleries and getting to know our neighbors, especially the Chagalls — Marc, his beautiful and intelligent wife Bella and little daughter Ida, who adored you. Bella was a Rosenfeld, which was also the family name of my father's mother.

Because it is the ultimate incivility to interrupt an artist at work, we were very careful about privacy. Even though life at *la ruche* was informal, no one would think to enter a room without knocking. This was especially important at the Chagalls' because Marc liked to paint in the nude. "*Attendez!*" he would shout, and we waited while he got his trousers on. It became the cry of the neighborhood, "*Attendez!*"

In retrospect, I realise it may be our common cultural heritage, but the work of artists like Chagall and Modigliani moved me more than the more intellectual painters. Like them, I worship the material world, the sensuality of nature, and the blessing of children. It is so sad that Modigliani died before his child was born. He could have painted exquisite Madonna and child portraits. Now that miracle is not to be. His girlfriend killed herself the day after his death.

Even though my friends in Paris were mostly figurative painters, I could experience the garden through them. In Marc's floating humans and animals, I revisited my own dreams. That was a kind of surrealism I could embrace. It had none of the hard edges and cynicism I felt in the work of Dali and the Cubists, Braque and Picasso, whose paintings of women I found disturbingly misogynistic.

We all experimented with Cubism, but we weren't comfortable with the mathematical archetypes. It was good for me to try it on and put it aside. As I watched my Paris friends at work, I understood Emily's struggle to find her voice in painting. Reducing nature to geometry is quite different from finding its elemental shapes and expressing its outward appearance in the language of dreams. What a privilege it was to walk in my neighbourhood and see canvases by Cézanne, van Gogh, Renoir and Matisse in the shop windows. Emily might forgive me for leaving if she could see how much I learned in that milieu.

My new friends and I had many discussions about realism and surrealism, our different perceptions of nature. I told Marc what Margot Asquith had said to Cecil Beaton, "I have no face, only two profiles" and he laughed. The next day he drew me with three. I think I have several secret personalities, and I was surprised that each aspect Marc drew revealed different parts of me.

Everyone in Paris was crazy for "indigenous" art and music. Seeing the influence of folk art on the painters here, I have also grown in my understanding of Emily's very strong identification with our aboriginal people. She once told me that her effort to make life drawings in Haida villages was regarded as spirit-snatching. That may have as much to do with her general avoidance of figurative art as does misanthropy.

We had fun in Paris. If I were to choose my rebirth, I think it might be as a Russian. The exuberance, the passionate intellectuality and family-centred lives of our Russian friends were a beautiful balance to our English experience. Marc would put his pixie face close to mine and actually spit out his passionately held beliefs. Even as a young man, he had begun writing the story of his life and he was trying his ideas on all of us. Like a wise old prophet, he often spoke in proverbs. "In art, as in life," he said, "everything is possible provided it is based on love." That is an amazing affirmation coming from someone who had witnessed the Cossacks burning Jewish villages.

In France, where there were fields filled with the bodies of young men like Alec who gave their lives for no reason, I wondered why everyone couldn't absorb that simple lesson. About his paintings created in reaction to war in France and pogroms in his own country, Marc insisted he wanted to breathe the breath of prayer into them — for redemption and resurrection.

He introduced me to a friend of his, a Madame Guerin who was making poppy pins out of red cloth and selling them to raise money for children who were victims of the Great War. She told me the killing fields looked like a sea of blood when the poppies bloomed in the lime rich soil.

"Could we go to see them?" I asked. "Perhaps we could hire a car and drive to Vimy Ridge."

We made a picnic the following Saturday. I was not prepared for what we saw in the fields and cemeteries outside Paris, the thousands upon thousands of graves and fields starting to bloom as if summer were still possible in this fallen world.

"Why are they all red, Poppy?" You asked.

"It's the soldiers' blood," I told her. "They are refusing to die."

I picked one for Alec and fixed it with the barrette in your hair.

None of us ate lunch. The following day, I began a series of poppy paintings using every colour but red. They were for the children. We all gave paintings to Madame Guerin for her art auction.

"We must work with seven fingers," Marc told me, using an unfamiliar Jewish expression, even though I had noticed this anatomical anomaly in his paintings. I realised that he meant giving one hundred and forty per cent of myself to my painting and regretted that my weakened heart wouldn't let me work as hard as I wished. That meant that however small my oeuvre I must put every ounce of energy and belief into it that I could muster. I would paint with seven fingers too, in my own way.

"*Attendons!*" we said in unison when one of us slipped into English. You would put your little hand over my mouth, "*Parles en francais, Poppy!*"

Our French improved greatly over those two months. Chattering with Ida, you were a sponge for the musicality of French, and by the end of our visit, I could hold my own in an abstract conversation. Mostly I stayed away from the Americans in Paris. I didn't want to drink with the English-speaking painters and writers and I had no desire to sleep with the rich American lesbians who seemed to be buying up all the intellectual property on the Left Bank. I met them a few times and that was enough. My Russian friends didn't speak English, so I assimilated French as quickly as I could. One night, when the children were asleep, I told Marc and Bella about my life. I admired the way they faced the world together and the strength they found in love and spirituality. Would I ever find a love like theirs?

What about Chou? Was I just *lo fan* to him even though we had been family for years? This was an amazing concept to assimilate. Since I had been raised in a climate of condescension to indentured Chinese workers, the idea that I was unacceptable, even repugnant to them, was a stunning reversal of the conventional wisdom. I had resisted such judgments; and for the first time I suspected they were made about me.

15

My Poor Wandering One,

There is a spa on the boat, which Tony discovered this morning. He made an appointment for me to have a full body rub. Since I decided against the steam bath because that would be dangerous to my heart, why not indulge myself? A very nice young man called William has taken all the kinks and unkindnesses out of my neck and shoulders, and I could feel my troubles leaving my body as he worked the tension down my arms and out through my hands.

William promised to try to locate Mr. Lee for us. Quite a few of the Chinese gentlemen have been in for massages. William, whom Tony and I are now calling Mr. Handsome, must know the backstairs of the *Empress of Asia* as well as anyone. I am sure William has left his shoes under quite a few bunks. I don't know who liked Mr. Handsome better, Tony, or me, but I suspect Tony will be booking a massage for himself before this voyage is finished.

Now we are back to the time we crossed the English Channel on our return from France, and the ride was rough. On that sailing, you and I were as sick as dogs. When we returned to London, I had two desiderata. I would try to make my marriage work, but I would not waver in my intention to return to Victoria and say farewell to my loved ones, Soong Chou and Boulie. While embracing my new life, I would not let the old one slip away unremarked. When he picked us up at Victoria Station, Olivier asked the driver to take us home by a different route.

"Surprise," he said. "Surprise." We stopped in front of a Georgian building in Chelsea. "Get out, girls!"

The flat, or I should say house, even though I still think of a house as free standing with its own garden around it, was stunning. Olivier had obviously been scheming for some time. He had sent us out of town so he could have free time to manufacture his tremendous surprise. I was touched and a little irritated. It was so typical of Olivier to think he should make all the decisions about where we would live and how the house would be decorated without consulting me.

The entry hall took my breath away. Its marble surfaces, seamless from floor to ceiling, were only interrupted by the horizontality of the silver stairs, silver deco wall lamps, and a chrome and glass table holding a large crystal vase filled with calla lilies. I soon discovered the whole house was decorated in shades of white, gray blue, silver and glass, very much like his mother's flat. Even your wooden sleigh bed was overlaid with silver leaf and had a white satin quilt. You, of course, took your shoes off right away and jumped on it.

The matrimonial bedroom was a temple of delight. How ironic, I thought, as I ran my hand over the Syrie Maugham gilded mahogany and camphor dressing table with ivory and crystal drawer pulls with silk tassels and glass and bronze screen, the pleated silk quilt, and the daybed shaped like a slice of the moon with its ermine throw. Olivier didn't forget a thing. My clothes hung in the mirrored armoire. My paintings hung on the walls. Even my photos in their silver frames were lined up on the mantle over the fireplace in our bedroom. Stunned and hurt, I nevertheless resolved to settle down in this thoughtful fugue as easily as I sank into my first bubble bath in our outrageously luxurious bathroom. Olivier meant well.

Since I had promised you that you could decorate your own walls when you next had a room of your own, I offered you the attic instead. Neither of us had the heart to compromise the wintry paradise Olivier had designed for us. You agreed to my plan and we got to work converting the bare attic walls into an imaginary world of animals and people living in a garden of gigantic proportions. I loved the role of *sous*-painter, taking orders. "This is what Emily does to her rooms," I told you, deciding that someday we would have our very own house and bloody well have the rooms painted the way we wanted them.

They say there is a moment in marriage when one of the partners hears a ripping noise, as if cloth had been rent, and that sound is the marriage being torn to pieces. Seeing the perfect house that I had no say in was that moment for me. I said nothing to Olivier because he wouldn't have understood.

After Easter, you went back to school and I got to work in my half of the attic, which Olivier equipped with easel, paints, pre-stretched canvases and sable brushes. There was no honeymoon between Olivier and me, but our house bubbled with vitality. The rooms reflected light pouring in floor to ceiling north-facing French windows, as he had intended they would. Friends came and went. We ate and slept and worked. I made my plans. Tallulah and Dola came for tea when Olivier was away.

Tallulah has such a way with words. She is the perfect tragic moment, every promise compromised. Another sharp fragment found its way from her mouth to my brain, and fit my mosaic of found truths. In her cups one evening, she let slip that my mother had killed my father. I wanted to tear off her lips, but I let her continue. It had been an accident. Hadn't Nora used just those words herself? There were cat burglars who followed café society around the world. Jewel thievery was a lucrative sport. Her older husband indulged her. She was beautiful, and precious things deserved to be worn by a woman as lovely as his wife. My father had given my mother a gun.

My parents slept apart. One night my father came into her room without knocking. Startled awake, she had shot him. My mother couldn't see who was approaching her in the dark. She was not charged, but the court of opinion decided it didn't want her around. Not in New York. Not in San Francisco.

Like Boulie, Tallulah was a veritable encyclopaedia of sin. I didn't want to believe her, but I knew she was right. Her story explained so much of mother's behaviour. When my friend filled me in, I wondered if the bullet that killed my father had also been seeking me out. Had that intelligent bullet followed me all the way to London? My hands and feet went numb. I remembered to breathe.

It made sense. Nora had kept her distance and infantilised me because she couldn't answer the questions I would ask. That terrible accident had put a curse on us, something Nora had translated into the language of fairies. I desperately wanted to talk to my mother, but it would have to wait until I arrived back in Victoria. Some things can't be put in a letter.

Late one spring morning, Ethel, our new cook, huffed and puffed up four flights of stairs up to the attic of the new house to tell me a weeping woman had asked for me at the kitchen door. As she had no idea who the stranger was, I told Ethel to keep this person in the kitchen and make her a cup of tea while I cleaned up. Cook was not to take the visitor to the drawing room, or to the little sitting room off Olivier's and my bedroom. I cleaned my brushes and my hands impatiently, resenting the interruption, and took my time going downstairs, stopping in front of a mirror to smooth my hair and my temper, wondering who would announce herself that way. At least I had the comfort of knowing there was no chance the woman would be my husband's disconsolate, pregnant mistress, something other women I knew had dealt with.

As I passed through the green baize door from the pantry to the kitchen, I heard sobbing and the comforting murmur of Cook's consolation.

"Daphne!" I stood still, paralyzed by the puddle of golden girl sitting at my kitchen table in a bloodstained ivory silk evening dress with a panel of beaded dragons around the waist, her arms and chest dripping blood. "What ever happened to you?"

"Fiona," she barely managed to get out, her shoulders shaking.

"Oh my God. Cook, get the first-aid kit, please." I found some neatly folded tea towels in a drawer, poured warm water over them and carefully began to wash her wounds. "Shouldn't you have gone to a doctor?"

"How could I?" She began sobbing harder.

"I thought men did this to us, not women." She had been cut in several places, but, as far as I could see, there was no need for stitches. She winced when I applied iodine. "Why did she hurt you?"

"I was dancing with a girl at *The Oasis* and Fiona came raging in, grabbed me by the wrist and dragged me outside, where she proceeded to scream at me and cut me with her knife. When I fell to the ground, she kicked me. I really didn't know she minded so much."

"Were you there together?"

"No. Fiona took the train down from Scotland. She was still wearing her traveling clothes. I imagine she started drinking on the train."

"Come upstairs and have a rest. I'll give you something comfortable to put on." I kissed Daphne's hands and half-lifted her out of the chair, knocking over her cup and saucer, while Ethel, no doubt ruminating on the behaviour of the privileged classes, stirred a pot on the stove. "Cook, would you please bring us some broth and Melba toast in about half an hour?"

There was an expression going around London at that time, "Oh my dear, it is too, too Chelsea". The phrase had started as a euphemism for women in romantic relationships, but had sinister overtones when sexual flirtation between girls turned to obsession.

"You know Daphne," I said in as calm a voice as I could muster. "We really should call the police."

. Daphne's face went gray. "Oh no, Poppy," She clutched my arm. "I couldn't bear it."

Daphne clearly enjoyed being cared for and I must admit I had a terrible premonition that she might try to move in. The last time she had stayed over, after the dinner party where I had found the unborn child in the toilet, we'd had a hell of a time getting her to leave the next day.

"Do you have anyplace to stay?" I asked.

"I'm going back to Scotland."

"You're what?"

"I have to get my things."

"What if she decides to kill you?"

"She won't. She'll be sorry by now."

"Oh Daphne." She had a bath and, wearing one of my dressing gowns, lay down on the chaise. I spoon fed her the broth, closed the curtains and laid out a summer frock and some sandals for her to put on when she awakened. Then I went back to the attic to paint until Daphne woke up or it was time to fetch you from school. I half wished Daphne would be long gone before you would have to see her like that.

When I didn't hear from Daphne, I tiptoed out of the house, resigning myself to explaining her appearance to you. All the way home, I wondered how much I should tell you, but, by the time we arrived, she had gone. No one had seen her leave, but there was a note thanking me for my kindness beside my neatly folded dressing gown.

I was unsettled. Now was the right time to talk to you about going home. Except for Chou and the dogs, you rarely mentioned Victoria; and my mother hadn't been once to visit us.

Olivier was, as ever, wonderful with you. A brilliant storyteller, he was your Stanford. It is astonishing to me that some people who have endured childhoods of neglect or abuse can maintain such beautiful childlike perspectives on life. Olivier knew exactly how to be with children. For a while, he had you believing he had a wooden leg. He hid from you as you relentlessly pursued him to his dressing room and his bath, begging for a look at his prosthetic limb. Somehow he made his leg sound hollow when he tapped it. Do you remember him producing chocolate coins wrapped in gold foil, telling you he had hidden his money in his wooden leg?

"I got the idea from an old lady I knew," he said with a straight face. "She couldn't move very fast and her grandchildren stole her chocolate and ran away from her. The only place she could hide it was in her hollow leg."

Your eyes got bigger and bigger and his confabulating spiraled further and further into the improbable.

Just when we seemed to have adjusted to London, it was time to leave. Olivier was bereft, which surprised me. Apart from the fact that I had served as his beard, I think he realised then that he did love me. When I asked him once, he did say, "I love you, but I am not *in* love with you." Neither of us said, "I love you." Instead, we said cute things like, "Oh you adorable you!"

Olivier was thoughtful, but not given to the impulsive purchase of presents, which I believed lovers did because they could not help themselves. I know Chou was in love with me when he stopped by the roadside to pick some wildflowers or when he brought me treats from Chinatown. His offerings had not been motivated by obligation or guilt. Giving me things was a compulsive and potentially dangerous manifestation of his feelings. When it looked as though I really was leaving London, Olivier began buying flowers and leaving notes and surprises under my pillow. Nothing has value in the absence of love. I hope that one day you marry someone who loves you above everything, Precious.

Tallu told me that every joke was an epitaph for a feeling and I think she was right. There is no one funnier than Miss Bankhead.

I have seen so many people destroyed by their feelings, it could be that the jokers live longer, if not better.

One evening shortly before we left, Olivier invited me out for dinner. In case we were out late, we had Miss Brown sleep over in her little maid's room. We were going on a mystery tour, he told me. I didn't know whether to expect a night at the opera or a gay ball in Chelsea. As it happened, he had rented rooms on one of the top floors at the Savoy and ordered dinner brought up.

Earlier in the day, Olivier had dropped off his own records. He played some of our favourite songs on the Victrola — "Tea for Two," "China Boy," "Cuban Moon," "Oh, How I Hate To Get up in the Morning," and "Honolulu Eyes." We got up and danced. He was a splendid dancer — so graceful he made even me feel airy and light as a soufflé. He nibbled my neck. And I tried not to laugh, because romance between us was so incongruous. Then he led me into the bedroom, which was filled with the exotic scent of a large bouquet of lilies.

I was wearing my new Molyneux dress, a gray-blue silk with a dropped waist and a floating handkerchief hem. Olivier began to undo the buttons. I asked what he was doing and he said he wanted to make me a proper wife.

It was too late, but what could I do? I felt my heart drop on the floor with the weight of my dress. What is it they say about the soul? It weighs twenty-one grams, I think — less than a dress. Olivier disrobed and folded his clothes neatly on the chair. Then he turned down the bed and asked me to get in. I did, and I lay there waiting for the next, or last, chapter in my married life. We kissed. We embraced. I waited for the telltale nudge of his little man, the infamous willy-nilly, against my body. Perhaps he would need encouragement. Patiently, I kissed his chest, his stomach, and his thighs. I brushed his shy member with my hair, which aroused him. "Let me come inside you," he said and he tried, but as soon as he entered me, his gentleman's treasure tiptoed away into the darkness.

"Sorry," he apologized, falling back on the incredibly soft and luxuriously appointed bed.

"I'm fine," I said, taking his hand. Poor Olivier didn't have a clue how to make love to a woman and I was past showing him. It was for him to find out if he wanted so badly to save our marriage. To think that I had married Olivier believing that holy matrimony would be the same as having my own vegetable garden, available at all time to satisfy my hunger — now a tender young carrot, now a ripe tomato warm from the vine.

"Draw a card and make a wish," Daphne keeps a deck in her purse at all times. Some of us remember the proverb that tells us to be careful what we wish for. Careful or not, every choice is careless in the end, and the end is invariably painful, as there is nothing as violent as the rending of a family. From fate, from evildoers, we expect violence, but not from our loved ones. Loved ones make jagged wounds, the hardest to heal. I was determined to leave Olivier gently.

After our near honeymoon, we lay in the dark with such thoughts going through our heads until the tears dried on our faces and the first light of morning peeked through the opening in the dove-coloured velvet curtains.

"Did you know about that night, Tony?" I ask as Tony leaves to get dressed for dinner.

"Yes," Tony answers.

16

MAY 21, 4 PM, YOKOHAMA, ABOARD THE *EMPRESS OF ASIA*

My Darling Daughter,
What a relief it is to be able to say those words at last. Tony keeps
making me repeat the word "daughter," my mantra.

Ten days out and we have had rough seas only once, praise
Neptune. The ship arrived at Yokohama late last night. Over
twenty years ago Boulie passed through Yokohama on her way
to whatever passes for safety in this troubled world. You were on
board just a heartbeat ago. I am your eye and your mind looking at
the hills around Yokohama and wondering what they know that
would help me find you. We have maps for everything, including
journeys of the heart. I have tried to follow my sputtering little
engine, but so many obstacles have got in the way.

I didn't want to leave the *Empress of Asia*. It might be superstition, but I won't touch land unless you are there. What if I got
lost or ill in Yokohama and missed the boat before it left for
Shanghai? Five years ago there was a terrible earthquake here. One
of the trans-Pacific liners sank in the harbour. However, I am more

willing to take my chances on the boat than in a city that might fall
to pieces again.

Mr. Lee has still not shown himself. Tony disembarked today
and rented a car and driver, who took him to British House in the
foreign zone. He hoped to get diplomatic help, but unfortunately,
because of political unrest in China, there is no reliable information
available. He did confirm that the Soong family is based in Hong
Kong and the Han family in Peking. If one of our suspicions is
correct and your disappearance is connected to bad feeling between
the Soong and Han families, then perhaps Shanghai has been
chosen as a neutral place to negotiate your return.

"I will break Chou's neck if he has done this to you," Tony said
when he returned, bringing me pale yellow roses from the British
consulate garden and a wrapped gift. "I saw camellias as well.
I didn't expect to see camellias and roses in Japan."

I sniffed the roses, hiding my smile as I thought of the two
quintessentially gentle men in combat. "What a welcome smell of
home, Tony."

I have put the flowers in my silver water jug and will continue
with the story in my stateroom until it is time to dress for dinner.
Tony's gift, a red silk pillow embroidered with a gold Chinese good
luck symbol, is tucked behind my back.

OLIVIER GAVE UP wooing me after our sad honeymoon at the Savoy.
You and I were sailing, regardless, on the appointed day. It was
1926. Seven years had passed since Boulie's death. He had not
asked to come with us, but we did promise to return. As a final
concession, I invited him to visit us, perhaps next year after Chou
left for China. "Distance" was beginning to sound like a recurring
theme in my life.

Our return crossing from England to New York, again on the
Aquitania, was uneventful in terms of weather. The sea was calm

and we spent most of our time lounging in deck chairs, reading, sketching and chatting. This time, you got to swim in the beautiful Egyptian pool. It was mid-June and the sun shone every day. One afternoon you lay on the chair beside me, your nose covered with cream so it wouldn't burn, asking questions about your real mother and father.

When you were small, my mother and I had conspired in make believe. Everything from your appearance inside a fairy ring in the garden one morning to my marriage to Olivier was "pretend". I had sketched in an acceptable story that I hoped would segue into the truth someday, telling you that we were blood family.

Putting your hand on my arm, you asked a stunning question.

"What if I were Chinese? Would I have been valued?"

"Why on earth would you ask a question like that?"

"At school we learned that they kill girl babies in China."

"Not all the girls, Precious, just the extras. If they killed all of them, there wouldn't be any."

"That's the thing. Why are some girls extra?"

I felt panic. "You are not an extra, Precious."

"You have to admit that I could be. It is possible"

"Is what possible?"

"That my parents didn't want me."

I said, holding both your arms in a grip so tight I left marks, "Your family adores you." Did you notice that I spoke of the present tense? I almost told you then, but I didn't because I was afraid you would hate me. There are many things I could have confided to you that day. You were almost but not quite old enough. I think mothers should talk to their daughters about intimate matters so that they won't repeat their mistakes. That is why I am writing to you so frankly now.

You looked out at the sea for a long time and then you stared so hard at me I thought you were reading my mind. "You have taught me that lies are bad. Why do I have the feeling that you lie to me?"

"I have not lied to you."

"But you haven't told me the whole truth."

"I will when I understand it myself."

The last sleepless night, I stood by the rail watching the full moon on the water, remembering the first time you had said the word. Moon Lily. Moon doors. We could sail a ship through the word with its O's as wide open as the sinks that swallow lost children. Moonshine, mother, my mother under the same moon, doing what? I looked at my watch. It was midnight. We were halfway home.

In Victoria, it would be almost dinnertime. My mother would be dressing, even if she were having dinner alone, or else she would be making sure everything was ready for guests, filling the cigarette boxes, running to the garden for one more flower as I had seen her do so many times to balance an arrangement. By the time I was asleep in our stateroom, she would be pouring coffee and liqueurs, one ear tuned to the water, listening for the purr of a powerful boat.

There was no possibility of keeping a boat in our cove. It would have been smashed on the rocks. She might be worrying about the lack of cloud cover, wondering if it was safe to deliver the bootleg liquor she sent across the water to America. She would be drumming her fingers on the inside of her forearm, perhaps pacing. If she were wearing trousers, she would be nervously jingling the keys in her pocket.

By morning, she would know. We were all floating from danger to danger. By morning, our ship might be passing the last of the icebergs floating south from the Arctic. You had insisted on going to bed with your clothes on so that you would be ready to jump up, and made me promise to wake you at dawn.

I was more homesick on the trip back to Victoria than I had been at any time during the five years we spent in England. Breathing the clean ocean breezes after the filth of London I especially longed for the smells of home. I closed my eyes and tasted the dirt that clung to the baby carrots Alec, Boulie and I had thinned in Fong's vegetable garden. I counted the thrums of the ship's engines and the click of metal wheels on the train tracks, wondering how close to infinity I would get before I would open my bedroom windows and see my ocean, my mountains and my islands again.

I had left Soong Chou's little songbird *tabatière* behind, thinking it would make me too sad in London. Now I longed to hear it sing. I visualized my room and my things as I had left them. Then I moved through the house, taking inventory of every piece of furniture, every painting, every porcelain bowl, every carpet. The garden also has rooms. I wandered through them, touching and smelling my way in the dark. The hardest thing to visualize was my mother's face.

We passed the house en route to the inner harbour. I stood at the rail, remembering how Duffie would stand on the balcony and wave a sheet in greeting as we sailed past. To my surprise, it happened. As we went by Casanora, someone, who later turned out to be Miss Beach, flagged us home. I was still in tears when Nora appeared by herself to pick us up at the C.P.R. dock after we landed with a bump at eight o'clock in the morning.

You and I stood on the deck watching my mother get bigger and bigger as we pulled in beside the word Victoria planted in marigolds and geraniums on the sloping bank beside the terminal. She smelled familiar when I embraced her. You kissed her on both cheeks, the way you had learned overseas, and Nora laughed. You are in many ways the image of my mother. While we stood in the sun waiting for our luggage, I breathed in the clean salty air of Victoria harbour and knew we were home. I watched my mother as she delighted in you and noticed the fine lines in her alabaster skin.

Chou had been out late the night before, my mother said, without explanation. I was glad she had come to the boat alone. There was still something inherently humiliating about his public role in our household.

As usual, we drove up Fort Street and I was surprised by the changes to the city. The open spaces were filling in with buildings and houses. There were more cars. Unlike London, even the smallest house had a garden. I couldn't wait to get to Casanora. I closed my eyes as we passed through the gates and listened to the crunching gravel as we rolled to the bottom of the driveway. When I opened them again, I saw everything in place — the majestic oak trees, sprinklers making rainbows on the green lawns, gardeners deadheading spent rhododendrons and hoeing between plantings of annual and perennial flowers.

The three of us had breakfast on the terrace, while Daisy and Guan Sing took our trunks upstairs to our bedrooms. A beaming Fong made fresh orange juice and French toast, your favourite breakfast. Miss Beach came in from the garden holding an armful of dahlias for our bedrooms.

When you had finished your food, you asked permission to go down to the fairy glen, giving Nora and me our first opportunity to talk. Life at home seemed so determinedly unchanged; I thought I would suffocate in the musty old deceptions if I didn't blow the dust away.

"Mother," I started, "We must talk."

"Whatever do you mean?" Her delicate eyebrows raised slightly as her mouth shut tight.

"For one thing, I've realised for years that there has been illegal activity in this house."

"Ah." She didn't seem to be breathing.

"The more elusive you were, the more determined I was to find answers."

"One is hardly going to tell a child that one is a smuggler."

"We all knew. Actually, Boulie told me first. I didn't want to believe her."

"Oh, my God." Nora reached for a cigarette and lit it.

"I was obsessed with you."

"There were things you couldn't know."

"Now Precious is asking questions."

I started by asking about Stanford. My mother had been to the hospital in Connecticut to see him. Because he was sedated, she said, she felt as if he wasn't there. He did ask to come home, which, of course, was impossible.

"What do they give him?" I asked.

"Oh, Laudanum, I imagine" she answered. "His drug of choice."

It was my perfect opportunity. "Is opium the reason we came here?"

"Partly." My mother looked to the sea.

"Do you use it? Boulie said you did."

"I used to, but not anymore. I have had a difficult life, Poppy."

"What's going on now?"

My mother didn't answer me directly. She started instead by telling me that Stanford had made some unwise investments. She had no longer been able to support Duffie and Alec. That is why she let Duffie go and why Alec couldn't go to university. I was stunned. For so long, I had been angered by what appeared to be her cold rejection of them.

"I'm sorry. I had no idea. The lawyer I consulted said that I had inherited plenty of money."

"He would only have seen the will. Things changed after that. Your lawyer misinformed you. Smuggling, which began as an adventure, became a necessity."

"People are making ridiculous amounts of money now." I ventured into new territory.

"And so are we. I am paying back debts and investing."

In the beginning, she and Stanford had played at being pirates. Their semi-legitimate business was exciting and fun. All they were doing was avoiding the American import taxes. They had been taking opium to the San Juan Islands where it was picked up by Chinese fisherman and transported to Seattle and San Francisco for distribution. Then, after the law prohibiting the sale of opium in Canada, it became more and more difficult to procure both the raw resin from China and India and the manufactured product. Slowly, the factories in Chinatown shut down. For a while, they processed their opium at home. I told her I knew that. We had been in the tunnel. We smelled it.

"I had to keep going," she told me. "By then, we needed the money. Stanford requires expensive care and then there are the servants and their families in China."

"What about Soong Chou?"

"Chou came through Lady Cowes-Wentworth-Cowes. He is the youngest brother of Boulie's mother."

I let out my breath slowly. So, it was true. The artery in my neck twitched.

"The Cowes-Wentworth-Cowes' left China with Boulie and Soong Chou. In order to get Chou into the country, he had to be classified as a domestic and the head tax paid. If they hadn't taken Boulie from her mother before she was executed, she might have suffered a similar fate. Boulie's very existence was an insult to her mother's husband and his family."

"Boulie told me they made her watch when her mother was thrown down the well."

"She was too small, Poppy, a newborn. Her mother's servant took her directly to the Cowes. Boulie must have heard the story and fabricated her own memory."

"Why did Chou come to Canada with her?"

"The Soong family is in the import-export business. His reasons for coming were partly personal and partly business."

"Drugs."

"Don't forget it was legal. Opium is a pharmaceutical."

"I thought they used a better grade from Turkey for medicine." I had done my homework in London, but I had to keep her talking. There was so much I had to know.

"Mostly, yes. In any case, Chou was sent by his family to watch over Boulie and also to keep an eye on the family business."

"I see, and does the business end when he takes Boulie's bones home?"

"Yes." The word came down like a hammer.

"Chou must have suffered terribly when Boulie died."

"Yes, he did. He felt responsible. It was his job to protect Boulie and bring her back when it was safe. Now that there has been so much political change in China, the Han family wouldn't have much reason to go after her. It would have been time for her to go home."

"If she had wanted to."

I wondered if Boulie would have been able to make the transition to Moon Lily. I couldn't see her kowtowing and submitting to the family imperatives. The thought made me smile. Then, watching my daughter climbing on the rocks, a surge of grief and love and appreciation for Boulie flooded me.

"Poor Boulie." I wiped my eyes with my napkin and my mother briefly covered my hand with hers.

I barely listened as she went on explaining that after the Volstead Act was passed in the United States, she got requests for liquor. Since liquor was available in Canada, it was less complicated and more lucrative than continuing to smuggle opium. She was able to continue keeping up the house, employing the help and sending me money in London. It was imperative to keep a clear head, so she had given up opium.

"Why did you ever start?" I asked.

"Because of my guilt about your father."

"You told me his death was an accident."

"It was."

"Tallulah Bankhead told me what happened. Once again, a friend knew more about our family than I did."

"Oh, Poppy." she paused and drew a big breath; "I feared that someone would tell you, eventually. I was afraid of that. Did she tell you there had been robberies in the hotel?"

"Yes."

"I would do anything to change what happened."

"Did you hate my father?"

"No. He was more like a parent to me than a husband."

"What about Stanford?"

"Stanford was just a friend, a dear friend. I wouldn't have left your father for him."

"I see." Of course I saw.

"Did you know Nanny told me that my father died of a nosebleed?"

"No! Why on earth would she do that? She must have frightened you half to death."

"She did. If I could ask her one question, that would be it. Why tell a child who has nosebleeds such a terrible lie?"

"Do you hate me?"

"No, Nora. If anything I feel badly about the burden you have been carrying."

All the time I'd been judging her, she'd been punishing herself. While I was feeling self-righteous in London, I was living off the proceeds from bootleg whiskey. My mother was risking her freedom so that I could live at Claridge's.

"Why did you do that? I didn't need so much money. Besides, I thought it was my own."

"Stanford got careless and bought on margin. I couldn't deny you your inheritance. That's the story," she said. "There is no revising it now."

"What will happen when Chou goes back to China?"

"He is not indispensable. I am quite good at this business." She smiled. "We are in the chips again."

"Why don't you quit now?"

"I will when Prohibition ends. Blue chip stocks are a very safe place for money, Poppy. We can't go wrong."

"What makes you think Prohibition will end?"

"I know it will."

"I've heard it's awfully dangerous."

"That makes it exciting," she said. "But we don't take a lot of risks. We're at the high end, delivering good whiskey to floating bars just outside American waters. We don't cut our whiskey and the customers appreciate that. The profits are huge, a thousand per cent, and the criminals are more interested in hijacking truck-loads as opposed to boatloads of liquor, or intercepting the alcohol being delivered to the mother-ships waiting in rum rows outside the legal limits."

"How do you do it? Except for the dinghy, you don't own a boat."

"We have several. We just can't keep them here. As you know, there is no safe moorage here and, because our cove is exposed, a boathouse would be obvious to anyone with a pair of binoculars. We keep the boats in a secure location and store the boxes here."

"We?"

"I go sometimes. I like it. Besides, I need to make sure business is properly done. Chou doesn't go out on the water because his family doesn't want him directly connected with the risky part of the business."

"What about the gardeners?"

"The men came back when business improved."

I should have known from her ferocity in the garden that my mother was a finisher. Perhaps I am too, in my own way. If it weren't for my heart, I might have had her astonishing energy. She left me to see to her roses, some of which had black spot, and I sat in the sun absorbing the heat and her fantastic story. This was the longest conversation we'd ever had. My mother, who neglected to tell me about sex, or religion, or child raising had finally revealed herself to me. My brain ached.

I called you back from the beach, went up to my room, where Daisy was putting away my clothes, and lay down on my bed, pulling you down beside me.

"Doesn't it wear you out?" I asked you.

"What Poppy?" You put your hand on my heart.

"This house."

I looked around at my familiar things — pictures by Boulie, Alec, Emily, you and me, our photographs, the changing landscape of the sea outside my windows and wondered why it was that my mother was willing to take such risks. We didn't need a huge house or servants, or expensive possessions. If any of her friends in Victoria knew what she was about, they would drop her in an instant.

That evening after dinner, you and I took our instruments over to the garage to meet Chou. You have a gift for music that even my mother understood. My heart was pounding. I had to stop twice on the stairs to get my breath. Eager to show off your skills, you bounded past me. Chou was at the door before you knocked. You looked at one another shyly for a moment and then you held out your free hand to shake his.

I know I am telling you things that you may recall perfectly, but if you learn anything about the ways in which you are loved, then they bear repetition.

Chou looked at me over your head, as you bounded past him into his apartment. His face was an open astonishment.

"Precious is mine," he whispered, his voice breaking. "Boulie was right."

I fell back in amazement, slumped onto the bench on his porch and put my head between my knees. *Mine.* My head spun. I gasped for air. There is never enough air.

Soong Chou brought me a glass of water. "We will talk later," he said.

I dug my nails into my hands to keep myself steady as I went inside and sat near you. "I used to keep my *liuqin* in the stable," I choked. Soong Chou gave me a look that said, "Calm down."

"Why Poppy?" You asked gently because you are so sensitive to my feelings.

"Because Nora wouldn't have approved and so I practised in secret."

"Tell me all your secrets."

"Not now, Precious. Let me come home first," I laughed unsteadily.

Because we had been away for so long, your father must have seen you differently. As a young adult you may resemble his favourite sister or an aunt. How can I not have known? I think the only reason is that I didn't want to. Much as I love your father, we are from separate continents and there is an ocean between us. If we kept silent then, it was to protect you. Now is different. That is why I am writing these letters.

When you sat side by side on Chou's cherry wood bench, I could see that you and your father played with what I call family intuition; the special way musicians who are related know how to make music together. Used to listening to my heart, I quickly recognized the synchronicity of blood.

Chou had sacrificed himself for his sister's child and now there would be further sadness as he wrestled with other loyalties — his wife and you. You were his. Now I could see it as clearly as he did. Much as I love Chou, I hadn't been looking for him in you.

I didn't play that day. I couldn't. My fingers were numb. We had tea and you chattered with your father. On the way out of his apartment, I handed him a small package wrapped in brown paper and told him not to open it until we had gone back to the house. It was one of the paintings from Paris that I'd had framed — a field of poppies in the rain.

"I am glad," I said.

Chou squeezed my arm as he helped me down the stairs.

17

Mon Petit Chou,

After all these years, little cabbage, I saw that I had been calling you by your father's name all along! I had to stop writing last night. It was too emotional. This morning, Tony got me started with a question.

"Is that moment in the garage *really* the first time you realised Chou was Precious' father?" Tony speaks as he finishes reading.

"She was Alec's. In my innocence, I believed people had babies from making love once. I *wanted* her to be Alec's. It was bad enough that she was illegitimate without subjecting her to racism as well. When Alec died, I thought it was so unfair. Why should the boys go? Why should the poor go first?"

"The rich went too, Poppy."

"Yes, but you know what they mean when they say 'cannon fodder.'"

"Perhaps you're still fighting the war."

"My whole life has been a battle, Tony, with all the lies and loyalties. It was such a relief to talk it through with my mother."

While we were in London, Nora had left things as they were in the attic ballroom. Even though it was an effort for me to climb the stairs, I was determined to start painting again. Smelling the paints and brushes, the turpentine, I felt an overwhelming sadness, grieving for Boulie and Alec and missing Emily.

Knowing her fondness for children, especially little girls, I hoped that I might be able to inveigle Emily to come to Casanora and give you drawing and painting classes. She said no to my written entreaty, but I could bring you to her house for tea. I warned you, my little calling card, that Miss Carr was special. She smelled funny and she could be rude, but she was a great artist and a wonderfully kind human being underneath her tough crust.

While I had no trouble deciding which paintings to bring home for my mother and Chou, I agonized over what to give Emily. An ordinary garden painting would not do. She would dismiss it as dilettante fluff or a Sunday picture. In London, I had walked round and round the sitting room, choosing one and then another. Olivier said I was going to wear a hole in the carpet.

Finally, I decided on a picture of a plinth at Stonehenge with wildflowers growing in the cracks. I had painted my own shadow on the rock. Hopefully, Emily would recognize that we were women breaking out of stone, connected by our own struggles to the worshippers who erected it.

Emily loved the painting and she adored you. We had tea and biscuits from a tin in her studio, while you played with her dogs and her monkey. I don't know if you recall that she was about to have a big exhibition in Ottawa at the National Gallery. At last, she was getting the recognition she deserved. The new paintings, intense and quintessentially feminine landscapes, were the best she had done. This was her motherhood.

If Emily suspected what Chou had seen, she didn't let on. She told me she would be happy to take you on as a student after her tour of the east. Until then, she was focusing on her own work and her other bread and butter businesses, the dog breeding and her boarding house. She was thrilled with the notes you sent her and I have saved the letters and drawings she has mailed to you so you will have them to keep.

Since Nora had been frank with me, I knew it would be best to do my own housekeeping, sooner rather than later. One morning, you went with Chou to Lady Cowes-Wentworth-Cowes with a basket of currents and some roses from our garden. My mother was doing her mail in the library. I pulled up a chair beside her and started by confessing about my marriage to Olivier.

"You married without telling me?"

"I was going to, but his mother was difficult and it seemed best not to complicate things."

"You might have died in childbirth."

"That wasn't going to be a problem."

My mother knew all about lavender marriages. She'd clearly had one with Stanford. Since mine wasn't likely to last, I hadn't thought it was necessary to tell anyone outside of our circle of friends in London. I told Nora that Olivier might come to visit in a year or so. He was very attached to you.

"What about Precious?" she asked. "Are you going to tell her?"

"Yes, of course."

"Everything?"

"Yes, what do you mean?"

"I mean Chou."

"Ah," I tried to continue breathing. It was an effort. "How long have you known?"

"I saw her Mongolian spot when she was born. It was faint, but it was there, the little cabbage at the base of her spine."

"I thought it was a bruise. It went away."

"They always go away."

I drew a large breath. "Did Chou ever tell you that he suspected she was his?"

"It never came up and it won't. Chou is discreet and so am I.

Be careful, Poppy. Don't ruin your daughter's life." She was right. I
could hear the tittle-tattling in Oak Bay drawing rooms. How many
times had I heard "Nigger in the woodpile" whispered over a tea
caddy? A mixture of relief and sadness overwhelmed me.

"Are you angry, ashamed, what?"

"Precious is my grandchild. Chou is my associate. His father was
an old friend."

"And you never discussed Precious with her father?"

"Just before you left for England, I told him that you had confessed that she was Alec's."

"Do you mind having a Chinese grandchild?"

"How absurd. Whatever made you think that?"

"I am sorry, but this is a racist city and London is even worse."

"Cities are made up of individuals, Poppy. You can't generalize."

"What am I going to do?"

"You're an adult. I can't direct you. Chou has a wife and you
have a husband. You have to remember that."

"What does it mean, though? He married because he was
obligated."

"The world doesn't operate on impulse." I wondered if she was
going to say it ran on duty, remembering what she had said about
Alec going to war.

"What would you do about Precious if you were me?"

"I would wait and see. Why make it harder for her? Her alleged
father is dead. Her stepfather is in England. Do you want to give
her another who will leave?"

"She doesn't think of Olivier as her stepfather."

Nora said nothing, just looked out the window. The car was
pulling up to the *porte cochère*. You got out and were overtaken by
my mother's dogs, which were jumping up and licking you, while
Chou drove away.

"How can he do this?"

"What?"

"Be a servant."

"Chou will do whatever is best for his family. This job has given him the opportunity to keep his head down, watch out for his sister's child and manage other business for his family."

"What about face?"

"Face is serving his family."

"And smuggling?"

"I told you, Chou doesn't go out in the boats."

"Who does exactly?"

"Sing and his gardeners, me. We have very powerful launches. Nothing in the American coast guard can come anywhere near them for speed or maneuverability. The authorities are not interested in small fish in any case. It is the big suppliers and real criminals they are after. Our boats are works of art, low and sleek with powerful engines and lots of storage room. I will show them to you sometime. They are perfectly safe."

I still do not feel safe in small vessels. Perhaps I am a failed fish, like the baby in the toilet.

I am in tears again. Tony wants me to look out the porthole. He is a master of distraction. It is hard to believe we will be in Shanghai in one more day. Shanghai "the whore of Asia," the "Paris of the East." How many times have I longed to visit the graceful port city, her culture, and her beautiful gardens? Now I dread what might happen.

Tony made plans for us while he was in Yokohama. His friend Victor Sassoon is building a hotel in Shanghai. We can stay in the first completed rooms. Shanghai is a cosmopolitan city. People are *Yangjingbang*, westernized, and we will be able to get around easily. English is spoken almost everywhere. If you are there, we will have less difficulty locating you than we would in Peking. Tony is trying to calm me, I know, but I am not going to relax until this is over. If only Mr. Lee would show himself again.

Last night, I lay awake in bed thinking of Duffie's forbidden Bible stories; the quests that men and women like Jonah and Ruth were sent on to test their faith. What am I *supposed* to believe in? I think I know, but it has everything to do with parents and children, the importance of childhood. I am a child inside a whale, alarmed and comforted by its noises, things being digested, the great heart of the ship pressing on at all costs, as Tallulah liked to say. Pressing on. There is music in that.

"We each have our own music," my unmusical mother told me.

She was telling me that I should listen to you and it would do more harm than good if I laid bare all of our deceptions when we returned from England. I still had most of a year to sort things out. In the meantime, you began school and kept improving on the *liuqin*.

It was hard for me to think of your father as a criminal. Chou is a man who loves poetry and music. He is above all a gentleman, albeit an enigmatic gentleman. Nora was easier to understand. I realise that there are different categories of lawbreakers. I know there are still countries where women are stoned to death for having children out of wedlock. Who can judge a man for providing drink to the thirsty, opiates to the addicted?

I frequently lay in my bed at night and wondered what would happen if I went out to the garage and painted Chou's eyes with pansy juice, then softly blew on his face until he woke up. Would he reach up and take me in his arms. Would he finally admit that he loved me? Would he forsake all others as I had intended when I married Olivier?

Driven by a restless energy, I had returned to my painting, but by the time I climbed to the top of the attic steps, I would have to sit down. My body felt like lead. There was no energy left for work. Nora and Daisy converted the yellow guest room into a studio. This worked better for me because of the ensuite bathroom where I could clean my brushes and relieve myself without going up and down the stairs.

As soon as Chou drove you to school, I painted urgently, with several canvases going at once. It was fall. I painted the death of the earth, dug up soil with smoldering leaf fires. At noon, my mother and I had lunch together in her sitting room. That way I wouldn't have to go downstairs to the dining room. We were almost relaxed with one another. She told me that my father had adored me.

"I felt guilty when you were sick. I thought it had happened because I hadn't loved you enough."

Why not? My question hung in the air, waiting for me to take possession of it, and ask. But I couldn't.

I was happy to be working. The finished canvases dried and were put away or sent to friends. I wasn't in a hurry to have another show. More and more, painting was becoming a private experience, something intimate to share with those I wanted to understand how I felt. I had no *ars poetica*, no statement beyond life itself.

Emily disagrees with me, but then she *is* disagreeable. She regards herself as a feminist and yet Lawren Harris and his boy's club, who condescend to her, cow her. They have convinced her she has to have an aesthetic philosophy, a political purpose. She says she isn't interested in fashion in art and yet she wants approval from the boys.

I liked my lonely little art world. I didn't have to apologize to anyone. Having said that, I missed Emily's presence more and more. Emily was my spirit wrestler. Even her disapproval made me strong. I painted to contradict her. In the end I was exhausted but content that I had given it everything I knew about living.

At night, I'd listen for the powerful engines that meant shipments were going out. Nora said nothing of her business to me, and Chou gave no indication that he was privy to our earlier conversations. When I heard the boats coming in, I went out to my balcony and looked for the phosphorus in their wake. Sometimes I watched my mother's shadowy figure cross the lawn and return. Often I was asleep by the time she came into the house. Those were the mornings she slept late. Perhaps she was right. Bootlegging was just a business.

On the afternoon of October eleventh, Nora came into my

bedroom and asked if I would like to go out with her that evening. She and the men were taking a run in just one boat to a private customer who was meeting them half way to Port Angeles. The moon was full and the water would be calm. Pleased as I was to be invited, I said no.

I was turning my light out when she popped her head in my doorway to say goodnight, "You can still change your mind."

"No, but thanks for asking me." She rushed off. I opened the door to my balcony. The moon was full. I could just barely see her walking quickly across the lawn. She disappeared into the dark and I went back to bed, where I dreamed I was in a mountain meadow with Nora and you, the three of us in matching blue cotton dresses with full skirts. We were minding goats and reading to one another in the field of wild flowers. I watched the goats climbing rocks near dangerous crevasses.

When Chou woke me up in the middle of the night, I was still dreaming. I heard the clock strike three. He stood beside my bed, holding both my wrists. At first I smiled, feeling my body reach up to him, then reading his face in the moonlight, realised he had come as a messenger.

"What is it?" I asked, fear crowding my sleep.

"Your mother didn't come back," he said.

"Maybe she stayed for a drink. She said she was meeting friends."

"No Poppy, she isn't coming back. She has been shot."

"How do you know?" I sat up in bed.

"The others have returned."

My whole body went cold. My mother was dead. I began to weep and tear at my bedding and my nightgown.

"You must be calm," he said, "for Precious."

Chou poured me a hot bath and helped me into it. I couldn't stop crying. Fong brought a cup of tea with Scotch, while Chou waited. I drank my tea and got out of the bath and into my nightgown. I was still shivering. My nose bled. Chou brought me ice in a towel for my nose and sat on the edge of my bed, explaining what we must do. My mother had been betrayed and he would see to it that she was avenged. No one in the household was to know what happened apart from those who already did. In a few hours, I would phone the police and say that she was missing and that her bed had not been slept in. She was in the habit of taking our little rowboat out at night when it was calm. He would set the boat adrift further along the beach. It will turn up somewhere and she will not be in it.

He brought extra blankets from the linen closet. I could not get warm.

"We will grieve later, Poppy. For now, we must think clearly and work quickly."

"What about the tunnel?" I asked.

"We have planned for this. The men are already making sure the police won't find it. There is no reason for them to look for it."

When I finished my tea, Chou picked up the cup and saucer and started to leave my room.

"Don't go," I said, and began weeping again.

"I can't stay. Everything must go on as usual, Poppy. Please try, for Precious if not for yourself."

I'm surprised I can recall anything about the time around my mother's death. I don't remember if I slept or not. Foolishly, I had let myself believe that once I had understood and forgiven my mother, the curse would be lifted. Daylight came with the suddenness of a sharp pain in my chest. Miss Beach opened my curtains at eight o' clock, telling me that Chou had taken you to school. My mother wasn't at home and her bed hadn't been slept in.

"Perhaps she made it," I said, foolishly. Nora wouldn't know one end of a blanket from the other.

"She's gone, Poppy. I'm going to make some calls."

I waited while Miss Beach called around on the telephone. She was preparing our alibi. When she came back to report, I asked if she thought we should call the police. She offered to do it. By then, I was shaking so hard I doubt I could have spoken coherently. She came back with tea and Melba toast and told me a policeman was coming. He had been informed that I was an invalid and should not be upset by any speculation about the whereabouts of my mother.

She had given me my cue not to get up. While I lay in bed waiting for the policeman, I wondered what had been going on below stairs. No doubt Chou and the others had put their plan in place. I couldn't worry about that. We each had to take care of our own part of the business. Chou was right. The grieving would have to come later.

For now, we had you to think of, and the safety of our family, which included the servants. Nora's reputation wasn't important to her anymore. Part of me would have liked to see the expressions on the faces of the stuffed shirts in Oak Bay when they found out one of them was shot and killed in a bootlegging operation. From what I have heard, hers wasn't the only stately home with a tunnel.

The policeman, Constable Godsell, took off his shoes before he walked on my bedroom carpet. In better times, I would have smiled at the sight of him standing at the end of my bed with a pair of brogues in his hand. He only asked me two questions: did I know where my mother was, and when did I last see her. I told him I had no idea where she had gone and that she had been in to say goodnight to me yesterday evening at about nine o'clock. I was surprised he didn't ask if she was in the habit of going out in the boat by herself, but that may have fallen in the category of perilously upsetting a heart patient.

We have two eyes, two ears, two kidneys, two ovaries, so many parts with spares, but only one heart. It is amazing to me that such an important muscle, one that has to bear all the emotions and pump all the blood, should have no backup. I have learned that heart disease is a romantic affliction. It isn't unhygienic like cancer or leprosy. Being treated differently from others gives me no satisfaction. However, if it meant our family would be treated with kid gloves, then so be it. It was also obvious that Constable Godsell at least was under the impression that a household of women born with silver spoons in their mouths would be an unlikely crime maven. Between my heart and my mother's address, we were going to be treated with deference.

Constable Godsell reassured me that Nora would likely turn up. In the meantime, the police would investigate. Chou told me later that meant they would have someone come to the morgue if any female bodies washed up on the beach. The policeman told him that the boat very likely floated out to sea by itself after being improperly secured on the beach. The implication was that a woman wouldn't have the strength to haul it up far enough.

After he left, I went to the pantry on the pretext of getting some baking soda for my bath and saw that the trap door to the tunnel had been covered with a piece of linoleum. When I opened the hatch outside the house and looked inside, I saw that the beginning of the tunnel had been transformed into a root cellar with four walls covered with shelves holding jars of preserves. The false wall must have been there all along.

Chou caught up to me while I walked to the beach. "The opening to the tunnel is closed," he said.

"Where are the men?"

"They have gone to Chinatown."

"I can't believe she is gone," I felt my throat closing again.

Soong Chou half carried me up the stairs, "In my culture, we say the dead come back to say goodbye after three days. Watch for her, Poppy, and bless her journey."

He helped me get back into bed. Moments later, Lady Cowes came to see me. We would have to tell you something. Decisions had to be made. The dogs had to be taken care of. Ling Ling and Moo Pei whimpered for my mother and both of them refused to leave her bed, where they lay all day long, their faces on her pillows. They had to be carried outside to toilet. Lady Cowes was very kind to them. She brought her own pair of Pekingese and said she would stay in the blue guest room as long as we needed her. Once again, I berated myself for underestimating her incredible reserves of strength. She took over everything from our finances to arranging a memorial service.

Lady Cowes offered to talk to you, but I told you myself that Nora had gone out in a boat and hadn't returned. That was all true. You became very quiet, and held my hand. After a while, you said, "You will miss your mother." You paused. "I miss mine." The water crashing on the rocks below our house might as well have been my blood.

On the third day, I waited for my mother to reappear. I think I expected a ghost. I wanted her to tell me she loved me, but that didn't happen. A bullet had found her and now my father might rest. Perhaps this would be the end of his curse. Before lunch, you came into my bedroom carrying a trillium you'd found in the fairy glen.

"Look, Poppy. Why did this bloom now?" You gave it to me.

I knew. "I think it is Nora, telling us she is at peace. Shall we press it in a book?"

"Yes, let's."

We kissed the flower; then we pressed it in my copy of *A Child's Garden of Verses*.

Sometimes, at night, I tiptoed through the linen closet and went to my mother's rooms. I opened her closets and smelled her things. Someone else would have to give them away. I couldn't do it.

The London dinner party where I'd found the foetus in the toilet became a recurring dream. As soon as I closed my eyes, I saw babies swimming in schools like luminous pink fish. Slowly, they morphed into soldiers. There were no girls, just boys in uniform with smooth baby faces. All of them looked surprised. Where was my mother? I wanted to ask her why the boys had been left unattended. Who let this happen to them? As I swam with the dead to a deeper sleep, I looked for her, but she was nowhere to be found.

When I had told Nora about the toilet incident at the dinner party shortly before the night she died, she said she didn't understand why

I was obsessing on someone else's private moment. "It was just an accident. Best ignored. You make yourself sick by worrying, Poppy."

"Write about the party. Maybe it will help." Tony is massaging my neck.

There were fourteen people at the party: myself, Tony, Olivier, Daphne, The Prince of Wales, who made himself available after my marriage to Olivier, Freda Dudley-Ward, The Duke and Duchess of York, Dola, Tallulah, Edward and Doulie Molyneux, and a war hero whose name was Edward Campion. I remember thinking how unusual it was to have an even number of ladies and gentlemen at dinner.

The men wore white tie because we were going on to a dance afterward. Edward Campion had on his medals. He was the only one. In between the shrimp aspic and the cold cucumber soup, he nudged my leg. "Sorry," he said. "It's only made of wood, but it has a mind of its own." The others laughed. I thought of Alec. They should have set a place for Alec. Sometimes I did.

When I came back from the powder room, I caught Daphne's eye. "What is it," she whispered. "There was a foetus in the toilet," I said. She put her fingers to her lips. Was she telling me that Canadians, like Americans, were too open? Of course she was. The British ignore unpleasantness. I wasn't going to open my mouth and ask, can you imagine, in front of the Prince of Wales, his girlfriend and his brother, the Duke of York, how an unborn child got in a water closet.

I wondered whether the woman who left it was feeling ill and needed a ride home. Would it be too conspicuous if I asked a footman to inquire if one of the women could accompany me to my house, as I was tired? I told Olivier to go on to the dance without me. He was used to me retiring early. It gave him an opportunity to have a social life without me.

"I have a confession to make," Tony has interrupted.

"You left the baby?" I laugh.

"Not exactly, but I know whose it was."

"No!"

"Yes."

"Who then?"

"Daphne."

"Daphne?"

"She wanted to have a baby."

"Oh my God. In the end, it was Daphne who came home with me. I had no idea. I booted her out the next morning."

"It was for the best, don't you think?"

Now he tells me! It was Daphne's baby I see in my sleep, poor little thing.

"Why are you telling me now?"

"I want to help. If this is a puzzle, then you'll need all the pieces."

"Who was the father?"

"I was."

"You."

"I contributed. It was quite clinical."

"Were you sad?"

"In a way, yes — for Daphne, for my poor mother. But Daphne was utterly unsuitable, don't you think?"

What does it take to make a good mother? I am the last person to answer that question. One thing I do know is that there has been too much dying. I must force myself back to the story because I do believe I will see you when it is finished.

Officially, Nora von Stronheim Slocum was another missing person. Until she was officially dead, we were in limbo. There would be no funeral, no reading of the will, no obituary. Her assets were frozen and there was only my allowance to support our extended family. Since some of us knew she was dead, we had to do something to commemorate her life. Otherwise, our lives would stop. Lady Cowes suggested a memorial garden. How perfect. She thought of everything. We decided that her empty grave should look over the sea, toward America, and chose a site at the highest point of the fairy glen, where a large arbutus leans over the rocks into the water. I had Mortimer's Monuments make a flat stone with her name and no dates carved into it, and a quotation from a Shakespeare sonnet — *Nora, for precious friends hid in death's dateless night.* Remembering all the graveyards I had seen covered with snowdrops after my mother had stopped me from bringing them into the house, I asked Guan Sing to bring us bulbs to plant in the meadow.

We had the ceremony at eleven on November the eleventh, the day Armistice had been declared between Germany and the Allies in 1919. It was a clear, sunny morning. Mount Baker rose magnificent on the other side of the Straight. We could see all the way to my mother's ocean grave. The mourners were you, Miss Beach, Daisy, Fong, Chou, Wash Martha, Lady Cowes-Wentworth-Cowes, Quon Sam, the gardeners, who came from Chinatown in shiny suits and with combed hair, the four dogs and me. Nora's stone was already in place. We took turns digging holes with a little shovel and putting in the bulbs. Lady Cowes read the whole Shakespeare sonnet in her stout English voice. You put a posy of winter pansies next to the stone, and you and your father sat side by side on a rock playing a haunting song on your *pipas*. How could anyone seeing you together not know?

I bowed my head and wept, thinking of Alec, Boulie, Duffie, my mother, all my dear friends hiding in the grim shadows. Someone in London told me that Monet, the great painter of light, had very poor vision. I thought of him laying strokes of colour side by side without seeing them individually. Perhaps that is the meaning of life, the apparent confusion of unrelated colour and absence of line. We are all lost, the children, the mothers, and the soldiers, but somehow in the light we are found and redeemed. My mother was redeemed by her garden.

After the ceremony, I went down to the beach and found a few pieces of blue glass, which I threw into the sea. Then I followed the others into the house for lunch. We had a fire in the drawing room and all of us sat together drinking Scotch whiskey, the gardeners' favourite drink, and eating smoked salmon sandwiches. Wash Martha had brought the fish as a gift from the Songhees people. I looked around at our eclectic family — one aboriginal, two women of limited circumstance, two handfuls of "Coolies," and one English Lady — and smiled. I am sure Nora would have approved.

18

My Precious,
There are times when music drives me mad, and this is one of them.
We can't get away from it. The decks are a plague of brass bands.
It's as if they are trying to drive us off the ship. Today is the day.
Either I will see you or we will be plunged even deeper into mystery
and uncertainty.

Tony and I are going to persevere through the afternoon. By
evening, we will be in Shanghai. Our bags are packed. We are ready
to disembark. This long letter (or letters) is almost at an end.

"Tony, dear. We are not moving fast enough. I want to jump off
the ship and swim to Precious."

"Poppy, you don't know how to swim," Tony laughs. "Stay with
the story. It is nearly done."

It seems my whole life has been about endings. I am determined
you won't live yours the same way.

WHILE OUR HOUSEHOLD mourned my mother's death and the police dithered, the rest of Victoria stayed away from us. There was no longer a row of engraved invitations on my mantle. You were not asked to birthday parties. The von Stronheim Slocum family was a scandal. It is not quite on to fall out of one's rowboat at night. That screams of drunkenness. There were also rumours, reported to me by Daisy who has her own information network of people in service.

The shock gradually sapped my energy. At the end of November, I had a recurrence of rheumatic fever. I knew what that meant the morning I woke up with a sore throat and a fever. Each attack would further weaken my heart. In some ways, the diagnosis was a relief. There was no need to fear what was already happening. It became imperative to think clearly.

At Christmas, Lady Cowes and her dogs went back to live in their own house after she hired a day nurse, Alice Burns, who, along with Miss Beach, took over my care. I no longer wished to paint.

Emily started visiting me again right after Nora died. I don't know if she saw Nora as a rival out of the way or if she was attracted by the *frisson* of intrigue and our new status as social lepers. She was determined to get me going again. When I think about our relationship over the years, I realise that many of our difficulties and misunderstandings have arisen from her affection for me. Emily thought I should rig up my bed so that I could draw and paint while lying down or sitting up on the days when I just couldn't manage getting up. She gave me a lovely sketchbook and charcoal pencils for Christmas. I know what that meant to her, because she couldn't afford any luxuries. When I had the strength to hold a pencil, I sketched.

As if we hadn't had enough bereavement, Nora's dogs died within hours of one another shortly before Christmas. They had given up waiting for Nora to come back with fresh chocolates and, besides, they were old. I wrote Stanford about the dogs as I had told him about my mother. The barking twins had grown on me. It wasn't their fault that my mother was mad about them. When Ling Ling and Moo Pei died, it was as if we had lost family members. You made your beautiful painting of Pekingese with wings flying over the ocean, toward my mother.

I told you the story of the Lion Dogs of the Forbidden City, the Pekingese that had been bred to resemble Imperial lions because lions couldn't survive in China.

"Lord Buddha was attended by Pekingese who transformed into lions when he was attacked."

"Who would attack a holy person, Poppy?"

"Holy people are the most vulnerable."

"Why?"

"You will have to find out for yourself."

"Wouldn't it save a lot of trouble if you just told me what you know?"

"Would you listen?"

"Of course."

Tony has a question. "Do you think it is possible that Precious guessed early on that you and Chou were her parents?"

"Why would you ask that?" I am incredulous.

"She is a wise and intuitive girl. Children know more than they are credited. Just as you began painting for your mother, perhaps she did the same for you. For her father, she plays music."

"We may find out." Oh please, dear God, make it soon. I am beside myself.

Chou had slipped away in the New Year to attend to some family business. I hadn't paid attention to his promise of vengeance the night my mother was shot, but I was reminded when he returned a week later and told me that he had gone to Seattle on a fishing boat and found out what had happened. "Your honour has been restored," he said, and, when I asked him if he had blood on his hands, he said no.

The chance that Nora's body could wash up on a beach in either

Canada or the United States was left unsaid between us. We had to live with the tension of not knowing. There would be no denying a bullet hole through her forehead. That would lead to further investigation and might even implicate our friend down the road.

I now knew that Lady Cowes-Wentworth-Cowes and her husband had also been involved in the legal export of opium. This sensibly dressed middle-aged English lady with her tweed suits and double strands of pearls had a double life.

Chou helped me with accounts. He found other jobs for all the gardeners but Guan Sing and got Daisy, Fong and Miss Beach to stay on with us for room and board until my mother was found or declared dead. Chou took no salary.

From a financial point of view, it would have been helpful if my mother's body were found. We would have to be patient. Fong, who relied heavily on produce from the garden at the best of times, found new ways to improvise. He made deals with friends in Chinatown, trading produce for chicken and pork. He bought elderly chicken and boiled the carcass before baking it. We ate less frivolously than before — no more French pâté and Russian caviar on the thin slices of Melba toast that Fong dried in the warming oven. We heated only the rooms we used. Daisy and Miss Beach moved down from the servant's rooms on the third floor and shared the blue guest room after Lady Cowes-Wentworth-Cowes left. The car was off limits unless it was absolutely necessary. This voyage is a gift from Olivier and Tony.

I hated having to make the decision to let all but the vegetable garden go. The garden was my mother's life's work. Between them, Chou and Sing did the best they could. The first winter, it didn't matter that they lacked help. The beds mostly lay fallow, except for raking the leaves and lifting the dahlias and putting them away until spring.

In spring, it was different. What ten people had done previously was now left to poor Sing, who despaired. I told him that a garden is an organic thing with a life of its own. Now was the time for ours to be wild. Sometimes I watched him from my window, standing alone in the garden, his head bowed over a rake or a shovel and I grieved for him.

Miss Beach has been a great comfort. The intimacy that began in San Francisco has grown and I now regard her as an aunt or older sister. She is the only one who has known all of us. I am ashamed that there was a time when I resented her for doing her job so well. It was Miss Beach who made sure I turned over in bed when the fever returned. When I was too weak to be helped to the tub, she gave me sponge baths and massages.

"You have given us the best part of your life," I said one evening while she rubbed warm lavender oil on my legs.

"This family is my life."

"Do you actually love us, Miss Beach? Is that possible?"

"What choice did I have? I was a woman without options and now I live in a grand house with a park around it. I eat well and I have family to care about."

"You weren't always. Remember when you went out in my mother's clothes. You must have been very angry with her to do that."

"Yes and no. Your mother was good to me. More than anything else I wanted not to be invisible. When I wore her things, I had substance."

"What did you do? Did you go out with men?"

"No, I went to nice shops and restaurants. When I dressed like my lady, I was actually seen by people, and treated well."

"Aren't human beings incredibly awful."

"They can be."

"Were you romantically in love with my mother?"

"You asked me that before. I told you then and I'll tell you again. I was her maid. I did my best to make her happy. That was my job."

"Is sex in the job description?"

"It wasn't sex. It was comfort. I was taught that women looked and felt better when they were sexually satisfied. A proper orgasm helps to keep the skin clear and the eyes sparkling. When we don't have that release we get anxious and nervous."

"What about you, Miss Beach? Who helps you?"

"I help myself."

Dola wrote weekly from London, telling me the news. She has been two-timing Tallulah with "Dish" Cavendish. Don't tell anyone, she confided, as if I had anyone to tell, but she thought he was going to ask her to marry him. It wasn't hard to imagine Dola as a wife. She would dote. I wondered if she had noticed that Dish was something other than a roaring hearty? Would she care, as I had, or was she just using him for his title and the chance to put Tallulah in her place? I can't imagine Dola thinking that way. She worships Tallulah. I imagine both of them are complicit in this.

Olivier's letters were wonderful. He was affectionate and asked about you. I often wondered if there was some way in which I could have made a better marriage with him. Perhaps I was too eager to accept failure, too uncharitable to exempt him from my judgments about his bigoted mother. He was coming in the summer, with Tony, he wrote, acting as chaperone. Seeing Tony and Olivier would be a tonic for us.

One rainy morning, there was a touching surprise on my breakfast tray. Tucked in a business envelope that appeared to be a bill from Stanford's hospital there was a note written by him. From lines that looked more like a barometer chart since most of the words were illegible, a few words reached out from his letter to embrace me. The word "love" was clearly written three times and "family" twice. His signature was as steady and legible as it ever had been. I held his note to my heart and I have it with me now. I will leave it in this letter for you, so you will know how pleased I was to be surprised by love.

In February, on Valentine's Day to be exact, Quon Sam came to tell us Lady Cowes-Wentworth-Cowes had smothered in her own pillow. Dr. Creighton wrote that she'd had an aneurysm on her death certificate. He told me privately she could have been intoxicated. She was only sixty-eight years old and still in the best of health, as far as I knew. I was hollow, desolate. None of it made sense. Poor Lady Cowes had no family here to mourn her. We had her cremated and her old friend Quon Sam scattered her ashes in the garden.

All my life, I have suffered from anxiety, but something new was feeding my terror. As I lay in bed day after day, the feeling grew as I reviewed my life. Alec died. Boulie died. Duffie died. My mother died. Now Lady Cowes-Wentworth-Cowes. None of them got near fourscore and ten. Why hadn't I been able to talk Alec out of going to war? Why had I humiliated Chou on the day of the fire? Why did Boulie have to save you? I should have gone first into the burning house. If I had turned my mother in to the police when I knew about her illicit activities, then she would still be alive. Was it hubris to think I could have changed anything?

Haunted by these thoughts, nothing comforted me, especially not the knowledge it was past the time when Chou should have left to return Boulie's bones to her family.

"They clean them with wine, Precious." You wanted to know what preparations were being made for the return of her bones. Already taller than me, you were an exceptionally wise and observant girl. I noticed your nipples were beginning to swell. That meant the end of your infancy. I was happy I had been there for your childhood, but sad that it was passing without your knowing that I was your mother. You were becoming moody and sometimes cried for no reason.

"It is a natural part of adolescence," I said to Chou who reported to me that you had wept over a particularly difficult passage during a music lesson.

"She is a perfectionist," he observed.

"Like my mother," I said ruefully.

"Like *my* mother," Chou laughed.

"Soong Chou taught me a prayer for the dead," you reported. By then he was teaching you Chinese in addition to your music lessons. More and more, you were going out to the garage to visit your father. There wasn't much to hold you in the house. I worried that you would be devastated when he left. What could I offer you? Sometimes I barely had the energy to breathe.

"Will you miss him when he goes back to China?" I asked.

"He'll come back. He promised he would come back."

"He has a wife in China, Precious. It isn't fair to keep a family apart."

"We're his family too." You were so right, more than you knew, or did you understand on some deeper, intuitive level that you were connected to him biologically?

Stanford told me that whales kept track of one another under the sea by making soundings, high-pitched noises that indicated their location. When I am alone in my stateroom, I whistle to you. The only thing that stops me from whistling all the way across the Pacific is that someone might think I am barking mad and have me put off the ship. We did a lot of whistling those last few months at home. It was a great comfort to me lying in bed or on my chaise to hear you in bed, in the bath, or going off to school.

Dola wrote to me during the winter and told me her wedding would be in Victoria the following summer. Would you like to be a junior bridesmaid? I wonder if Dola consulted her mother. If Laura was hearing the gossip about Nora's disappearance, I am sure she wouldn't want any of us in her daughter's wedding party, especially as she was marrying into minor aristocracy, and despite the fact that her only remaining son was a drug addict hiding out in Singapore.

Dola wondered if The Prince of Wales would give her a wedding present with his crest on it like the decanter and glasses he had given to Olivier and me. I imagined that she was still a virgin. Dish was probably feeding her fairytales about the nobility of chastity before marriage.

The spring after my mother and Lady Cowes-Wentworth-Cowes had died was especially glorious. First to appear were the snowdrops on Nora's empty grave. I couldn't see them from my window, but you reported the first sighting in late February. I tried drawing them from memory. The problem is that when I drew or painted I became passionately involved in the process and that was exhausting. By March, the fruit trees and first rhododendrons were in bloom. The garden, even when it became overgrown, would continue without my mother.

Invalids are very aware of sound. For the first few months after my mother's death, every ring of the phone, every knock at the door could have been the police coming to report they had found her body. I shuddered when I heard strange footfalls on the stairs. My mother's file was open, but, without a body, what could they do? Constable Godsell even suggested she might have vanished for romantic reasons and left us behind.

Chou visited my bedroom every afternoon. We talked about business and your progress in your lessons. I had papers to sign handing over the management of our household accounts and Stanford's care to a trust company. Everything would be taken care of. His boat was sailing at the end of May. I wasn't sure I would live to see him again.

Wash Martha came to sit by me and tell me fascinating stories about the salmon people, the bear, the eagle and the Songhees that belonged to her family. Miss Beach read aloud from new books by old favourites and the new American writers Faulkner, Hemingway and Fitzgerald. They were a distraction, but I could not stop fretting. I worried that I was no more available to you than Nora had been to me. You could, it was true, go back to England with Olivier, who did cherish you. But then there was Olivier's horrible mother. What would that woman do to violate your beautiful spirit?

Wash Martha told me not to worry so much. You were a hummingbird. They were female tricksters with intelligence and speed compensating for their lack of power.

I tried to visualize you as a hummingbird, but I was convinced

that I was a curse and that you would be the next victim. I decided
that I would send you to Olivier, where you would be safe from the
bad fairies in our garden. Taking Olivier's mother into considera-
tion, it wasn't an easy decision to make. I put off telling you and
dreaded informing Chou. Clearly, the chemistry was better between
the two of you than with me at this unsettled time in your life.

Chou's Chinese wife became my imaginary companion as I lay
in bed at home listening to the sea, conjuring a woman in China
hearing the same rhyming waves, wondering what troubles they
would bring her. I thought of the beaches in France washing themselves clean of the blood of Canadian soldiers. I thought of my
mother floating somewhere, unrecognizable, just a body, her real
spirit remaining in her living garden. I thought of Boulie's mother,
her bones cleaned by the acidic water in a Chinese well. I thought
of Tony's mother, hearing the cry of a seagull and wishing it were
that of a grandchild.

Chou listened while I told him that I could not live. I was
resigned to that. Being confined to my bed, short of breath and the
energy to do anything meaningful with my time, was not a life. It
was no life for you watching it happen. I told him of my fears that
I was part of a curse and begged him to understand my reasons for
sending you to England.

He sat with his face in his hands for a very long time. When he
looked up again, his cheeks were wet. I thought what a gift he was
and remembered the lines we had read from *As You Like It* the
night before: "Sweet are the uses of adversity, which like the toad,
ugly and venomous, wears yet a precious jewel in his head."

"It is the wrong thing to do, Poppy," he said, and then left me.

I decided to leave the idea alone for a while. Chou would spend
his final weeks with us and then he would go. I would tell you
about my plans after he left.

We went along as before, taking care of practical matters. I loved
the evenings when you and your father came to my room and

played music together. One night, Chou returned after the household was asleep, and lay beside me. He whispered to me in the dark that he loved you and me more than life itself.

"When you leave," I said, "My life will stop."

"Poppy. You have lived so well. Why wouldn't you go on? Paint. Show us the way. Have I ever told you the story of Ruan Xian, one of the seven great scholars of the third century?"

"No."

"The old style *pipa* is named after him. When he refused to serve the barbarian emperor Sima, he was sentenced to death. Just before execution, he performed his composition "Guang Ling San" for his students and friends, to bid them farewell. Ruan Xian died but his music lived on."

We kissed and wept as the house sighed and settled around us, and then we slowly undressed one another. This was the most beautiful and leisurely lovemaking. We had everything to cherish now, passion and grief, tenderness and pain — our child. I breathed him in, slowly, carefully, memorizing all the parts of his body. We visited one another as if we were maps of the world and the parts of our bodies were countries we would not visit again.

That night, I felt at once the greatest happiness and sadness I have ever known. How many people know when it is happening that this is the last time, a sacrament? In our perfect moment, we cried out as the seagulls began to call to one another over the water. We lay together a bit longer, feeling the warmth of our bodies side by side, and I fell asleep.

When I woke up, Chou had gone, leaving his scent and a dent in my pillow, and you were sitting on the end of my bed. I smiled and invited you in for a sisterly snuggle. Would you remember this some day and understand that what you felt in the warmth of my bed was the mingling of your parents? I hoped so. "How would you like to go for a holiday in England?" I asked you impulsively.

"No!" You shot up. "Are you crazy? I'm not going there."

"Well," I nervously straightened my sheet. "You are!"

"Says who?"

"Says me."

"Why?" You actually stamped your foot, my reasonable girl.

"Because I say so." I sat up.

Precious, my precious, you looked at me with an expression of pure rage. "You can't make me, Poppy. You are not my mother!"

The room turned white and began to spin. I lay back on my pillow, biting my lip so hard it bled. Why didn't I tell you then?

"You can't stay here," I insisted.

"Why not?"

"Because it isn't good for you. I'm not well. You need to be with people who are alive, like Olivier."

"I love Olivier, Poppy, but I don't want to go to London. If I go anywhere, I'll go to China with Soong Chou."

"China!"

"Yes, China. He's going anyway. It's only a week by ship. I can play music. There is so much I could learn." Your cheeks were bright pink and your eyes shone.

"What would Chou think about all this?"

"He knows. We've talked about it."

"He had no business."

"It was my idea. I said I'd like to go with him. I didn't expect he would agree, but he did."

"I thought you wanted to stay here."

"I do, but it's just a holiday. The Soongs would treat me like family," you begged. "Besides, it is my duty to take Boulie home to her family since she died saving my life."

"Did Chou tell you to say that?" I asked.

"Yes," you replied.

I felt the east wind blowing. My tiles surrendered to theirs. You had a right. You loved Chou and your *pipa*. You were proud of your progress in Cantonese, and absorbed by the Chinese fairy tales your father told you. You once told me how similar Chou's Chinese stories were to the Aboriginal legends that Wash Martha told us.

"Are they related?" you asked me then. The only prayer we said was "All my relations," which we had borrowed from the Songhees people.

You lay down beside me again, resting your case. "We're all related, Precious." I said, parting your hair with my fingers.

"I could almost whistle to you from Hong Kong."

"Almost."

It was done. I made you promise to write to me once a week and tell me everything about Hong Kong. You were to draw pictures of all the rooms in Chou's family house and tell me about his relations. I wanted to know what you ate and how you were doing with your Chinese lessons.

"It won't be forever, Poppy," you said.

Forever, I thought. What a strange word, the distance between stars, the length of the body of water between Canada and the Orient, the depth of the water where my mother lay.

I couldn't go to the boat with you. Chou carried me down the stairs and set me down in a wicker chair on the lawn. It was a warm May morning. Birds were singing. I watched Fong and Chou carry the trunks and the "golden pagoda" that held Boulie's bones out to the waiting cab and held one of your hands. Miss Beach hung on to the other.

You wore your new sky blue coat and hat. I could see the graceful woman that you would become. Hong Kong was secure. You would adapt and there was the comfort of the English presence to fall back on when you missed home. You would fit in. I handed you some forget-me-nots that Fong had picked for me from the rockery along the driveway

"I love you, Precious," I said, my tears falling on your hands.

"I love you too, Poppy," you said, but you were not weeping. You sparkled. "*Joy geen!*"

When it was time to go, Chou kissed me tenderly on the lips and both hands. Then he put his arm around you and led you to the car. You rolled down the window and whistled when the cab started up.

My heart was breaking. As you drove away, you blew kisses from the rear window and I waved at you. When you were gone, Miss Beach and Alice helped me back to bed, where I stayed with the curtains shut for weeks.

Because you and I had been on ocean liners together, magical thinking helped to visualize your journey with your father. For the ten or so days of the voyage, I was with you, imagining your staterooms, two bedrooms and a sitting room decorated in the CPR style with blue carpets and sturdy but handsome wooden furnishings. I saw you at dinner, making shy conversation, slowly becoming more intimate as you released your secrets. You are a careful girl, but you have a wonderful sense of humour. Chou would have allowed himself to laugh a lot with you as he became more relaxed, more of his own man as he approached his family and his country. He would have been working to improve your Chinese and playing music with you. His family would be pleased with your musicality and artistic skills. You would make a delightful *mah jong* partner during the long intervals between lunch and dinner.

The hardest part was after I knew that you had landed in Hong Kong. Chou sent a wire. It said, "Arrived safely. No seasickness. We both send love." I clung to that. The telegram is as worn as an old flannel now. I have wet it with my tears and kissed it a thousand times at least. When you began to live in the family house, I had no way of orienting myself. I could not imagine the smell, the texture, the sounds or the colours of your new life.

That was when I began to lose you. Because I didn't want to overwhelm you with anxious letters, I wrote notes begging you to be well and happy and had Miss Beach take them to the wall.

Two months after you sailed to China, Olivier and Tony arrived in Victoria and took over the house. By the time they came, there was no water left in my body. Chou sent a letter saying that you were making a good transition. Reassured by his letter, I began to recover.

Toujours gai, Olivier and Tony tried so hard to make living an art again. They played records and danced, carried me up and down the stairs so I could enjoy the garden and have dinner in the dining room with them. My guests pitched in with the gardening, helping Guan Sing with the weeding, mowing, deadheading, and cultivation of vegetables. We may be gentry on the surface, they said, but we are peasants at heart.

I could see that those two really loved one another and that in Victoria — thousands of miles away from home — they were free to be themselves. Our marriage was, at the end of the day, a good thing. Olivier had been and would continue to be a dear friend. The boys took over my mother's bedroom and they hooted and splashed in her huge bathtub as I had with Boulie and Alec years ago. I heard them rummaging in my mother's closets, exclaiming over her beautiful things. Sometimes they came into my bedroom wearing hats and dresses and we laughed. Our home holiday was an ongoing pyjama party. At night and first thing in the morning, we called back and forth to one another. The doors to the linen closet were left open at both ends.

Up until the moment our quasi-idyllic life was smashed apart by terrible news, our year was as good as it could be without you. I was relatively content, and Olivier and Tony had a wonderful time discovering Victoria. We giggled and gossiped and played endless lazy games of *mah jong*. The ocean and its secret was no longer a threat to my family. You were safe in China. I would be safe in the arms of whatever took me next. If Nora's body should surface, its discovery would only contribute to her legend. I looked out the window at the changing sea and sky and listened to the bird in my *tabatière* sing the song Chou had chosen for me when I was the same age you are now.

Before you left, Chou brought me the singing fountain bowl and left it on the table beside my bed. He told me the story of the Sung dynasty poet Li Po who drank a whole bowlful of wine, then leaned out of his rowboat to embrace the reflection of the moon on the water. Li Po fell out of his boat and drowned, a happy man.

"I would like to die that way," I said, and I believed I meant it. I rubbed the handles on the singing bowl and saw the faces of my loved ones in it. Perhaps the East Wind would gather me in its arms and fly me over China. I would have my chance to see the Great Wall, the Forbidden City and my living family before I met with the others.

Some days I barely moved, just lay in bed listening to the rhyming waves and imagined the sex lives of fishes. Laughter was the only exercise left to me. Tallu sent me a letter describing how she had done cartwheels, no underpants, at a posh party given by Cecil Beaton, the snobbish young photographer. He was outraged, of course. That's why she did it. Beaton was foolishly infatuated with Greta Garbo, who was, Tallulah assured me, a boy or at the very least an androgyne.

"I want to try everything once," Tallulah told me more than once. That was the problem. She was repeating herself and I imagine she still is. I think I have been luckier. My mother taught me one important thing. A garden is made up of annuals and perennials. I am an annual.

My bedroom was my world, as it has been most of my life. I listened to our stairs. I could hear my ghosts on them — Duffie running up and down with trays, Stanford in his monogrammed velvet house slippers, Alec, his head heavy with his mother's expectations, Boulie, hungry as fire, swallowing all the oxygen in her path, my mother's whispering gait, Soong Chou bringing his sad music, and you my Precious, the soft footfalls of hope.

I waited for more letters from Hong Kong. When we were in England, remember, I had you write every week — to my mother, to Miss Beach and Chou. China is a long way away, but the CPR boats go back and forth constantly with the mail.

When I woke up in the middle of the night, I lay in the dark trying to imagine the rooms you inhabited. You had described

Chou's family house, but I had hoped that you would draw it for me. I pictured your pensive face taking in everything around you; the house — built around a garden with a pond, lilies, peonies, and chrysanthemums — your own room, a big wooden bed with dragons carved in the posts and silk hangings, photos of me, Nora and the dogs, Duffie, Olivier and Boulie. I saw you walking arm in arm with your father and your father's wife. I could hear you playing music together. You had a busy life, I was sure, but why was there no time to write to me? In my sleep, I scattered rose petals on the ocean between Hong Kong and Victoria, the charm that brought loved ones home.

On the first of April, I had my answer. You had gone with your aunt to take Boulie's bones to the Han family in Peking. While you were there, officers of the *Kuomintang* had raided the house. The Han family had gone into hiding and you, presumably, with them. Soong Chou was looking for you. Helpless, I was tormented by all the awful possibilities.

I came clean with Olivier, telling him all about you and me — admitting every single lie and omission. He was kind. We had misled one another. This was not the time for recriminations or feelings of guilt. We had to find you. Olivier persevered in trying to contact Chou. After some thought and consultation with my doctor, he and Tony developed a plan, which they presented to me after they had already bought tickets on the *Empress of Asia*. They proposed that Olivier stay behind to look after the house and co-ordinate efforts with the police and diplomatic channels. Tony would accompany me to China. If I were to lie in bed and wait, it would drive me completely mad.

We are steaming into Shanghai now, and I am leaving my body. Shanghai has a beautiful waterfront. The city could be a larger Victoria, the *bund*, its street of dreams, stepping gracefully up to the sea, hopefully offering you.

Miracolo, Mr. Lee has just joined us on deck. We didn't imagine him. I want to grab him by the shoulders and shake his secrets out. That would, I know, be futile. Having exchanged his western business suit for a blue brocade tunic and skirt, he appears even more enigmatic than he did the first time we saw him. We wait for him to speak. Stanford, the mad genius whose typewriter kept me sane on this journey, has delivered me to this moment. Someday soon I will thank him. My hands are shaking and Tony has taken over the typing.

Now Mr. Lee tells us we cannot stay in Shanghai. It is too dangerous. The *Kuomintang* rebellion has come this far. I would ask why Chou risked sending you to Peking, but I know I can't question their decision. In China, women listen. It was a question of face, a girl for a girl, he explains. You and your aunt had to *kowtow* on behalf of the Soong family. The Soongs expected you back within a month, but you didn't return. Because of financial reverses suffered in the political upheaval, the Hans required money in addition to an apology and the gifts you and your aunt had brought.

"The money was paid right away," Mr. Lee looks away. He is clearly not a man who likes to fail at his business. "But it became almost impossible to travel. In addition to the followers of Chiang Kai-shek, the Japanese are politically active in the north, taking advantage of the unrest in China. Chou went himself to Peking, but the Han family had already fled. We were assured that Precious left at the same time. I went to Hawaii where some relatives of the Hans own land, and found the family there, but Precious and my wife were not with them."

"Your *wife*?" I ask.

"My wife is Precious' second aunt. I am Soong Tso-li. I have been on the boat since it left Honolulu. If there had been helpful information, I would have told you. I have had telegrams from Hong Kong each day."

"Why couldn't we find you? Tony searched the boat."

"I didn't want to be found until I heard the answer we both sought. I used the name Mr. Lee because Occidentals rearrange my name in any case." Mr. Soong smiled.

"Chou wrote that she was not in danger."

"We had assurances, which turned out to be true. He gave me the letter before we both left Hong Kong so you wouldn't worry unnecessarily."

"I have done nothing but worry. How do you know my daughter is here, in Shanghai?"

"Because my brother Chou has sent a telegram."

"Why didn't you tell me all this before?"

"I didn't know. Chou sent a wire just this morning, telling me he will be boarding the *Empress of Asia* with Precious and my wife as soon as we dock. This boat will only be in Shanghai long enough to drop off the mail and take on passengers. There will be no shore leaves. Only Shanghai residents will be allowed off the ship."

My hands fly to my hair, to my skirt. Am I all right? Am I presentable enough to meet you? Moving his fingers over the keys with exaggerated grace, Tony looks more like a concert pianist than an amanuensis. "Take a bow, Tony," I dictate, "You are the two-fingered genius of friendship."

I take the risk. "Why, Mr. Soong, would you ever risk sending your wife and a child into danger?"

"We have been in danger for many years and now the situation is resolved. We sent them to Peking for the family."

Of course, everything is for the family. How can I argue with that when you are safe, if I am to believe him, and I think I do? I suppose I should rejoice that you were sent to represent the Soong family. That is progress. Foot-bound girls your age are still sold into arranged marriages in China, and you have been a plenipotentiary for peace. Perhaps I should get over thinking of you as a child. I am afraid you will be so changed, so *Chinese*, so womanly that I won't know you after a year.

Chou once told me the Chinese have a bride expression — "sitting happiness in." The newlywed is left alone on the matrimonial *kang* to calm her nerves. Restlessness is not considered a positive attribute in Chinese wives. I am trying to be calm. But I am not a Chinese wife; I am a mother, and my heart is a bird in my chest.

We are very close to the dock now. The story of our voyage is almost over. Am I imagining that the wind is bringing me the fresh scent of your hair and skin? When I close my eyes, I feel you close to me, almost touching. I feel in my pocket for the brocade purse and decide that I will wear my jade and pearl earrings and the dragon choker, just this once. I will not dishonour Chou's wife by wearing them in her house, but this moment is ours. Mr. Soong wants to help me out of my deck chair. We will stand at the rail as the ship berths, watching the crowd, hoping one of us will see you right away. On the chance that you might hear me before we see one another, I will whistle. When I see you, I will shout, "Precious, *n'attendes pas, mon coeur!*" We will start our new lives with an old joke.

Years ago, when he was teaching me to play, Soong Chou told me that *mah jong* was a test of patience and that someday I would understand that every game was a life. Trust the East Wind, he said. Four times, she will come to your aid. He was right. The East Wind is powerful. When Tony plays his last chord and our gangplank slams on the dock, the last tile in my game will play itself and I can relax and dream of the day when you will read my letters, sealed with love, and call me Mother.

ACKNOWLEDGEMENTS

I would like to thank Cormorant editor Marc Côté, Shannon Badcock, copy editor Adam Moldenhauer, designer Angel Guerra, Walter Quan, the muffin man, the BC Arts Council and Canada Council who supported the writing of this book, my husband and cyber support Rick van Krugel, Gorge historian Dennis Minnaker, Charlayne Thornton-Joe, guardian angel of the Chinese Cemetery in Victoria, expert readers writer Rhonda Batchelor, herbalist Bonnie Elandiuk, historian Doug Henderson, Captain Paddy Hernon, Kathryn Mulders, my mother Patricia Hall, Joan Seidl, curator of the Vancouver Museum, who let me into the opium exhibit on a dark day, Charlene Simon for her psychological insights, my sheltering brother and brother-in-law Dana Hall and Brad Macivor, designers Charles and Patricia Lester for sharing their Welsh gardens, Patricia Young for explicating her mother's "Scottishisms," fact sleuth Jim Munro, The Palace Hotel in San Francisco, The Royal Hawaiian Hotel, Honolulu, *ne plus ultra* hair stylist Frederick Roesner, who owns Tallulah Bankhead's cigarette case, Harry Locke, still the paradigm good teacher and good person, my imaginative grandchildren Sophie, Sage, and Olive, and my inspirational great-grandmother, Baroness Hélène von Rosenfeld, "Garden" to us.